REST IN PEACE

Albert Campion lay on the floor, breathing regularly as though he were asleep. The man who bent over him completed his arrangements hurriedly. He opened the oven door and forced Mr. Campion's head and one shoulder into the tiny cavity. The gas jets poured choking death into the small space. Then the man drew a card from his pocket and tucked it into Mr. Campion's livid hand. It read "Amanda: You won't forget me. Albert."

Just the sort of laconic suicide note Albert Campion would be expected to write. The murderer counted on that. . . .

Margery Allingham

THE FASHION IN SHROUDS

BANTAM BOOKS
Toronto • New York • London • Sydney • Auckland

THE FASHION IN SHROUDS
A Bantam Book / published by arrangement with
Doubleday & Co., Inc.

PRINTING HISTORY
Doubleday edition published October 1938
A Selection of Dollar Mystery Guild, 1961
Bantam edition / November 1985

ISBN 0-553-25412-X

Published simultaneously in the United States and Canada

PRINTED IN THE UNITED STATES OF AMERICA

O   0 9 8 7 6 5 4 3 2 1

THE FASHION
IN SHROUDS

Chapter One

Probably the most exasperating thing about the Fashion is its elusiveness. Even the word has a dozen definitions, and when it is pinned down and qualified, as "the Fashion in woman's dress," it becomes ridiculous and stilted and is gone again.

To catch at its skirts it is safest to say that it is a kind of miracle, a familiar phenomenon. Why it is that a garment which is honestly attractive in, say, 1910 should be honestly ridiculous a few years later and honestly charming again a few years later still is one of those things which are not satisfactorily to be explained and are therefore jolly and exciting and an addition to the perennial interest of life.

When the last Roland Papendeik died, after receiving a knighthood for a royal wedding dress—having thus scaled the heights of his ambition as a great couturier—the ancient firm declined and might well have faded into one of the amusing legends Fashion leaves behind her had it not been for a certain phoenix quality possessed by Lady Papendeik.

At the moment when descent became apparent and dissolution likely Lady Papendeik discovered Val, and from the day that the Valentine cape in Lincoln-green facecloth flickered across the salon and won the hearts of twenty-five professional buyers and subsequently five hundred private purchasers Val climbed steadily, and behind her rose up the firm of Papendeik again like a great silk tent.

At the moment she was standing in a fitting room whither she had dragged a visitor who had come on private business of his own and was surveying herself in a wall-wide mirror with earnest criticism.

Like most of those people whose personality has to be consciously expressed in the things they create, she was a little more of a person, a little more clear in outline than is usual. She had no suggestion of overemphasis, but she was a sharp, vivid entity, and when one first saw her the immediate thing one realised was that it had not happened before.

As she stood before the mirror considering her burgundy-red suit from every angle she looked about twenty-three, which was not the fact. Her slenderness was slenderness personified and her yellow hair, folding softly into the nape of her neck at the back and combed into a ridiculous roll in front, could have belonged to no one else and would have suited no other face.

It occurred to her visitor, who was regarding her with the detached affection of a relation, that she was dressed up to look like a female, and he said so affably.

She turned and grinned at him, her unexpectedly warm grey eyes, which saved her whole appearance from affectation, dancing at him happily.

"I am," she said. "I am, my darling. I'm female as a cartload of monkeys."

"Or a kettle of fish, of course," observed Mr. Albert Campion, unfolding his long thin legs and rising from an inadequate gilt chair to look in the mirror also. "Do you like my new suit?"

"Very good indeed." Her approval was professional. "Jamieson and Fellowes? I thought so. They're so mercifully uninspired. Inspiration in men's clothes is stomach-turning. People ought to be shot for it."

Campion raised his eyebrows at her. She had a charming voice which was high and clear and so unlike his own in tone and colour that it gave him a sense of acquisition whenever he heard it.

"Too extreme," he said. "I like your garment, but let's forget it now."

"Do you? I was wondering if it wasn't a bit 'intelligent.'"
He looked interested.

"I wanted to talk to you before these people come. Aren't we lunching alone?"

Val swung slowly round in only partially amused surprise. For a moment she looked her full age, which was thirty, and there was character and intelligence in her face.

"You're too clever altogether, aren't you?" she said. "Go away. You take me out of my stride."

"Who is he? It's not to be a lovely surprise, I trust?" Campion put an arm round her shoulders and they stood for a moment admiring themselves with the bland unself-consciousness of the nursery. "If I didn't look so half-witted we should be very much alike," he remarked presently. "There's a distinct resemblance. Thank God we took after Mother and not the other side. Red hair would sink either of us, even Father's celebrated variety. Poor old Herbert used to look like nothing on earth."

He paused and considered her dispassionately in the mirror, while it occurred to him suddenly that the relationship between brother and sister was the one association of the sexes that was intrinsically personal.

"If one resents one's sister or even loathes the sight of her," he remarked presently, "it's for familiar faults or virtues which one either has or hasn't got oneself and one likes the little beast for the same rather personal reasons. I think you're better than I am in one or two ways, but I'm always glad to note that you have sufficient feminine weaknesses to make you thoroughly inferior on the whole. This is a serious, valuable thought, by the way. See what I mean?"

"Yes," she said with an irritating lack of appreciation, "but I don't think it's very new. What feminine weaknesses have I got?"

He beamed at her. In spite of her astonishing success she could always be relied upon to make him feel comfortingly superior.

"Who's coming to lunch?"

"Alan Dell—Alandel aeroplanes."

"Really? That's unexpected. I've heard of him, of course, but we've never met. Nice fellow?"

She did not answer immediately and he glanced at her sharply.

"I don't know," she said at last and met his eyes. "I think so, very."

Campion grimaced. "Valentine the valiant."

She was suddenly hurt and colour came into her face.

"No, darling, not necessarily," she objected a little too vehemently. "Only twice shy, you know, only twice, not forever."

There was dignity in the protest. It brought him down to earth and reminded him effectively that she was after all a distinguished and important woman with every right to her own private life. He changed the conversation, feeling, as he sometimes did, that she was older than he was for all her femininity.

"Can I smoke in this clothespress without sacrilege?" he enquired. "I came up here once to a reception when I was very young. The Perownes had it then as their town house. That was in the days before the street went down and a Perowne could live in Park Lane. I don't remember much about it except that there were golden cream horns bursting with fruit all round the cornice. You've transformed the place. Does Tante Marthe like the change of address?"

"Lady Papendeik finds herself enchanted," said Val cheerfully, her mind still on her clothes. "She thinks it a pity trade should have come so near the park but she's consoling herself by concentrating on 'our mission to glorify the Essential Goddess.' This is a temple, my boy, not a shop. When it's not a temple it's that damned draughty hole of Maude Perowne's. But on the whole it's just exactly what she always wanted. It has the grand manner, the authentic Papa Papendeik touch. Did you see her little black pages downstairs?"

"The objects in the turbans? Are they recent?"

"Almost temporary," said Val, turning from the mirror and slipping her arm through his. "Let's go up and wait. We're lunching on the roof."

As he came through the wide doorway from a hushed and breathless world whose self-conscious good taste was almost over-powering to the upper, or workshop, part of the Papendeik establishment, Mr. Campion felt a gratifying return to reality. A narrow uncarpeted corridor, still bearing traces of the Perowne era in wallpaper and paint, was lit by half-a-dozen open doorways through which came a variety of sounds, from the chiming of cups to the hiss of the pressing iron, while above all there predominated the strident, sibilant chatter of female voices, which is perhaps the most unpleasant noise in the world.

An elderly woman in a shabby navy-blue dress came bustling along towards them, a black pincushion bumping ridiculously on her hipbone as she walked. She did not stop but smiled and passed them, radiating a solid obstinacy as definite as the clatter of her old-lady shoes on the boards. Behind her trotted a man in a costume in which Campion recognised at once Val's conception of the term "inspired."

He was breathless and angry and yet managed to look pathetic, with doggy brown eyes and the cares of the world on his compact little shoulders.

"She won't let me have it," he said without preamble. "I hate any sort of unpleasantness, but the two girls are waiting to go down to the house and I distinctly promised that the white model should go with the other. It's the one with the draped corsage."

He sketched a design with his two hands on his own chest with surprising vividness.

"The vendeuse is in tears."

He seemed not far off them himself and Mr. Campion felt sorry for him.

"Coax her," said Val without slackening pace and they hurried on, leaving him sighing. "Rex," she said as they mounted the narrow uncarpeted staircase amid a labyrinth of corridors. "Tante says he's not quite a lady. It's one of her filthy remarks that gets more true the longer you know him."

Campion made no comment. They were passing through a group of untidy girls who had stepped aside as they appeared.

"Seamstresses," Val explained as they came up on to the landing. "Tante prefers the word to 'workwomen.' This is their room."

She threw open a door which faced them and he looked into a vast attic where solid felt-covered tables made a mighty horseshoe whose well was peopled with dreadful brown headless figures each fretted with pinpricks and labelled with the name of the lady whose secret faults of contour it so uncompromisingly reproduced.

Reflecting that easily the most terrifying thing about women was their practical realism, he withdrew uneasily and followed her up a final staircase to a small roof garden set among the chimney-pots, where a table had been laid beneath a striped awning.

It was early summer and the trees in the park were round and green above the formal flower beds, so that the view, as they looked down upon it, was like a coloured panoramic print of eighteenth-century London, with the houses of the Bayswater Road making a grey cloud on the horizon.

He sat down on a white basketwork settee and blinked at her in the sunlight.

"I want to meet Georgia Wells. You're sure she's coming?"

"My dear, they're all coming." Val spoke soothingly. "Her husband, the leading man, Ferdie Paul himself and heaven knows who else. It's partly mutual publicity and partly a genuine inspection of dresses for *The Lover*, now in rehearsal. You'll see Georgia all right."

"Good," he said and his lean face was unusually thoughtful. "I shall try not to be vulgar or indiscreet, of course, but I must get to know her if I can. Was she actually engaged to Portland-Smith at the time he disappeared, or was it already off by then?"

Val considered and her eyes strayed to the doorway through which they had come.

"It's almost three years ago, isn't it?" she said. "My impression is that it was still on, but I can't swear to it. It was all kept so decently quiet until the family decided that they really had better look for him, and by then she was stalking Ramillies. It's funny you never found that man, Albert. He's your one entire failure, isn't he?"

Apparently Mr. Campion did not care to comment.

"How long has she been Lady Ramillies?"

"Over two years, I think."

"Shall I get a black eye if I lead round to Portland-Smith?"

"No, I don't think so. Georgia's not renowned for good taste. If she stares at you blankly it'll only mean that she's forgotten the poor beast's name."

He laughed. "You don't like the woman?"

Val hesitated. She looked very feminine.

"Georgia's our most important client, 'the best-dressed actress in the world gowned by the most famous couturier.' We're a mutual benefit society."

"What's the matter with her?"

"Nothing." She glanced at the door again and then out over the park. "I admire her. She's witty, beautiful, predatory, intrinsically vulgar and utterly charming."

Mr. Campion became diffident.

"You're not jealous of her?"

"No, no, of course not. I'm as successful as she is—more."

"Frightened of her?"

Val looked at him and he was embarrassed to see in her for an instant the candid-eyed child of his youth.

"Thoroughly."

"Why?"

"She's so charming," she said with uncharacteristic naïveté. "She's got *my* charm."

"That's unforgivable," he agreed sympathetically. "Which one?"

"The only one there is, my good ape. She makes you think she likes you. Forget her. You'll see her this afternoon. I like her really. She's fundamentally sadistic and not nearly so brilliant as she sounds, but she's all right. I like her. I do like her."

Mr. Campion thought it wisest not to press the subject and would doubtless have started some other topic had he not discovered that Val was no longer listening to him. The door to the staircase had opened and her second guest had arrived.

As he rose to greet the newcomer Campion was aware of a fleeting sense of disappointment.

In common with many other people he cherished the secret conviction that a celebrity should look peculiar, at the very least, and had hitherto been happy to note that a great number did.

Dell was an exception. He was a bony thirty-five-year-old with greying hair and the recently scoured appearance of one intimately associated with machinery. It was only when he spoke, revealing a cultured mobile voice of unexpected authority, that his personality became apparent. He came forward shyly and it occurred to Campion that he was a little put out to find that he was not the only guest.

"Your brother?" he said. "I had no idea Albert Campion was your brother."

"Oh, we're a distinguished family," murmured Val brightly, but an underlying note of uncertainty in her voice made Campion glance at her shrewdly. He was a little startled by the change in her. She looked younger and less elegant, more charming and far more vulnerable. He looked at the man and was relieved to see that he was very much aware of her.

"You've kept each other very dark," said Dell. "Why is that?"

Val was preoccupied at the moment with two waiters who had arrived with the luncheon from the giant hotel next door, but she spoke over her shoulder.

"We haven't. Our professions haven't clashed yet, that's all. We nod to each other in the street and send birthday

7

cards. We're the half of the family that is on speaking terms, as a matter of fact.''

"We're the bones under the ancestral staircase."

Campion embarked upon the explanation solely because it was expected of him. It was a reason he would never have considered sufficient in the ordinary way, but there was something about Alan Dell, with his unusually bright blue eyes and sudden smile, which seemed to demand that extra consideration which is given automatically to important children, as if he were somehow special and it was to everyone's interest that he should be accurately informed.

"I was asked to leave first—in a nice way, of course. We all have charming manners. Val followed a few years later, and now, whenever our names crop up at home, someone steps into the library and dashes off another note to the family solicitor disinheriting us. Considering their passion for self-expression, they always seem to me a little unreasonable about ours.''

"That's not quite true about me." Val leant across the table and spoke with determined frankness. "I left home to marry a man whom no one liked, and after I married I didn't like him either. Lady Papendeik, who used to make my mother's clothes, saw some of my designs and gave me a job——''

"Since when you've revolutionised the business," put in Campion hastily with some vague idea of saving the situation. He was shocked. Since Sidney Ferris had died the death he deserved in a burnt-out motorcar with which, in a fit of alcoholic exuberance, he had attempted to fell a tree, he had never heard his widow mention his name.

Val seemed quite unconscious of anything unusual in her behavior. She was looking across at Dell with anxious eyes.

"Yes," he said, "I've been hearing about you. I didn't realise how long Papendeik's had been going. You've performed an extraordinary feat in putting them back on the map. I thought change was the essence of fashion.''

Val flushed.

"It would have been easier to start afresh," she admitted. "There was a lot of prejudice at first. But as the new designs were attractive they sold, and the solidarity of the name was a great help on the business side.''

"It would be, of course." He regarded her with interest. "That's true. If the things one makes are better than the other

8

man's, one does get the contracts. That's the most comforting discovery I've ever made.''

They laughed at each other, mutually admiring and entirely comprehending, and Campion, who had work of his own to do, felt oddly out of it.

"When do you expect Georgia Wells?" he ventured. "About three?"

He felt the remark was hardly tactful as soon as he had made it, and Val's careless nod strengthened the impression. Dell was interested, however.

"Georgia Wells?" he said quickly. "Did you design her clothes for *The Little Sacrifice*?"

"Did you see them?" Val was openly pleased. Her sophistication seemed to have deserted her entirely. "She looked magnificent, didn't she?"

"Amazing." He glanced at the green treetops across the road. "I rarely go to the theatre," he went on after a pause, "and I was practically forced into that visit, but once I'd seen her I went again alone."

He made the statement with a complete unself-consciousness which was almost embarrassing and sat regarding them seriously.

"Amazing," he repeated. "I never heard such depth of feeling in my life. I'd like to meet that woman. She had some sort of tragedy in her life, I think? The same sort of thing as in the play."

Mr. Campion blinked. Unexpected naïveté in a delightful stranger whose ordinary intelligence is obviously equal to or beyond one's own always comes as something of a shock. He glanced at Val apprehensively. She was sitting up, her mouth smiling.

"She divorced her husband, the actor, some years ago, and there was a barrister fiancé who disappeared mysteriously a few months before she married Ramillies," she said. "I don't know which incident reminded you of the play."

Alan Dell stared at her with such transparent disappointment and surprise that she blushed, and Campion began to understand the attraction he had for her.

"I mean," she said helplessly, "*The Little Sacrifice* was about a woman relinquishing the only man she ever loved to marry the father of her eighteen-year-old daughter. Wasn't that it?"

"It was about a woman losing the man she loved in an

attempt to do something rather fine," said Dell and looked unhappy, as if he felt he had been forced into an admission.

"Georgia was brilliant. She always is. There's no one like her." Val was protesting too much and realising it too late, in Campion's opinion, and he was sorry for her.

"I saw the show," he put in. "It was a very impressive performance, I thought."

"It was, wasn't it?" The other man turned to him gratefully. "It got one. She was so utterly comprehendable. I don't like emotional stuff as a rule. If it's good I feel I'm butting in on strangers, and if it's bad it's unbearably embarrassing. But she was so—so confiding, if you see what I mean. There *was* some tragedy, wasn't there, before she married Ramillies? Who was this barrister fiancé?"

"A man called Portland-Smith," said Campion slowly.

"He disappeared?"

"He vanished," said Val. "Georgia may have been terribly upset; I think she probably was. I was only being smart and silly about it."

Dell smiled at her. He had a sort of chuckleheaded and shy affection towards her that was very disarming.

"That sort of shock can go very deep, you know," he said awkwardly. "It's the element of shame in it—the man clearing off suddenly and publicly like that."

"Oh, but you're wrong. It wasn't that kind of disappearance at all." Val was struggling between the very feminine desire to remove any misapprehension under which he might be suffering and the instinctive conviction that it would be wiser to leave the subject altogether. "He simply vanished into the air. He left his practice, his money in the bank and his clothes on the peg. It couldn't have been anything to do with Georgia. He'd been to a party at which I don't think she was even present, and he left early because he'd got to get back and read a brief before the morning. He left the hotel about ten o'clock and didn't get to his chambers. Somewhere between the two he disappeared. That's the story, isn't it, Albert?"

The thin young man in the horn-rimmed spectacles did not speak at once, and Dell glanced at him enquiringly.

"You took it up professionally?"

"Yes, about two years later." Mr. Campion appeared to be anxious to excuse his failure. "Portland-Smith's career was

10

heading towards a recordership," he explained, "and at the time he seemed pretty well certain to become a county court judge eventually, so his relatives were naturally wary of any publicity. In fact they covered his tracks, what there were of them, in case he turned up after a month or so with loss of memory. He was a lonely bird at the best of times, a great walker and naturalist, a curious type to have appealed so strongly to a successful woman. Anyway, the police weren't notified until it was too late for them to do anything, and I was approached after they'd given up. I didn't trouble Miss Wells because that angle had been explored very thoroughly by the authorities and they were quite satisfied that she knew nothing at all about the business."

Dell nodded. He seemed gratified by the final piece of information, which evidently corroborated his own convinced opinion.

"Interesting," he remarked after a pause. "That sort of thing's always happening. I mean one often hears a story like that."

Val looked up in surprise.

"About people walking out into the blue?"

"Yes," he said and smiled at her again. "I've heard of quite half-a-dozen cases in my time. It's quite understandable, of course, but every time it crops up it gives one a jolt, a new vision, like putting on a pair of long-sighted spectacles."

Val was visibly puzzled. She looked very sane sitting up and watching him with something like concern in her eyes.

"How do you mean? What happened to him?"

Dell laughed. He was embarrassed and glanced at Campion for support.

"Well," he said, the colour in his face making his eyes more vivid, "we all do get the feeling that we'd like to walk out, don't we? I mean we all feel at times an insane impulse to vanish, to abandon the great rattling caravan we're driving and walk off down the road with nothing but our own weight to carry. It's not always a question of concrete responsibilities; it's ambitions and conventions and especially affections which seem to get too much at moments. One often feels one'd like to ditch them all and just walk away. The odd thing is that so few of us do, and so when one hears of someone actually succumbing to that most familiar impulse one gets a sort of personal jolt. Portland-Smith is probably selling vacuum cleaners in Philadelphia by now."

Val shook her head.

"Women don't feel like that," she said. "Not alone."

Mr. Campion felt there might be something in this observation but he was not concerning himself with the abstract just then.

Months of careful investigation had led him late the previous afternoon to a little estate in Kent where the young Portland-Smith had spent a summer holiday at the age of nine. During the past ten years the old house had been deserted and had fallen into disrepair, creepers and brambles making of the garden a Sleeping Beauty thicket. There in a natural den in the midst of a shrubbery, the sort of hide-out that any nine-year-old would cherish forever as his own private place, Mr. Campion had found the thirty-eight-year-old Portland-Smith, or all that was left of him after three years. The skeleton had been lying face downward, the left arm pillowing the head and the knees drawn up in a feather bed of dried leaves.

Chapter Two

Val's office was one of the more original features of Papendeik's new establishment in Park Lane. Reynarde, who had been responsible for the transformation of the mansion, had indulged in one of his celebrated "strokes of genius" in its construction and Colin Greenleaf's photographs of the white wrought-iron basket of a studio slung under the centre cupola above the well of the grand staircase had appeared in all the more expensive illustrated periodicals at the time of the move.

In spite of its affected design the room was proving unexpectedly useful, much to everyone's relief, for its glass walls afforded a view not only of the visitors' part of the building but a clear vision down the two main workshop corridors and permitted Lady Papendeik to keep an eye on her house.

Although it was technically Val's own domain and contained a drawing table, Marthe Papendeik sat there most of the day "in the midst of her web," as Rex had once said in a fit of petulance, "looking like a spider, seeing itself a queen bee."

When Marthe Lafranc had come to London in the days when Victorian exuberance was bursting through its confining laces and drawing its breath for the skyrocketing and subsequent crash which were to follow, she had been an acute French businesswoman, hard and brittle as glass and volatile as ether. Her evolution had been accomplished by Papendeik, the great artist. He had taken her as if she had been a bale of tinsel cloth and had created from her something quite unique and individual to himself. "He taught me how to mellow," she said once with a tenderness which was certainly not Gallic, "the *grand seigneur*."

At sixty she was a small, dark, ugly woman with black silk hair, a lifted face and the gift of making a grace of every fold she wore. She was at her little writing table making great illegible characters with a ridiculous pen when Mr. Campion wandered in after lunch and she greeted him with genuine welcome in her narrow eyes.

"The little Albert," she said. "My dear, the ensemble! Very distinguished. Turn round. Delightful. That is the part of a man one remembers always with affection, his back from the shoulders to the waist. Is Val still on the roof with that mechanic?"

Mr. Campion seated himself and beamed. They were old friends and without the least disrespect he always thought she looked like a little wet newt, she was so sleek and lizardlike with her sharp eyes and swift movements.

"I rather liked him," he said, "but I felt a little superfluous so I came down."

Tante Marthe's bright eyes rested for a moment on two mannequins who were talking together some distance down the southern corridor. The glass walls of the room were soundproof so there was no means of telling if they were actually saying the things to each other which appearances would suggest, but when one of them caught sight of the little figure silhouetted against the brightness of the further wall there was a hurried adjournment.

Lady Papendeik shrugged her shoulders and made a note of two names on her blotting pad.

"Val is in love with that man," she remarked. "He is very masculine. I hope it is not merely a most natural reaction. We are too many women here. There is no 'body' in the place."

Mr. Campion shied away from the subject.

"You don't like women, Tante Marthe?"

"My dear, it is not a question of liking." The vehemence in her deep, ugly voice startled him. "One does not dislike the half of everything. You bore me, you young people, when you talk about one sex or the other, as if they were separate things. There is only one human entity and that is a man and a woman. The man is the silhouette, the woman is the detail. The one often spoils or makes the other. But apart they are so much material. Don't be a fool."

She turned over the sheet of paper on which she had been writing and drew a little house on it.

"*Did* you like him?" she demanded suddenly, shooting a direct and surprisingly youthful glance at him.

"Yes," he said seriously, "yes. He's a personality and a curiously simple chap, but I liked him."

"The family would raise no difficulty?"

"Val's family?"

"Naturally."

He began to laugh.

"Darling, you're slipping back through the ages, aren't you?"

Lady Papendeik smiled at herself.

"It's marriage, my dear," she confided. "Where marriage is concerned, Albert, I am still French. It is so much better in France. There marriage is always the contract and nobody forgets that, even in the beginning. It makes it so proper. Here no one thinks of his signature until he wants to cross it out."

Mr. Campion stirred uneasily.

"I don't want to be offensive," he murmured, "but I think all this is a bit premature."

"Ah." To his relief she followed him instantly. "I wondered. Perhaps so. Very likely. We will forget it. Why are you here?''

"Come about a body.'' His tone was diffident. "Nothing indelicate or bad for business, naturally. I want to meet Georgia Wells.''

Tante Marthe sat up.

"Georgia Wells,'' she said. "Of course! I could not think if Portland-Smith was the name of the man or not. Have you seen the evening paper?''

"Oh, Lord, have they got it already?'' He took up the early racing edition from the desk and turned it over. In the Stop Press he found a little paragraph in blurred, irregular type.

SKELETON IN BUSHES. Papers found near a skeleton of a man discovered in the shrubbery of a house near Wellferry, Kent, suggest that body may be that of Mr. Richard Portland-Smith, who disappeared from his home nearly three years ago.

He refolded the paper and smiled at her wryly.

"Yes, well, that's a pity,'' he said.

Lady Papendeik was curious but years of solid experience had taught her discretion.

"It is a professional affair for you?''

"I found the poor chap.''

"Ah.'' She sat nibbling her pen, her small back straight and her inquisitive eyes fixed upon his face. "It is undoubtedly the body of the fiancé?''

"Oh yes, it's Portland-Smith all right. Tante Marthe, was that engagement on or off when he vanished? Do you remember?''

"Oh,'' said the old lady firmly. "Ramillies had appeared upon the scene, you understand, but Georgia was still engaged. How long after he disappeared did the wretched man die? Can you tell that?''

"Not from the state of the body . . . at least I shouldn't think so. It must have been fairly soon but I don't think any pathologist could swear to it within a month or so. However, I fancy the police will be able to pin it down because of the fragments of the clothes. He seems to have been in evening dress.''

Tante Marthe nodded. She looked her full age and her lips moved in a little soundless murmur of pity.

15

"And the cause? That will be difficult too?"

"No. He was shot."

She moved her hands and clicked her tongue.

"Very unpleasant," she pronounced and added maliciously: "It will be interesting to see Ferdie Paul turn it into good publicity."

Campion rose and stood looking down at her, his long thin figure drooping a little.

"I'd better fade away," he said regretfully. "I can't very well butt in on her now."

Lady Papendeik stretched out a restraining hand.

"No, don't go," she said. "You stay. Be intelligent of course; the woman's a client. But I'd like someone to see them all. We are putting up some of the money for Caesar's Court. I would like your advice. Paul and Ramillies will be here and so will Laminoff."

"Caesar's Court?" Campion was surprised. "You too? Everyone I meet seems to have a finger in that pie. You're sitting pretty. It's going to be a Tom Tiddler's ground."

"I think so." She smiled complacently. "London has never had that kind of luxury on the doorstep and we can afford it. It was never possible in the old days because of the transport difficulty and when the transport did come there wasn't the money. Now the two have arrived together. Have you been out there yet? It's hardly a journey at all by car."

"No," said Mr. Campion, grinning. "I don't want to picnic in Naples, take a foam bath, improve my game, eat a lotus or mix with the elite. Also, frankly, the idea of spending six or seven hundred on a week-end party makes me feel physically sick. However, I realise that there are people who do, and I must say I like the wholesale magnificence of the scheme. These things usually flop because the promoters will rely on one or two good features to carry the others. This show *is* solid leather all through. The chef from the Virginia, Teddy Quoit's band, Andy Bullard in charge of the golf course, the Crannis woman doing the swimming and Waugh the tennis, while it was genius to make the place the headquarters of the beauty king chap, what's-his-name."

"Mirabeau," she supplied. "He's an artist. Ditte, his coiffeuse, designed my hair. Yes, the idea was excellent, but the execution has been extraordinary. That's Laminoff. Laminoff was the maître d'hôtel at the Poire d'Or. Bjornson let him in when he crashed. He's incredible, and Madame is no fool. It was Laminoff who insisted that the flying field must be made a customs port. Alan Dell arranged that."

"Dell? Is he in it too?"

"Naturally. All the club planes are Alandel machines and his pilots are in charge. His works are only a mile or so away on the other side of the river. He has a big interest in the whole hotel. That's how Val met him."

"I see." Mr. Campion blinked. "It's quite a neat little miracle of organisation, isn't it? Who's the clever lad in the background? Who woke up in the night with the great idea?"

Tante Marthe hesitated.

"Ferdie Paul. Don't mention it. It's not generally known." She pursed her lips and looked down her long nose. "Do you know Paul?"

"No. I thought he was a stage man. He's a producer, surely?"

"He's very clever," said Lady Papendeik. "He made Georgia Wells and he holds the leases of the Sovereign and the Venture theatres. The Cherry Orchard Club is his and he has a half share in the Tulip Restaurant."

Campion laughed. "And that's all you've been able to find out about him?"

She grimaced at him. "It's not enough, is it?" she said. "After all, we're not made of money—who is? Oh, they're here, are they? We'll go down."

She nodded and dismissed a page boy who had barely entered the room and had not had time to open his mouth.

"Now," she said without the slightest trace of conscious affectation, "we will see what beautiful dresses can do to a woman. One of these gowns is so lovely that I burst into tears when I first saw it and Rex would have fainted if he hadn't controlled himself, the poor neurotic."

Finding himself incapable of suitable comment, Mr. Campion said nothing and followed her dutifully down the grand staircase.

Chapter Three

It was never Mr. Campion's custom to make an entrance. In early youth he had perfected the difficult art of getting into and out of rooms without fuss, avoiding both the defensive flourish and the despicable creep, but he swept into Papendeik's grand salon like the rear guard of a conqueror, which in a way, of course, he was.

Lady Papendeik at work was a very different person from Tante Marthe in Val's office. She appeared to be a good two inches higher, for one thing, and she achieved a curious sailing motion which was as far removed from ordinary walking as is the goose step in an exactly opposite direction. Mr. Campion found himself stalking behind her as though to fast and martial music. It was quite an experience.

The salon was golden. Val held that a true conceit is only a vulgarity in the right place and had done the thing thoroughly.

The room itself had been conceived in the grand manner. It was very long and high, with seven great windows leading out on to a stone terrace with bronzes, so that the general effect might easily have become period had not the very pale gold monotone of the walls, floor and furnishings given it a certain conscious peculiarity which, although satisfactory to the eye, was yet not sufficiently familiar to breed any hint of ignorant contempt.

The practical side of the colour scheme, which had really determined the two ladies to adopt it and which was now quite honestly forgotten by both of them, was that as a background for fine silk or wool material there is nothing so flattering as a warm, polished metal. Also, as Tante Marthe had remarked in an unguarded moment, "gold is so *comforting*, my dears, if you can really make it unimportant."

So Mr. Campion tramped through pale golden pile and was

18

confronted at last by a vivid group of very human people, all silhouetted, framed and set and thus brought into startling relief against a pale golden wall. He was aware first of a dark face and then a fair one, a small boy of all unexpected things and afterwards, principally and completely, of Georgia Wells.

She was bigger than he had thought from the auditorium and now, without losing charm, more coarse. She was made up under the skin, as it were, designed by nature as a poster rather than a pen drawing.

He was aware that her eyes were large and grey, with long strong lashes and thick pale skin round them. Even the brown flecks in the grey irises seemed bolder and larger than is common and her expression was bright and shrewd and so frank that he felt she must have known him for some time.

She kissed Lady Papendeik ritualistically upon both cheeks but the gesture was performed absently and he felt that her attention was never diverted an instant from himself.

"Mr. Campion?" she echoed. "Really? Albert Campion?"

Her voice, which, like everything else about her, was far stronger and more flexible than the average, conveyed a certain wondering interest and he understood at once that she knew who he was, that she had seen the newspapers and was now considering if there was some fortunate coincidence in their meeting or if it were not fortunate or not a coincidence.

"Ferdie, this is Mr. Campion. *You* know. Mr. Campion, this is Ferdie Paul."

The dark face resolved itself into a person. Ferdie Paul was younger than Mr. Campion had expected. He was a large, plumpish man who looked like Byron. He had the same dark curling hair that was unreasonably inadequate on crown and temples, the same proud, curling mouth which would have been charming on a girl and was not on Mr. Paul, and the same short, strong, uniform features which made him just a little ridiculous, like a pretty bull.

When he spoke, however, the indolence which should have been a part and parcel of his make-up was surprisingly absent. He was a vigorous personality, his voice high and almost squeaky, with a nervous energy in it which never descended into irritability.

There was also something else about him which Campion noticed and could not define. It was a peculiar uncertainty of power, like pinking in a car engine, a quality of labour under

19

difficulties which was odd and more in keeping with his voice than his appearance or personality.

He glanced at Campion with quick, intelligent interest, decided he did not know or need him, and dismissed him from his mind in a perfectly friendly fashion.

"We can begin at once, can't we?" he said to Lady Papendeik. "It's absolutely imperative that they should be quite right."

"They are exquisite," announced Tante Marthe coldly, conveying her irrevocable attitude in one single stroke.

Paul grinned at her. His amusement changed his entire appearance. His mouth became more masculine and the fleeting glimpse of gold stopping in his side teeth made him look for some reason more human and fallible.

"You're a dear, aren't you?" he said and sounded as if he meant it.

Lady Papendeik's narrow eyes, which seemed to be all pupil, flickered at him. She did not smile but her thin mouth quirked and it occurred to Campion, who was watching them, that they were the working brains of the gathering. Neither of them were artists but they were the masters of artists, the Prosperos of their respective Ariels, and they had a very healthy admiration for one another.

By this time new visitors had arrived and were drifting towards the quilted settees between the windows. Rex was very much in evidence. He had lost his anger but retained his pathos, interrupting it at times with little boy exuberances always subdued to the right degree of ingratiating affability.

Campion noticed one woman in particular, a very correctly dressed little matron whose excellent sartorial taste could not quite lend her elegance, finding him very comforting. He wondered who she was and why she should receive such deference. Rex, he felt certain, would genuinely only find charm where it was politic that charm should be found, yet she did not by her manner appear to be very rich nor did she seem to belong to anybody. He had little time to observe her or anyone else, however, for Georgia returned to him.

"I'm so interested in you," she said with a frankness which he found a little overwhelming. "I'm not at all sure you couldn't be useful to me."

The naïveté of the final remark was so complete that for a second he wondered if she had really made it, but her eyes, which were as grey as tweed suiting and rather like it, were fixed on his own and her broad, beautiful face was earnest and friendly.

"Something rather awful has happened to me this afternoon," she went on, her voice husky. "They've found the skeleton of a man I adored. I can't help talking about it to somebody. Do forgive me. It's a shock, you know."

She gave him a faint apologetic smile and it came to him with surprise that she was perfectly sincere. He learnt a great deal about Georgia Wells at that moment and was interested in her. The ordinary hysteric who dramatises everything until she loses all sense of proportion and becomes a menace to the unsuspecting stranger was familiar to him, but this was something new. For the moment at any rate Georgia Wells was genuine in her despair and she seemed to be regarding him not as an audience but as a possible ally, which was at least disarming.

"I ought not to blurt it out like this to a stranger," she said. "I only realise how terrible these things are when I hear myself saying them. It's disgusting. Do forgive me."

She paused and looked up into his face with sudden childlike honesty.

"It is a frightful shock, you know."

"Of course it is," Campion heard himself saying earnestly. "Terrible. Didn't you know he was dead?"

"No, I had no idea." The protest was hearty and convincing but it lacked the confiding quality of her earlier announcements and he glanced at her sharply. She closed her eyes and opened them again.

"I'm behaving damnably," she said. "It's because I've heard so much about you I feel I know you. This news about Richard has taken me off my balance. Come and meet my husband."

He followed her obediently and it occurred to him as they crossed the room that she had that rare gift, so rare that he had some difficulty in remembering that it was only a gift, of being able to talk directly to the essential individual lurking behind the civilised façade of the man before her, so that it was impossible for him to evade or disappoint her without feeling personally responsible.

"Here he is," said Georgia. "Mr. Campion, this is my husband."

Campion's involuntary thought on first meeting Sir Raymond Ramillies was that he would be a particularly nasty drunk. This thought came out of the air and was not inspired by anything faintly suggestive of the alcoholic in the man himself. From Ramillies' actual appearance there was nothing to indicate that he ever drank at all, yet when Campion was first confronted by that arrogant brown face with the light eyes set too close together and that general air of irresponsible power the first thing that came into his mind was that it was as well that the fellow was at least sober.

They shook hands and Ramillies stood looking at him in a way that could only be called impudent. He did not speak at all but seemed amused and superior without troubling to be even faintly antagonistic.

Mr. Campion continued to regard him with misgiving and all the odd stories he had heard about this youthful middle-aged man with the fine-sounding name returned to his mind. Ramillies had retired from a famous regiment after the Irish trouble, at which times fantastic and rather horrible rumours had been floating about in connection with his name. There had been a brief period of sporting life in the shires and then he had been given the governorship of Ulangi, an unhealthy spot on the West Coast, a tiny serpent of country separating two foreign possessions. There the climate was so inclement that he was forced to spend three months of the year at home, but it was hinted that he contrived to make his exile not unexciting. Campion particularly remembered a pallid youngster who had been one of a party to spend a month at the Ulangi Residency and who had been strangely loth to discuss his adventures there on his return. One remark had stuck in Campion's mind: "Ramillies is a funny bird. All the time you're with him you feel he's going to get himself hanged or win the V.C. then and there before your eyes. Wonderful lad. Puts the wind up you."

Ramillies was quiet enough at the moment. He had made no remark of any kind since their arrival, but had remained standing with his feet apart and his hands behind him. He was swinging a little on his toes and his alert face wore an expression of innocence which was blatantly deceptive. Campion received the uncomfortable impression that he was thinking of something to do.

"I've just blurted out all my misery about Richard."

22

Georgia's deep voice was devoid of any affectation and indeed achieved a note of rather startling sincerity. "I had no idea how frightfully shaken up I am. You know who Mr. Campion is, don't you, Raymond?"

"Yes, of course I do." Ramillies glanced at his wife as he spoke and his thin sharp voice, which had yet nothing effeminate about it, was amused. He looked at Campion and spoke to him as though from a slight distance. "Do you find that sort of thing terribly interesting? I suppose you do or you wouldn't do it. There's a thrill in it, is there, hunting down fellows?"

The interesting thing was that he was not rude. His voice, manner and even the words were all sufficiently offensive to warrant one knocking him down, but the general effect was somehow naïve. There was no antagonism there at all, rather something wistful in the final question.

Mr. Campion suddenly remembered him at school, a much older boy who had gone on to Sandhurst at the end of Campion's first term, leaving a banner of legend behind him. With a touch of snobbism which he recognised as childish at the time he refrained from mentioning the fact.

"The thrill is terrific," he agreed solemnly. "I frequently frighten myself into a fit with it."

"Do you?" Again there was the faint trace of real interest.

Georgia put her arm through Campion's, an unself-conscious gesture designed to attract his attention, which it did.

"Why did you come to see this dress show?"

He felt her shaking a little as she clung to him.

"I wanted to meet you," he said truthfully. "I wanted to talk to you."

"About Richard? I'll tell you anything I know. I want to talk about him."

While there was no doubt about her sincerity there was a suggestion of daring in her manner, an awareness of danger without the comprehension of it, which gave him his first real insight into her essential character and incidentally half startled the life out of him.

"You said he was dead, Raymond." There was a definite challenge in her voice and Campion felt her quivering like a discharging battery at his side.

"Oh yes, I knew the chap was dead." Ramillies was remarkably matter of fact and Campion stared at him.

"How did you know?"

"Thought he must be, else he'd have turned up once I'd gone back to Africa and Georgia was alone." He made the statement casually but with conviction and it dawned upon the other man that he was not only indifferent to any construction that might be put upon his words, but incapable of seeing that they might convey any other meaning.

Georgia shuddered. Campion felt the involuntary movement and was puzzled again, since it did not seem to be inspired purely by fear or disgust. He had the unreasonable impression that there was something more like pleasure at the root of it.

"If it wouldn't upset you to talk about him," he ventured, looking down at her, "I'd like to hear your impression of his mental condition the last time you saw him . . . if you're sure you don't mind."

"My dear, I *must* talk!" Georgia's cry came from the heart, or seemed to do so, but the next instant her grip on his arm loosened and she said in an entirely different tone: "Who's that coming over here with Val?"

Campion glanced up and was aware of a faint sense of calamity.

"That?" he murmured guiltily. "Oh, that's Alan Dell, the aeroplane chap."

"Introduce us," said Georgia. "I think he wants to meet me."

Val came across the room purposefully and it occurred to Mr. Campion that she looked like the Revenge sailing resolutely into battle with her pennants flying. She looked very fine with her little yellow coxcomb held high and every line of her body flowing with that particular kind of femininity which is neat and precisely graceful. He sighed for her. He was prepared to back the Spanish galleon every time.

Alan Dell came beside her. Having once met the man, Campion discovered that his shy and peculiarly masculine personality was now completely apparent and that his first superficial impression of him had vanished.

Georgia put about.

"My pretty," she said, stretching out both hands. "Come and comfort me with clothes. I'm in a tragedy."

Her fine strong body was beautiful as she swung forward

and a warmth of friendliness went out to meet the other girl.
Val responded to it cautiously.

"I've got just the dress for it, whatever it is," she said
lightly. "The ultimate garment of all time."

Georgia drew back. She looked pathetically hurt behind her
smile.

"I'm afraid it's a real tragedy," she said reproachfully.

"My pet, I'm so sorry. What is it?" Val made the apology
so unjustly forced from her and her eyes grew wary.

Georgia glanced over her shoulder before she spoke. Ramillies
still stood swinging on his toes, his glance resting consideringly
upon the small boy in the corner. Georgia shook her head.

"Tell me about the lovely dresses," she said, and added
before Val or Campion could speak, "Who is this?" a
demand which brought Dell forward with the conviction that
there had been a general disinclination to present him.

He shook hands with unexpected gaucherie and stood
blinking at her, suffering no doubt from that misapprehension
so common to shy folk, that he was not quite so clearly
visible to her as she was to him.

Georgia regarded him with that glowing and intelligent
interest which was her chief weapon of attack.

"The second last person on earth to find in a dress shop,"
she said. "My dear, are you going to enjoy all this? Have you
ever been to this sort of show before?"

"No," he said and laughed. "I stayed to see you."

Georgia blushed. The colour flowed up her throat and over
her face with a charm no seventeen-year-old could have
touched.

"That's very nice of you," she said. "I'm afraid I'm going
to be very dull. Something rather beastly has happened to me
and I'm just behaving disgustingly and blurting it out to
everyone."

It was a dangerous opening and might well have proved
disastrous but that her gift of utter directness was a lodestone.
Dell's sudden gratified sense of kindly superiority was com-
municated to them all and he murmured something bald about
seeing her in trouble once more.

"*The Little Sacrifice*?" she said quickly. "Oh, I adored
that woman Jacynth. I found myself putting all I'd ever
known or ever felt into her, poor sweetie. It was very nice of
you to go and see me."

From that moment her manner changed subtly. It was such a gradual metamorphosis, so exquisitely done, that Campion only just noticed it, but the fact remained that she began to remind him strongly of the heroine in *The Little Sacrifice*. Touches of the character crept into her voice, into helpless little gestures, into her very attitude of mind, and he thought ungenerously that it would have been even more interesting, besides being much more easy to follow, if the original part had only been played in some strong foreign accent.

Dell was openly enchanted. He remained watching her with fascinated attention, his blue eyes smiling and very kind.

"It was a long time ago and all very sad and silly even then." Georgia sounded both brave and helplessly apologetic. "He was such a dear, my sweet moody Richard. I knew him so awfully well. We were both innately lonely people and ... well, we were very fond of one another. When he simply vanished I was broken-hearted, but naturally I couldn't admit it. Could I?"

She made a little fluttering appeal to them all to understand.

"One doesn't, does one?" she demanded with that sudden frankness which, if it is as embarrassing, is also as entirely disarming as nakedness. "I mean, when one really is in love one's so painfully self-conscious, so miserably mistrustful of one's own strength. I'm talking about the real, rather tragic thing, of course. Then one's so horribly afraid that this exquisite, precious, deliriously lovely sanctuary one's somehow achieved may not be really solid, may not be one's own for keeps. One's so conscious all the time that one can be hurt beyond the bounds of bearing that in one's natural pessimism one dreads disaster all the time, and so when something does happen one accepts it and crawls away somewhere. You do know what I mean, don't you?"

They did, of course, being all adult and reasonably experienced, and Mr. Campion, who was shocked, was yet grudgingly impressed. Her tremendous physical health and that quality which Dell had called "confiding" had clothed an embarrassing revelation of the ordinary with something rather charming. He glanced at Val.

She looked past him and did not speak aloud, although her lips moved. He thought he read the words "strip tease," and regarded her with sudden respect.

Georgia did not let the scene drop.

"I'm so sorry," she said helplessly. "This is all so disgustingly vulgar of me, but oh, my dears!—suddenly to see it on the placards, to make Ferdie leap out of the car and get a paper, to snatch it away from him and then to look and find it all true! They've found his skeleton, you see."

Her eyes were holding them all and there was real wretchedness in the grey shadows.

"You never think of people you know having skeletons, do you?"

"My dear, how horrible!" Val's ejaculation was startled out of her. "When did all this happen?"

"Now," said Georgia miserably. "Now, just as I was coming here. I'd have gone home, my pet, but I couldn't let you and everybody else down just when we were all so rushed. I didn't realise it was going to have this dreadful loquacious effect upon me."

"Darling, what are you talking about?" Ferdie Paul slipped his arm round her and drew her back against him. His face over her shoulder was dark and amused, but there was more in his voice than tolerance. "Forget it. You'll upset yourself."

Georgia shivered, smiled and released herself with a gentle dignity, directed, Campion felt, at himself and Dell. She glanced at her husband, who came forward promptly, his natural springy walk lending him a jauntiness which added considerably to his disturbing air of active irresponsibility.

"That's right, Georgia," he said in his flat staccato voice. "Forget the fellow if you can, and if you can't don't make an ass of yourself."

Even he seemed to feel that this admonition might sound a trifle harsh to the uninitiated, for he suddenly smiled with that transfiguring, sunny happiness usually associated with early childhood. "What I mean to say is, a lovely girl looks very touching grizzling over a corpse but she looks damned silly doing it over a skeleton. She's missed the boat. The great lover's not merely dead, dearest; he's dead and gone. Should I be a bounder if I asked for a drink?"

The last remark was directed towards Val with a quick-eyed charm which was ingratiating.

"Certainly not. You must all need one." Val sounded thoroughly startled. She glanced at Rex, who had been hovering on the edge of the group, and he nodded and disappeared. Ferdie Paul resumed his hold on Georgia. He had a gently contemptuous way with her, as if she were a difficult elderly relative of whom he was fond.

"We're going to see the great dress for the third act first," he said. "I want to make sure that when Pendleton gets you by the throat he can only tear the left shoulder out. It's got to be restrained and dignified. I don't want you running about in your brassière. The whole danger of that scene is that it may go a bit *vieux jeu* if we don't look out . . . nineteen twenty-sixish or so. Lady Papendeik wants us to see the dress on the model first because apparently it's pretty hot. Then I want you to get into it and we'll run through that bit."

Georgia stiffened.

"I'm not going to rehearse here in front of a lot of strangers," she protested. "God knows I'm not temperamental, sweetheart, but there are limits. You're not going to ask me to do that, Ferdie, not this afternoon of all times?"

"Georgia." Paul's arm had tightened, and Campion saw his round brown eyes fixed firmly upon the woman's own with a terrifying quality of intelligence in them, as if he were trying to hypnotise some sense into her. "Georgia, you're not going to be silly, are you, *dear*?"

It was an idiotic little scene, reminding Campion irresistibly of a jockey he had once heard talking to a refractory horse.

"We'll go. Mr. Campion and I will go, Miss Wells." Alan Dell spoke hastily and Paul, looking up, seemed to see him for the first time.

"Oh no, that's all right," he said. "There's only a few of us here. It's a purely technical matter. You're going to be reasonable, aren't you, darling? You're only a bit jittery because of the boy friend."

Georgia smiled at him with unexpected tolerance and turned to Dell with a little deprecating grimace.

"My nerves have gone to pieces," she said and it occurred to Mr. Campion that she might easily be more accurate than she realised.

It was at this moment that Tante Marthe came over with one of her small coloured pages at her elbow.

"The *Trumpet* is on the phone, my dear," she said. "Will you speak to them?"

Georgia's hunted expression would have been entirely convincing if it had not been so much what one might have expected.

"All right," she said heavily. "This is the horrible part of it all. This is what I've been dreading. Yes, I'll come."

"No." Ramillies and Paul spoke together and paused to look at one another afterwards. It was the briefest interchange of glances and Mr. Campion, who was watching them both, became aware for the first time that the undercurrent which he had been trying to define throughout the entire afternoon was an unusual, and in the circumstances incomprehensible, combination of alarm and excitement.

"No," said Ramillies again. "Don't say a thing."

"Do you mean that?" She turned to him almost with eagerness and he did not look at her.

"No, dear, I don't think I would." Ferdie Paul spoke casually. "We'll put out some sort of statement later if it's necessary. It's not a particularly good story so they won't get excited. Tell them Miss Wells is not here. She left half an hour ago."

The page went off obediently and Paul watched the child until it disappeared, his figure drooping and his prominent eyes thoughtful. Georgia looked at Dell, who moved over to her.

"That must be a very great relief to you," he said.

She stared at him. "You understand, don't you?" she said with sudden earnestness. "You really do."

Mr. Campion turned away rather sadly and became aware of Val. She was looking at the other woman and he caught her unawares. Once again she surprised him. Jealousy is one emotion but hatred is quite another and much more rare in a civilised community. Once it is seen it is not easily forgotten.

Chapter Four

The gentle art of putting things over had always interested Mr. Campion, but as he sat down beside Alan Dell to watch the house of Papendeik at work he was aware of a sudden sense of irritation. There was so much going on under his nose that needed explanation. The strangers were vivid personalities but not types he recognised and at the moment he did not understand their reactions at all.

Meanwhile an impressive if informal performance was beginning. Val and Tante Marthe were staging an act and he was entertained to note that they worked together with the precision of a first-class vaudeville turn.

Tante Marthe had seated herself on the largest of the settees between the two most central windows and had made room for Ferdie Paul beside her, while Georgia had been provided by Rex with a wide-seated gilt chair thrust out into the room a little.

She sat in it regally, her dark head thrown back and her lovely broad face tilted expectantly. Even so she contrived to look a little tragic, making it clear that she was a woman with a background of deep emotional experience.

Val stood behind her, slender and exquisite and very much the brilliant young artist about to display something that might well prove to be the masterpiece of a century.

The rest of the conversation piece was furnished by the staff. Every available saleswoman had assembled together at one end of the room, as though for prayers in an old-fashioned household. There was a flutter of expectancy among them, a gathering together to admire a creation for which they all took a small degree of personal responsibility. Their very presence indicated a big moment.

Dell caught Campion's eye and leant forward.

"Wonderfully interesting," he whispered with professional appreciation.

There was a moment of silence and Rex slid forward to give an entirely unnecessary flick to the folds of a curtain. Lady Papendeik glanced round her and raised a small dark paw. The staff sighed and the dress appeared.

At this point Mr. Campion felt somewhat out of his depth. He looked at the dress and saw that it was long and white, with a satisfactory arrangement of drapery at the front, and that it had an extraordinary-looking girl in it. She caught his attention because she was beautiful without being in any way real or desirable. She had a strong superficial likeness to Georgia inasmuch as she was not small and was dark with broad cheekbones, but there all similarity ended. Where Georgia was coarse the newcomer was exquisite, where Georgia was vital the other girl was dead.

30

Campion glanced at Tante Martha and was delighted to see her sitting back, her hands in her lap, her eyes half closed and an outrageous expression of fainting ecstasy on her face. Ferdie Paul looked thoughtful but by no means unimpressed and the staff whispered and preened itself.

Campion and Alan Dell looked at the gown again, each trying to discover why it should be so particularly pleasing, and were both on the verge of making the same thundering mistake by deciding that its charm lay in its simplicity when Georgia dropped the bomb.

"Val, my angel," she said, her lovely husky voice sounding clearly through the room, "it's breath-taking! It's *you*. It's *me*. But, my pet, it's not *new*. I saw it last night at the Dudley Club."

There was a moment of scandalised silence. The Greek chorus in the corner gaped and Rex's nervous giggle echoed inopportunely from the background. The formal conversation piece had turned into a Gluyas Williams picture.

Lady Papendeik rose.

"My dear," she said, "my dear." Her voice was not very loud or even particularly severe but instantly all the humour went out of the situation and Georgia was on the defensive.

"Oh, my dear, I'm so sorry." She turned to Val impulsively and the most ungenerous among them could not have doubted her honesty. "There's been some hideous mistake, of course. This whole day is like a nightmare. I did see it. I saw it last night and it fascinated me. I can even prove it, unfortunately. There's a photograph of the Blaxill woman wearing it in one of the morning papers ... the *Range Finder*, I think ... on the back page. She's dancing with a cabinet minister. I noticed it, naturally. It wiped the floor with everything else."

Val said nothing. Her face was quite expressionless as she nodded to the horrified group at the other end of the room. There was a discreet scurrying towards the door and a rustle of chatter as they reached the hall. Georgia stood up. Her tall, graceful body towered over Val, making the other girl look as if she belonged to some smaller and neater world.

"Of course it hadn't your cut," she said earnestly, "and I don't think it was in that material, but it was white."

31

Lady Papendeik shrugged her shoulders.

"That is Bouleau's *Caresse*," she said, "woven to our design."

Georgia looked like helpless apology personified.

"I had to tell you," she said.

"Of course you did, my dear," murmured Lady Papendeik without thawing. "Of course."

There was no doubt that the incident was a major catastrophe. Everybody began to talk and Paul crossed the room to Val's side, with Ramillies, casual and unaccountable, at his heels.

Mr. Campion was puzzled. In his experience the duplication of a design, although the most dispiriting of all disasters to the artist concerned, is seldom taken seriously by anyone else, unless hard money has already been involved, and he began to wonder if this explosion was not in the nature of a safety valve, seized upon gratefully because it was a legitimate excuse for excitement actually engendered by something less politic to talk about.

The other person who might possibly have shared Mr. Campion's own Alice in Wonderland view of the situation was the small boy. He sat staring into the inside of his Haverleigh cap, his forehead wrinkled, and was apparently unaware of any crisis.

The return of Rex was dramatic. He came hurrying in with a perfectly white face, a newspaper in his outstretched hand. Lady Papendeik stood looking at the photograph for some moments and when she spoke her comment was typical.

"Only a thief would permit a woman with a stomach to commit such sacrilege. Who dresses her?"

The others crowded round and Dell turned to Campion again.

"It's a leakage," he murmured. "You can't stop it in any show where designs are secret. It's an infuriating thing."

"It's a miracle the photograph is so clear," said Georgia forlornly. "They're usually so vague. But you can't miss that, can you? It was in ribbed silk. I couldn't take my eyes off it." She put an arm round Val's shoulders. "You poor sweet," she said.

Val released herself gently and turned to Rex.

"Who is that woman's couturier?"

"Ring her up." Ramillies made the outrageously impolitic

suggestion with all the vigorous irresponsibility which turned him into such a peculiarly disturbing element. "Say you're a magazine. Georgia, you do it . . . or I will. Shall I?"

"No, darling, of course not. Don't be an ass." Georgia had spoken casually and he turned to her.

"Ass be damned!" he exploded with a violence which startled everyone. "It's the only intelligent suggestion that's been put forward so far. What's the woman's name? She'll be in the book, I suppose."

His fury was so entirely unexpected that for a moment the main disaster was forgotten. Campion stared at him in astonishment. His thin jaws were clenched and the little pulses in them throbbed visibly. The reaction was so entirely out of proportion to the occurrence that Campion was inclined to suspect that the man was drunk after all, when he caught a glimpse of Ferdie Paul. Both he and Georgia were eyeing Ramillies with definite apprehension.

"Wait a moment, old boy." Paul sounded cautious. "You never know. We may be able to pin it down here."

"You may be in an hour or so of fooling about." Ramillies' contempt was bitter. "But that's the straightforward, elementary way of finding a thing out . . . ask."

"Just one little moment," murmured Tante Marthe over her shoulder. "This is not a thing that has never happened before."

Ramillies shrugged his shoulders. "As you please. But I still think the intelligent thing to do is to get on the phone to the woman. Tell her all about it if you must. But if I was doing it myself I should say I was a magazine and get it out of her that way. However, it's nothing to do with me, thank God."

He swung on his heel and made for the door.

"Ray, where are you going?" Georgia still sounded apprehensive.

He paused on the threshold and regarded her with cold dislike which was uncomfortably convincing.

"I'm simply going downstairs to see if they've got a telephone book," he said and went out.

Val glanced at Georgia, a startled question in her eyes, but it was Ferdie Paul who answered her.

"Oh no, that's all right. He won't phone," he said and looked across at the small boy, who nodded reassuringly and,

33

sliding off his chair, passed unobtrusively out of the room. It was an odd incident and Dell glanced at Campion.

"Astonishing chap," he said under his breath and regarded Georgia with increased interest.

Meanwhile Rex, who had been permitted to get a word in at last, was talking earnestly to Tante Marthe. He had a nervous habit of wriggling ingratiatingly and now, all the time he was talking, he seemed to be making surreptitious attempts to stroke his calves by leaning over backwards to get at them. But his observations were to the point.

"I know Leonard Lôke used to dress her," he said, "and if the design has gone there, of course it means it'll be turned over to the worst kind of wholesalers and produced by the hundred. It's a tragedy."

"The premier who made it, the vendeuse, Mrs. Saluski, the child in the fitting room, you, myself and Val," murmured Lady Papendeik, shooting her little lizard head up. "No one else saw the finished dress. The sketch was never completed. Val cut it on the living model."

Rex straightened.

"Wait," he said in an altered voice. "I've remembered. Leonard Lôke has two partners, Pretzger and Morris. Pretzger had a brother-in-law in the fur trade. You may remember him, madame; we've dealt with him once or twice. A fortnight ago I saw that man dining at the Borgia in Greek Street and he had Miss Adamson with him."

The dramatic point of this statement was not clear to Mr. Campion at first but, as all eyes were slowly turned upon the one person in the room who had hitherto taken no interest whatever in the proceedings, the inference dawned slowly upon him.

The mannequin had remained exactly where she was when the general attention had first been distracted from her. She was standing in the middle of the room, beautiful, serene and entirely remote. Her lack of reality was almost unpleasant and it occurred to Campion that her personality was as secret as if she had been a corpse. Now, with everyone staring at her rather than her dress, she did not come to life but remained looking at them blankly with brilliant, foolish eyes.

"Caroline, is this true?" demanded Tante Marthe.

"Is what true, madame?" Her voice, a jew's-harp, with a Croydon accent, came as a shock to some of them. Campion, who knew from experience that the beauty of porcelain lies too often in the glaze, was not so much surprised as regretfully confirmed in an opinion.

"Don't be a fool, my dear." Lady Papendeik betrayed unexpected heartiness. "You must know if you've eaten with a man or not. Do not let us waste time."

"I didn't know whose brother-in-law he was," protested Miss Adamson sulkily.

"Did you describe the model? Did it slip out by accident? These things have happened."

"No, I didn't tell him, madame."

"You understand what has occurred?"

Miss Adamson did not change her expression. Her dark eyes were liquid and devastatingly unintelligent.

"I didn't tell him anything. I swear it, I didn't."

Tante Marthe sighed. "Very well. Go and take it off."

As the girl floated from the room Val made a gesture of resignation.

"That's all we shall ever know," she said to Dell, who was standing beside her. "There's a direct link there, of course, but she was quite emphatic."

Campion joined them.

"I thought I noticed a certain clinging to the letter," he ventured.

"That was the diagnosis that leapt to my mind but I didn't care to mention it," Dell said, and added with the smile which made him attractive, "She's too lovely to be that kind of fool."

"No one's too lovely to be mental, in my experience," remarked Lady Papendeik briskly. "What diagnosis is this?"

"We thought she might be a letter-of-the-law liar," Dell said, glancing at Campion for support. "She didn't tell the man, she drew it for him. They're the most impossible people in the world to deal with. If you pin them down they get more and more evasive and convince themselves all the time that they're speaking the literal truth . . . which they are, of course, in a way. In my experience the only thing to do is to get rid of them, however valuable they are. Still, I shouldn't like to convict the girl on that evidence alone."

Tante Marthe hesitated and it went through Campion's mind that she was suppressing a remark that might possibly turn out to be indiscreet.

Ferdie Paul, who had remained silent throughout the interview, looked down at her.

"Send her to Caesar's Court," he said. "She's too lovely to lose. Margaret is down there, isn't she? Turn this kid over to her. She can talk about the gowns there as much as she likes; she won't see them until they're ready to be shown."

"Perhaps so," said Tante Marthe and her black eyes wavered.

Georgia resumed her seat.

"I think you're very generous, Val," she began. "I'm broken-hearted. I could weep. You'll never make me anything so deliriously lovely again."

"No," Val said, a cloud passing over her face, "I don't suppose I ever shall."

Georgia stretched out a strong hand and drew the other girl towards her.

"Darling, that was mean," she said with a sweet gentleness which was out of period, let alone character. "You're upset because your lovely design has been stolen. You're naturally livid and I understand that. But you're lucky, you know. After all, Val, it's such a little thing. I hate to repeat all this but I can't get it off my mind. Richard's poor murdered body has been found and here are we all fooling about stupid idiot dresses for a stupid idiot play."

She did not turn away but sat looking at them and her eyes slowly filled with tears and brimmed over. If she had only sounded insincere, only been not quite so unanswerably in the right, the outburst would have been forgivable: as it was, they all stood round uncomfortably until Mr. Campion elected to drop his little brick.

"I say, you know, you're wrong there," he said in his quiet, slightly nervous voice. "I don't think the word 'murder' has gone through any official mind. Portland-Smith committed suicide; that's absolutely obvious, to the police at any rate."

Val, who knew him, guessed from his expression of affable innocence that he hoped for some interesting reaction to this announcement, but neither of them was prepared for what actually took place. Georgia sat up stiffly in her chair and stared at him, while a dark stream of colour rose up her throat, swelling the veins in her neck and passing over her expressionless face.

"That's not true," she said.

With what appeared to be well-meaningness of the most unenlightened kind, Mr. Campion persisted in his point, ignoring all the danger signals.

"Honestly," he said. "I can reassure you on that question. I'm hand in glove with the fellow who found the body. As a matter of fact I was actually on the spot myself this morning. The poor chap had killed himself all right. . . . At least that's what the coroner will decide; I'm sure of it."

The quiet plausible voice was conversational and convincing.

"No." Georgia made the word a statement. "I don't believe it. It's not true." She was controlling herself with difficulty and when she stood up her body was trembling with the effort. There was no doubt at all about her principal emotion and it was so unaccountable and unreasonable in the circumstances that even Mr. Campion showed some of the astonishment he felt. She was angry, beside herself with ordinary, unadulterated rage.

Campion looked to Ferdie Paul for assistance, but he did not intervene. He stood regarding her speculatively, almost, it seemed to Campion, with the same sort of puzzled conjecture that he felt himself.

It was left to Tante Marthe to make the enquiry that was on the tip of everybody's tongue.

"My dear child," she said with faint reproof in her tone, "why be so annoyed? The poor man has been dead these three years. Had he been murdered it must have meant that someone killed him and that would entail trouble for everyone who knew him. If he killed himself no one need think of him with anything except pity."

"Oh, don't be so silly, angel." Georgia turned on the old woman in exasperation. "Can't you see the damage a story like that can do once it gets about? I won't believe it. I know it's not true."

"You *know*?" Campion's eyes were mild behind his spectacles but they did not disarm her into answering him impulsively.

"Richard was not a suicidal type," she said after a pause which lasted too long. "This is the final insufferable straw. I can't bear it. You must all forgive me and manage as best you can. I must go home."

"Going home?" Ramillies' voice sounded disappointed in the doorway. "Why? What's the matter now?" He seemed to have forgotten his flamboyant exit of ten minutes before, and came in jauntily pleased with himself as ever.

Georgia stood looking at him steadily.

"Albert Campion says Richard committed suicide. He seems to think there's no doubt about it."

"Oh?" Ramillies' casualness was remarkable and Campion wished he knew the man better. From what he had seen of him so far the reaction might mean absolutely anything, even genuine disinterest. Since no one else spoke it came to Ramillies somewhat belatedly that further comment was expected. "It's a long time ago anyhow," he remarked with singularly unhappy effect. "There'll be no ferreting about either, which is one good thing. That's the one advantage of suicide; everyone knows who did it," he ended lamely, and remained looking at his wife.

Georgia kept her eyes upon him for almost a minute and, having subdued him, turned to Dell.

"Would you be most terribly kind and drive me home?"

"Why, yes. Yes, of course." He looked a little startled. "Of course," he repeated. "I'd like to."

"Bless you," said Georgia and smiled at him faintly.

"Oh, I'll take you home if you really want to go," put in Ramillies without much enthusiasm.

She drew away from him.

"I'm not sure if I ever want to speak to you again," she said distinctly and went out, taking Dell with her.

"What on earth did she mean by that?" demanded Ferdie Paul.

Ramillies turned to look at him and there was, incongruously, the suggestion of a smile in the many creases round his eyes.

"God knows, my dear fellow," he said. "God knows."

Chapter Five

There is a distinct difference between the state of believing something to be true and knowing it to be so with the paid stamp of an official opinion affixed to the knowledge.

When the embarrassed foreman of the coroner's jury stood up in the cool dark village hall at Wellferry and stated that he and his confreres were convinced that the skeleton found in the bushes at Eves Hall on the Shelley road was the skeleton of Richard Portland-Smith, who had died by his own hand—a hand which had first thrust the barrel of a revolver into his mouth and then pulled the trigger—and that in their considered opinion he must have been of unsound mind at the time to have done such a thing, Mr. Campion felt aware of a distinct wave of relief, a comforting confirmation and a full stop, as it were.

He was sitting beside the man who was his friend and client at the end of a row of church chairs arranged against a wall of the converted army hut, and the scene before him was melancholy and very human. It was a coroner's court in essence, the bare practical bones of that judicial proceeding which has remained sound and useful from far-off simple times. A man had died mysteriously and nine of his countrymen had met together on the common ground of their patrial birth to decide how such a calamity had befallen him. There had been no decoration, no merciful arabesques of judicial pomp to smother the stark proceedings. The witnesses had come to the T-shaped table and muttered their depositions with nervous humility, while the jury had listened stolidly and afterwards shuffled out to the little cloakroom behind the stage on which the Conservative Concerts were held in the spring, and had returned, self-conscious and unhappy, to give their verdict.

Now the coroner with the patchy pink face and the unfortunate air of being unaccustomed to his job wriggled in his chair. He glanced shyly at the four pressmen at the far end of the table, almost, it would seem, in the hope of getting a little appreciation from them, or at least some indication that he had been "all right," and returned to his formalities with the jury.

The witnesses, who had been sitting with their friends around the walls, began to file out into the sunlight and the inspector came across to ask Mr. Campion's companion about the funeral. He was not tactful but he was kindly, and his pleasant Kentish voice rumbled on, explaining with simple practicalness that the shed where the remains now lay was not public property and the owner needed it for his handcart, whose paint was even now blistering in the sun. He added that the local builder, who had been on the jury, was also the undertaker and he had no doubt but that he would be over in a minute, so that no time would be lost.

While the sad little details were being arranged Mr. Campion had leisure to reflect on the evidence which had brought the Sunday-suited jury, with their perpetual jingle of darts medals and their solid, sensible faces, to their conclusions.

The identification had provided the most interesting fifteen minutes of the morning. The brown paper parcels of grey-green rags, the mildewed wallet complete with discoloured notes and visiting cards, and the rusty gun had been first displayed and sworn to by tailor and manservant. Afterwards, even more gruesome, had come the evidence of the self-important little dentist, who had rushed in to rattle off his formidable list of degrees and testify that the dental work in the remains of the dead man's jaw was his own and that it corresponded to his records of Portland-Smith's mouth. He had given place to the county pathologist, who had described the wound in detail and given his opinions on the length of time during which the body must have lain undiscovered.

Finally Mr. Campion's companion had walked to the table, his enormous shoulders held erect and the light from a window high in the wall falling on his white hair, which was silky and theatrically handsome. He had given his word that as far as he knew his son had no worries of sufficient magnitude to drive him to take his life. That had been all. The coroner had summed up and the jury had shambled out. Richard Portland-Smith had retired from the round dance of life while his measure in it was yet incomplete and nobody knew why.

Mr. Campion and his companion walked down the road to the inn where lunch was awaiting them. It was bright and clean in the sunlight, with summer in the air and all that promise of breathless festivity just round the corner which is the spirit of that time of year.

Campion did not speak, since his companion showed no desire to do so, but he glanced at the man out of the corner of his eye and thought that he was taking it very well.

In his own sphere Sir Henry Portland-Smith was a great man. In his hospital in South London he was a hard-working

THE FASHION IN SHROUDS

god whose every half-hour was earmarked for some separate and important purpose. This was probably the first morning he had set aside for purely personal considerations during the past twenty years.

Like many great physicians, he had a fine presence allied to enormous physical strength, and although he was nearly seventy his movements were vigorous and decisive. He did not talk until they sat down together in an alcove of the big dining room, which smelt faintly of creosote and plaster from recent restoring. The place was very quiet. They were early and a fleet of little tables, which looked homely and countrified in spite of an effort at sophistication, spread out before them.

"Satisfied?" The old man looked at Campion directly. He had taken off his spectacles and his cold but rather fine grey eyes had that pathetic, naked look which eyes which are normally hidden behind lenses achieve when the barrier is down.

"I think it was a true verdict."

"Unsound mind?"

Campion shrugged his shoulders.

"What *is* unsound mind?" he said helplessly. "It means nothing."

"Merely a form to get round the Christian burial difficulty?" There was bitterness in the query, which was unusual and slightly shocking to find in the old, and Campion, looking up, found himself thinking irrelevantly that if over-busy people keep young they also keep raw, retaining the prejudices and sophistries of their first period. He prepared to listen to an outburst against the hypocrisy of the law and the Church, but it did not come. Sir Henry planted his great elbows on the table and pushed his hands over his face as if he were cleansing it. He had the long, fine hands of the man who does not use them and the younger man remembered that he was not a surgeon.

"I'm trying to make up my mind," he said presently. "I appreciate what you've done, Albert. I like your reticence and your quiet persistence. I'm grateful to you for finding the boy. It's all over now with the least possible scandal. In a few months now he might never have been born."

This time the bitterness was savage and Campion, meeting those old, chilly, naked eyes, was suddenly ashamed of

41

himself for his smugness. He caught one of those sudden panoramic glimpses of a whole thirty-eight-year life and was aware for an instant of the paralysingly infuriating tragedy of waste.

"I want to know," said the old man. "For my own satisfaction I want to know. Now look here, my boy, this is a private matter between you and me. The public aspect of this affair is fixed and finished. Richard is dead. Everybody knows he shot himself. And that is the end. But I want to know why he did it and I want you to find out."

Mr. Campion's pale eyes were intelligent behind his spectacles but he looked uncomfortable.

"You're thinking he may have had a brainstorm?" Sir Henry made the query an accusation. "You're ready to believe in the form, are you? Well, you may be right. But I want to know."

Mr. Campion was an adroit young man and the present situation was not one he had not encountered before.

"I'll do anything I can," he said slowly. "But, after all, we've covered a lot of ground already. You say yourself he must have been extravagant. He was earning money and could have carried on, but he *had* no money when he died. You think he spent all his mother's legacy on Miss Wells? That is very probable but it is a thing we shall never find out. No one can find out how a man spent the money he drew out in cash three years before. I will do all I can but I can't promise results."

Sir Henry leant back in his chair and surveyed his companion consideringly. He was smiling a little and his magnificent head had never looked more imposing.

"My boy," he said, "I'm going to tell you something. This is a secret. Never let it out of your mouth, whatever happens, but when I tell you, you'll see why I am so anxious that you should carry on."

He hesitated and Campion was puzzled. It was impossible not to be impressed by the other man's manner, nor had he any reason to suspect him of anything faintly theatrical or unsound. In his experience Sir Henry was a sophisticated and in many ways a hard man.

"Yes?" he invited.

"You've seen this girl Georgia Wells, as I asked you?"

"Yes."

"Are you taken with her?"

The question was so unexpected that Campion blinked.

"No," he said truthfully. "I see her attraction but I should never be bowled over by her myself."

"Did she strike you as being a clever woman? Not a bluestocking, of course, but a really clever woman? Clever in the extraordinary way women sometimes are? Clever enough to get a man to do anything she wanted him to by reasoning with him?"

Campion gave the matter serious consideration.

"Not unless he was a fool," he said at last.

"Ah!" The old man pounced on the admission. "I thought not. That's what makes this so very interesting. Richard was not a fool. I would admit it if he was. I haven't been a physician all my life without learning that you can't make a true diagnosis if you falsify the symptoms. Richard was not a fool in that way. He was a virile type, the type to lose his head over a woman for a night but not for a month or two. Once he got his mind working again it would work, whatever his physical inclinations were. Do you follow me?"

"Yes," said Mr. Campion dubiously. "But—forgive me—I don't think that is getting us very far. You see, there's no evidence even of a quarrel. She seems to have been happily engaged to him right up to the time he disappeared."

"Campion"—the old man was leaning across the table—"you've seen that girl and you know her history. Do you honestly think she was the type of woman to be engaged to anybody?"

The younger man stared at him. The question had jerked him round to face a problem which had been chipping away at the back of his mind for some time. Now that it was out, unprotected by the automatic acceptance that is given to a fact that is known to everybody, the whole matter did strike him as extraordinary.

"A woman once through the divorce courts, important in a bohemian profession, doesn't go and get herself involved in a long engagement." Sir Henry's voice was contemptuous. "She gets married, my boy. She gets married."

Campion sat up.

"They were married!" he said blankly. "But that's incredible. She married again. What about Ramillies?"

"Yes, that was six months after Richard disappeared." The

old man was speaking earnestly. "After he disappeared, mind you, not after he died. No one knows when he died, although the likelihood is that the two events coincided. But the point I want you to realise is that the woman knew Richard was dead more than two years before we did. She must have known it. Why was she so quiet about it?"

He leant back in his chair and surveyed Campion steadily, his fierce cold eyes hard and intelligent.

Mr. Campion passed his hand over his fair hair.

"Are you sure of this?"

"Absolutely."

"You could prove it?"

"Yes."

"Why didn't you tell me before?"

"I didn't know it for certain until three or four weeks ago and by then I felt sure the boy was dead. Now that I know roughly when he died, I am wondering. Whatever we find out, I don't want it made public. I see no point in that. The publicity would hardly hurt me or his memory, but I have daughters and they have children, so I see no reason why the tale should linger on. Let it die with Richard. But I want to know."

Mr. Campion did not look at ease. His thin, good-humoured face with the twisted mouth was grave and his eyes thoughtful.

"You put me in a very awkward position," he said at last. "When I undertook this search for your son I simply felt I was making myself useful to an old friend of Belle Lafcadio's, and I've been more than glad to do it, but now I'm afraid I can't go any farther. This woman Georgia Wells is an important client of my sister's. To get hold of her I must abuse hospitality there. You see how it is."

He paused apologetically, and the old man watched him, a faint smile playing round the corners of his mouth.

"I'm hardly contemplating revenge," he observed.

"No. I did realise that." Campion was hesitating and unhappy. "But this marriage alters the whole complexion of the business."

"I think so. It makes it very curious."

Campion was silent, and after a while Sir Henry went on.

"My boy," he said, "I'm an old man who's seen a great deal, and I don't like mysteries. My son's death was a shock to my affections, of course, but it was also a shock of surprise. I simply want to know what the circumstances were that induced Richard, who was no neurotic, to take his life, and why that woman should never have told what she must have known. Don't make a mouthful of it, but if you should ever find out, remember I want to know.''

Campion raised his head.

"I'll do what I can," he said, "but don't rely on me.''

"Very well," said the old physician, and changed the subject abruptly.

For the rest of the meal they discussed the Abominable Snowmen and other sedate fripperies, but as Campion drove back to London a thought slipped quietly into his mind and sat there nagging at him.

Georgia Wells had not been sure of Portland-Smith's death until the day on which the discovery of his body had been reported in the newspapers: of that Campion was only fairly certain; but there was one point upon which he was prepared to stake his all, and that was that she had no idea that her ex-husband had committed suicide until Campion himself had told her.

Chapter Six

It was a little over six weeks later, one evening when the summer was at its height and London was sprawling, dirty and happily voluptuous, in the yellow evening sun, that Mr. Campion, letting himself into the flat, was accosted by a hoarse voice from the bathroom.

"Your sis rang up. She's coming round with a Frog of some sort.''

Not wishing to snub, but at the same time hoping to convey some disapproval at the lack of ceremony, Mr. Campion passed on to the sitting room without comment.

He had seated himself at the desk, found some cigarettes and pulled a sheet of notepaper towards him before there was a lumbering in the passage outside and a vast, melancholy figure in a black velvet coat surged breathily into the room.

Mr. Lugg, Mr. Campion's "male person's gentleman," regarded his employer with reproachful little black eyes.

"You 'eard," he said, and added with charming confiding, "I was cleanin' meself up. You'd do well to put on a dressing gown and a belt."

"A belt?" enquired Campion, taken off his guard.

"Braces is low, except when worn with a white waistcoat for billiards." Lugg made the pronouncement with justifiable pride. "I picked that up down at the club today. You'll 'ave to get a new robe, too. Mr. Tuke's young feller has a different-coloured one for every day of the week. What d'you say to that idea?"

"Slightly disgusting."

Lugg considered, his eyes flickering.

"I tell 'im it was pansy," he admitted, "but I couldn't be sure. It was a shot in the dark. 'Robe,' though; make a note of that. 'Robe's' the new name for dressing gown. I'm learnin' a lot from Mr. Tuke. He lent me 'is book, for one thing."

Campion threw down his pen.

"You're learning to read, are you?" he said pleasantly. "That's good. That'll keep us both quiet."

Mr. Lugg let down the flap of the cocktail cabinet with elaborate care before he deigned to reply.

"Silence is like sleep," he observed with unnatural solemnity. "It refreshes wisdom."

"Eh?" said Mr. Campion.

A slow, smug smile passed over the great white face and Mr. Lugg coughed.

"That give you something to think about," he said with satisfaction. "D'you know 'oo thought of it? Walter Plato."

"Really?" Mr. Campion was gratified. "And who was he?"

"A bloke." The scholar did not seem anxious to pursue the matter further, but afterwards, unwilling to lessen any impression he might have made, he spurred himself to a further flight. " 'Im what give 'is name to the term 'platitude.' " He threw the piece of information over his shoulder with all the nonchalance of the finest academic tradition and peered round to see the effect.

He was rewarded. Mr. Campion appeared to have been stricken dumb.

"Is that in the book?" he enquired humbly after a pause.

"I expec' so," said Lugg, adding magnificently, "I read it somewhere. Mr. Tuke's getting me interested in education. Education is the final stamp of good class, that's what 'e says."

"And a belt," murmured Campion. "Don't forget that."

The fat man heaved himself towards the desk.

"Look 'ere," he said belligerently, "I expected somethin' like this. Every step I've took in an upward direction you've done your best to nark. Now I'm on to somethin' useful. I'm goin' to educate myself, and then I'll never feel inferior, not with anybody, see?"

"My dear chap——" Mr. Campion was touched. "You don't feel inferior with anybody now, surely, do you? Lay off, Lugg. This is a horrible line."

The other man regarded him shrewdly. His little black eyes were winking, and there was a certain sheepishness in his expression which was out of character.

"Not with you, of course, cock," he conceded affectionately. "But I do with Mr. Tuke. 'E thinks about it. Still, let 'im wait."

"Is it *all* in the book?" enquired Mr. Campion, whom the idea seemed to fascinate.

"A ruddy great lot of it is." Mr. Lugg wrestled with his pocket. "I'll be as hot as most when I get this on board." He produced a small dictionary of quotations and laid it metaphorically at Mr. Campion's feet. "I'm leavin' out the Yiddish," he remarked as they turned over the pages together. "See that bit there? And there's another over 'ere."

Campion sighed.

"It may be Yiddish to you, guv'nor," he murmured, "but it's Greek to me. These two lads Milt and Shakes get an unfair look-in, don't they?"

"They're all all right." Lugg was magnanimous. "But when I get good I'll do me own quotations. A quotation's only a short neat way of sayin' somethin' everybody knows, like *It's crackers to slip a rozzer the dropsy in snide.* That's the sort of thing. Only you want it to be about somethin' less 'omely . . . women and such."

Mr. Campion seemed rather taken with the idea of running

47

a line in personal quotations on the system of "every man his own poet," and Lugg was gratified.

"I don't often get you goin'," he observed with satisfaction. "Lucky I 'it on this; it might have been religion. There's a bloke at the club——"

"No," said Mr. Campion, pulling himself together. "No, old boy. No, really. Not now."

"That's what I tell 'im." Lugg was cheerful. "I'll come to it, I says, but not now. I'm sorry, mate, but I don't see yer as a brother yet. Which reminds me—what about your sis? She'll be 'ere any minute. What's she up to? She's in with a funny crowd, isn't she?"

"Val? I don't think so."

Lugg sniffed. "I do. Mr. Tuke tell me in confidence that 'e 'eard someone pass a remark about seein' 'er at a luncheon party at the Tulip with a very funny lot . . . that bloke Ramillies, for one."

Once more Mr. Campion pushed his letter aside, faint distaste on his face.

"Of course we don't want to go listenin' to servants' gossip," continued Lugg happily, "but I like that girl and I wouldn't like to see 'er mixed up with a chap like Ramillies."

He pronounced the name with such a wealth of disgust that his employer's interest was stirred in spite of himself.

"I've met Sir Raymond Ramillies," he said.

" 'Ave yer?" The black eyes expressed disapproval. "I ain't and I don't want to. A ruddy awful chap. 'Ide your wife in a ditch rather than let 'im set eyes on her. 'E's a proper blot. I tell you want, if you 'ad to set in public court and 'ear a beak talkin' to 'im after the sentence you'd 'ave to turn your 'ead away. You'd blush; that's a fact."

"That's slander," said Campion mildly. "The man's never been in the dock in his life."

"And wot's that?" Lugg was virtuous. "As you very well know, there's a lot of people walkin' about today 'oo ought to be in the jug by rights. 'E 'appens to be one of them, that's all."

Long experience had taught Mr. Campion not to argue with his aide in this mood, but he felt bound to protest.

"You mustn't drivel libel about people. You're like a woman."

"Ho!" The insult penetrated the skin and Mr. Lugg's

mountainous form quivered. "You've got no right to say a thing like that, cock," he said earnestly. "I know what I'm sayin'. Sir Ramillies is mud, not so good as mud. He's done one man in, to my certain knowledge, and the army tales about 'im make my 'air curl, wherever it may be now. 'Ere's an instance. Take the time of the Irish trouble. There was a couple of fellers come over to England after 'im. They were lookin' for 'im, I admit that, but neither of 'em 'ad a gun. They lay for 'im up in Hampstead where 'e used to live. 'E spotted 'em and went for 'em quick as a flash. 'E caught one chap and killed 'im with 'is bare 'ands—broke 'is neck. The bloke was on the run, mind you, but Ramillies got 'im by the 'air and forced 'is chin up until 'e 'eard 'is neck go. 'E was only a little feller. It was 'ushed up when they found out the lads were reely after 'im and it was self-defence, and Ramillies was ruddy pleased with 'imself. Saw 'imself a Tarzan. I don't know what you think about it but it don't sound quite nice to me; not at all the article. It's downright brutish, look at it how you like. Put me off the chap for life. It's not respectable to lose your temper like that. Makes you no better than an animal. It's dangerous, for one thing."

The story was certainly not attractive, and it occurred to Mr. Campion that it was unfortunate that, having met Ramillies, it did not strike him as being obviously untrue.

"Do you know this for a fact?"

"Of course I do." Lugg was contemptuous. "I 'ad a drink with the other bloke. 'E *was* in a state—not frightened, you know, but shook. There's other tales about Ramillies not as pretty as that. I wouldn't soil yer ears with 'em. 'E's not the bloke for your sis to sit down to table with, not if she was in Salvation Army uniform, take it from me."

Mr. Campion said no more. He remained sitting at his desk with his head slightly on one side and an introspective expression in his eyes.

He was still there, drumming idly on the blotter with his long thin fingers, when the doorbell buzzed and a subtle change came over Mr. Lugg.

He straightened his back from his ministrations at the cocktail cabinet and padded over to the wall mirror, where he settled his collar, arranging his chins upon its white pedestal with great care. Having thus set the stage, he pulled a silk

handkerchief out of his side pocket and gave his glistening
head a good rub with it, using it immediately afterwards to
give a flick to the toe of each patent-leather pump. Then he
pulled himself up to attention and, turning all in one piece
with his plump hands flat against his sides, he tottered from
the room.

A moment or so later he returned with an expressionless
face and the words "This way, please. 'E'll see you and be
'appy to," uttered in a voice so affected in tone and quality
that the announcement was barely comprehensible.

Val came in hurriedly. She looked very charming in her
black suit with the faintly military air about it, and with her
came all that fragrance and flutter which has been the hall-
mark of the "lovely lady" since Mme de Maintenon discovered
it. She was so vivacious and determinedly gay that Campion
did not notice any change in her for some time.

Behind her came a stranger whose personality was instantly
and engagingly apparent.

Georgy Laminoff, or Gaiogi, as his friends called him, with
the g's hard, was a delightful person. The art of being
delightful was with him a life study, and, since he was no fool
and at heart a prince, he achieved an excellence in it. To look
at, he was round and gracious, with a small white beard and
bright circular eyes in sockets as arched and sombre as
Norman gateways.

He took Mr. Campion's hand with a murmur of apology
which came from his soul. It was an intrusion, he insisted, an
abominable and disgusting thing, but Val had assured him that
it would be forgiven and he was happy to note from the very
amiability of his host's expression that it was indeed miraculously
so. He seated himself when bidden, conveying without saying
so that the chair was incomparably comfortable and that he
knew and appreciated the superb quality of the sherry which
had been offered him.

Within five minutes of his arrival they were sitting round in
pleasant intimacy. The ice had melted rather than broken, and
yet his behaviour had never deviated for a moment from that
exact formality which is the rightful protection of every man
against the stranger within his doors.

Val leant back in the winged chair, unaware that she was
irritating her brother, who, for some reason of his own, did
not like to see a woman sitting in it.

"We've got a nice new job for you, my lamb," she said. "Something easy and vulgar. How would you like to bring your boots and have a slap-up week end with all the comforts of the rich, and the rare intellectual treat of mingling with the best people—all for nothing? What about it?"

Laminoff made a deprecating gesture with a spade-shaped hand.

"I am embarrassed," he said. "We are unpleasant, ignorant people. I shall commit suicide." He chuckled with sudden happiness. "I talk like all the best plays."

"Anything except divorce," said Campion cheerfully. "Divorce and the joke's over. I'd rather go back to my people."

"Oh, no." Gaiogi was shocked. "No, no, we are not indecent. Good God, no. This is at least honest vulgarity. Mr. Campion, will you come and stay in my house over the week end? I ask you so that, should I have need to call upon my guest for assistance, assistance he cannot by all the laws of hospitality refuse me, I shall have in him someone who will be an asset and not an encumbrance."

He leant back and laughed until his eyes were shining with tears.

"I rehearsed that coming along. It sounds a little false."

They both looked at him, Val with tolerant amusement and Mr. Campion with simple interest.

"Having trouble?"

"No." Gaiogi was still laughing, and he glanced at Val with that shyness which comes from the intellect rather than from any social embarrassment. "We are here on false pretences."

"Not at all." Val spoke briskly, her voice a little harder than usual. "It's Ramillies," she said.

"Really?" Mr. Campion hoped he did not sound cautious. "What's he done now?"

"Nothing yet, thank God." Val was obstinately bright. "He's going to Boohoo Land, or wherever it is, on Sunday, in a gold aeroplane, and we just thought we'd like you about to see he does go."

"In a gold aeroplane?"

"Gold. The propeller hub may be studded with diamonds." Gaiogi made the announcement gravely and Campion raised his eyebrows.

"Quite the gent," he commented politely. "How serious is all this?"

Val rose, and as the light fell upon her face her brother looked at her sharply. He had not seen her quite so fine drawn before.

"I'm not very clear about all this," he said. "Explain it all to me without effects. Ramillies is going back to Ulangi, is he? Alone?"

"Yes. Georgia is going out to join him in six weeks time, with a wild party. The Taretons and that lot."

"That should be jolly." Campion spoke without enthusiasm.

"Riotous," she agreed. "Paul Tareton is taking 'three girls from totally different environments,' and Mrs. has selected one rather beastly little boy called Waffle. Still, that's their *après-midi,* not ours. Our concern is that nothing goes wrong with the flight. Gaiogi was telling Tante Marthe his troubles and she sent us both along to you."

"Ah yes, the flight," said Campion. "Start at the flight."

"The flight is not exactly an attempt upon the record" —Val's brightness was growing more and more artificial— "except that no one has ever taken the trouble to fly from England to Ulangi before. I wonder you haven't heard about all this, Albert. There's been enough publicity."

At the mention of the magic word Campion began to see a little daylight.

"The plane is being sent out as a present to the native ruler," she said. "It's an Alandel machine, and it's taking off from the Caesar's Court flying ground at six o'clock on Sunday night. In it go the pilot and a navigator and Ramillies. He insisted that they paint it gold. He said the man would like it better, and pointed out that if you paint a thing silver there's no reason why you shouldn't paint it gold. I think Gaiogi made up the diamonds. Anyway, the airmen will stay and instruct the coloured gentleman how not to break his neck, and Ramillies will tidy the house up ready for Georgia. On Sunday there is to be a semiofficial send-off, with Towser from the Colonial Office and one or two other bigwigs, and the whole thing is to be stage-managed gracefully. Gaiogi is anxious that nothing shall go wrong."

"I can understand that." Campion sounded sympathetic. "Is there any reason why anything should?"

Val glanced at the Russian before she spoke.

"No," she said at last but without conviction. "No, I don't think so. No, none at all. You just come down for the week end. We shall all be there. You can even bring Lugg, if he'll behave."

"I'm sorry, my dear. It sounds fishy." Campion filled her glass as he spoke. "Don't think me inquisitive, but I must have a bit more to go on. It's my luggage I'm worrying about. Do I bring a knuckle-duster and a chloroform spray, or merely my etiquette book?"

"The chloroform spray, I should say, wouldn't you, Gaiogi?" Val was not entirely flippant, and the old man laughed at her before he turned his round eyes towards Campion.

"I hope not," he said, "but who can tell? That is the difference between the world of my youth and the world of today. Then I was bored because nothing could happen; now I am apprehensive because nothing couldn't. I am living my life backwards, my exciting youth last."

"Gaiogi doesn't feel Ramillies is quite safe," Val remarked. "I know what he means."

So did Campion, but he made no comment and she continued.

"There's been some little trouble about a gun already. He wants to take one out with him and the flying people are jibbing about the weight. Anyhow, it's not the sort of thing he ought to want out there, is it?"

"I don't know. It's not a cannon, I suppose?"

"Sir Raymond wishes to take out a Filmer 5A," said Laminoff calmly. "He does not see why he should not take it to pieces and stow it under the seat, together with enough ammunition to kill every elephant in Africa. Do you know the new 5A, Mr. Campion?"

"Good Lord, that's not the big one, is it? The mounted one with the magazine? Really? What does he want that for?"

"No one likes to ask," said Val dryly. "Anyway, he can't take it. Alan Dell had to make that clear to him himself. Ramillies flew into one of his idiotic rages, came out of it, and is now sulking with a watch-what-I'm-going-to-do air about him, which is disturbing. We don't want him making a scene just when everything is set for the take-off, or getting tight and trying to take the machine up himself ten minutes before the official time. I'd like you down there anyway. Don't be a cad."

"My dear girl, I'm coming. Nothing would keep me

53

away." Campion sounded sincere. "The suggestion is that
Ramillies is slightly barmy, I take it?"

"No, no, spoilt," murmured Gaiogi tolerantly. "Too much
money all his life, mental age thirteen. A superb soldier, no
doubt."

Val wriggled her shoulders under her severe little coat.

"He's abnormal," she said. "I dislike having him in the
house in case something awful happens to him while he's
there. A thunderbolt, perhaps. You know what I mean."

Gaiogi was delighted.

"Val is right. He has an impious challenge," he agreed,
grinning at the phrase. "That is the analysis of my own
alarm. He should be exorcised."

"He should be watched," said Val, who seemed to have
set her heart on being practical at all costs. "That's fixed
then, is it, Albert? We can rely on you to come on Saturday?
You're a pet. We're terribly grateful. Gaiogi has to rush off
now to catch Ferdie Paul, but I'll stay half an hour with you if
I may."

Her announcement was so brusque that it constituted a
dismissal and Campion regarded her with respectful astonishment. Laminoff rose.

"We shall be delighted to see you," he said earnestly.
"My wife and I have a little cottage in the grounds and we
will entertain you there." He glanced at Val and smiled shyly.
"It is more comfortable than in the hotel."

"It's the loveliest house in the world," she assured him
and he seemed pleased.

He left them gracefully, making the awkward business of
departure a charming experience for everyone concerned, and
went away, leaving them liking him and, for some inexplicable reason, gratified by the interview, although it had simply
served to arrange something he desired.

"Nice old boy," Mr. Campion observed when they were
alone.

"A dear. The only genuine Russian prince I've ever met."
Val wandered down the room to look out of the window as
she spoke. "He lived in Mentone before the Revolution,
toddling home now and again for the wolfing or the ballet or
whatever they had at home. His wife said that they were
miserable, really miserable; you know w t wet blankets
Russians were."

"Cried each other to sleep every night," suggested Mr. Campion helpfully.

"That sort of thing." Val was not listening to him. "Then they lost all and life began anew. Gaiogi has princely ideas, real ones. He understands organisation as well as magnificence. Just the man for a luxury hotel. He's a prince with a point to him and he's hysterically happy. I'd hate anything really unpleasant to happen in that little kingdom."

Mr. Campion took up the decanter.

"Sit down," he said. "I'm not being critical but do you think you're being a bit nervy? I mean, old Ramillies may have a spot of the devil in him, but the horns haven't actually appeared yet. He evidently understands his job. That gilded aeroplane idea shows a certain amount of practical insight. You can't convince a Gold Coast nigger that silver isn't an inferior metal. He's probably quite all right in a limited way, once you get to know him. Don't think I'm not going down to Caesar's Court; I am. I want to. I only felt it was a bit hysterical, this roaring round here yourself to bring Laminoff and making a great to-do about it. You could have phoned me."

Val sat down on the couch and closed her eyes.

"It's amazing about relations," she observed after a pause. "You're a pleasant, reasonable person. You'd never be so cruelly hyper-critical of any other woman. Why shouldn't I be hysterical? I'm not, as it happens, but if I was why shouldn't I?"

Mr. Campion was temporarily taken aback.

"One naturally expects one's relatives to behave with the decorum one demands of oneself," he said primly. "Hysteria doesn't run in our family."

"Oh, doesn't it?" said Val. "Like to hear me scream the place down? Give me something to drink."

"Have some gin in it and have a lovely sick?" he suggested.

She laughed and sat up. She had pulled off her ridiculous hat and her yellow hair was very slightly dishevelled. She looked young and clever and tolerantly disgusted with herself. She glanced up at him and spoke wearily.

"'Ardy, 'Ardy, I am wownded."

"Not seriously, I 'ope?" enquired Campion solicitously, dropping into the nursery joke of their youth without noticing it.

"Mort-u-ally, I fear."

"Really? What's up?"

"Unrequited love." She was still speaking lightly but with a certain breathlessness which made the words uncertain.

"Oh?" He did not sound very sympathetic. "If I may say so without being indelicate, it looked very healthy last time I saw you both."

"Did it? You're a detective of some sort, aren't you?" A change in her voice, a certain hardness, almost a cheapness, that was a stranger there, caught Mr. Campion's attention and silenced the flippant remark on his lips. He had known that sickening deterioration himself in his time and, while he still found it infuriating in himself or anyone else who might be part of his own personal secret dignity, he was not entirely without pity for it.

"These things happen," he said awkwardly, trying to sound sympathetic without inviting confidence. "It's all part of the dance."

Val laughed at him. She was genuinely amused and he was relieved to notice a slackening of the emotional tension in her voice.

"You're just the person not to come and cry to, aren't you?" she said. "You look as though you're going to be ill already. I'm all right, ducky. I'm only telling you I'm feeling like suicide because Georgia Wells has pinched my young man. You might at least say you're sorry. If I told you I was broke or had a twisted ankle you'd be flapping about like a mother chicken."

"Hen," said Campion absently. "Hen is the word you want. What do you mean when you say pinched? Has Georgia merely abducted Dell? Or has she dazzled him? I mean, has the situation come about because the fellow wants to hang round or because he's too polite to slash his way out of the palisade?"

Val lay back again. She was having great difficulty with the cigarette between her lips and her eyes were startled at her own weakness.

"No," she said at last. "No, I think it's quite genuine. It does happen, you know. She's simply knocked him off his feet. He's rather added what he *knows* of me to what he's *seen* of her, if you see what I mean."

Mr. Campion did see and he looked at her with one of

56

those sharp glances which betrayed his surprise. Her insight was always astonishing him. It was misleading, he reminded himself hastily; a sort of inspired guesswork or, rather, an intermittent contact with truth.

"He certainly didn't know much about women," he remarked. "He'll learn a bit from Georgia."

Val did not speak and he went on without thinking of her in any objective way. He was aware of her, of course, but only as of someone whom he considered another facet of himself.

"A man like that ought to fall in love a few times. It matures the mind. He can't marry her, of course, because of Ramillies. In a way that's almost a pity because, in a case like that, that type of decent, rather sentimental chap is apt to go off and nurse a lovely pie-eyed dream of tragical frustration for a hell of a time."

He caught sight of her white face with the two tears on her cheekbones and jerked himself up with sudden contrition.

"My dear girl, forgive me. I was thinking aloud. I forgot you were in this. I'm mental. Oi! Val! Val, I'm sorry. I'm a tick. What shall we do? Go and chuck the woman in the Regent's Canal? What's she doing, by the way? Accepting it all with fashionable languor?"

"Oh no." Val's lips twisted. "You underestimate her. Georgia doesn't do things like that. Georgia loves. She always does. She's riotously, deliriously, ecstatically in love at the moment. She's a fire, a whirlwind. She comes and tells me about it by the hour. I rushed off with Gaiogi this afternoon to get away from her. She's so heartrendingly genuine, Albert, like all the worst in one's self."

Mr. Campion looked scandalised and his sympathy for his sister increased.

"That's not quite decent," he remarked. "How startlingly vulgar you women are."

"It's not vulgarity. It's cheating," said Val calmly. "You do so hope you're not really hurting, but you do want to do it so much. I know the instinct. It's a feeling, not a 'think' at all."

Mr. Campion made no direct comment.

"Is Ramillies in on all this?" he enquired at last.

"Oh yes. Georgia's like a house on fire. It can't be kept a secret for the rest of the street, much less from the master in the library. Ramillies knows more about it than anyone."

"What's he doing? Anything?"

"I don't know." Val sounded uneasy. "He's a very curious person. When I can bring myself to listen to her Georgia seems to be taking him very seriously. She says he's frightfully jealous and frighteningly quiet, but that may mean anything or nothing. He seems to have set his heart on having this party out there with the Taretons. Georgia's not so keen. She says that once she gets out there he'll make her stay. That'll be awkward because *The Lover* looks like settling down, and whereas they could risk dropping her out for a month, if it was running away, I doubt whether it would carry on for a full season without her. It might, of course. It's a success."

"In six weeks time," said Mr. Campion thoughtfully. "I'm not at all sure that my estimation of Sieur Ramillies doesn't go up. The grand passion should just about reach the wobbling point by then. These thundering fires die down pretty fast, don't they?"

He paused. Val was looking at him with a speculative expression that was not altogether sympathetic.

"You've forgotten Alan," she said. "Alan's in it too. He's a different kettle of fish altogether. It's not so simple, my dear. Frankly I wish it were. They're not children. It might so easily be very serious."

"You mean Ramillies might divorce her?"

"Not because of Alan. He'd never get grounds. You don't know Alan at all. He's an idealist."

"Well, then, it'll come to a quiet, uncomfortable end and you'll have to stand by and pick up the pieces," said Campion, a little irritated by what he felt was an unjust estimation of his powers of comprehension.

"Yes," said Val slowly. She shivered and stretched herself with a graceful, furtive movement like a little cat. "I envy those women who just love normally and nobly with their bodies," she observed unexpectedly. "Then they're only engulfed by a sort of lovely high tragedy. The hero persists. That's at least decent. Once you cultivate your mind you lay yourself open to low tragedy, the mingy, dirty little tragedy of making an ass of yourself over an ordinary poor little bloke. Female women love so abjectly that a reasonable hard-working mind becomes a responsibility. It's a cruelty that shouldn't have to be endured. I tell you I'd rather die than have to face it that he was neither better nor even more intelligent than I am!"

Her passionate sincerity demanded his consideration and he looked at her helplessly.

"You're asking rather a lot of him, old girl, aren't you?"

"Yes, I know." Val rose to her feet. "That's what I'm kicking at. I'm asking much too much of most men. I've so constructed myself that I've either got to ask too much or go maternal. Anyway, that's how it looks to me when I pull myself together and remember that I'm one of the most important business women in Europe, with a reputation to keep up and a staff to look after."

She looked very slim and small standing on his hearthrug and it came to him with something of a shock that she was not overestimating herself.

"Do you always see your—er—passion in this slightly inhuman light?"

"No." She glanced down at her exquisitely cut shoes, which a Viennese manufacturer had materialised from her design. "No, my other viewpoint is ordinary and howlingly undignified. I wish she were dead."

She met his eyes with sudden fire.

"My God, I hate her," she said.

Mr. Campion blinked. "I can't do her in," he said.

"Of course not. Don't be an ape." She was laughing. "Don't take any notice of me. I am nervy, very nervy. I had no idea I could behave like this. It's come rather late—I ought to be twenty-two to feel like this and enjoy it—and it's frightened me for the time being. Look here, all I want you to do is to see that Ramillies goes quietly out of the country without any fuss on Sunday. Then Georgia will follow him in six weeks time and meanwhile——"

She broke off so sharply that he was startled.

"Meanwhile what?"

"Meanwhile Alan will at least be safe physically."

"Who from? Ramillies? My poor girl, you're cuckoo. Husbands don't go around pigsticking their rivals these days. They seize another woman and sit showing off with her at the other end of the drawing room until the wife's boy friend leaves out of sheer embarrassment."

Val was not disarmed.

"You're *vieux jeu*, my pet," she said. "Like most men you're between three and five years out of date. Don't you notice a change in the fashion? Gaiogi's right. Today anything

59

can happen. People can wear *anything*, say *anything*, do *anything*. It's the motif of the moment; look at the waistline. Besides, consider Ramillies. He's a man who might have taken up a blasé attitude if he thought it would be in any way shocking. Nowadays it's not. It's dull, it's ordinary, it's provincial. D'you know, last week the most fashionable woman in London rushed in to tell me that her husband had thrashed her within an inch of her life and pitched her boy friend through a first-story window into a holly hedge. She was scandalised but terribly excited.''

"Dear me,'' said Mr. Campion mildly. "You matched up her black eye in your new *peau de pêche noir*, I hope? Oh well, you surprise me. The old man must catch up on his homework. Let me get this straight. You seriously think that Sir Raymond Ramillies is capable of making a physical assault on Alan Dell?''

"I know he's capable of it,'' said Val bluntly. "I'm telling you that I'm haunted by the idea that it's likely. Naturally I'm bothered because I can't tell if my worry is reasonable or just some silly physical reaction. I do have to explain things in detail to you. I thought you were so hot on understanding people.''

"I've been cheating all these years. I'm really Alice in Wonderland,'' said Mr. Campion humbly. "Still, I'm picking up a crumb or two now in my fiddling little way. What am I expected to do? Stand by to plant my body between them to stop the bullet?''

"Oh, darling, don't be a lout.'' Val was at her sweedling best. "I don't know what I want. Can't you see that? Just be about. I'm frightened of Ramillies. I don't think he'd simply hit out like a Christian, but I think he might do something— something—well, elaborate. That's the impression he gives me. I'm uneasy with him. After all, there was Portland-Smith, you know.''

Mr. Campion's eyelids drooped.

"What about Portland-Smith?'' he said. "He committed suicide.''

"How do you know?''

"I do. There's no doubt about it.''

Val shrugged her shoulders.

"It was very convenient for Ramillies, wasn't it?'' she said, sweeping away the facts with a carelessness that left him helpless. "There's no end of chatter about it in the last few weeks."

"Then someone will get into trouble," Campion insisted firmly. "That's pure slander."

"You can't have smoke without fire, my dear," said Val, and he could have slapped her because she was both unreasonable and quite right. "Now I'm going," she said. "Don't come down with me. I'm sorry I've behaved like a neurotic. You ought to fall in love yourself sometime and get the angle."

He did not answer her immediately but when he looked up his eyes were apologetic.

"It wouldn't take me like that, you know," he remarked seriously.

"Evidently not."

"Why?"

"Well, where is she?" Val's glance round the room was expressive and she went off, leaving him reflecting that the gentle, conservative dog with his taboos, his conscience and his ideals was a rather pathetic, defenceless animal beside his ruthless, hag-ridden sister, the cat.

Lugg's stomach appeared round the doorway.

"Sex rearin' its ugly 'ead again, eh?" he remarked, coming into fuller view. "I didn't 'ear 'er speak because I kep' in the kitchen like a gent, but you can see it in 'er face, can't you? Funny, we seem to 'ave struck a patch of it lately. It's pitch, sex is. Once you touch it, it clings to you. Why don't you sneak off and come on this cruise we're always talking about? Crime's vulgar enough, but sex crime is common. There's no other word for it. 'Oo's she in love with? 'Andle to 'is name?"

Mr. Campion regarded him with disgust.

"You turn my stomach," he said. "I believe if you had a fortune you'd try to buy a title."

"No, I wouldn't." Lugg appeared to be giving the suggestion more serious thought than it warranted. "Not a title. I wouldn't mind being a councillor of a nice classy little burrow. That's about my mark. I'm sorry about your sis but we can't 'elp 'er troubles. You look out. I don't like sex. Remember the setout we 'ad down in the country. Which reminds me, I 'ad a note from my little mate the other day. Like to see it? She's at boarding school."

He waddled over to the bureau and pulled open the bottom drawer.

" 'Ere you are," he said with the nonchalance that ill disguises bursting pride. "Not bad for a kid, is it?"

Mr. Campion took the inky square of expensive notepaper and glanced at the embossed address.

The Convent of the Holy Sepulchre
Lording
Dorset

DEAR MR LUGG [the handwriting was enormous and abominable] *I am at school. Here we speak French. Some of the nuns like the tricks you showed me and some do not. I have written "I must not swindle" 50 times for S. Mary Therese but S. Mary Anna laffed. I am going to read the Gompleat works of William Shakespeare.*

Lots and lots of love from
SARAH.

Mr. Lugg put the note back among his better shirts, which he insisted on keeping in the bureau in defiance of all objections.

"I could 'ave done a lot with that poor little bit if I'd 'ad the educatin' of 'er," he remarked regretfully. "Still, she'd 'ave bin a nuisance, you know. Per'aps she's better off, reely, with them nuns."

"Indeed, perhaps so," said Mr. Campion not without derision.

Lugg straightened his back and regarded his employer under fat white eyelids.

"I found this 'ere in one of yer suits," he said, feeling in his waistcoat pocket. "I've bin waitin' for an opportunity to give it to you. There you are: a little yeller button. It came off one of Mrs. Sutane's dresses, I think. Correc' me if I'm wrong."

Mr. Campion took the button, turned it over and pitched it out of the open window into the street below. He said nothing and his face was an amiable blank.

Mr. Lugg's complacent expression vanished and he pulled his collar off.

"I'm more comfortable without it," he remarked in the tone of one making pleasant conversation under difficulties.

"Now the company's gone I can let out the compression. Blest came in while you was talkin' to your sis. I tell 'im you was busy. I give 'im the end of one of my old bottles and made 'im leave a message."

"Oh?" Mr. Campion seemed mildly interested. "And how did the ex-inspector take that from the ex-Borstal prefect?"

"Drunk up every drop like a starvin' kitty." Mr. Lugg's conversational powers increased with his anxiety. "It did me good to see 'im. ''Ave another mite of the wages of virtue, mate,' I said, smellin' another 'arf empty, but he wouldn't stop. Said 'e'd phone you, and meanwhile you might like to know that 'e'd found a little church down in Putney with some very interesting records of a wedding three and a 'alf years ago. 'E wouldn't tell me 'oo the parties were; said you'd know and that it was all okay, he'd got the doings."

"Anything else?"

"Yus. Wait a minute. 'Ullo, that's the bell. It would be." Mr. Lugg fumbled with his collar again. "It's comin' back to me," he said breathlessly in the midst of his struggle. "He said did you know there was someone else snouting around for the same information less than a week ago, and if it was news to you, did you think it funny?"

He lumbered out into the passage. Mr. Campion's eyebrows rose.

"Damn funny," he said.

He was still lost in unquiet thought when the fat man reappeared, his face shining.

"Look 'ere," he said with even less ceremony than usual, "look 'ere. Look what I've found on the door step. 'Ere's a bottle o' milk for you."

Mr. Campion raised his eyes to the newcomer and for an instant he did not recognise the heart-shaped face with the triangular smile and the expression that was as resourceful, as eager and as infinitely young as when he had last seen it six years before.

"Hullo, Orph," said Amanda Fitton. "The lieut has come to report. This is a nice thing to get in my face when I look up at your window for the first time in six years."

She held out a small brown paw and displayed a yellow button with a rose painted on it lying in the palm.

"Thank you, Amanda." Mr. Campion took the button and pocketed it. "It burst off my waistcoat as my heart leapt at your approach. A most extraordinary phenomenon. I wondered what on earth it was. Why did you come? I mean, nothing wrong, I hope?"

Amanda pulled off her hat and the full glory of the Pontisbright hair glowed in the evening light.

"It's about my chief, Alan Dell," she said, "and frightfully confidential. I say, Albert, you don't know a man called Ramillies, do you?"

Chapter Seven

Mr. Campion leant back in the taxicab, which smelt like the inside of the dressing-up trunk in the attic of his childhood's home, and glanced at the shadowy form beside him with a return of a respect he had forgotten. The six years between eighteen and twenty-four had certainly not robbed Amanda of her pep. On the whole he was inclined to think they must have added power to her elbow.

It was now a little after twelve, and the night, it seemed, was yet a babe.

"What I still don't understand is how you got there," he said. "I thought aeroplane works were holies of holies."

"So they are." Amanda sounded cheerful in the darkness. "It took me three and a half years to do it, but I'm a pretty good engineer, you know. I went straight into the shops when I got some money. I hadn't a sufficiently decent education to take an ordinary degree so I had to go the back way. My title helped, though," she added honestly.

"Did it? What does your brother say about it?"

"The little earl?" Lady Amanda Fitton's respect for young Hal did not seem to have increased. "He's still at Oxford. He seemed to be dying of old age last time I saw him. He's given me up for the time being. Aunt Hat says he's gathering strength. Meanwhile don't take your mind off the business in hand. This is serious. I'm up here on a sacred mission. You don't seem to realise that. The man Ramillies and his crowd must be called off A.D. What am I going to tell the boys?''

Mr. Campion stirred.

"Amanda," he enquired, "was I a hero in my youth?"

"A hero? No, of course not. What's the matter with you?" She was surprised. "You've got introspective or had a serious illness or something. You were a useful, dependable sort of person and the only soul I could think of to come to in this idiotic mess. Besides, in view of one thing and another, I thought you might know something about it already. Look here, you forget about yourself for a minute and consider the situation. Here's a man—a genius, Albert; there's no one like him—and in the middle of serious and important work he's got hold of by the wretched Ramillies and his crowd and taken completely off his course. It's a frightful calamity; you must see that. We can't get on without him. The whole machine room is held up. Drawings are waiting for his okay. Specimen parts are ready to be tried out. All kinds of details you wouldn't understand. . . . And it's not only that. There's the morale of the whole place to consider. He's endangering it. We stuck it as long as we could and then Sid sent me up to find out how bad things really were. We talked it all over and decided that real loyalty isn't just sentimental and unpractical. A.D. has been got at. He's a child in some things. He must be persuaded back to work.''

Mr. Campion, thirty-eight next birthday, was aware of a chill. It began in the soles of his feet and swept up over him in a tingling wave. Behind Amanda's story he had caught a glimpse of a world which he had practically forgotten. In many ways it was an idiotic, exasperating but tremendously exciting world wherein incredible dreams fed fine enthusiasms and led to fierce consultations, pathetically noble sacrifices and astounding feats of endeavour, to say nothing of heights of impudence which made one giddy even in considering them.

"You're all pretty young down there, I suppose?" he ventured.

"A lot of us are. A.D.'s wonderful like that." Amanda's eyes were shining in the dusk. "It's just ability that counts with him. Of course there are a few old people too, but they're all fanatically keen on the work and that keeps them young. We're all so helplessly worried, Albert, or at least all those of us are who realise what's up. It's such a wizard show. We're all behind him, you see. We'd do anything for the work, absolutely anything. We all would. He *couldn't* let us all down, could he?''

Her voice was wonderfully young and clear and he was reminded of the first time he had ever heard it in the drawing room at Pontisbright Mill when the curtains had been drawn to hide the tears in the furniture. A lot of water had gone through the wheel since then, he reflected.

"It all depends," he said cautiously. "A man has a private life, you know, apart from his work."

"Not A.D." Amanda was vehement. "His work's his life and he's a very great man. That's why we all depend on him so. He's a genius."

It went through Mr. Campion's mind that he had had a spot of trouble with geniuses before but he thought it politic not to say so. He continued with his diffident questioning.

"What put you on to Ramillies?"

"That's the only telephone number that seems to reach Dell. He's got some money in Caesar's Court, you know, and he must have picked up that crowd down there. Ramillies is all right really, I believe; I mean his family is all right and he's a governor on the West Coast somewhere; but he's wild and in with a wild crowd. A.D. has probably never met anything like him before and is going into some idiotic scheme for setting up an airport in an African swamp. He gets wrapped up in things like that sometimes. The only alarming thing is that he's never neglected us before and we are so hoping that there aren't any sharks in Ramillies' lot. You don't know, do you? Sometimes these clever crooks get hold of wild hearties like Ramillies and impress them. A.D. wouldn't fall in the ordinary way but if they approached him through a county mug he might just possibly be taken in."

Mr. Campion's eyebrows rose in the darkness.

"I say," he murmured, "don't you think you may be getting a bit melodramatic? No offence, of course, but if a lad doesn't turn up at the office for a day or two it doesn't always mean that he's in the hands of what counsel calls 'a wicked and unscrupulous gang.'"

"An office, yes," conceded Amanda with contempt, "but not our works. You don't seem to understand at all. He's neglecting his *work*. We haven't seen him at all for a fortnight and before then he was vague and preoccupied. Sid and I diagnosed a succession of hangovers. It really is serious. Sid has sent me to find out and I must. Then if things don't improve we must have it out with him and get him back to normal."

"I see," said Mr. Campion a little helplessly. "Who is Sid?"

Amanda chuckled. "Sid's my immediate boss. A grand chap. He was born in Wallington and went to the Polytechnic and starved through the shops, finally got his M.I.M.E. and is one of the finest men in his own line in the kingdom. He's only twenty-nine and an awful snob, but so absolutely honest as a workman."

"A snob?"

"Yes, bless him. He's batty about my title. He's always getting at me for it just so he can hear himself use it. I like Sid. He's got enthusiasm. Where is this place, the Tulip? What makes you think they may be there?"

"Intuition backed by the law of elimination." Mr. Campion sounded dogged. "If they're not here, my child, we shall have to start knocking at doors and asking. London is a largish town for that method, but since you've made up your mind I see no other course."

"I hope you're not getting old," said Amanda dubiously. "If the worst comes to the worst we'll begin at Hampstead and work our way south."

The Tulip had been flowering for a little over seven months and was therefore nearing its zenith in the fashionable sunlight. Jules Parroquet, whose golden rule for the exploitation of a successful restaurant and night club was simple—a new name and orchestra to every two changes of paint—already considered it one of his triumphs. The ceiling of flowers was still noticed and admired and the silly little striped canvas canopies every now and again were as fresh and piquant as when they had first been erected.

Mr. Campion and Amanda stood for a moment looking over the broad silver rail above the orchestra before going down to the dance-floor level, where Campion was relying on the headwaiter, the lean Ulysse, the one permanent husband-man in Parroquet's ever-changing flower garden, to find them a respectably prominent table.

He did not find Georgia immediately but was relieved to see that the place was filled with likely people. Stage and society were well represented, and Money hung about with Art in the corners, while the mass attempt at complete unself-consciousness provided the familiar atmosphere of feverish effort.

Young Hennessy, sitting at a table with a duchess, an actor-manager and two complete strangers, made an importunate attempt to attract his attention, and it was not until then that Campion, normally the most observant of men, glanced at Amanda and noticed that she had grown astonishingly good to look at. She saw his expression and grinned.

"I put my best frock on," she said. "Hal chooses all my things. Hal says good undergraduate taste is the only safe criterion of modern clothes. He takes it terribly seriously. Do you see anybody you know or have we got to go on somewhere else?"

"No, this'll do." Mr. Campion's tone contained not only relief but a note of resignation. Amanda, he foresaw, was about to discover the worst.

Ulysse received them with all that wealth of unspoken satisfaction which was his principal professional asset and conducted them to the small but not ill-placed table which he swore he had been keeping up his sleeve for just such an eventuality. The worst of the cabaret was over, he confided with that carefully cultivated contempt for everything that interfered with beautiful food, which was another of his more valuable affectations. He also spent some time considering the best meal for Amanda at that time of night.

As soon as they were at peace again Mr. Campion took it upon himself to rearrange his companion's chair so that her view across the room was not impeded. Then he sat down beside her.

"There you are, lady," he said. "Once more the veteran conjuror staggers out with the rabbit. There's the situation for you in the proverbial nut."

Georgia and Alan Dell had a table on the edge of the dance floor and from where she now sat Amanda had clear view of

the two profiles. Georgia's slightly blunt features and magnificent shoulders were thrown up against the moving kaleido-
scope of colour, and Dell sat staring at her with fifteen years
off his age and the lost, slightly dazed expression of the man
who, whether his trouble be love, drink or merely loss of
blood, has honestly no idea that he is surrounded by strangers.

Infatuation is one of those slightly comic illnesses which
are at once so undignified and so painful that a nice-minded
world does its best to ignore their existence altogether, refer-
ring to them only under provocation and then with apology,
but, like its more material brother, this boil on the neck of the
spirit can hardly be forgotten either by the sufferer or anyone
else in his vicinity. The malady is ludicrous, sad, excruciating
and, above all, instantly diagnosable.

Mr. Campion glanced at Amanda and was sorry. Illusions
may deserve to be broken, young enthusiasts may have to take
what is coming to them, and heroes may desert their causes as
life dictates, but it is always an unhappy business to watch.
Amanda sat up, her round white neck very stiff and the jut of
her flaming curls dangerous. Her face was expressionless, and
the absence of any animation brought into sudden prominence
the natural hauteur stamped into the fine bones of her head.
She regarded the two for a long candid minute and then,
turning away, changed the conversation with that flat delibera-
tion which is a gift.

"This is excellent fish," she said.

Mr. Campion, who had the uncomfortable feeling that he
had been a little vulgar, laboured to make amends.

"It's dudgeon," he said. "Very rare. They have great
difficulty in keeping it. Hence the term 'high——'"

"Yes, I know." Amanda met his eyes. "We lived on it
down at the mill one year. Do you remember? Who is that
woman?"

"Georgia Wells, the actress."

Amanda's fine eyebrows rose.

"I thought that was Lady Ramillies?"

"Yes," said Mr. Campion.

She was silent. There was no possible way of divining what
was in her mind, but he reflected that the younger generation
was notoriously severe.

"It wears off, you know," he said, trying not to sound
avuncular. "He can't help the out-in-the-street-in-the-nude

effect, poor chap, at the moment. Nothing can be done. The work will have to wait.''

"No, nothing can be done," agreed Amanda politely. "That's what I have to explain to Sid. Thank you very much for bringing me.''

She moved her chair a little to shut out Dell, and set herself to be entertaining. Mr. Campion approved. He remembered enough of the hard-working, hero-worshipping, ecstatic days of his own youth to realise some of the shame, the sneaking jealousy and horrified sense of injustice and neglect that comes when the great man lets his fiery disciples down. But if Amanda was conscious of any of this she was not inflicting it upon him. Her manners were irreproachable. Amanda was, as ever, the perfect gent.

It occurred to him also that both Val and Amanda had intrinsically the same quarrel with Dell inasmuch as they both dreaded his loss of dignity. He sighed. The man had his sincere sympathy.

He glanced across the dance floor and caught a fleeting glimpse of Georgia dancing. It was only a momentary impression but he recognised her by her distinctive silver dress and the ridiculous but charming spray of swallows on her dark crown. His astonishment was considerable, therefore, when his glance, travelling back, lighted upon her still sitting at the table, her face radiant, her eyes shining, and the whole warmth of her magnificent, fraudulent personality glowing at the man before her. He sat up and looked out at the floor again and his expression changed. His mistake was triumphantly justified.

Another woman of Georgia's type was wearing a replica of Georgia's silver dress and Georgia's silver swallows. Her dark curls were dressed in Georgia's style and at that distance the two faces were indistinguishable. Mr. Campion recognised Miss Adamson with difficulty and reflected that the girl was a fool as well as a knave. Then he caught sight of her partner, and once again experienced that faint sense of outrage which thundering bad taste invariably produced in him.

Dancing with Miss Adamson, his small head held at a slight angle and his whole body expressing his tremendous satisfaction, was Sir Raymond Ramillies.

Chapter Eight

Ulysse had settled Sir Raymond and Miss Adamson safely at the table immediately behind Georgia, and Ramillies was grinning happily at his success in acquiring it before the good maître d'hôtel noticed the phenomenon of the two Miss Wells.

Mr. Campion, who found himself watching the scene with the fascinated apprehension of a village idiot at a dangerous crossing, almost laughed aloud at the expression of incredulity which spread over Ulysse's face as his glance took in the two women. His small bright eyes flickered and he thrashed the menu card which he happened to be holding as if it had been a tail and he a labrador. It was a comic moment but it passed too soon, leaving only a growing sense of embarrassment as half-a-dozen diners at other tables swung round to stare with that insolence which comes from an attempt to look casual, or perhaps invisible, before they returned to warn their companions not to look round immediately.

Amanda looked at Campion and for the first time in their entire acquaintance he saw her rattled.

"That *is* Ramillies," she said. "What can we do?"

"Fire at the lights," he suggested, his wide mouth twisting with brief amusement. "No, it's no good, old lady; this is grown-up vulgarity. We sit and watch. Oh, Lord!"

The final exclamation was occasioned by a movement at Georgia's table. Alan Dell had dragged his dazzled eyes away from Lady Ramillies for an instant, only to be confronted immediately by Miss Adamson, seated directly behind her. Georgia noted the sudden deflection of interest and turned her head impulsively. Ramillies met her eyes and grinned with bland self-satisfaction.

She gave him a single offended and reproving glance, natural if unreasonable in the circumstances, and turned her eyes to his companion with an expression half condescending, half curious. The next moment, however, as the full insult

THE FASHION IN SHROUDS

became apparent, she was reduced to elementary emotions. The colour rose over her chest and flowed up her neck to her face in an angry flood. There was a sudden cessation of conversation at all the tables round about and she sat for a moment in a little oasis of silence in the desert of hissing sound.

Mr. Campion dropped his hand over Amanda's but she drew it away from him and began to eat as resolutely and angrily as her Victorian grandfather might have done in similar circumstances.

Ramillies bent forward and said something to his wife and she pushed back her chair, her face as pale as it had been red, while Alan Dell sprang up and fumbled for her bag and flowers.

It was a dangerous moment. There was something not quite ordinary in the quality of the contretemps—an ultimate degree of outrage, the quintessence of going a bit too far—so that the situation became vaguely alarming even to those least concerned. At the very instant when the clash of many emotions was still tingling in the air and everyone in that half of the room was waiting uncomfortably for Georgia's exit, a preserving angel appeared somewhat heavily disguised as Solly Batemann.

When Solly was described as an ornament to the theatrical profession, the word was never meant to be taken in its literal or decorative sense. He looked like a cross between a frog and a bulldog and was reputed to have the hide and warts of a rhino, but his personality was as full and generous as his voice, which was sweet and caressing without any of the oiliness which one was led to expect from his appearance. He was very pleased with himself at the moment. Three of his theatres were playing to capacity and the fourth production, which had flopped, had been by far the least expensive of them all. He surged across the floor to Georgia, his great stomach thrown out, his little eyes popping out of the top of his head, and his many grey-blue jowls quivering with bonhomie.

"Ah, my darling, you are a clever girl," he said when he was within hailing distance. "If we were only alone I should kiss you. I saw the show tonight. I sat and cried all over my shirt. Fact. No, not that spot; that's minestrone—this one."

Solly's irresistibility was the irresistibility of a tidal wave. Even Georgia could only succumb. She had no need to speak. He swept a chair from another table and planted it squarely between her and Dell. Then, with one elephantine knee resting on its velvet seat, he held forth, pouring unstinted

72

praise upon her as though from some vast cornucopia. It was a performance and its genuineness was Georgia's own. In spite of herself she warmed under it and within three minutes he had her laughing.

Mr. Campion was bewildered. Since Solly's interests were concentrated solely upon musical and spectacular shows and Georgia was well known to be under a long contract with Ferdie Paul, there could scarcely be any ulterior motive in the display, so that the tribute became sincere and heaven sent.

Mr. Campion glanced at the other table and his eyebrows rose. In fact heaven seemed to be sending all sorts of things. As soon as general interest had become focussed upon Solly, Ramillies had turned in his chair like an unnoticed child with every intention of joining in the new conversation, but now a waiter appeared at his elbow with a card on a salver. Ramillies took the pasteboard absently. His interest was still centred on his wife, but a glance at the message distracted him. He looked up eagerly, his dazzling childlike smile appearing, and making a brief excuse to Miss Adamson, he set off across the room after the waiter without a backward glance. The next moment, as if these two dispensations of Providence were not enough, Ramon Starr, the Tulip's most promising gigolo, sidled over to the deserted girl and she jumped at his murmured proposal. They floated away together to the strains of "Little Old Lady."

Dell himself had remained standing, regarding the exuberant Solly with growing disapproval, but before Georgia could become preoccupied with his discomfort yet another minor miracle occurred, taking the whole thing out of the happy-coincidence class altogether. Tante Marthe herself came sweeping by, looking like a famous elderly ballerina in her severe black gown, her head crowned by a ridiculous little beaded turban which only Val could have devised.

She nodded to Georgia, who did not see her, which was not surprising since Solly still filled every arc of her horizon, and, passing on, pounced upon Alan. She said something to him in which the name of "Gaiogi" alone was audible and laid her small yellow hand familiarly on his arm. From the little distance at which Campion and Amanda sat it was not possible to hear his reply, but Lady Papendeik's lizard glance darted round the room and came to rest on the two with a sparkle of satisfaction. A minute or two later she bore down upon them with Alan Dell following reluctantly at her heels, but she still had him by the cuff so that he could hardly escape her without brusquerie.

There was no time to warn Amanda with words and Campion kicked her gently under the table as he rose to greet the newcomer.

"Albert, my dear, I hear you're going to join our party at Caesar's Court. I am so glad, my dear boy. You and Mr. Dell have met, I think?"

Tante Marthe looked him full in the eyes as she spoke and he read there a command that he should be helpful. He made a suitable rejoinder and turned to Dell.

The conventional words faded on his lips as he saw the other man's face, however, and once more the whole situation became real and painful. Dell was staring helplessly at Amanda. There was colour in his face and his eyes were indescribably hurt, almost bewildered, as if he could scarcely credit the astonishing cruelty of the mischance. Mr. Campion felt very sorry for him.

Amanda took the situation in hand.

"Hallo, A.D.," she said with charming embarrassment. "I'm having a night on the tiles. This is my fourth meal this evening. The food is good. Come and have some. You haven't eaten yet, have you?"

"I'm afraid I have." He was looking at her suspiciously. "I've been sitting just over there all the evening."

"Really? Where?" She stared across the room with such regretful astonishment that she convinced even Mr. Campion, who thought for an instant that she was out of her mind. "I'm so sorry. I didn't notice you. I was engrossed in my fiancé. Do you know him?"

Mr. Campion received a mental thump between the shoulder blades and saved himself from blinking just in time.

"Albert?" Lady Papendeik was startled. "My children, congratulations! Why haven't we heard of this before? It's Amanda Fitton, isn't it? My dears, this is great news. Does Val know?"

"Engaged?" Alan Dell peered at Amanda. "You? Really? Is it recent? Tonight?"

Mr. Campion glanced at his companion from under his eyelashes. He hoped she knew what she was doing and would let him in on it. So far she had certainly succeeded in changing the conversation, albeit somewhat drastically.

"But how long has this been a fact?" Dell persisted, seizing on the point as though it had been the only solid spar in the conversational sea.

Amanda glanced at Campion demurely.

"We shall have to explain," she said.

"I think so," he agreed affably. "You do it."

"Well, it's my brother," she confided unexpectedly. "Do sit down. We ought to drink some champagne to this, you know, darling," she added, looking Campion firmly in the face and rubbing her chin thoughtfully with one finger, a gesture that fogged him utterly until he recollected that it was a secret sign in the Fitton family indicating that the speaker was there and then possessed of sufficient funds to cover the proposed extravagance.

Tante Marthe seated herself at once, and Dell, with a backward glance at Georgia, who was still monopolised, sat down in the opposite chair. As they drank, Mr. Campion met Lady Papendeik's eyes. He read vigorous approval in them and was alarmed.

Dell was even more embarrassing.

"You're extremely lucky, Campion," he said seriously. "She's a very remarkable girl. We shall feel the draught without her. When is the wrench to be, Amanda?"

"Not for quite a time, I'm afraid." The bride-to-be spoke regretfully. "It's Hal, you know. He's young and frightfully self-opinionated. Of course he's head of the family and I don't want to hurt him by flouting his authority. He'll come round in time. Meanwhile the engagement is more or less secret—as much as these things ever are. It's simply not announced; that's what it amounts to. It's a howling pity but we're both such very busy people that we can—er—bear to wait about a bit."

Lady Papendeik approved.

"So sensible," she said. "So French. You have been very sly, Albert. This has been going on some time. You're both so composed, so friendly. The coy period is over, thank God. When was the grande passion?"

Amanda smiled at her and her honey-brown eyes were guileless.

"That's all a bit shy-making in a crowd," she said. "I'll leave you with Albert for a bit. He'll tell you the worst. A.D., would you like to dance with me?"

Dell carried her off unwillingly and Tante Marthe looked after their retreating figures. "Well, that's astonishing but very nice," she said with a sigh. "You took our breath away. She is so fresh, so charming, so really young. Val will design her a wedding dress that will make her look like a Botticelli angel. She has taste, too. That is a Lelong she is wearing."

Campion regarded the old woman thoughtfully.

"You came along remarkably opportunely just now," he observed.

"I?" Her face was completely innocent but the narrow black eyes flickered. "Oh, to hear your news? Yes. I shall have some gossip again at last."

"I didn't mean that, as you know very well. You and Solly Batemann did a remarkably neat stroke of peace-preserving between you just now, didn't you? That wasn't pure act of God, was it?"

Lady Papendeik stared at him, her thin mouth widening.

"You detectives," she said with good-humoured contempt. "What a lot you see. My dear, I was simply sitting over there with the Bensons and Donald Tweed when I caught sight of Alan Dell across the room. I wanted to make sure that he was coming down on Saturday to Ramillies' farewell party at Caesar's Court and so I stepped across to speak to him. Georgia looks very exuberant, doesn't she? A woman who wears birds in her hair ceases to look like Primavera after thirty and simply reminds one of that song they will keep playing."

Mr. Campion reflected.

"You're thinking of a nest of robins, my dear," he said. "A very different caper; someone didn't consult his nature notes when he wrote that. Miss Adamson also favours swallows, I saw."

Lady Papendeik did not look at him. She sat up, her small shoulders compact and severe.

"That is the end of that little girl," she remarked briefly. "Tell me about your engagement. It is so entirely unexpected."

"It is, rather, isn't it?" he agreed. "Still, Amanda's an unexpected young person."

"She's sweet." Tante Marthe glanced across the table to the dance floor. "She looks so lovely. Her figure is completely natural. How does she keep her stockings up?"

Mr. Campion gave the matter his serious consideration.

"I tremble to think. Two magnets and a dry battery, if I know her, or perhaps something complicated on the grid system."

The old woman leant back in her chair.

"Delightful," she murmured. "You love her so comfortably. There is no unhappy excitement. I am glad, my dear boy. I hope the brother is reasonable. What is his objection?"

"Age," supplied Mr. Campion promptly. He made the first excuse that came into his head and was amused to find that he was irritated when she accepted it without incredulity.

"You are old for your years," she said. "You'll grow out of it. My God, I nearly died of old age when I was thirty-three, yet look at me now. There they are."

Campion glanced round and saw that Dell and Amanda had paused at Georgia's table. Ramillies was still absent and Miss Adamson seemed to have disappeared altogether, since there was no sign of her on the dance floor. He watched the little scene round Georgia with interest. It was not possible to hear any remark save from Solly, but his were enlightening.

"When I was married you know what my mama said? She said: 'Have your photograph taken, Solly; you'll never look the same again.' Such a pretty little flower! It is a pity to pick her so soon."

He almost chucked Amanda under the chin, and Lady Papendeik laughed softly at Campion's side as he changed his mind and the plump hand, fluttering uncertainly, accomplished the chucking an inch or so above the red head.

Amanda appeared to be enjoying herself. She smiled at Solly, whom she seemed to like, and was gracefully deferential to Georgia. The brief gathering broke up with Lady Ramillies embracing the younger girl with a sort of fine, generous spirituality which made Mr. Campion think of Britannia in the cartoons of Sir Bernard Partridge, and Solly trotting off across the dance floor waving and nodding like a Bacchus in a triumphal car.

Dell and Georgia settled down again and Amanda came back to her seat. Lady Papendeik rose.

"Good night, my dears," she said. "This is only a secret, isn't it? I mean, I can tell it in confidence? Felicitations, Albert. You are a very clever young man."

Amanda watched her depart before she spoke.

"He *is* a mess, isn't he?" she said gloomily. "It wasn't too good over there. He was hoping I wouldn't notice anything and she was trying to tell me all about it. I concentrated on the hearty old party with the chins and talked about my own engagement. I'm afraid that Georgia woman's a sweep."

"I think she's genuinely very much in love at the moment." Campion put forward the excuse in all fairness.

"She's not," said Amanda. "If you're in love with a man the one thing you're frightened of is doing him any harm. That's the whole principle of the thing. She's not thinking of A.D. at all. She's using him to make herself feel emotional and that means that there are at least two or three hundred other men who would do just as well. I don't mind her going on in her natural way if she's that sort of person, but she's a sweep to pick on A.D., who has work to do."

Mr. Campion regarded her with amusement.

"Taking up philosophy in your old age?"

"That's not philosophy; that's elementary common sense," said Amanda. "Have you got enough money on you to pay for the champagne? If you haven't, that's going to be the next problem. I thought I had thirty bob with me but I see it's only ten."

"No, it's all right. They know me," he assured her, reflecting that Hal and his colleagues must find her a relief to entertain. "That was inspirational."

"It was, wasn't it?" Amanda was never modest in her self-appreciation. "There's nothing to take your mind off an embarrassing situation of your own like being asked to celebrate someone else's engagement. It's partly the champagne and partly the feeling that you're not responsible in any way for the setout. Poor chap, I thought he was going to be sick when he saw me. I felt like the blue-eyed toddler who had staggered in when Daddy was making a beast of himself. Look here, we've got to go. I excused you from that crowd by saying that you had to be in bed early after your illness."

"What illness?" demanded Mr. Campion, startled into bald enquiry.

Amanda sat looking at him, her round brown eyes curious.

"You have been rather ill, haven't you?" she enquired seriously. "You're quieter than you used to be and you look a bit bleached. I took it you'd had tonsillitis or something on the chest."

"I'm perfectly healthy and always have been," declared

Mr. Campion with an outraged dignity that was at least half genuine, "and I'll thank you, miss, to keep your dispiriting remarks to yourself. I'm damned if I want to be rejuvenated, either," he added, a note of genuine resentment which he had not quite intended creeping into his tone.

"Perhaps you're sickening for something," she murmured with intent to comfort. "Come on. We shall have to stay engaged for a week or two. It was a nuisance in a way but it seemed the best thing to do. I couldn't let A.D. feel we'd been spying on him. I thought he was simply being rooked, you see. I didn't dream it was anything like this. I knew you'd back me up so I got out of the situation as neatly as possible. We can let the betrothal excitement die down gradually. I've got a ring of Aunt Flo's somewhere, so you needn't bother about that."

"Splendid." Mr. Campion seemed relieved. "Then it's just my wife to square and we're all set."

"Yes, well, you can do that," said Amanda. "I've done all the dirty work so far. Put me in a cab and I'll go down to Boot's Hotel on my own. It's right out of your way. You do look rather tired, you know."

Mr. Campion prepared to depart.

"You're stewing up for a thick ear," he remarked. "I never raise my hand against a woman save in anger."

Amanda sighed and he had the uncomfortable impression that it was with relief. Her smile vanished immediately, however, and he caught her looking a trifle older herself.

"I'm behaving like a goat mainly because I feel so miserable, you know," she remarked presently. "Can you see the sort of blazing shame this all is?"

"Yes," he said gravely, catching her mood. "It's not good. Rotten for Sid and all of you. The death of a hero but not a hero's death, so to speak."

"Oh, you're still all right." She was grinning at him with a warmth that no Georgia could ever counterfeit. "Up here, away from it all, I can understand some people feeling that this angle of ours is all a bit 'footy' and small, but down there . . . ! We all *live* from him, Albert. He's the spark that lights the fires. That woman's not so much a sweep, you know, as an enemy. Ramillies is a bit of a tick, too, isn't he? That incident might have been most indelicate. It was rather miraculous how it all cleared up in a moment."

79

"Rather miraculous? My poor young woman..." Mr. Campion regarded her with affection. "That was not merely a miracle; that was fishy. I've never actually believed in a guardian angel, but when I observe such a veritable cloud of feathers I do suspect something of the sort. You don't seem to realise I've been sitting here watching a conjuring trick that leaves Caligari cold. There's someone around here to whom I take off my hat—all my hats."

He was still pondering over the phenomenon as they went out and as they crossed into the wide aisle behind the pillars someone nodded to him from a table not too well placed in a corner. He returned the nod and comprehension came to him with recognition.

Ferdie Paul lay back idly in his chair looking more like a bored gilt Byron than ever. There was an air of great weariness and disinterest about him, but his smile was friendly and he raised a pale hand in salute. There were two women at his table and a deserted chair. Campion recognised one of his companions as the very well-dressed but ill-at-ease little person whom Rex had been so anxious to placate at Papendeik's dress show, while the other, a big-boned good-tempered blonde, was unmistakably Mrs. Solly Batemann. At the moment she was talking to Gaiogi, who was standing at her side.

Campion glanced round him. As he thought, Tante Marthe was seated not so very far away.

Chapter Nine

When the seventh Earl Hurrell rebuilt Caesar's Court in the late eighteenth century he incorporated a great many of the brighter ideas of the day into the construction of the house and grounds. The Pinery, the ice house, the Vine Palace and the useful gazebo were all much admired at the time, and the sloping lawn, which not only ran down to the Thames but presumably continued under it, since it reappeared on the opposite bank and went on and on for the best part of a mile like a strip of gigantic stair carpet, had been commented on by George IV ("Impressive, Hurrell, ain't it? What? What?").

Since that time the succeeding Hurrells had been fully occupied keeping the monstrous property a going concern, let alone improving it, so that when Gaiogi Laminoff took charge the place was, as the estate agent said, delightfully unspoilt.

At eleven o'clock on the Sunday morning following the farewell party given for Sir Raymond Ramillies, Mr. Campion sat on a little footbridge over the river and considered Gaiogi's alterations with sober admiration.

The rosy building itself had retained the dignity of a great private palace but had miraculously lost its pomposity. Even at this distance it exuded a party atmosphere and it occurred to Mr. Campion that it looked like some millionaire child's play pen magnified up to an impossible scale. There were expensive toys everywhere. Little silver aeroplanes taxied off the green turf on the other side of the river. Glossy hacks and shiny motorcars paraded on the gravel drives, and everywhere there were flowers and casually elegant clothes, with a suggestion of music in the background. The general effect was expensive, exclusive and very pleasant; the Royal Enclosure at Home sort of atmosphere.

There was much activity on the flying field, especially round the hangar where the new plane had been housed the night before, and Campion did not notice the two who came striding towards him until Amanda spoke. She looked very like herself in a brown suit, better cut than her working clothes of old but the same in general effect, and her heart-shaped face was alive and interested with all the freshness of a sixteen-year-old.

"Hallo," she said. "Has the old cad turned up yet?"

"Ramillies? No, I'm afraid not."

"Where on earth is he? Oh, Albert, I quite forget. This is Sid."

They had reached the middle of the bridge by this time and Mr. Campion found himself confronted by a tall, bull-necked young man with very black hair, which he wore practically shaved save for a solid thatch on the very top of his head. He shook hands with deep resentment and said with patent insincerity that he was pleased to meet Mr. Campion.

"Well, I'll get back," he said immediately with an assumption of ease which was ridiculous or heroic according to the way one's mind worked. "If you can find out when Sir Raymond returns, Lady Amanda, send a message over to us. The broadcasting blokes are twittering away like spadgers over there."

"I thought you were coming up to the bar?" Amanda was surprised. "He'll be there if he's back."

"No, I don't think I will, thanks awfully." Sid had his hands in his pockets and the skirts of his brown jacket, which were a trifle too fluted, jutted out behind him like a cape. "I'll get back. So long. Take care of yourself."

He seemed to mistrust the social tone of the final admonition as soon as he had made it, for he reddened and, nodding to Campion without looking at him, strode off with his broad shoulders hunched and his trousers flapping. Amanda looked after him, her eyebrows raised. She glanced at Campion appealingly.

"He's all right, really," she said. "Or don't you think so?"

"Dear chap," murmured Mr. Campion. "Not quite sure of himself, that's all. That's nothing."

"Don't you believe it," said Amanda gloomily. "Class is like sex or the electric light supply, not worth thinking about as long as yours is all right but embarrassingly inconvenient if there's anything wrong with it. Sid *will* feel he's lowish, and so he is, and nothing much can be done about it. It doesn't worry other people at all, of course, but it's lousy for him. What about Ramillies?"

"He hasn't shown up yet but I don't think there's much point in worrying. He'll appear when the time comes."

She glanced at him sharply. "You think he's simply doing this to put everybody in a flap?"

"It wouldn't be astounding, would it?"

"No. Disgustingly likely. What a crowd they all are. . . ." Amanda sounded tolerant. "It was a bad show clearing off in the middle of his own farewell do like that. He's too old to go roaring off into the night at two o'clock in the morning as if he were twenty. It's so old-fashioned."

Mr. Campion was inclined to agree but he could not forget that there had been extenuating circumstances.

"Georgia wasn't helping," he ventured.

Amanda sniffed. She was wandering along beside him, her hands clasped behind her and her head bent.

"D'you know, I can't believe it of A.D.," she said suddenly. "When I actually see it I can't believe it. It's—well, it's shocking, isn't it? That's a spoilt word but you see what I mean."

He laughed.

"What's the reaction among the disciples?"

"I don't know. I mentioned it to Sid but he didn't believe me until yesterday when he came over here and got the gossip. He's just murderous towards the woman, of course. Sid sees things in black and white. It doesn't seem to be a bad idea. It saves him no end of bother. Where are we going?"

They had turned aside and taken a path which led through a rose garden to a shrubbery interspersed with several high trees, all very brave and gay in their summer finery.

"I'm staying with the Laminoffs," he explained. "They're having a small hangover party at a quarter to twelve. I promised I'd bring my fiancée if I could find her. You're getting on nicely with my family, aren't you?"

"I think I do you credit," agreed Amanda complacently. "You asked me to marry you at the Olympia Circus last year. It was just like the pictures. We came together over a game of darts in the amusement park afterwards. I don't suppose Val will ask you about it but you may as well know what she's talking about if she does. I like Val. I came to you about this business in the first place because I had an idea that A.D. was a friend of hers. He was, wasn't he?"

"They seemed to like each other."

Amanda sighed. "Then you do know about it. I only wondered. Relations are sometimes dense. It shows, you know. I noticed it as soon as I saw them together. That makes Georgia more of a sweep than ever, don't you think?"

Mr. Campion had not the opportunity to reply. They had turned a corner in the shrubbery path and now came to an unexpected wicket gate which gave on to one of the seventh earl's prettier follies. The seventh earl had seen the Petit Trianon and it had taken his fancy. His recollection had been shorter than the French king's, but he had achieved a little house. It sat solid and white, like an upended box of bricks, with pillars and steps and a fine flat lead roof. The little trees, which had once matched its miniature magnificence, had now grown to big trees and the tiny terrace was moss grown and charming.

So much for the earl. Gaiogi had added gaiety. The pompous windows were wide, and pink and apple-green curtains billowed in their dark eyes. There were chairs on the steps, and cushions and great stone urns of flowers. It was a party house and Gaiogi was the perfect party host. His head appeared through a window as soon as they entered the gate.

"The sun has come out," he shouted to Amanda. "How are you?"

"Excited," said Amanda obligingly.

Gaiogi met her eyes and laughed, and it occurred to Campion that it was the meeting and mutual recognition of two persons of resource.

Mme Laminoff met them in the hall, which would have been a grim box with a black-and-white squared marble floor if Gaiogi had not taken it into his head to have a set of red chessmen painted on the stones and to enliven an alcove with a red glass lobster in place of the seventh earl's bust of Cicero. Sofya Laminoff was herself unexpected. She was plump and gracious and succeeded in looking like a very exotic film star unsuccessfully disguised as Queen Victoria. She was far more placid than her husband, but her eyes, which were theatrically black against her magnificent white hair, had a twinkle in them and her small fat hands fluttered charmingly as she talked.

"Still no news of him?" Her anxious enquiry stood out from the flurry of welcome as though it had leapt into blacker type. "No? Never mind. He'll come. I tell Gaiogi he will come. He is simply a man who likes to make himself interesting. Come in."

She swept them into the salon, where the hangover party was already in progress. The room itself was charming. It ran through to the back of the house and ended in wide windows giving on to a small formal garden. Here again the seventh earl had not been so much suppressed as made a little tipsy. His graceful fireplace and flat-fluted columns remained, while much of the furniture was pure Georgian, but the rest was Gaiogi's own collection of interesting pieces, many of which were of the frankly bought-for-fun variety. It was all remarkably comfortable. Tante Marthe sat in a rocking chair in a patch of sunlight, and Val, looking like one of her own advertisements in Vogue, was curled up on a Mme Récamier chaise longue. There were four or five strangers present: an affable young man from the B.B.C., a gloomy youngster with a big nose whose name was Wivenhoe and who seemed to be something to do with Towser of the Colonial Office, two quiet little men who talked together respectfully and might have had "Money" neatly embroidered on sashes round their middles, and a large gentleman with a Guardee moustache who devoted himself to Val and turned out most unexpectedly to be the managing editor of one of the larger dailies.

Gaiogi himself was happy, playing apothecary, and he dispensed his three sovereign remedies, champagne, tea or iced draught beer, according to the condition of the individual patient.

Campion wandered over to him.

"I've phoned his house, his clubs and every Turkish bath in London," he said quietly. "We'll give him another couple of hours and then I'll go to town and get the bloodhounds out. We can't very well do a thing like that too soon. I also tried to get hold of a Miss Adamson but apparently Annie doesn't live there any more."

"Ah? Oh yes, *that* girl." Gaiogi hunched his shoulders and looked vaguely introspective. "Yes, a pretty girl. No head. No perception. No, she doesn't live here or at Papendeik's any more."

"Nor with her aunt Maggie either, it would appear."

"Really?" Gaiogi did not seem interested. "That may be. Very likely. We will give him until after lunch. Meanwhile, my dear fellow, don't let it distress you. What will you drink? Let us all forget the miserable chap. Towser is coming to the lunch. He wants a round of golf before the ceremony. I had hoped that Ramillies would be here to help entertain him, but from what Wivenhoe tells me perhaps it is almost as well. Not all these charming people like one another."

He exploded with laughter on the last word and his round brown eyes met Campion's shyly.

"That fellow Wivenhoe is a bit of a stick. Marthe Papendeik keeps talking to him about his chief, Pluto. He is quite offended. She is innocent. It is a natural slip. I thought I'd warn you."

"Thank you. I'll remember that." Campion spoke gravely and it sent through his mind that more than half Gaiogi's secret lay in his naïveté and the rest was deep understanding of important fun. There was an air of magnificent goings on about this morning's party, much of which was justified if one accepted the all-importance of the success of Caesar's Court.

"I talked to Ferdie Paul on the telephone just now," Gaiogi went on. "He says don't worry. In his opinion the fellow is something of an exhibitionist. He knows him well. That is between friends, of course. He says like all these people, when the moment on which their job depends actually arrives, they are always there."

"There's a lot in that," said Campion. "Is Paul coming down this afternoon?"

"No, unfortunately no. He is just off to Paris. He has interests over there and must be back in London tomorrow."

'He's a clever chap," Campion remarked absently.

"Oh, extraordinary." Gaiogi pronounced each syllable of the word in his admiration. "Brilliant. If only he weren't so lazy he'd be a force, a power."

"Lazy? I should hardly have thought that."

Gaiogi filled a glass.

"There is a phrase for him in English," he said. "Do you know it? He is 'born tired.' He never does anything at all if he can get someone to do it for him. Will your beautiful betrothed drink champagne?"

Mr. Campion glanced at his beautiful betrothed with a certain amount of apprehension. She was talking to Val and Tante Marthe and the older woman's little lizard head was cocked on one side and her eyes were dancing.

"You're both darling to want to help," Amanda was saying firmly, "but you don't know my brother. We've decided to let him grow. His mind will expand. Meanwhile we're perfectly happy, aren't we, Albert?"

"You have your aeroplanes, my dear," said Mr. Campion with caddish resignation.

Amanda blinked. "That's terribly true," she agreed earnestly. "I must try not to be selfish—or vulgar," she added warningly.

Campion caught Val's eye and turned away hastily. She had looked a little sorry for him.

"You didn't find him?" Tante Marthe put the question in an undertone and she grimaced when he shook his head. "He expected to find that girl here last night. That is why he went off. He was piqued, like a child. I told Gaiogi so. Georgia was being thoughtless, I know, but he's been married to her for over two years. He must be used to that sort of thing by this time. Who's that coming now?''

There was a stir in the room and Gaiogi hurried to the window and they caught over his plump shoulders a fleeting vision of a small vehicle passing up the drive. It was a calash, one of the pneumatic-tired electric cars like glorified bath chairs for two which Gaiogi had acquired to transport his lazier lotus-eaters about the grounds and which were proving very popular in this little world of toys. Val glanced at Campion questioningly and once again he avoided her eyes.

"Georgia," he said briefly.

"And Alan?"

"Yes, I think so."

She did not speak but glanced out across the little flower garden as if she were half a mind to escape into it, but there was no sign of any emotion on her face.

With the sound of Georgia's warm happy voice in the hall outside a flatness passed over the company. For the first time the title of the party became apt, as though everyone had just remembered that he had taken part in an uproarious ceremony the night before.

Georgia came in with Dell in attendance. She was beautiful, alive and blatantly triumphant. In any other circumstances her naïve delight in her captive would have been disarming, but this morning, in view of everything, it was not quite forgivable and succeeded in striking a démodé note in that aware community. Campion caught Amanda regarding them speculatively and, as was his gift, saw them for a moment through her eyes. He was startled. She was thinking that they were poor old things.

Georgia crossed the room, her white silk sports suit emphasising the warmth of her skin and the strong grace of her figure. She kissed Tante Marthe, nodded to the two decent young men and sat down beside Val with an arm round her shoulders. Dell remained by the door talking to Gaiogi. There was a distinct air of defiance about him which was young and sat oddly upon him, destroying his dignity, but when he came over at Georgia's imperious command they saw that his eyes were bewildered and unhappy.

"Something will have to be done," said Georgia clearly

above the chatter. "He's got to go in that plane. Where on earth is he?"

It was the first time that the subject of Ramillies' absence had been mentioned in any tone above a whisper and the effect upon the whole room was interesting. Everybody stopped talking and Campion realised for the first time that every member of the party had a definite reason for being present. It was another evidence of Gaiogi's celebrated diplomacy and was, for some obscure psychological reason, faintly disturbing, as if one had accidentally discovered that the floor was laid over a well.

"Didn't he leave any message when he went off last night, Lady Ramillies?" enquired Wivenhoe, who seemed constitutionally incapable of grasping the unconventional. "Surely he said something to somebody? I mean a man doesn't go off into the night like that without a word."

Georgia looked at him steadily, holding his eyes while she laughed.

"It does sometimes happen, my pet," she said, and the large man with the moustache chuckled and the two little men who had been talking about money smiled at each other.

"Well, darlings," said Georgia, looking round the room and conveying, most unjustifiably, that they were all in the family, "we were all at the party last night, weren't we? Did anyone notice anything peculiar about the old villain? I rather lost sight of him myself." She glanced under her lashes at Dell, who blushed. The colour rushed into his face and suffused his very eyes. He was so mature for such an exhibition, so entirely the wrong sort of person for the reaction, that he could scarcely have been more obvious or caused more embarrassment if he had burst into tears. Everybody began to talk again.

As Mr. Campion turned his head he saw two profiles, Amanda as red as her hero and Val so white that her face looked stony. Georgia seemed surprised.

"It's all all right," she said. "He probably realised he was getting a bit tight and trotted off to a Turkish bath in town. He'll turn up very clean and hungry half an hour late for lunch. He hasn't been frightfully fit, as a mater of fact. He went to a specialist a fortnight ago. He knows he ought not to drink. His sins are finding him out, wicked old thing."

Why these revelations should set everyone's mind at rest

was not very clear, but conversation became general again, indicating that everyone had found out that no one knew much more than he did and had decided to wait a little longer.

Georgia's attention returned to Dell, who was standing by the windows looking into the little garden. He came when she called him and paused before her. Georgia appeared to have forgotten what she wanted him for and was clearly about to tell the tasselled gentle so when Val intervened.

"What's that in your coat?" she said. "I've been trying to place it. May I ask?"

The ordinary question was a relief to him and he seized on it.

"This?" he enquired, pulling his lapel and squinting down at it. "That's the Quentin Clear."

"Good heavens, I never noticed it." Georgia's tone was vigorously possessive and her arm tightened about the other woman unconsciously, so that she was virtually holding Val back by main force. "My dear man, you can't go about like that. You look like a darts champion. Whatever is it, pet? Give it here."

She held out her free hand and, after fidgeting with the split pin that held it in place, he gave it to her unwillingly. It was a small silver medallion, not particularly distinguished in design but of exquisite workmanship, as these things sometimes are. Georgia turned it over.

"It's rather sweet," she said. "I like the little propeller things, don't you, Val? But you can't wear it, dear, you simply can't. I'll keep it."

Dell hesitated. He looked profoundly uncomfortable.

"I'm afraid you mustn't," he said awkwardly. "I'll put it back."

"You won't." Georgia was laughing. "If anyone wears it I will. It looks rather sweet on this revers."

There was a force in her voice that he seemed to find unanswerable and Mr. Campion felt himself led firmly out into the garden.

"Sorry, but I thought I was going to protest," said Amanda, striding across the grass plot. "That's the Quentin Clear. The woman must be nuts. He is, God knows."

"That's rather special, isn't it?"

"Special?" Amanda made a noise like an angry old gentleman. "It's it. It's *the* one. Only about three men in the world have it. A.D. wouldn't wear it if it wasn't for this 'do' this afternoon. She's simply ignorant, of course, and evidently doesn't understand that he isn't just anybody, which is what I've complained of all along. He ought to be taken home and given a sedative, of course, but if Sid or any of the boys see her wearing that thing there'll be a riot. It's a howling insult. Can't we tell her?''

"I'm afraid that's his pigeon, my dear." Mr. Campion spoke mildly. "Anything we do reflects on him, doesn't it?"

Amanda kicked the edge of the lawn with a small neat toe and glanced up at him.

"The older one gets the more one understands and the smaller the things are that matter," she remarked. "It doesn't get easier, does it? I'm sorry I cleared out. I suddenly felt it was all a bit beyond me. Hullo."

Her final remark was addressed to a small boy who was seated on a wooden settle against a southern wall. He had been hidden from them as they came out by the angle of the house and was sitting very quietly all by himself, a book on his knee. He rose politely and pulled off his Haverleigh cap as Amanda spoke and Campion recognised him as the child he had seen at Papendeik's. He looked now much as he had done then, self-contained and patient, like somebody waiting on a railway station.

"It's very pleasant out here in the sun," he remarked, more, they felt, in an attempt to put them at their ease than in an attempt to cover any embarrassment of his own. "I like this little garden."

He was an undersized fourteen, Campion judged, and he tried somewhat hurriedly to remember his own mentality at that age. Meanwhile, however, Amanda came to the rescue.

"Haverleigh is shut, isn't it?" she said. "What was it? I.P. in the village? Do you think you'll get back at half?"

He shrugged his shoulders and smiled wryly.

"We hope so. The last case was reported three weeks ago. Meanwhile one can only wait. It's rather rotten. It's only my second term."

The confidence was the first sign of immaturity he had shown and Campion was relieved to notice it.

"I saw you in town the other day," he said, trying to avoid the accusing tone one so often uses to children.

The boy looked up with interest.

"With Georgia and Raymond at Papendeik's?" he said. "Yes, I remember you. I'm afraid I'm not as interested in clothes as I should be," he added apologetically. "Mother— that's Georgia, you know—is doing her best with me but I'm not really keen. That sort of interest grows on one later, don't you think?"

"It's not a thing you're born with, necessarily," remarked Amanda cheerfully. "We're going back to the party. Are you coming?"

"No, I don't think I will, thank you very much," he said, reseating himself. "I've got this that I must read, and it's very warm out here in the sun."

Amanda eyed the solid green volume on his knee.

"Holiday task?"

He nodded. *"Ivanhoe,"* he admitted, a touch of amused embarrassment in his eyes.

"Heavy going?" enquired Campion sympathetically.

"Well, he wrote in a hurry, didn't he?" There was no affectation in the pronouncement, nor did he censure, but appeared to be offering an explanation merely. "It's a bit theatrical, you know, or at least I think so. The people aren't like anyone I've met." He paused and added, "So far," with a cautiousness which gave his age away again.

"That's all very true," said Mr. Campion, "but I shouldn't put it in your essay if I were you."

The child met his eyes with a startled expression.

"Good Lord, no," he said fervently and smiled at Campion as if he felt they shared a secret about schoolmasters.

They had been longer in the garden than they realised and the party had broken up when they returned. The room was deserted and the debris of empty glasses and overfilled ashtrays made it look forlorn in spite of its essential gaiety. Through the front window the departing crowd was visible, straggling towards the wicket gate.

Amanda turned aside to look for her handbag and Campion went on to the hall alone. In the doorway he paused. Georgia was standing with her back to him looking up the staircase, and as he appeared she spoke to Dell over her shoulder.

"I shan't be a moment. You start the little bath chair thing."

With some vague idea of allowing them to get away first Campion remained where he was and he was still in the salon doorway when Val came hurrying downstairs, a small square box in her outstretched hand.

"There's only one left," she said. "You know how to take it? Soften it in water and gulp it down."

"Bless you, darling, you've saved my life." Georgia took the box without glancing at the other woman. "I must fly. He's waiting for me like a little dog on the step, the sweetie. Thanks so much."

She hurried across the hall and Val stood on the lowest stair looking after her. There was a startled expression upon her face and her lips were parted. Campion stared at her and she turned and saw him.

She did not speak but started violently, made a little inarticulate sound and, turning, fled up the staircase, leaving him bewildered and, in spite of every ounce of common sense that he possessed, alarmed. He had half a mind to follow her, and would, of course, have altered a great many things had he obeyed the impulse, but Georgia's precipitate return drove the incident from his mind.

"Where's Gaiogi?" she demanded, flying into the hall, her eyes bright with excitement. "My dear, he's turned up! Raymond's back. They say he's tight as forty owls, the abominable old brute. He must have been drinking like a fish all night. He's gone straight to his room. He says he'll sleep for an hour. I think it's best to let him, don't you? He's got to go on that plane. If it's the last thing he does he's got to go back today."

Chapter Ten

The Ulangi Flight Luncheon given by Alan Dell in the Degas Room at Caesar's Court was, as is the fashion, strictly informal. In spite of the fact that Towser spoke, Dell spoke, the heads of the various departments in the huge Alandel works responsible for the machine spoke, a wit from Towser's party who *could* speak spoke, and even the pilot drawled a few shy, halting words, the informality was strictly preserved.

In spite of the amusing aeroplane of flowers suspended in a block of ice on a pillar in the centre of the horseshoe table, in spite of the silver-gilt souvenirs that Gaiogi had so thoughtfully provided, in spite of the Ulangi pears, a rather dreadful fruit imported at great trouble and expense for the occasion and served mercifully soaked in kirsch to deaden their own unpalatable flavour, the happy family party atmosphere was firmly maintained.

The one genuinely unconventional note was provided by Ramillies' absence and a great many excuses were offered, both publicly and privately, for that omission.

Towser, who was one of the older school of politicians with a big head and such an affectation of plain-manishness on top of a natural bent in that direction that one automatically suspected him, most unjustly, of every sort of insincerity, explained at laborious length what he honestly understood about Sir Raymond's slight indisposition. It came out an overpowering story, hinting at sickly relatives dying in inaccessible parts of the island, cross-country journeys, and a noble if exhausted Ramillies crawling gamely home to be persuaded by an adoring wife to snatch what rest he might before attempting the feat of endurance which lay before him as a passenger on an almost epic flight.

It was unfortunate that the impression which this recital conveyed to that experienced audience was even worse than the facts. By the time the distinguished speaker had gone on to something else there was a universal conviction that Sir Raymond had been brought in drunk on a police stretcher and was even now lying unconscious on the floor of a private cell in the barber's shop. The pilot and the navigator exchanged glances and shrugged their shoulders philosophically. They were both lean stringy youngsters with faded hair and the curious clear-eyed, unimaginative stare of that new and magnificent breed that seems to have been created by or for the air. So long as their cargo avoided delirium tremens they did not care.

Sir Raymond's adoring wife, who was getting on very nicely in her place of honour between the minister and the host, looked properly tolerant of her husband's misfortunes, and the meal progressed happily with everyone being as charming as possible to the one uncertain element in their midst, the bored but ungullible Press.

Mr. Campion was not present. He lunched alone in the open-air restaurant in the water garden and avoided the eyes of more acquaintances than he had realised he possessed. Caesar's Court was flourishing. Gaiogi's principality was in its golden age.

With Ramillies safely in his room recovering from a night out his own immediate charge was at a standstill. Like all professionals who are doing a little work on the side to oblige a friend, he felt at a disadvantage. Friendship is a hampering thing at the best of times, and the demands made in its name are often unreasonable. As far as he could see, everybody in his immediate circle was beseeching him to avert something different. Looking round this pleasant and expensive scene, it struck him forcibly that such universal alarm was quite extraordinary. Ramillies appeared to be the focal point of the general anxiety. Ramillies was clearly expected to do something spiteful or sensational or both. So far, it seemed to Campion, he had simply behaved like a spoilt undergraduate with a gift for the offensive yet neither Val nor Gaiogi was unduly nervous or even inexperienced. He reminded himself that he knew all these decorative, volatile people very slightly. They were all such natural exhibitionists, all so busy presenting various aspects of themselves, that to meet them was like watching a play in which by the end of the evening all the actors seem old friends and yet in the back of one's mind there is the conviction that ten minutes behind the scenes would make them all strangers again. He decided to wander up and take a look at the patient.

He located the bedroom and was bearing down upon the door when it opened six inches or so and remained dark and ajar. He paused. Of all the minor incidents of life a door which opens at one's approach is perhaps the most disconcerting. An eye regarded him through the aperture.

"Campion."

"Yes?"

"Come in. Are the others still eating? Come in, will you?"

The thin sharp voice was not so strident as usual but the note of insolence was still there. Campion walked into a room whose only light crept in round the edges of drawn curtains and the door closed behind him. A shadowy figure laid an unsteady hand on his arm.

"I'm going to take my things down to the plane now."
Ramillies sounded excited and the confidential tone was new
in him. "I'm not travelling much. They're sticky about the
weight because she's carrying so much extra juice. My man's
gone on by sea and rail like a Christian and I don't want any
damned hotel servants touching my stuff. That's natural, isn't
it?"

A querulous anxiety in the question confirmed the general
diagnosis, and his visitor made haste to reassure him. Ramillies
tittered. It was an unpleasant sound in the gloom and reminded
Mr. Campion that he never had liked the man.

"I'm going to shift it myself," Georgia's husband continued huskily. "You come down with me and see it weighed.
You bear witness that I haven't got that gun. I've had my head
talked off about that gun and I'm bloody sick of it. You come
along. I've been on the lookout for a stranger but you're
better. You'll do nicely."

Campion disengaged himself from the gripping fingers.

"Anything you like," he said easily. "Are you all right? I
thought you weren't feeling too good."

"I've been drunk. God, I've been drunk!" He made the
words a breathy little prayer of satisfaction. "I'm sobering up
now. It's rotten sobering up but it won't last. Nothing gets me
down for long. Besides, I've got something to do. I've got
something on. I can always snap out of it if I've got
something on. It doesn't really affect me."

The bravado sounded a trifle forlorn to Campion.

"Have you packed?" he enquired.

"Lord, yes, packed in town. What the hell are we doing
chattering here in the dark?"

This was a question which had occurred to Mr. Campion
himself and he said so.

"Georgia pulled the curtains to keep the blasted light out of
my eyes." Ramillies was blundering slowly across the room
as he spoke. "She's full of wifely concern, isn't she? Have
you noticed it?"

He turned round suspiciously on the last word, letting in a
shaft of sun with the same movement, but apparently the
younger man's expression was satisfactory, for he seemed
content.

"I've only got one little case and some coats," he said.
"We'll take them down and show them. Then I'll come back

and sleep. I'll be all right by the time we leave. We go at five, they say, not four; weather or something damned silly. What are you looking at? Do I show it much? I do sometimes.''

He lurched unsteadily towards a mirror and stared at himself, and Campion felt a twinge of pity for him. The man was grey and positively sweating, and his eyes had sunk into his head.

"Where on earth did you get the stuff at two in the morning?" he demanded involuntarily.

Ramillies looked round and for an instant there was a flicker of his old childlike smile.

"She had a cellar," he said. "Come on. I'm going to put on one coat. They'll weigh me as well as the baggage. I dislike those fellows. I dislike people who live for machinery. I dislike Dell himself. Not for the reason you think, Campion. Not for that reason. I dislike Dell because he's a mechanic and a blasted prig.''

He found the coat he wanted and struggled slowly into it.

"A blasted sentimental petrol-scented prig," he added, standing swaying in the shaft of sunlight with the ulster flapping against his calves. "Georgia needs a sense of proportion. She'll get one when she comes out to me with the Taretons. I shall probably have my gun by then. I'm going to show them some sport. You're not the kind of chap who'd like what I call sport, Campion."

"No," said Mr. Campion, remembering him at school. "No, I don't think I am."

Ramillies began to laugh but thought better of it and presently they began a weary descent. Side by side in a calash they set off for the footbridge and a hangar. Ramillies looked like a great tweed parcel and a death's-head, and sat balancing a small suitcase on his knee while Campion drove the flimsy machine. It was nearly three quarters of a mile over gravel and turf and they took it slowly to avoid jolting. Ramillies sat silent, hunched up in his coat in the blazing sun, and Campion glanced at his beaded forehead with apprehension.

"I should take that thing off if I were you," he remarked. "You'll suffocate yourself."

"That would suit Dell, wouldn't it?" said Ramillies. "I expect he prays, don't you? That sort of chap hugs his virtue and prays I'll die—blasted prig! Damned fool, too. I'll tell you something, Campion. You're sitting there thinking I'm more offensive drunk than sober, aren't you?''

"Well," said Mr. Campion, not wishing to be offensive himself, "roughly that sort of thought, you know."

"I am," said Ramillies modestly, as if he had received a much-prized compliment. "I am. D'you know why I ever thought of leaving my wife here with that fellow hanging around her? Nobody knows Georgia. That's the cream of the joke. She's out of date. She's the 1902 chorus-girl type. It's damned low-class blood in her. She's got the careful-virgin mentality. I know. My God, I know! She wears a *ceinture de chasteté* with a wedding-ring key. She'll come out with the Taretons in six weeks time and when I get her there she'll give up the stage. This is a prophecy. You listen to it. Write it down somewhere. Georgia won't come back to the stage. I've got something on, you know. I'm not the complacent husband. I've got a surprise for Georgia and that fellow Dell. Sorry I'm being so vulgar. I don't know you well, do I?''

"We're not buddies," said Mr. Campion mildly. "You're tight."

"Yes," Sir Raymond agreed in his thin flat voice. "I'm very, very tight." He laughed. "These government fellows," he said, "they wouldn't stand me for ten minutes if it wasn't for one thing. Do you know what that is? I'm a genius with my niggers. My province is the most damned degenerate hole in the entire creation. My niggers would make your hair stand on end. They even startle me at times and I like 'em. The rest of the West Coast doesn't mention us when it writes home. It doesn't want to be associated with us. But my niggers and I understand one another. I suit them and they suit me. I'm not afraid, you know. I'm not afraid of anything on earth.''

"Jolly for you," murmured Mr. Campion politely.

Ramillies nodded. "I've never tolerated fear. There's only one thing I'm afraid of and I've overcome that," he said earnestly and with that naïveté which Campion had noticed in him once before, "and I have just a touch of the miraculous with my two dirty little tribes. You look at this plane."

They were admitted somewhat grudgingly into the hangar. The plane stood half in and half out of the shed and was certainly something to see. It was a pretty four-seater single-engined machine of the Alandel Seraphim class, with the typical sharp nose and a specially designed undercarriage in anticipation of the Ulangi landing grounds, but by far the most sensational feature to the lay observer was the yellow metal paint which transformed the whole thing into a gaudy toy.

The mechanics who surrounded her each wore the slightly sullen expression reserved by the conscientious workman for anything unconventional in the way of decoration and one of them made so bold as to comment upon it.

" 'Is Coloured 'Ighness will find this 'ere all colours o' the rainbow in three months," he observed ostensibly to a colleague but with a sidelong glance at Ramillies.

"He'll have broken his neck in it long before then or sold it to a dangerous relation," muttered Sir Raymond under his breath to Campion. "Where do I get myself weighed?"

Since practically everyone of authority was at the lunch there was a certain amount of confusion over this preliminary, and Mr. Campion fancied that he detected a certain transparency in his charge's motive in choosing this particular moment to make his arrangements. There was a brief delay, and he had leisure to observe the preparations for the official send-off. A narrow wooden platform had been erected against the wall just inside the hangar, and while at the moment this was smothered in cables and batteries in anticipation for the broadcast, a cut-glass water carafe and two enormous pots of hydrangeas standing precariously in a corner indicated the general effect desired.

Meanwhile Ramillies had got himself in the centre of a small group and Campion was summoned to be a witness to the fact that his small suitcase contained nothing to which anyone could possibly take exception. It was also sealed, an unnecessary precaution embarrassing to everyone except its owner, who insisted upon it being taken. Ramillies then clambered upon the scales himself while the old dangerous and irresponsible expression returned to his pallid face.

Since there appeared to be no deception here, either, everything was being very satisfactorily concluded when there was an unexpected interruption as Georgia appeared, very sweet and gracious and maternal.

"Darling," she said earnestly, hurrying over to her husband, "you ought to be lying down. I nearly had a fit when I found you'd gone. I'm going to take you back at once. My dear man, you're starting in a couple of hours. You must get some rest. Mr. Campion, you do agree, don't you?''

It was a charming little domestic scene and the group of interested minor officials were properly impressed. Ramillies proclaimed "night out" as clearly as if the words had been stamped all over him, and Georgia did much to counteract the gossip which had been floating about by as charming an exhibition of wifely devotion as the most sentimental British workingman could have wished to see. She no longer wore the Quentin Clear, Campion was relieved to notice.

Ramillies eyed her narrowly and Campion, who was watching him, was startled to see a sudden docility come into his face. He smiled at her happily, almost triumphantly, and tucked her arm into his.

"We'll go back together," he said. "Campion won't mind us taking the calash."

They went off arm in arm and Mr. Campion added another interesting and contradictory fact to his collection. Ramillies was genuinely in love with his wife and was therefore, presumably, deeply jealous of her.

He was strolling back across the turf when he encountered Amanda, who greeted him enthusiastically and seemed disposed to gossip.

"A.D.'s gone golfing with Towser," she said, "and I've just passed Georgia and Ramillies sitting side by side in a bath chair. It was very pretty. 'Having ten minutes to spare, I spent them with my husband.' I almost like her, don't you? She's so comfortingly obvious. The lunch was good—the food, I mean. Did you like the plane? It's only one of the Seraphim, of course. You should come and see the new Archangels we're building.''

"I'd like it," he said gravely. "Tell me, do you do Cherubim as well?"

"Yes, we did, but the model wasn't too satisfactory." She shook her head over the failure.

"Too short in the tail, perhaps?" he suggested, sympathetically. "Nothing to—er—catch hold of."

"That's right," she agreed, eyeing him admiringly. "You're picking up, aren't you? The pink feathers came off the wings, too, just as you were going to say. Did you know Val was ill?''

"Ill?"

Amanda nodded and her big honey-coloured eyes were thoughtful.

"Not seriously. But she looked pretty white and sort of hunted at lunch and afterwards she went off to lie down." She hesitated and shot him one of those odd direct glances which were peculiarly her own. "It's terrifying and ludicrous and ugly, isn't it?" she said. "Not Val, of course, but the thing itself; cake love."

"Cake love?" he enquired, remembering her interest in food. Amanda raised her eyebrows at him.

"Oh, use your head," she said. "Don't embarrass me. This thing they've all got that's hurting them so and making us all feel they may blow up. Cake love as opposed to the bread-and-butter kind."

"Oh, I see. You're plumping for bread and butter, are you, my young hopeful?"

"I'm full of bread and butter," said Amanda with content.

Campion looked down at her. "You're very young," he remarked.

She grunted contemptuously.

"Please God I'll stay like it, you poor old gent," she said. "Let's sit on the terrace and digest. We can keep our eye on 'em all from there. Ramillies is up to something, isn't he? You don't think he's going to pop his head out of the plane and pick Georgia off just as they start to taxi?"

"Relying on the engine row to hide the shot?" Campion laughed. "That would be rather pretty. If he wasn't seen doing the deed the body wouldn't be noticed till they were away, and nobody would suspect him."

"Except us," agreed Amanda complacently. "It's not such a batty idea. It's the kind of childish thing he might do. Fancy dressing that girl up as his wife the other night."

They sat chatting on the edge of the terrace until the sun passed over the edge of the house. Amanda was a stimulating conversationalist. Her complete lack of self-consciousness rendered no subject taboo, and he found her philosophy, which appeared to be part common sense and part mechanics, refreshing after the purely medical variety on which his generation had fed so long.

The ceremony was timed for a quarter to five, and by four o'clock there was a fair-sized crowd round the hangar, far away over the river at the end of the lawn. Amanda sat silent, considering the view. The scene was peaceful, there was a light wind, and the treetops were golden against an eggshell sky.

"There goes Ramillies," she said, nodding towards his tweed-coated figure gliding over the gravel in a calash. "He's in good time. Since he's alone, I suppose that means that A.D. is back."

Mr. Campion looked surprised. Traces of femininity in Amanda were rare. She smiled at him.

"I'm not one of your beastly 'kind women,'" she said. "I don't go round shedding grace. That was quite justified. There goes that little ape Wivenhoe with his nose."

They sat where they were for another half-hour, and then, when Georgia and Dell, Tante Marthe, Gaiogi and the rest of the morning's party had joined the stream winding over the bridge and across the turf, they rose themselves and wandered after the others. Campion was content. He felt rested and at ease. The air was soft and pleasant, and that tranquil mood which is induced by the contemplation of the derring-do of others was upon him.

The two boys with the faded hair and level eyes were going to fly Ramillies over the Sahara, and all Mr. Campion had to do was to watch them go. The hundred-year-old turf was spongy beneath his feet, and Amanda, the least exacting woman in the world to entertain, was by his side. In his own mind he had dismissed Ramillies as a possible source of disturbance. He felt sure that any project Ramillies had in mind was being preserved for his party with the Taretons.

The awakening came a minute or two later. Dell appeared, hurrying back with Georgia just behind him.

"Have you seen Ramillies?" he demanded. "We thought he was down here. The—the fellow seems to have gone again. The ceremony begins in a minute."

"Oh, but he's there," said Amanda inexplicitly. "We saw him go into the hangar, didn't we, Albert?"

"He certainly came down this way just over half an hour ago, just before Wivenhoe," said Campion more cautiously. "Are you sure you haven't missed him?"

"There's a lot of people there, darling," said Georgia nervously, pulling at Dell's sleeve. "He may be among them."

"My dear girl, that's impossible." Dell stood hesitating. "Time's so short," he said.

"But I saw him," insisted Amanda, and set off for the aeroplane shed at a run, with Campion behind her.

There was the usual excitement in the crowd round the entrance, and the platform was a seething jumble of privileged guests, guests who were not privileged, and experts who were trying to protect their untidy paraphernalia. Everyone seemed to have heard that Ramillies was missing again, and the long sibilant name sounded from all sides. Campion hoisted himself on the dais and looked around him. It seemed impossible that the man should be there unobserved. He pushed his way over to a mechanic.

"He *was* 'ere." The man looked over his shoulder as if he expected to find the lost sheep behind him. "'E come in about 'alf an hour ago, just before the gentleman from the government who wanted everything altered. No, I ain't seen 'im since."

"Albert." Amanda came round from behind the plane, which had been wheeled out into the sunlight. She was dragging behind her a bespectacled young man in oily dungarees. "Jimmy says Ramillies *was* here," she said. "He wanted to see the seating accommodation again, and they let him in the plane. Then Wivenhoe came along and took everyone's attention, and they think Ramillies went off then."

Campion glanced at the gaudy little Seraphim spreading its golden wings to the evening.

"Let's have a look," he suggested.

"He's not *in* there," said Jimmy, revealing a stammer and a public-school accent. "Don't be absurd, old man. I've c-c-called him."

"Let's have a look."

They found Ramillies cramped in the back seat. His tweed ulster billowed round him, and beneath it, strapped to his body, were the dismantled parts of the Filmer 5A together with two hundred rounds of ammunition. He was quite dead.

Chapter Eleven

Mr. Campion's first thought as he looked down at the body was that if Ramillies merely intended to reawaken his wife's interest he had overdone the effort considerably. After that he had little time for reflection.

A dead man in a gilded aeroplane in the midst of a crowd, with a broadcast imminent, an African flight about to begin, and in authority a cabinet minister who does not wish to be convinced that anything unpleasant has occurred, is a responsibility which absorbs all one's attention.

The magic words "taken ill" circulated through the inquisitive gathering inside the hangar and acted, as they always do, as a temporary sedative. No doctor appeared but Georgia hurried forward, all grace and anxiety, and the photographers obtained their one useful picture of the afternoon when she stood looking up at Wivenhoe in the doorway of the plane.

It was Wivenhoe, supported by Dell and a white-faced Gaiogi, who made the situation clear to Campion.

"My dear fellow, he can't die here," he whispered urgently, indicating by a single expressive lift of his shoulder the fidgety crowd, the weaving pressmen, and the mechanics and groundsmen who were at bay round their precious plane. "He can't. The Old Man wouldn't stand for it for a moment. Sir Ray must be taken up to the house and a doctor must see him there." He leant forward, his big nose bringing his face much nearer the other man's own than he seemed to realise. "He's alive. The Old Man is convinced that he's alive. I'll bring Lady Ramillies along after you. I'll explain he's very ill, so she'll be prepared for anything."

Mr. Campion said no more. He was barely on speaking terms with himself, let alone anyone else. To spend an entire day watching a man to see that he does not make a nuisance of himself and, in the furtherance of one's object, to connive at the most obvious piece of smuggling one has ever seen, only to be so entirely frustrated at the eleventh hour, is an exasperating experience. His frame of mind did not encourage him to insist on the letter of police procedure. He hoped he knew a corpse when he saw one, but if the government wished its servant, Sir Raymond Ramillies, to die in a bed, who was Albert Campion to protest? He was, also, very sorry for Ramillies.

Actually there seemed little reason why this particular body should not be moved. There were no signs of wounding, and the possibility that the man had been shot in that confined space, firstly without sound and secondly without any smell of cordite, seemed more than unlikely.

The lean head with the doormat hair lolled forward on the chest, the weight of the skull dragging the tendons of the neck horribly. The skin was still clammy with sweat and the flesh was not quite cold. Campion was curious to see the eyes and as he lifted one flaccid lid he was surprised to find the pupil almost normal. There were one or two other curious circumstances and he made a note of them.

The arrival of the ambulance provided a few grim moments. All that had to be done was accomplished in whispers, since the broadcast, which waits for no man, had begun and Towser's resonant voice, a trifle shaken but otherwise normally monotonous, had embarked upon the prearranged speech.

Georgia climbed into the ambulance and was persuaded out of it by the resourceful Wivenhoe, while Mr. Campion took her place on the spare leather bench. The stretcher was hoisted gently into position, the doors closed, and the wheels began to move. It was a very discreet departure.

Ramillies lay on his back beside the dark glass windows and Mr. Campion and the attendant sat and looked at him.

A uniform can make a man the next best thing to invisible, and when someone sucked a tooth with a sound both human and ingratiating Mr. Campion started and turned to see, for the first time, a small, sharp-featured, red face lit with the bright ghoul's eyes of the professional calamity fancier.

"You're a relative I expect," observed a wistful voice.

"No, no, I'm not, I'm afraid." Campion felt for a cigarette and changed his mind.

The attendant got up and stood looking down at Ramillies with fascination.

"You're just a friend, are you?" he said regretfully. "Well,

I dare say it'll be a bit of a shock for you. You've got to prepare yourself, you know. I thought that as soon as I set eyes on 'im. I've seen too many of 'em. You get used to 'em in our work. As soon as I see 'im I said to myself, 'This is goin' to be a shock for someone.' I thought it might be you."

He conveyed considerable reproach and unconsciously Mr. Campion did his best for him, as was his nature.

"I knew him quite well."

"Knew? So you know he's a goner?" Reproach had become disappointment. "You're right, 'e is dead. I see it the moment I saw 'im. 'E's nearly cold. Still, you can't be too sure. When we git up to the 'ouse we'll do one or two of the tests, although I expect there'll be a doctor there by then."

There was not so much relief as contempt in the last phrase.

"Once a doctor gets 'old of a patient you're nowhere. They think they know everything. And yet a man like me, who's seen serious cases every day of 'is life, he knows quite as much as any doctor. Look at this chap 'ere, now. D'you know what I notice about 'im? I wouldn't say it if you were a relative, but as you're only a friend I shan't 'ave to be so tactful. (We're taught that, you know: be tactful with relatives. That's part of our training.) Looking at 'im, I should say, 'You've 'ad a seizure, my lad, a sort of fit, and, though I couldn't say for certain without openin' you up, in my opinion you've got a clot of blood over the 'eart or in the 'ead, and if it's not that, then it's fatty degeneration. You've had trouble with your arteries for a long time and you've bin livin' a bit too 'ard and now the excitement of getting ready for this 'ere trip's bin too much for you, and I'd give you my certificate . . . after I'd done the tests to see you *was* dead.'"

He paused and looked at Mr. Campion brightly.

"That's what I'd say and I'd be right," he said.

Mr. Campion considered him with distaste, but there was something forgivable in those bright, excited eyes. The man was a ghoul, but a good-natured one, and the dreadful thought came to Campion that if Ramillies' truculent spirit should by chance be hanging about its late abode its reply to the address might be worth hearing. There is a lot of talk about the dignity of death, yet it is but a negative kind of dignity. Ramillies alive would have made short work of this impertinence.

Meanwhile the ambulance had bumped off the flying field onto the lower road and had passed the main entrance gates of Caesar's Court.

"We're goin' round to the cottage, you know," said the ghoul. "That's standing orders. Nothing unpleasant near the main 'otel. It's very sensible reelly. As soon as you get a bit o' class there's no sympathy with illness. 'Ave you noticed that? In a different neighbour'ood a thing like this 'd be an attraction, but not with the smart people you get 'ere. No, it's all 'ush, 'ush 'ere. Coo, 'e's ill! Shut 'im in a nursing 'ome and don't let me see 'im. That's the cry everytime. Did you know this gentleman very well, sir? Would you say 'e was an 'ard liver? I don't want to sound inquisitive. It's just a professional question. I like to know if my diagnosis is correct. 'E's bit 'is tongue. That's a seizure, isn't it?"

Mr. Campion breathed deeply.

"I really can't tell you," he said. He was not naturally squeamish, but a ghoul is a ghoul and to suffer them gladly is not in everybody's capacity.

"I'm sorry, I'm sure," said the attendant stuffily and was silent for a while.

Presently, however, Mr. Campion, who had forgotten him, turned to find him looking down at one of the rather fine brown hands which lay upon the cover. He had tied a small piece of string very tightly round the lower phalanx of the forefinger and was studying the effect.

"That's the only test you can do in the ambulance," he said. "You can't go mucking about with saucers of water on the chest in 'ere. There you are, you see; there's no pinky glow. 'E's dead. I knew 'e was dead as soon as I saw 'im. I expect 'e was all right this afternoon, was 'e? Must 'ave been a shock for you."

"Yes, he was all right this afternoon." A certain lack of decision in Mr. Campion's tone brought the bright eyes up again.

"Then you did notice something? 'E was 'eavy, was 'e? Very likely. P'raps 'e was a bit appre'ensive? A lot of people are 'oo die sudden. It's a funny thing and the doctors say there's nothing in it, but I've noticed it time and again. Time and again I've 'ad a sobbing relative sittin' where you're sittin' now and they've told me the same thing. Just before a seizure, just before someone's took off sudden, they've bin overcast, as you might say. Felt there was somethin' 'angin' over them. Of course that's psychic; that's not medicine; and I don't suppose there's anything in it. But it does 'appen. Would you say it 'ad 'appened in this case? Would you say this gentleman 'ad any premonition? D'you think it went through 'is 'ead that 'e was goin' to die?"

"No," said Mr. Campion soberly. "No. I don't think it occurred to him for a moment."

The heavy tires scrunched on gravel and the ghoul looked out of the window.

"'Ere we are," he said. "Well, there'll be a doctor 'ere, but 'e'll tell you the same as me and get paid more for it."

It was during the next twenty minutes that Mr. Campion received the key to the entire story. At the time he did not recognise it, but afterwards, when he looked back, he saw that it was then that the shadowy words were formed and spread out for him to recognise.

Gaiogi was waiting on the cushion-strewn steps of his doll's house when the ambulance arrived and only the presence of a calash, abandoned on the path, indicated that he had not flown there. Already evidences of his extraordinary organisation were apparent. There was even a woman in nurse's uniform in the doorway behind him and a houseman, with blankets and hot-water bottles, appeared in the hall as the two ambulance men carried the stretcher inside.

"I'm afraid all that is useless," murmured Campion, trying not to be nettled by the reproachful expression in his host's shiny brown eyes. "He was quite dead when I found him."

Gaiogi took his arm.

"Oh no, my dear fellow," he said pleadingly. "Oh *no*. Be careful, be careful, you two men. Take the stairs carefully—carefully. No jolting, please."

The nurse superintended the ascent and he watched her critically, still holding Campion's arm.

"His doctor will be here in a moment," he whispered. "Then we shall see. I've been talking to him on the phone. He's coming at once."

"From town?"

"No. Oh no. He was here this afternoon, playing tennis. He's Buxton-Coltness, of Upper Brook Street, a very distinguished fellow. Very good. Do you know him? He's just coming.''

Gaiogi made the announcement blandly and with the faintest suggestion of a smile behind his anxiety. He was like a man throwing off a small conjuring trick in the midst of some other major manoeuvre.

''Wasn't it fortunate that he should have been here?''

''Miraculous,'' said Mr. Campion involuntarily. ''One's every want anticipated. There'll be an inquest, of course.''

''An inquest? An inquest at Caesar's Court?''

There is one expression that is the same upon every countenance. It is the slow, incredulous stare of disgust which is reserved for him who reveals the ultimate depths, the mortal insult, the utterly unforgivable error of taste and morals. Gaiogi wore it now and Mr. Campion was almost apologetic until he pulled himself together and grasped at his fleeting sense of proportion.

''My dear chap, it's a sudden death,'' he protested.

''I doubt it,'' said Gaiogi calmly. ''You are a good chap, Campion, a sensible fellow, but you jump to conclusions. We do not know if this man is dead. Let us hope he is not. It is for his doctor to say.''

Mr. Campion blinked and was prevented from implicating himself still further by the arrival of a second calash bearing Georgia and Wivenhoe. Georgia came to Campion, her hands outstretched. She was pale but controlled, and there was something about her manner that made him think of suppressed excitement before he put the idea aside as unworthy.

''My dear, how is he?'' she said, her eyes meeting his frankly. ''Don't be afraid to tell me. Is it terribly bad? I'm being as sensible as I possibly can and you can rely on me. This dear boy here has been preparing me for the worst and I'm not a child. I can stand it if you tell me. How is he?''

''Georgia, we don't know.'' Gaiogi seemed to have caught her mood and for the first time Mr. Campion felt slightly nauseated. Everybody was behaving too well for anything. ''The doctor is coming. Don't go up yet. There is a nurse with him, an excellent girl. You are wonderfully brave. You are taking it just as I knew you would. Look, we will go into my little room and sit down.''

''He's quite right, you know, Lady Ramillies.'' Wivenhoe's solicitude was charming. ''You can see the door from the

108

window. The moment the doctor arrives we shall know everything.''

The living room had been tidied after the hangover party and a decanter of old brandy and glasses had been set out on a small table as though ready for some emergency. Gaiogi dispensed the cordial with an air.

''I've told Dell to keep everybody down here,'' he said. ''Meanwhile this house is positively surrounded, so we shan't have any Press for a little while at least. Ah, there is someone now. That will be Doctor Buxton-Coltness.''

Everyone so far forgot his manners as to stare out of the window at the newcomer. Even in flannels and a blazer Dr. Harvey Buxton-Coltness managed to convey that he was a distinguished man. The white scarf round his throat was folded with precision and his step was firm and purposeful. His voice floated in to them from the hall. It was deep and reassuring. Here, at any rate, was a man with a manner, the kind of doctor who was entirely in keeping with Caesar's Court.

Georgia and Gaiogi hurried out to him. Wivenhoe gave them two minutes and then went out himself to bring her back. There was something familiar about her when she returned. Campion was reminded forcefully of the heroine in *The Little Sacrifice*. There was the same quiet, only-just-balanced movement, the same air of suppressed tragedy.

''I think I'll sit down,'' she said. She glanced at Campion and smiled wanly. ''They've promised to send for me the instant he's conscious.''

It was a horrible moment. The complete insincerity of the entire scene sickened Campion and he looked at Wivenhoe steadily. The young man frowned at him and bent over his glass.

Georgia went on playing her part for some little time. It was not an inspired performance; rather, a trifle mechanical, as if her thoughts were not on it.

''I can't imagine Ray ill,'' she said. ''He's not the kind of person who ought to suffer. Haven't you noticed it? There's something so vital about him, like a child. I think that's what I fell in love with first of all. He's been going the pace terribly lately. I persuaded him to go and see Buxton-Coltness only a little while ago. He didn't tell me what he said. He wouldn't, you know, not if it was anything serious. That's where Ray's rather sweet.''

Mr. Campion was not given to hating people but at that moment he conceived an active dislike for Georgia Ramillies and surprised himself in an impulse to take her by the shoulders and shake her till her teeth rattled. He felt she knew as well as he did, as well as Wivenhoe knew, as well as the ghoul knew, as well as Buxton-Coltness must know by this time, that Ramillies was dead, dead as mutton, and in appallingly fishy circumstances. He knew now what Val had meant when she had described Georgia as vulgar. Georgia's vulgarity was staggering. It was the overpowering, insufferable vulgarity to which nothing is sacred. It was also, he found, the vulgarity which breeds vulgarity; his own inclination to stand and shout the brutal truth at her until he forced her out of her performance was almost uncontrollable, and when someone came in he turned towards the door with physical relief.

It was Val. She had evidently just made up her face but her pallor made the colour look artificial and there were shadows round her large light eyes. She glanced from one to the other enquiringly.

"I met a servant on the landing," she said, "and he told me something quite incredible. It is true?"

The direct question in the clear, startled voice brought a draught of reality into the room. Georgia looked up at her and became, miraculously, a human being again.

"It's Ray," she said bluntly. "He was taken ill in the plane. The doctor is with him now. Everyone's being awfully kind but I'm afraid it's serious."

It was an odd situation. For a moment it was Georgia who was softening a staggering blow to the other woman. There was alarm in her eyes and something dreadfully like apology in her tone.

Like most men Mr. Campion was at heart conventional, and when he saw brutal, practical reality thrust under his very nose he could not bring himself to recognise it. He watched the two women with growing bewilderment. They were both entirely female, both sharp-witted, both realists, but whereas the one had a balanced intellect in control the other was as wanton and unexpected as a rudderless steamboat in a gale. Val sat down.

"Is he dead?"

Wivenhoe, even more out of his depth than Campion, made a disparaging sound, but for once Georgia did not respond to him. She seemed to be absorbed by the other woman.

"I think so," she said. "They've been preparing me for it. Oh, Val, isn't it *fantastic*? I mean it's frightful, terrible, the most ghastly thing that could have happened! But—it's amazing, isn't it?"

Mr. Campion felt his eyes widening. Now it was impossible to misunderstand. He and Wivenhoe had been forgotten as completely as if they had been children, to be ignored as soon as a grownup entered. Georgia was doing no play acting for Val. They were equals coming down to essentials in the face of the unexpected.

Val was sitting on a low chair, her hands folded in her lap. She was wearing a bright red dress of some smooth material which had been designed for her, and in it she made a complete and finished work of art, as artificial in appearance as any other ornament in that mannered room, but her personality was vivid and entirely human. She alone expressed that sense of shock and calamity which her brother now realised was the element he had missed throughout the entire incident.

"What happened?" she enquired quietly.

"I don't know." Georgia glanced at Wivenhoe. "What was it? Some sort of stroke? How did he die?"

"I say, you know—really. We—we must wait for the doctor." The young man was flustered. "I mean, we don't actually know yet, do we? He was breathing in the plane. I'm sure of it. That is definite. Otherwise he couldn't have been moved, do you see? It was probably some sort of embolism. He was getting on for fifty, wasn't he? I know that sort of thing does happen. An uncle of mine died the same way. It's dreadful when it does occur but it's very much kinder for the old boys. . . ."

He was drivelling and seemed to realise it. Neither of the two women was looking at him. Val's eyes were holding Georgia's.

"You saw him when he came in today, didn't you?" she said. "How was he? I thought he seemed so well last night."

There was no hint of accusation in her voice or in the words, but Georgia recoiled.

"He was in a fearful state this afternoon," she said

111

sharply. "He'd been drinking all night. He said so. He was thick and loquacious and—oh, Val, don't look at me like that! I'm broken-hearted, really I am. I'm holding myself together with tremendous difficulty, darling. I am sorry. I *am*. I am sorry. When you're married to a man, whatever you do, however you behave to one another, there is an affinity. There is. It's a frightful shock. I haven't begun to realise it yet. When I do I——"

"My dear Lady Ramillies!" Wivenhoe's startled voice was what she needed. She swung towards him, put both her hands in his and began to cry. Val blushed. The slow resentful colour spread over her face and neck and her eyes were sombre.

"You poor, poor darling," she said.

Georgia wiped her eyes.

"I hate hysterical women," she murmured, smiling wryly at Campion. "I'm all right, I'm all right now." She patted Wivenhoe's hands and released them. Then, rising, she went over to Val and sat down beside her with an arm round her shoulders. "You see, dearest, I don't know what's happened," she said earnestly. "Nobody knows yet. It's all so—so utterly extraordinary. It's incredible. But, Val, incredible things do happen to me, don't they? You know that, don't you? We're always commenting on it, aren't we?"

She seemed to be pleading with the fair girl, striving to force some reassurance out of her, and Campion saw the strong, capable fingers pressing into the shoulder of the red dress. Val laid a hand on Georgia's knee but she did not speak. She was rigid, and there was a short, unhappy silence before it was mercifully broken by footsteps in the hall.

Gaiogi and the doctor came in solemnly and shut the door behind them.

Chapter Twelve

The personal humility of all medical men is jeopardised throughout their career by the fact that one of the disadvantages of their profession is that they should be treated with much greater seriousness than any other visitor to the normal household. Their lightest words are hung upon and they receive every hour the flattery of absorbed attention. Some noble natures can stand up to this and some cannot, but there is a small class which turns a disadvantage into an asset and thrives upon the thing that should defeat it.

Dr. Harvey Buxton-Coltness was one of these. Critical colleagues told each other bitterly that it was Buxton-Coltness' conceit alone which kept him on the register. His head, they said, was like a balloon which lifted him gently over morass and crevice, bearing him gracefully from cocktail party to ducal bedroom, from exorbitant nursing home to fashionable funeral, with a grace and ease not afforded to any man with his feet set firmly upon the ground.

Mr. Campion recognised his type as soon as he saw him and another little detail in the key of the problem flickered under his nose.

The doctor was a large man with what is called a fine presence. His light grey eyes were entirely without humour in spite of the laughter lines beside them, and his shapely pink hands were graceful and expressive. He waited for Gaiogi to introduce him to Georgia and bestowed a general nod upon the rest of the room. When he judged the right moment had come he made his announcement tactfully.

"Lady Ramillies," he said, "I am afraid I have bad news for you. Can you bear it?"

Georgia nodded. Even she seemed to feel that a return to artificiality would be indecorous.

"I was so afraid," she said simply. "What—what was it, Doctor? His heart?"

"His heart—yes." Dr. Buxton-Coltness conveyed that he was making a very difficult thing very simple. He also seemed considerably relieved. "Yes, I think we may say in actual fact his heart." He took the hand which she had stretched out to him and stood looking down at her, his cold eyes cautious in spite of his general air of contented omnipotence. "Tell me, Lady Ramillies," he began, his voice rolling melodiously round the room, "is this quite the shock it might have been? Did Sir Raymond tell you nothing which might just conceivably have made you apprehensive?"

There was a pause and he glanced round him enquiringly.

"We are all in committee, are we not?"

"Oh yes," said Georgia hastily. "We're all very close friends."

She made some perfunctory introductions and returned to his question.

"He told me he'd been to see you. He'd been worried about himself and some of our friends advised him to go to you. He told me you thought he ought to go slow."

"I did. I did, most emphatically." The deep voice was thick with sad conviction. "There were distinct symptoms of chronic nephritis, a considerably raised blood pressure, and I diagnosed cardiovascular trouble. I warned Sir Raymond to be very careful of himself. I told him to avoid every sort of excess. I can't put it plainer than that, can I? Every sort of excess. I impressed it upon him that alcohol was definitely dangerous to him and I advised a visit to a spa. Now Mr. Laminoff tells me he can hardly have been said to have taken my advice. Do you agree with that?"

Georgia looked at him blankly and he, mistaking her reaction, fell back upon his charm.

"Forgive me," he said. "Of course this is a very great shock for you. Surely it's not necessary for you to give me these details yourself, is it? Isn't there some member of the family you can depute to act for you? If I might prescribe for *you*, Lady Ramillies, I should go to bed immediately. Keep warm. Take a sedative. What do you usually use? Aspirin? Or do you like luminol? Anything like that. Wrap yourself up. Get your maid to bring you plenty of hot water-bottles."

"No," said Georgia with sudden decision. "No, I'm all right. I can tell you. We can all tell you. Ray hasn't been looking after himself. He's been very gay during the last week or so—more, I think, than usual."

She glanced round at them for confirmation, and Gaiogi, who was watching the scene with the bright anxiety of a squirrel, made a reassuring noise. Georgia went on steadily.

"Then last night, in the middle of a farewell party, he went rushing off somewhere and came back this morning about lunchtime. He said he'd been drinking all night, and frankly that was obvious. He didn't come to the farewell luncheon and when I saw him afterwards I thought he was even worse.

He was unsteady, you know, and pale, and frightfully talkative and—well . . ." She threw out her hands expressively and the doctor nodded.

He glanced round at his small audience with sad resignation.

"There you are," he said. "There you are."

Georgia opened her mouth but did not speak. She stood staring at him. The matter-of-fact expression which he had used seemed to have jolted her. Presently she turned to Val, her eyes wide and dark.

"Dead," she said. "Ray is dead. Val, do you realise it? Ray is dead."

The doctor moved to her side with unexpected agility.

"Now, my dear lady," he began warningly, "my dear lady, sit down. I foresaw this. It was only to be expected. Sit down. Mr. Laminoff, I want some water, please."

"No." Georgia pushed him away. "No, really. I'm not hysterical. I suddenly saw it. That was all. Why did he die? What was it?"

She listened to his recital with deep attention and so did Campion.

The full medical definition of the words "arterial thrombosis" is impressive to the lay mind. It is one of those simple mechanical disasters which are easily comprehensible to anybody, and as Mr. Campion sat listening to the full, confident voice his brows rose.

In a well-ordered society it is easy to think of some things as concrete when they are nothing of the kind. After long years of experience Mr. Campion had come to consider a sudden and suspicious death as synonymous with a postmortem and a coroner's inquest, but now for the first time it was brought strongly to his mind that this was not so in actual fact. No ordinary hard-working general practitioner would dream of giving a certificate of natural death in the present case, for the excellent reason that should any talk arise afterwards, as well it might in ordinary circumstances, the consequences would be thunderingly inconvenient for him, and whereas he would have everything to lose he would have precious little to gain. But there was no earthly reason why a man like Harvey Buxton-Coltness should not give a certificate; rather, every reason that he should.

Buxton-Coltness' practice was not bounded by any district.

His patients were all wealthy folk recommended to him by each other. The more influential friends he made the better for him, and here he was in a nest of influential people. It was clearly to everyone's advantage that there should be no fuss over Ramillies' death. Towser, for one, would be more than grateful to hear that it was a natural tragedy. Gaiogi, Georgia herself, nobody wanted publicity. The ghoul's words returned to him forcefully:

"It's all 'ush, 'ush 'ere. . . . Coo, 'e's ill! Shut 'im in a nursing 'ome and don't let me see 'im. That's the cry every time."

It was horribly true and nobody could possibly know it better than the fashionable doctor with his partnership in Mayfair, his colossal fees and his magnificent manner. There was no reason why he should not issue a certificate of death from thrombosis of a main artery following kidney disease and cardiodilation, and attend the funeral at Willesden Cemetery, fixing himself in yet another twenty useful minds as that charming man who was "so clever and considerate when poor Ray died after getting so abominably tight." And if there was a little talk afterwards, what was the real danger? It would only be talk among people who would never risk seeing themselves in court on a slander charge. At worst it would be frivolous and meaningless talk, and not in any case detrimental to the doctor.

Mr. Campion blinked. He saw how it was going to be done. Buxton-Coltness was going to give the certificate and there was only one thing that would stop him. That was immediate talk. Talk now. He glanced round the room. He saw Gaiogi, Wivenhoe, Georgia and Val. Even Val was financially interested in the preservation of the peace and privacy of Caesar's Court. There remained himself. He was the sole representative of the general public who might demand to know more definitely the cause of Raymond Ramillies' extraordinarily opportune death. He alone was unsatisfied. He alone was curious to know exactly what sort of seizure had caused those last convulsions. It was up to him. He was the only disinterested agent.

The hesitant words were on the tip of his tongue when he saw the pitfall, and as it opened beneath his feet he experienced for the first time that deep anger which altered him so and changed him from the affable universal uncle to the man with an intolerable personal affront to avenge. How could he protest? He was the guest of a host who had expressly invited him to prevent just such trouble as he was preparing to make. Moreover, he had spent the day watching a man who had died under his nose. If the circumstances were suspicious, had he not had every opportunity to alter them as they occurred? Both his professional dignity and his natural ingrained reluctance to abuse his position as a guest prevented him from speaking. They were his two vulnerable spots, his two vanities. It was almost as though someone had sized him up and sized him up accurately, a degrading experience for anybody at the best of times.

Most people dislike to be made use of and resent being forced into a position wherein their hands are tied, but in some folk the experience raises a devil. Mr. Campion was one of these. Had he been sure of his ground, he flattered himself, he would have conquered his weaknesses and taken the strong, if oafish, course, but he was not sure. If Providence's celebrated Mysterious Ways Department was actually as blatantly at work as it appeared to be, then Ramillies might have died from a thrombosis, a cerebral hemorrhage or any other natural thunderbolt known to medicine.

As it was, Campion would do nothing. He saw that at once and his sense of personal outrage grew. He was trapped by himself, fettered by his own personality. The thing was mental jujitsu. The plaything-of-fate sensation was bad enough but he had an uncomfortable feeling that the fate in question had a human brain behind it, and there was insult as well as inconvenience to counter.

Mr. Campion's amiable brown face became dangerously blank and he stood looking at the company, his hands deep in his pockets and his pale eyes narrowed behind his spectacles.

The unexpected development came from Georgia. She was sitting on a corner of the couch under the window, her hands between her knees and her dark head bowed.

"I couldn't have done anything, could I?" she demanded, looking up.

"Nothing," Dr. Buxton-Coltness managed to give the word sympathy as well as conviction.

Georgia sighed.

"It's so extraordinary," she said. "It's so utterly extraordinary."

"It's very terrible." Gaiogi substituted the better word with gentle firmness.

"Of course," said Georgia sharply. "Of course. No one knows that better than I do, Gaiogi. But it is extraordinary, too, isn't it, Val?"

The fair woman did not reply and she hurried on.

"He didn't even take anything. He had nothing at all. He didn't even take a sleeping powder. I gave him a cachet blanc when I first saw him and he decided not to come down to lunch."

She seemed to find something surprising in her own words, for she broke off abruptly and sat up.

"It was that cachet you gave me, Val. I meant to take it myself. But when I saw him it seemed only charitable to hand it over. He took it at once. That's all he had."

Val regarded her steadily. She was cold and slightly contemptuous.

"It was a perfectly ordinary cachet blanc," she said.

"My dear, of course it was." Georgia was eyeing her. "Of course." She laughed and covered her face with her hands immediately afterwards. "I'm completely off my balance. I only suddenly remembered that that was the only thing he did take, and that you had meant it for me."

The words were out of her mouth before she realised their full significance and she looked as startled by them as anyone else in the room.

Val rose.

"You don't mean that, do you?" she said.

"No," said Georgia hastily. "No. No, of course not." But she spoiled the denial a moment afterwards by allowing a glimmer of ill-timed mischief to pass over her face. "After all, my pet, why should you want to get rid of me?"

That was all, but the trouble was made. The little flame flickered and grew. It flared in Gaiogi's eyes, passed over Wivenhoe's head, and revealed itself to Buxton-Coltness, who recognised it and retreated hastily, his cautious expression deepening. He coughed.

"Lady Ramillies," he began, "I've been thinking. This is a sudden death, you know, and if Sir Raymond had not been a patient I could never have considered giving a certificate. In that case a post-mortem and an inquest would have been automatic. You realise that, don't you?"

118

Georgia looked at him blankly.

"Don't you know how he died?" she said.

Dr. Buxton-Coltness smiled faintly with his small mouth and Gaiogi turned away.

"My dear lady." The doctor's beautiful voice was kind. "*I* am satisfied, but in a case of this sort there are certain formalities which can hardly be ignored. These things are very painful but they have to be endured."

Georgia saw Gaiogi's face.

"Not an inquest," she said. "Doctor, can't you have a post-mortem without an inquest? Isn't that possible?"

Wivenhoe cleared his throat.

"In such exceptional circumstances, sir," he said, "couldn't— I mean, couldn't the certificate be held up for an hour or two while the P.M. was rushed through?"

Campion watched the doctor curiously. The man was very tempted. After all, his entire scheme of life was to be obliging to the right people.

"I suppose it might be arranged," he was saying dubiously. "My partner, Rowlandson Blake, the surgeon, might possibly be persuaded. I don't know, really. I should have to telephone, of course."

It was at that moment that Campion caught sight of Val and her fixed expression and white face sent a thrill of unreasoning alarm trickling down his spine. He moved over to her, and, taking her by the arm, led her out into the little walled garden, lying smug in the warm evening sun. She went with him obediently, her hands clasped limply behind her back, but she did not speak and he missed her direct, confiding glance. They walked over the grass plot in silence and after a while he spoke himself.

"What are you thinking?"

"I'm not."

"Bad business."

"Frightful."

"I say, Val?"

"Yes?"

"What did you give that woman?"

"A cachet blanc."

There was a long pause and when Campion spoke again his tone was very casual.

"They're things in rice-paper cases, aren't they?"

"You know they are." The icy quality in her voice did not warn him, as it might have done. There is nothing like the blood tie to render ordinary sympathetic comprehension void.

"One could open a thing like that?"

"One could, easily."

"She simply asked for it, I suppose, and you just handed it over?"

"You know exactly what happened. You saw me."

"Yes," he said. "I did. That's what's worrying me. I did. Val, you wouldn't be an utter fool?"

"My God!" Her outburst startled him and he turned to her so that they faced each other on the turf.

"My dear girl," he said, "you behaved like an amateur actress registering stealth. It's no good being angry with me."

"I'm sorry." To his relief there was a glimmer of a smile on her mouth, although her eyes were heavy with an old pain which he was embarrassed to recognise and remember. "I'm sorry," she repeated. "But it all seems so blazingly silly. I gave Georgia a perfectly ordinary cachet blanc. She asked me if I had any after the party this morning, and I went up to get her one. When I put it into her hand I had one of those dreadful mad thoughts; insane impulses they call them, don't they? Anyway it went through my mind that a good dose of cyanide in that thing would silence her beastly, predatory vulgarity forever. And then, of course, as soon as I'd thought it I looked up and saw your ridiculous face. I felt I *was* mad and I suppose I shuddered or recoiled, as one would naturally. However, it doesn't matter. It was only one of those things."

Campion was silent and she laughed at him.

"Good heavens, you believe me, don't you?"

"I? Oh, Lord, yes." His tone was still troubled. "I was only thinking. If they find a good narcotic poison in that chap's belly you'll be very awkwardly placed. That woman has a mind like a demented eel; does she always say any mortal thing that comes into her head?"

"Usually, I think." Val spoke lightly. "It was the fashion to be daring some years ago, and the women who grew up at that period seem to have got it incorporated in their general make-up. The trouble is that when it's natural like that it becomes a negative thing. When it was deliberate it was considered a decoration, or at least a weapon. Now that it's natural it's just an ordinary unbridled tongue. It's dangerous, of course."

"Dangerous? My good girl, it's terrifying. If they find——"

Val laid a restraining hand on his arm.

"They won't find anything," she said.

Her complacency was irritating and he shrugged his shoulders and was silent.

Presently she shuddered. He felt the tremor run through the arm against his side.

"They won't find anything suspicious," she went on quietly. "I know that. I'm certain of it. If there was any real danger of that the whole thing would have worked out differently."

"Do you know what you're talking about, my sweet?"

"Yes, I do." He had succeeded in nettling her. "I know that Portland-Smith died very conveniently for Georgia, and now Ramillies has done the same thing. I know that it has been proved that Portland-Smith committed suicide, and I know it will be proved that Ramillies died naturally. There's no danger of a row because danger has been carefully eliminated. It's all working out. There's a superstition in the theatre that everything works out for Georgia. You must never cross Georgia. If you go with her you're on wheels. This is another evidence of the truth of it, that's all."

Campion frowned at his sister. His masculine mind revolted from this in-touch-with-the-stars attitude and he said so.

"This is all very fine and large," he added, "but there's obviously going to be a P.M.—Georgia brought that on her own head—and if the fellow died unnaturally everybody's going to know."

Val shook her head.

"I don't think so."

"But, my dear good girl!" Mr. Campion was restraining an impulse to jitter at her with difficulty. No one else in the world save the whole skein of his blood relations had this undignified effect upon him. "What do you mean? Do you think that that pompous ass of a doctor is going to risk his reputation saving anybody's skin? He'll spaniel round as long as everything is pretty, but did you see him when the first flicker of awkwardness showed? Did you see him?"

"I did. Don't shout at me."

"Darling, *am* I shouting?" The injustice of the accusation took his breath away. "You saw him. You know as well as I

121

do that he's only going to be obliging as far as it suits him and it doesn't suit any doctor on earth to hush up anything really serious unless he's personally involved. It's an ordinary question of value for risk. If Ramillies was poisoned, as I'm open to bet he was, the P.M. will uncover it and there'll be an almighty row."

"I don't agree with you."

Mr. Campion breathed deeply.

"Are you getting any fun out of baiting me or are you just not listening?"

She squeezed his arm and her head touched his shoulder.

"I can't argue," she said. "I'm only telling you. However Ramillies died, there won't be a row."

"If you think that doctor could be bribed I very much doubt it."

"I don't think that."

"Well then, Val, Val darling, put me out of my misery; how's it going to be done?"

"I don't know," she said frankly. "I just realise that if a P.M. will reveal anything unpleasant or dangerous there won't be a P.M."

"But there's *going* to be a P.M., woman!"

"Then they won't find anything."

"Do you think it was a natural death?"

She closed her eyes.

"I think someone hoped very much it would happen."

Mr. Campion sniffed. "And administered some dangerous drug unknown to science, no doubt," he murmured.

Val's expression was infuriatingly vague.

"Perhaps so," she agreed absently.

He looked down at her with a mixture of rage and affection and finally slid an arm round her shoulders.

"You're a dear little bloody, aren't you?" he said. "Let's be practical. You've got no access to anything dangerous yourself, have you? Nothing anyone could get silly about in case the dangerous drug wasn't unknown to science after all?"

Val considered and finally glanced up at him.

"I've got about half a pound of morphine crystals at the Park Lane house," she said.

"How much?"

"An enormous amount. About half a pound. A little under, perhaps."

"Don't play the fool, Val. This is fairly serious."

"I'm not, my dear. I'm telling you the literal truth. Tante Marthe knows about it. It's in a drawer at the back of my desk in a big cigarette tin. It's been there for two years at least."

She looked up at him and laughed softly.

"It came over from Lyons in the cardboard cylinder of a roll of taffeta which we hadn't ordered," she said. "Rex found there was one odd bale and the silk was put in my office to be returned. Tante Marthe knocked it over and the cap fell off. There were about twenty-five little packets of this stuff inside. We talked it over and decided that it was quite obvious that someone was using us as a cover, and we suspected a woman on the buying side. Naturally we didn't want a fuss, police in the place and that sort of horror, so we sacked the woman, kept the material and stuck the stuff in a drawer, where it still is, as far as I know."

"How do you know it was morphine?"

Val raised her eyebrows.

"I sent a little down to a chemist and asked, naturally."

"Weren't they curious?"

"No. I told some likely story about finding it in an old medicine chest I'd bought. I sent very little. And when I had the report I told them they needn't return it."

"I see," said Mr. Campion a trifle blankly. "You're an alarmingly matter-of-fact lot, you businesswomen, aren't you?"

"I suppose so." The depth of bitterness in her voice startled him and he felt again that old bewilderment at her range of thought and her staggering inconsistencies. His common sense reasserted itself.

"Look here," he said seriously, "I'm going to collect that stuff immediately and you forget you ever had it unless I tell you to come out with the whole story. I hope to God you can substantiate it."

"All right." He had the impression that she was laughing at him a little and he regarded her helplessly.

"I don't understand you," he said. "You come roaring to me in town, making a mountain out of a positive worm cast, and yet when a situation which is really unpleasant does arise you behave as if I were an overexcited Boy Scout."

"I'm sorry. I'm really very grateful." The clear high voice sounded flat and she bestirred herself. "It's a question of proportion," she said. "When I came to you in London I was afraid of losing something really important for always; now I think I have lost it. It's altered my entire perspective."

"Perspective?" he ejaculated, resenting the intolerance which she engendered in him without being able to suppress it. "Do you know the meaning of the word? Val, you're an intelligent woman. Your mind works, so do use it, darling. This may be a beastly situation."

"If there's a P.M. they won't find anything," she repeated placidly.

He caught his breath and resisted the impulse to shake her. "How can you possibly know that?"

"I do. You must leave it at that. Whatever we're up against, it's not something childish or careless. But I can't discuss it now. I can't be bothered with it. As far as I'm concerned it doesn't matter. I'm full, satiate, with my own personal aspect of this affair. I've got to pull myself together and behave, and I'm funking it. Now do you see what I mean by perspective?"

"I think you're off your head," said Mr. Campion frankly.

She looked at him with surprise.

"I am," she said. "I thought I'd explain all that pretty thoroughly. Oh, Albert, my dear good ape, do try and understand. You're a sensible, reasonable, masculine soul. If you fell in love and something went wrong you'd think it all out like a little gent and think it all quietly away, taking the conventional view and the intelligent path and saving yourself no end of bother because your head plus your training is much stronger than all your emotions put together. You're a civilised masculine product. But when it happens to me, when it happens to Georgia, our entire world slides round. We can't be conventional or take the intelligent path except by a superhuman mental effort. Our feeling is twice as strong as our heads and we haven't been trained for thousands of years. We're feminine, you fool! I'm trying to use my head constructively: she isn't. She's sailing with the tide."

"Oh," said Mr. Campion furiously, "This is damned silly introspective rot. What you need, my girl, is a good cry or a nice rape—either, I should think."

Val's laughter was spiteful.

"There's a section of your generation who talks about rape as a cure for all ills, like old Aunt Beth used to talk about flannel next to the skin," she said witheringly. "This mania for sex-to-do-you-good is idiotic. You'd far better get back to bloodletting or cod liver oil. No, my dear, you may have the mental discipline, but we're the realists. At least we don't kid ourselves even if we try to put on a decent performance for everyone else. When I heard Ramillies was dead I didn't think 'Oh, poor man, what a shock for his wife!' I thought, 'My God, now Georgia will be able to marry Alan.' I'm still thinking that. And so is she. It's disgusting and shocking to the sentimental or conventional mind, but at least it's not false. Georgia may change round suddenly. It all depends on whether she happens to see herself in some new drama-tic situation which demands a genuine regret for Ramil-lies."

"Hush," said Mr. Campion and swung her gently round. Georgia was advancing towards them across the grass. She was crying unaffectedly. There were tears on her cheeks and tears swimming in her eyes. She held out her hands to Val with a gesture that was oddly youthful.

"Val darling, where are you? Come and help me. I don't know what to do. I can't bear it alone—I can't! I've got to get on to Ferdie in Paris and I've got to tell Ray's half-brother, and there are some old aunts somewhere. Alan's still down at the hangar. They're not putting off the flight. There's no one, no one I can rely on at all. You must come. You must. Whatever you feel about me, you can't desert me. I couldn't help falling in love any more than you could."

Mr. Campion stared, wondering if his ears had deceived him. Georgia had flung her arms round Val and was crying like a child.

"Oh, come in," she sobbed, "do come in! There's a dreadful nurse there. She seems to think I ought to go up and look at him, and I don't want to. I'm terrified of him. What shall I do? What shall I do?"

"I'll come." Val sounded very cool and quiet after her revealing outburst of five minutes before and Campion saw that she looked as comfortingly calm and matter of fact as ever she did.

"When Alan comes he'll look after everything." There

was a naïve warning in Georgia's tearful announcement. "But until then you can't leave me, Val. You can't. I've no one to turn to."

"There, there," said Val. "There, there," and they went into the house together.

Campion stood looking after them. From the depth of his memory came a remark of old Belle Lafcadio's: "Women are terribly shocking to men, my dear. Don't understand them. Like them. It saves such a lot of hurting one way and the other."

That was all very well, he reflected, but in the present situation this feminine inability to adjust the viewpoint was appallingly dangerous. Now, without Val's level-eyed gaze to help convince him, her story of the morphine was terrifying, more especially when, having glimpsed her state of heart, he saw Georgia rubbing caustic into the wounds with a wanton recklessness which no man in his senses would risk. He shook his head impatiently. Val was getting him muddled with her intuitive convictions and airy statements. The facts were the thing. Had Ramillies died naturally? It seemed most unlikely. If he had been murdered, who had done it? Who had any motive? Georgia? Alan Dell? If, on the other hand, he had died from some noxious thing intended for his wife, who then?

He was pacing down the grass plot trying to force all personal considerations out of his reckoning when another thought occurred to him. To whose interest was it that Ramillies should be avenged if he deserved vengeance? Who in his entire circle minded if Ramillies died? Who, during the two hours since his death, had thought for an instant of Raymond Ramillies suddenly and tragically ended? Who cared?

As it happened it was at that particular moment that he heard the shuddering breaths in the shrubbery. Someone was weeping.

Chapter Thirteen

The boy sat on the edge of an ornate marble love seat hidden in the shrubbery. His feet were set squarely on the ground and his head rested in his hands. He was crying in that steady absorbed fashion which is peculiar to childhood. His grief engrossed him and he was blind and deaf to everything else in the world.

The hopvine growing over the high wall behind the seat made a yellow curtain and its scented folds hung down to spill over the stone. There were birds about and the lazy grumble of bees. Art was out of the way for once and Fashion might never have existed. There was life and reality in the garden and this ridiculous weeping figure was a part of it. Mr. Campion felt suddenly grateful to him. He sat down on the stone step and took out a cigarette. *Ivanhoe* lay at his feet and presently he turned over the pages, looking for the Black Knight.

He had been reading for several minutes when the shuddering breaths ceased and he glanced up to find a pair of fiery red eyes regarding him.

"It happens," he said when the silence had to be broken. "It's one of the things that do. It's beastly, but it's part of the experience of being alive."

"I know." The boy wiped his face and kicked the foot of the bench with his heel. "I know." He spoke with the resignation of a much older person. "This is silly. I just felt like it. That was all."

"My dear chap, it's perfectly natural. The weakness part of it is only shock. It's physical. That's nothing."

"Is it?" There was quick relief in the question. "One doesn't *know*, you know," he added presently and summed up the whole misery of youth in the statement.

Mr. Campion did his best to recount the physical effects of shock and Georgia's son listened to him with interest.

"That does explain it," he said at last. "That makes it understandable anyway. How about Georgia? Do you think I ought to go in to her? I don't want to. This—er—this shock might make me blub again and anyhow I should probably be in the way. Is Mr. Dell with her?"

"I don't know. She had my sister there with her the last time I saw her."

"Your sister? Oh, that's good. That's all right then. I'll get over the wall and sneak back to the hotel to wash in a minute. I'd better pack. She may want to get back to town."

Mr. Campion glanced at the small pointed face with interest. It was not unattractive but the son would never have his mother's dark handsomeness nor her magnificent physique. All his life he would be small and in age would look very much as he did now. He was a funny sort of child.

They sat in silence for a long time, both of them unexpectedly at ease.

"Ray wasn't my father, you know." The announcement was made bluntly and sounded like a confession. "My name's Sinclair."

"Fine. I didn't know what to call you. What's the other name?"

Campion was sorry for the question as soon as it was out of his mouth. His companion's embarrassment was considerable.

"I was christened 'Sonny,'" the boy said with a protective formality which was clearly of some years growth. "It seems to have been all right then. Fashionable, you know. Now, of course, it's ghastly. Everyone calls me Sinclair, even Mother."

"I was christened Rudolph," said Mr. Campion. "I get people to call me Albert."

"You have to, don't you?" said Sinclair with earnest sympathy. "Georgia says my father insisted on the name in case I went on the stage." His lip trembled and he scrubbed his face angrily with a sodden handkerchief.

"You're not attracted to the stage?"

"Oh, it's not that." The voice broke helplessly. "I wouldn't care, really. I wouldn't care about anything. I'd be *anything*, only—only I did think it was all settled at last. That's why I'm blubbing. It ought to be about Ray, but it's not. He was all right really—friendly, you know, and rather exciting when he got on to his adventures in Ireland, but he was an awful worry to you. You had to follow him around the whole time and play up to him and coax him into being reasonable and doing what Georgia wanted. I liked him sometimes and sometimes I got jolly tired of him. I was frightened when I heard he was dead. I mean I thought I was going to cat, like you said. But I was blubbing because of myself."

He sniffed violently and kicked the bench for support again.

128

"I thought I'd better tell you—not that I think you'd care, of course—but after all it's the truth and it's ghastly to have someone sympathise with you because he thinks you're cut up about your stepfather dying when you're really being selfish. I don't really care frightfully for anyone except Bunny Barnes-Chetwynd and old Grits. Grits is Georgia's housekeeper. She looked after me when I was a kid."

"Who is Bunny?"

Sinclair brightened.

"Bunny's a good chap. We came on from Tolleshurst Prep to Haverleigh last term. He has trouble with his people too. They keep on starting divorces and changing their minds. Bunny's all right. He'd be able to explain this better than I can. It's all so stinkingly mouldy. I don't want to be a snob or a squirt but when you're *in* a thing you've got to *be* in it, haven't you?"

The last question was a plea from the heart and Mr. Campion, who was ever honest, gave a considered reply.

"It's very unsettling if you're not."

"That's what I mean." There was despair in the red eyes. "Before Ray turned up I was always in such a *mess*. It began at Tolleshurst. It's a snoop sort of prep and at first I was a sort of curiosity because of Georgia being so well known, and then..." He paused. "Oh, things happened, you know," he said vaguely.

"Scandal, you mean?"

"Yes, I suppose so."

"About Georgia?"

"Yes. Nothing beastly, of course." Sinclair was scarlet with shame. "I didn't follow it very well at first, of course, because I was a little kid, but you know what prep schoolmasters are. They talk like a lot of old women and fellows' people take their kids on one side and put them off you and that sort of thing. It wasn't anything beastly. It was just a sort of feeling that we were a bit low. My father appeared in a rather hot sort of farce in the town one term while Georgia was having a lot of publicity and being photographed with one of the fighters."

He took a deep breath and leant forward.

"I didn't really care," he said earnestly, "but I wish they'd sent me to a lower place. I don't want to be bogus and pretend. I only want to be something definite. I find things

129

awfully confusing anyway. It's not the work; I like that. But it's not knowing ordinary things, like that shock business, for instance, and why you suddenly feel you must go and do something silly even though you know it's silly, like telling barmy lies or pretending you're awfully keen on poetry when you're not. *You* know.''

''Yes, I know,'' said Mr. Campion and saw for the first time the use of Raymond Ramillies. The advent of Ramillies must have made a great difference to Sinclair. Ramillies sounded all right. His family was good and his position unquestionable. As a step-father he must have been a rock. Much has been said against the English system of moulding young gentlemen to a certain pattern, but, whatever the arguments for and against it may be, the system itself when in operation is a formidable machine. The passage through it is painful anyway if one's corners are stubborn but to be jerked in and out of it by the capricious tricks and antics of one's parents' fluctuating whims or income is a mangling process not to be endured.

''Do you like Haverleigh?'' he asked.

Sinclair stared at his feet. His eyes were swimming.

''It's marvellous,'' he said. ''It's pretty good.''

''We used to play you,'' Mr. Campion observed. ''You were very strong in those days. You are still, aren't you?''

The boy nodded. ''We're the top,'' he said. ''It was foul at Tolleshurst, being not quite sound—presentable, you know— but here it would be hell. You'd let the place down, you see. They wouldn't chuck it at you, of course, but you'd feel you were doing it.''

Since the talk was an intimate one and complete frankness seemed in order Mr. Campion put forward a comforting suggestion somewhat baldly.

''Perhaps you'll get someone as good.''

''Yes,'' said Sinclair and let the air sizzle through his teeth. There was a flicker of hope in his eyes, stifled immediately, which was among the most genuinely pathetic sights Campion had ever seen. ''Mother was engaged to Portland-Smith once,'' the boy remarked presently. ''I liked him. He was hopelessly stiff and conventional but he did know what he wanted and what he was going to do next. He was going to be a county court judge. Georgia would have left the stage if she'd married him. I hoped she would but that was pretty low of me. I was only thinking of myself. He was a moody person, though. He shot himself. Did you know?''

"Yes. I found him, as a matter of fact.''

"Did you?'' Sinclair hesitated over the obvious question, instinctive to everyone and yet always false to the ear. Campion answered it for him.

"In a place very much like this,'' he said, looking round at the leaves.

Sinclair considered the astounding vagaries of life for some time and finally reverted to his own problems, which were at least concrete.

"It's filthy to sit and blub about oneself,'' he remarked. "A lot of what I've been saying is filthy. But I've started, you see. I've started to be one sort of chap. Ray said if I worked I could go to Oxford and have a shot at the diplomatic. I meant to hold him to that if it was possible. I tried to make it square with him by trailing round and doing what I could. It's putrid talking like this when he's just dead, and I liked him. I did like him, but it's my *life*, you see. It's all I've got. Now I may have to change everything again, and anyway I won't know what I'm doing for a bit. I wish I'd started on something where none of this mattered a hang. That's not quite true. I love Haverleigh and I'd miss Bunny.''

The name made him laugh.

"Bunny would burst if he heard me talking like this,'' he said with a chuckle. "Bunny's 'fearfully decent.' Sorry I told you. I'll go back and pack. She'll be going back to town, and if I'm not there when the car's ready I'll have to cadge a lift from someone. There's not a train for miles. Good-bye, Mr. Campion. Thank you for the tip about shock.''

Having no other convenient place to carry it, he stuffed Sir Walter's great romance into the seat of his flannels and hoisted himself up the wall. Perched on the top, he looked down at Campion.

"I've been talking like Ray did when he was tight,'' he said with a bravado which deceived neither of them. "Forget it, please, won't you? It was seeing things working again that put the wind up me. It does, doesn't it?''

"Things working again?'' echoed Mr. Campion sharply.

Sinclair seemed surprised.

"Things do work, don't they?'' he said. "Things happen and link up rather peculiarly. Haven't you noticed it? They do round Georgia and me anyway. Don't they do it every-where?''

"I don't know," said Mr. Campion slowly.

"I think they do," persisted Sinclair. "You'll jolly well see it if you watch, or at least I think you will. I do. I say, this wall's giving. Good-bye, sir.''

Raymond Ramillies' chief mourner dropped out of sight and Mr. Campion was left alone, thinking.

He was still there, sitting with his arms clasping his bent knees, when Amanda found him. She was dishevelled and almost weary, for once in her life.

"Gone to ground?" she enquired, pausing before him. "I don't altogether blame you. The plane's off at last. Nearly an hour late. What a show!''

She sat down on the step beside him and retied her shoelace, her red hair hanging over her face.

"How did that chap die?''

Mr. Campion related the entire story truthfully, omitting only Val's incredible admission about the morphine. He knew from experience that there was not much which could be hidden from Amanda for long and so made the rest of the tale as exact as possible.

She listened to him in complete silence and when he had finished began to whistle a little tune, very flat and breathy.

"Albert," she said suddenly, "I'll tell you something. I can *hear* machinery.''

He turned his head.

"It's getting a bit obvious, isn't it?" he murmured. "Even my great ears began to throb. Who's the little god in charge?''

Amanda hesitated, her hand still on her shoe and her skinny young body arched forward.

"Could she have the nerve?''

"Has she the organising ability? I know poison is supposed to be sacred to women, but she brought that P.M. on herself. Buxton-Coltness would have signed up like a lamb.''

Amanda grunted.

"Perhaps she overplayed the part," she said. "Or perhaps she knows she's safe.''

"How can she know she's safe? The Buxton-Coltness combine may be a gaggle of quacks, but they're not criminal and presumably they can do a P.M. between them.''

Amanda opened her mouth and thought better of it.

"I don't care about Ramillies," she said at last. "I thought the chap was close to being a bounder and he was certainly a dreadful old cad, but I don't like us being used. It's this Old Testament touch that frightens me. I don't like being caught up in the cogwheels if I think someone's doing it. It's bad enough when it's the Lord."

"Organised machinations of fate," murmured Mr. Campion, and felt for the first time that old swift trickle down the spine. It was astounding that three such very different people should have expressed so unusual a thought to him within the hour.

Meanwhile Amanda was still talking.

"What's going to happen next?" she said. "Something's up. When the pilot got into the Seraphim he found this lying on his seat and he gave it to me to attend to."

Campion glanced at the little silver model in her outstretched hand. It was the Quentin Clear. Amanda's brown fingers closed over it.

"I thought I'd better hang on to it, for a while anyway," she said. "What do you know about that?"

"Georgia wasn't wearing it when she came down to the hangar after lunch."

"I know she wasn't. Nor was A.D. And why should it be lying on the seat, right under the nose of one of the few men who would know what it was and whose it was when he saw it? It's a plant, another 'mysterious way.' "

Mr. Campion stirred.

"It's so damned insulting," he said. "Amanda, we'll get the impious god in this machine."

Chapter Fourteen

The post-mortem examination on the body of Sir Raymond Ramillies was performed and an examination of certain organs was rushed through, the Richmond Laboratories performing in twenty-four hours a task over which the public analyst might have been expected to take three weeks.

After the reports had been made Dr. Harvey Buxton-Coltness saw no reason to withdraw the certificate which he had given, and the funeral took place on the fifth day, Messrs. Huxley and Coyne, the big furnishing and warehouse people, making an excellent job of the arrangements.

The details in the box headed "Cause of Death" in the registrar's oblong black book read "Cardiac failure due to myocardial degeneration. Other conditions present: chronic nephritis," and meant, in much plainer English, that Sir Raymond's heart had ceased to beat and that there was no really satisfactory reason, as far as Dr. Buxton-Coltness, Mr. Rowlandson Blake, F.R.C.S., and the Richmond Laboratories could ascertain, why on earth this should have been so. It also meant, of course, that these three authorities were prepared to bet that no other experts could ascertain more, and there the official side of the matter rested.

Several people were surprised, Amanda among them, but Mr. Campion was also angry. His sense of outrage grew. His personal and professional dignity had been assailed, his reputation had been utilised, and Val's prophetic judgment confirmed. Moreover, the "mysterious drug unknown to science" seemed to have materialised at last. He became very affable and friendly and he and Amanda went everywhere together.

They went to the memorial service at St. Jude's-by-the-Wardrobe, near the Old Palace, and Val saw them there looking very charming and sleek in their black clothes, two rows behind Gaiogi. Val went with the widow. Georgia had phoned her in the morning.

"Darling, you must. I'm relying on you, Val. The only women in the family are the aunts and the half-brother's wife and they're all definitely hostile besides being frightful females who smell like puppy's breath. I've got Sinclair, of course, but I must have a woman, mustn't I? I thought of having Ferdie sit with me, but somehow I don't think . . . do you? He's not old enough. Alan's to go alone. He must appear but I can't have him near me. That would be too filthy. Darling?"

"Yes."

"Isn't it *amazing*?"

"Extraordinary."

"I'm terribly upset, you know."

"I'm sure you are."

"You don't sound as though you were. But I am, Val. I've cried myself to sleep every night since. I have. I really have. I did love him. Not like Alan, of course, but I did love Ray. Poor Ray! I miss him terribly. Come with me. I'll call for you at a quarter to. Not late or early, I think, don't you? Just on time."

"It's safest."

"Val, you sound chilly, almost distant. You're not angry with me by any chance, are you?"

"Angry with you? My dear, why should I be? What have you been up to?"

There had been a light, relieved laugh.

"Nothing. Of course not. I only wondered." And then, in a burlesqued cockney accent, "We girls are funny sometimes, duck. We imagine things, don't we? It's our natures, I suppose. Val?"

"Yes."

"You do like me a little bit, don't you? We are friends?"

"Darling, of course." Val was not a great actress and a hint of dogged determination came through the words.

"Honestly?"

"Oh, don't be a fool, woman. I'm at work. Of course we are."

"All right. You needn't be so very brittle, need you? It's a memorial service to my dead husband, you know. You don't understand, do you, pet? You're hard, Val."

The word had done the work it always does, and Val's face betrayed her, but the telephone had only carried her cool, high voice to the other woman.

"Am I? I don't think so. I don't know."

"Take it from me, then. But I don't blame you. I admire you for it. You don't know how much you save yourself by it. You miss a lot but you save more, I think. Look here, what about Lady Papendeik? Would she come with us? We don't want to look like a couple of floozies. Not that we should, of course. But we both do look so young. Who is she coming with?"

"She's not going, I'm afraid."

"Oh? Why not? I think she ought to."

"She doesn't feel like it," said Val. Tante Marthe had actually said that she knew Ramillies well enough to realise that mere praying for him was a waste of her own and the Bon Dieu's time, but there seemed no point in repeating it.

"Oh, I see. Then it's just you and me and, of course, Sinclair. I've tried on the entire ensemble again and I like it enormously. You don't think those millions of little black butterflies on the cap are a tiny bit pert for the occasion?"

"No, I don't think so. . . . After all, he liked you to look lovely."

"Are you laughing at me?"

"My dear, why should I?"

"I never know with you. You don't understand. I loved him. I adore Alan but I loved Ray. I did. I really did."

"You love us all," said Val. "God bless you. Good-bye, my pet."

"Good-bye, darling. A quarter to three, then. I say, Val, don't wear *all* black. *I'm* the widow. You don't mind me saying that, do you? I thought you wouldn't. That's why I love you. I can be myself with you. Val, do you think I'm vulgar?"

"Not more than we all are. Good-bye, my dear."

The memorial service was charmingly devised and, since the church specialised in such offices, well carried out. Glancing round the ancient greystone nave, it occurred to Mr. Campion that the familiar "friends of the bride" and "friends of the groom" division had been aptly translated into "relations and officials" and "friends of the deceased."

Towser, representing royalty, and a small brigade of supporters presumably representing Towser, sat on one side of the aisle with the aunts, the half-brother and a host of army and club folk, while Georgia and the Caesar's Court contingent formed the flower of the opposition. Sinclair stood by his mother, his small drawn face stoical.

Val had given her mind to her clothes and her femininity had triumphed. She was exquisite. Georgia's dark galleon was for once a little heavy, a little funereal, beside this dainty mourning skiff. Val had conceded to the not-all-black request in her own way, and carried, instead of the more ordinary enamel compactum, a pochette made from the chased silver binding of an old German missal, with three or four large real violets threaded through its solid clasp.

Many people looked at her and there were some who nudged their neighbours and pointed her out. Much of this notice was an ordinary tribute to a distinguished and beautiful woman, but not all. Val was sublimely unconscious of the general interest. She was acutely aware of Alan Dell seated five or six rows behind her and of Georgia kneeling and rising at her side, but save for them the rest of the church might have been empty as far as she was concerned.

Mr. Campion was aware of Dell also.

The vicar of St. Jude's-by-the-Wardrobe had been a soldier himself in his time and had decided to give an address. He was an oldish man with a failing memory, and once or twice during his discourse it became apparent that he had confused Ramillies with some other warrior, but his parsonical intonation robbed most of his words of any meaning whatsoever and fortunately embarrassment was thus avoided.

The homily provided an interlude, however, and during it Campion had leisure to look at Dell.

He was sitting forward, his silk hat hanging from his hand and his face clearly outlined against a pillar. From time to time he glanced towards the backs of the two women sitting far in front of him. Amanda kicked Campion.

"A.D. looks like that at work," she murmured.

He nodded and glanced at the face again. There was no shyness there now, nor was there weakness or uncertainty. The Alan Dell at Ramillies' memorial service was the Alan Dell of Alandel planes, Val's love, Sid's hero and Amanda's boss. Mr. Campion felt more than sorry for him.

He could just see Georgia, looking unapproachable in her beauty, her elegance and her grief. Val, he knew, was beside her, and the thought of her reminded him of the uncanny accuracy of her guesses. Most women were alarming in that way, he reflected again. They muddled through to truth in the most dangerous and infuriating fashion. All the same they were not quite so clever as they thought they were, which was as it should be, of course, but odd considering their remarkable penetration in most other practical matters.

It was astonishing how the simple, direct reactions of the ordinary male eluded them. In many cases he was their main interest and yet they invariably boggled over him, approaching a machine of the relative size and simplicity of a bicycle with an outfit which one might be expected to need to take a watch to pieces.

He glanced at Dell again and picked up some of the other

man's thought; he recognised the pail-of-water-over-the-head experience which Ramillies' sudden death and Georgia's sudden release must have been to him. That shock had been physical, of course, while the decent, well-behaved mind, which is always being bewildered by the body's antics, had no doubt reacted conventionally. The beloved was free and the beloved must therefore be claimed and married, so that, after making all allowances for natural regret at another human being's untimely end, the heart should be bounding. And yet did Dell's heart bound? Mr. Campion was inclined to bet his all that it did no such thing. In Mr. Campion's opinion Dell was probably disgusted, and, if he was as inexperienced as he appeared to be, disconcerted by himself. In his idle mind Mr. Campion addressed him across the church. "You'll ask the woman to marry you, old boy, insistently if you're pigheaded and half-heartedly if you're not, and if she agrees to do so with sufficient speed you will marry her, and you'll become one of the half-resentful, half-obstinately optimistic husbands that the Georgias of this world acquire. But, ever since Ramillies died, ever since the moment when the first word of his death reached you, although Georgia's body has remained sickeningly desirable and will remain so for some time, every other word that has escaped her, every little offensive trick of mind which she had betrayed and which until now has been muffled by you automatically because her deficiencies were not your affair, has suddenly become italicised. In fact, ever since Ramillies died Georgia has got on your nerves and you cannot bring yourself to believe that you are such an outsider, or love is so fragile, that the two events have any connection."

Mr. Campion read the label in his hat. It gave him a childish sense of satisfaction to reflect that this elementary mental process was one that neither Val nor Georgia would ever grasp until it had been bitten into their minds with the slow acid of the years. They would both of them pry and probe with their delicate little forceps, they would weigh intonations and pore over letters, forcing little pieces of jigsaw to fit into fantastic theories as ingenious and delightful as Chinese puzzles, and yet the elementary fact would sit and stare them in the face, defeating them by its very simplicity.

He looked down at Amanda. She was reading in a very old Prayer Book she had found in the pew a Form of Service for

Thanksgiving for the Delivery of King James from the Gunpowder Plot.

It was raining a little as they came out of the church and they paused for a moment in the half cupola of the pillared porch. Ferdie Paul joined them. He looked profoundly mournful and his curling mouth was drawn down. His eyes lit up at the sight of Amanda and he congratulated Campion heartily on his engagement, about which he seemed to know a good deal; but having completed these formalities, his gloom returned.

"It's bad," he said, his unexpectedly thin voice irritable. "Damn bad luck all round. Too near the other business. It's bad for Georgia. People will begin to think she's poisonous or something, poor girl. It's amazing what people *will* think, you know."

The last remark was uttered with sudden directness and the full brown eyes were intelligent.

"I don't know how half the lunatics in this world arrive at their beliefs. By the way, how is Val?"

The connection between the two remarks was not apparent and Mr. Campion looked blank. Ferdie Paul, who was watching him closely, seemed startled and then, if such a thing had been possible, almost confused.

"She's here, is she? That's good. Oh, with Georgia? Really? That's splendid. She's been a great comfort there, I know. Georgia's far more cut up than she shows. I can tell it when she's working. She's put up a stronger performance in some respects than I've even heard her give these last few nights, but you can tell she's running on her nerves."

He paused and a faint smile passed over his face.

"Thank God it's not a farce," he said, "or we'd have to come off. As it is, the 'gallant little woman' can carry on with entire propriety."

Mr. Campion was mildly surprised. The reference to Val had not been lost upon him in spite of the adroit cover-up.

"The whole thing was a great shock to everyone concerned," he said.

"Oh, my dear chap, frightful! Frightful!" There was no doubting Ferdie Paul's sincerity. The nervous energy in his voice was almost a touchable thing. "Frightful! I nearly had apoplexy myself when Georgia phoned me. I mean, think of the publicity. If poor old Ray had wanted to make a stink he couldn't have fixed it better, could he?"

"I suppose not. Gaiogi seemed upset."

"Oh, Gaiogi?" Ferdie laughed. "He took to his bed for three days afterwards. Did you know? He's in love with that hotel. My God, the fellow sleeps with it. It's indecent. Here he is. Czar Gaiogi, representing Caesar's Court."

The dig was unkind, but apt. Gaiogi Laminoff came out of the church door with the dignity of a sorrowing emperor. He bowed gravely to them and came over.

"Not a good address, did you think?" he remarked seriously as he joined them.

"Rotten. Not an ad in it," said Ferdie maliciously.

Gaiogi raised his eyebrows and turned to Amanda.

"You are a lovely thing on a sad day," he said simply. "I am so glad to see you."

Somewhat ungallantly Mr. Campion deserted his betrothed to deal with this sort of impasse as best she could and was relieved to hear her confessing that much the same notion had come into her head at the sight of Gaiogi. He went forward with Ferdie to meet Georgia, who had just appeared.

Val had become separated from her charge during their passage down the aisle and she was waiting with the rest of the fashionable crowd, on whom enforced silence had inflicted a certain simmering quality, when she caught sight of Dell looking at her anxiously.

Her first fleeting impression was that he had been waiting for her, but she dismissed it irritably and favoured him with a faint, cool smile of recognition. He came over to her, edging his way through the group clumsily, and was by her side as the crowd began to move. She was aware that he was making up his mind to speak to her and was suddenly unreasonably and degradingly elated, but when the words did come, blurted out huskily as they stepped into the rain, she was only puzzled by them.

"Val," he said, "you've got intelligence, my dear. You wouldn't blame the wrong person, would you?"

She had time to stare at him blankly and then Georgia was before them.

"Come with us, Val. We'll drop you. For God's sake don't smile. You know what photographs are. Where's Sinclair? Oh well, never mind. He can take a taxi. Come, we can't stand here. It looks terrible. Come, Alan. Sinclair is a little beast. I told him to stick to me."

Sir Raymond's chief mourner was in a pew at the back of the church. A thought had been tormenting him all the way down the aisle and at the last moment he had weakened and given way to it.

"O God, dear God," he prayed, "if so be it You do exist, hear me. I know they say there isn't a hell, but if there is, O God, dear God, kind God, don't let Ray burn. He was only silly, O God, dear God, only stinkingly silly. Don't let him burn."

Then, this last orison performed, he scrambled up, caught a verger looking at him suspiciously, and hurried out, his ears burning. The car had gone and he looked about for a cab and would have taken one had not Amanda and Campion met him on a street island and carried him off to tea with them.

Meanwhile Val and Georgia sat side by side in Georgia's car and Alan Dell sat opposite them.

Georgia was on edge. There was a certain quality of defence about her also which was new in her in Val's experience. She was working hard. Every ounce of her physical magnetism was forced into service and, because this was hardly necessary and even a large car is a confined space, the effect was overwhelming and uncomfortable.

Val became very quiet, almost sedate. She sat gracefully in her corner, one knee tucked up under the four-inch heel of her little shoe showing against the grey rep-covered seat.

Dell looked preoccupied and morose but Georgia was irresistibly warm. Her life flowed over him, forcing him to respond to it in spite of his inclination, which was towards peace.

"Oh, darlings, this is the first time that I've felt happy since that dreadful afternoon. You're the two people I rely on most. I couldn't live without either of you. I know I say and do the filthiest things but I don't mean it. Do you think I could take my hat off, Val? No one could see in here, could they? Not to recognize me, I mean."

Dell took her hat from her outstretched hand and put it down on the seat beside him. The little black butterflies on the crown attracted him and he filliped one of them idly. Georgia laughed.

"They're like aeroplane wings, aren't they?" she said. "Val's a genius. She's entirely brilliant. Do you realise that, Alan?"

He looked at the two of them dispassionately, his bright blue eyes reproving.

"Val is a good friend," he said. "The best friend you have."

Georgia shrank back like an abashed baby and there was new colour in her cheeks.

"Oh, but, darling, I *know*," she said with passionate reproach in her tone. She laid a hand on Val's wrist possessively. "I do know. Don't I know? Alan, why do you say that? I adore Val and Val likes me, don't you, Val? You do like me. We've been friends for years. We're all frightfully upset. The service was terribly emotional. That's why I dread these things. Let's stop and have a cocktail somewhere. Oh no, I suppose we can't like this. My God, I suppose we can't be seen out at all tonight. Where shall we go?"

"I must go back to Tante Marthe. She's waiting for me at Park Lane," said Val.

"Oh, must you." Georgia did not make the words a question. "What a frightful nuisance. I don't know what we shall do. Alan?"

"Yes."

"Take me up in a plane."

"What, now?"

"Yes, as soon as we've changed. Drive me out to Caesar's Court and take me up in a plane. I want to get away, right away, just for a little tiny while. Do. Please, Alan, because I ask you."

"All right," he said dubiously. "It'll be frightfully cold, you know, and it's raining."

"Oh, all right." Georgia shrugged her shoulders. "We'll light a fire and sit round it and talk, or dress up in old clothes and go to some dirty little Soho restaurant where we shan't be recognised. What shall we do?"

Val glanced at Dell. He was watching the other woman gravely. There was no telling what was the thought in his mind. He was regarding her earnestly and with evident interest, but his opinion was secret. Val blinked and turned her head.

"Here we are," she said with relief. "Will you come in? No? All right. I'll see you soon, Georgia. Good-bye, Alan."

Her small gloved hand rested in each of their own for an

instant and then she was gone. Georgia looked after her and smiled with genuine sadness.

"Poor pretty Val," she said. "Isn't she a dear?"

Dell did not answer her directly. He moved over into the seat Val had vacated and laid a hand on Georgia's·arm.

"I'm going to take you home now and then I'm going to leave you," he said. "I'll phone you tomorrow."

"Oh, but why?" She moved away and sat looking at him with the wide-open eyes of an injured child. It was Georgia at her most appealing, her warmest and most vulnerable. He hesitated.

"Don't you think I ought to?" he said at last.

"Ought to?" She was honestly bewildered and he laughed uneasily.

"I think I will," he said.

Georgia could see herself faintly mirrored in the glass between them and the chauffeur's dark back. It was a flattering reflector and she was reassured after a momentary misgiving. His obvious reason, which was a natural conventional distaste for the proximity of love and death, escaped her and she was puzzled. She slid an arm through his.

"I want to be with you this evening, Alan," she said. "I'm not playing tonight, you know, because of the service. No, my dear, this is the first time, the very first time, I've felt free." There was no mistaking her confiding. It was genuine, voluptuous and entirely generous.

He did not speak and she felt him stiffen. She looked up and was amazed. She had caught him unawares and there had been nausea on his face.

"All right," she said, releasing him. She was laughing but obviously deeply hurt. "All right. I shall be terribly rushed tomorrow. Phone me the day after."

He sighed and rubbed his hard, scrubbed hands over his face.

"You don't understand at all, do you?" he said.

"My dear, I do, of course I do," said Georgia with more conviction than truth, and sat looking at him with patent speculation in her tweed-grey eyes, so that he felt like a medical specimen and was revolted and ashamed of himself and very unhappy.

Meanwhile Val proceeded calmly to her office. Rex met her in the hall with two queries concerning dresses which she had forgotten and she dragged her mind out of its self-protective coma and considered them intelligently. He noticed nothing unusual about her and when she stepped into the little wrought-iron gazebo of a room, Lady Papendeik, who was sitting at her desk, thought she looked particularly well and was grateful for the circumstance in view of the letter before her.

They talked of trivialities for some moments and touched on business. Val pulled off her small black hat and her yellow hair shone in a stray shaft of sunlight cutting through to them from the west landing window, where the sun was breaking through after the rain.

"It was tiring," she explained, smiling in faint apology.

Tante Marthe's little black eyes glinted.

"Georgia played the leading part well, no doubt? Did she enjoy herself?"

"Oh, I think so. She behaved excellently."

"Did she? That must have been a comfort to her husband's ghost."

"Mustn't it?" Val agreed absently.

She had not seated herself and there was an undercurrent of restlessness in her movements which did not escape the old woman.

"Are you feeling irritable?"

"No, not particularly."

"Good." Lady Papendeik sniffed over the word. "I had a letter this afternoon from Emily."

"From Mother?" There is nothing like surprise to ease emotional tension and Val moved over to the desk with her natural step.

Lady Papendeik spread her small hands over the blotter.

"It is annoying."

"I can imagine it."

"I wonder. I hope not." Tante Marthe shrugged her shoulders. "Oh, read it," she said. "It must be true or she could never have heard of it. No one can do anything."

Val took up the thick cream double sheet with the well-known crimson heading, the single arrogant house name and county which had once been so familiar and which even now brought a far-off memory of a peach tree of all things, a sprawling peach tree on a rosy wall.

DEAR LADY PAPENDEIK,
  I am an old woman, [the letter had originally begun

144

''We are both,'' but the three words had been struck out
with a single broad line from the hard steel pen and
remained a shining example of British county tact at its
unhappiest,] *and I am writing to you instead of to my
daughter because I feel that you at least will appreciate
to the full my natural reactions to the monstrous situation which has arisen. This morning I received a letter
from Dorothy Phelps. She is a fool, of course, but I am
sure she wrote me out of the kindest of motives. She is a
distant relation of my husband's, a collateral branch of
his mother's family, and I am sure she would never do
anything to wound me maliciously. I enclose her letter,
which I hope you will return to me. You will see she says
"everyone is talking about it." This is quite intolerable.
I have suffered enough from my children, God knows,
but even they must see that this is the last straw. Will you
kindly see that Val has nothing more to do with this
woman? Val should never again visit this hotel, Caesar's
Court, and must be brought to realise that, even if she
has obstinately thrown away every advantage to which
her birth has entitled her, she cannot escape from the*
responsibility *which is hers as much as it is mine or any
other owner of our name or those few names like ours
which are left. They tell me times have changed,* but
they have not changed here. *This precious little part of
England is as it ever was, thank God, and until I die it
will remain so. After that I dare not contemplate. Of
course no* action *is possible. Val, I am sure, will recognise this in spite of the subversive influences of the past
few years, but in my opinion a threatened action might
have some effect, and I am instructing our solicitors to
put themselves at her disposal. I do not want to hear
from Val. Explanations do not interest me, as all my
children know. In my world explanations and excuses
have ever been taken, rightly or wrongly, as signs of
guilt or weakness. This abominable slander should never
have been uttered. No daughter of ours should ever have
put herself into a position which made its utterance
possible. Since it has been uttered, I am forced to take
steps to see that it is silenced and I appeal to you to
bring Val to her sense of responsibility in the matter. If
she can do nothing she should at least go abroad for six*

months. Meanwhile, you will oblige me by refusing, of
course, to have any future transactions with this woman,
Georgia Ramillies.

> *Believe me,*
> *Yours sincerely,*
> EMILY K——

The rest of the signature was illegible.

Val put the letter down quietly and picked up the enclosure,
which was written on single sheets with a club address and
was in an 1890 calligraphy.

DEAREST AUNT EMILY,

I do not know how to write to you, darling, without
hurting you much more than you could ever deserve, but
something has come to my ears which Kenneth and I feel
we ought to let you know about. I was playing bridge
here yesterday and a Mrs. Fellowes—her husband is one
of the Norfolk people, I think—was talking about poor
Val. Of course I listened and said nothing. Amy Fellowes
has a daughter who is in the stage set (many quite good
young people play at this nowadays, you know, dear)
and when the conversation turned to the death of Raymond
Ramillies (no doubt you read about it; it was very
sudden) Mrs. Fellowes came out with an extraordinary
story. According to this, Lady Ramillies, who is Georgia
Wells, the actress, actually said to Amy Fellowes' daugh-
ter, in front of several other people, that it was a very
extraordinary thing that her husband should have died
so suddenly after taking some aspirin which Val had
given Lady Ramillies for herself. What made it worse is
that she hinted that Val and this Ramillies woman had
some quarrel over a man whose name I did not hear
although several were mentioned. Of course this cannot
be true. Neither Kenneth nor I would believe it for a
moment. But I felt it was my duty to write you because it
is the kind of gossip which should be stopped. *Everyone*
is talking about it. Val, I know, is very clever and
probably very foolish. I am sure if she realised the pain
she gave you she would be more careful. Forgive me for
sending you such bad news but I thought it best to come

out in the open, and so did Kenneth. I expect your dear
garden is very beautiful now. How you must love it!
      Very affectionately, dear Auntie, yours,
              DOROTHY PHELPS

Val let the paper drop and her fingers fluttered over it in a
little gesture of distaste.

"A frightful old woman," she said. "I remember her. Yes,
well, that accounts for it."

"Accounts for what?" demanded Tante Marthe sharply.

"Oh—things." Val walked down the room and stood
looking across the landing to the west window blazing in the
evening sun.

"Georgia must have said this thing to someone," remarked
Tante Marthe.

"Oh, Lord, yes, she's said it." Val sounded weary. "She's
said it to everyone she's become confidential with in the last
fortnight. There must be dozens of them. You know what
Georgia is. She doesn't really mean it. She doesn't think I
tried to poison her. She simply knows it's a good story but
doesn't realise how good. She doesn't actually think at all.
She goes entirely by feel."

"It's dangerous, my dear."

"Is it?" The younger woman spoke bitterly. "There's been
a P.M. Ramillies is safely buried. It's all perfectly normal.
Am I likely to sue her?"

"You could."

"I could. But am I likely to? If she weren't one of our most
important clients would I be likely to admit I've even heard
that I am so much in love with Alan Dell that I attempted to
murder the woman he preferred?"

Lady Papendeik did not speak for a moment.

"It's very naughty of Georgia," she observed somewhat
inadequately, when the silence had gone on long enough.
"What shall one say to Emily?"

"She's seventy." Val sounded tolerant. "Say you'll do all
you can. She's a hundred and fifty miles away and a hundred
and fifty years off. She's living in the past, somewhere just
before the Napoleonic Wars. You get like that down there.
The house hasn't changed and neither has she. If she weren't
so gloriously hard it would be pathetic. Still, it's idiotic. You

can't believe like Queen Charlotte just because you live in a Georgian pile.''

Lady Papendeik nodded regretfully.

"Will you mention this to Georgia?"

"Oh no." Val was standing with her back to the room, the sun turning her hair into a blazing halo. "No. She'll forget it in a day or so. If I talk to her it'll give her something else to add to it, or else she'll be brokenhearted and contrite and have to confess to someone terribly confidentially, and the whole thing'll blaze up again.''

"You're very wise for your age." Lady Papendeik seemed to find the fact a pity. "Perhaps this niece of Emily's has exaggerated.''

"Perhaps so. Let us look on the bright side by all means.''

"You are afraid the man will hear of it?"

"I'm afraid he has." Val's tone was commendably matter of fact. Ever since she had read Dorothy Phelps's letter the full significance of Dell's muttered injunction on the church step had been slowly sinking into her mind. It is the little unexpected nicenesses which creep through the armour chinks, and suddenly her restraint shivered. She laid her forehead against the pane.

"My dear, oh, my dear, my dear, my love, oh, sweet, sweet, oh, my dear." The idiotic refrain made existence just bearable until the moment was over.

She turned away from the window and glanced at Tante Marthe.

"It passes," said the old woman, answering her thought. "Of all the things that pass that passes most completely. Enjoy it while you can.''

"Enjoy it?"

Lady Papendeik looked down at her hands with the little brown mottles on them.

"There's a great deal to be said for feeling anything," she remarked. "I don't.''

Val sat down at her table and began to scribble. Presently the other woman rose to look over her shoulder.

"What's that?" she demanded. "A nightgown?"

Van ran a pencil through the design. She looked up, her cheeks red and her eyes laughing.

"A tiddy little shroud," she said. "It should be made in

something rather heavy and expensive. Berthé's new corded chîne-chîne, I think.''

"Morbid and silly," said Lady Papendeik. "I like the little bows. What's the pocket for?"

"Indulgences," said Val cheerfully. "They're always in fashion."

Chapter Fifteen

"I tell you wot, cock," said Mr. Lugg, looking at an enormous gold hunter which had been entirely ruined, from his point of view, by an engraved tribute in the back which rendered it of little interest to pawnbrokers. "I tell you wot. She's not coming."

Mr. Campion turned away from his sitting-room window and wandered across the carpet, his lean dinner-jacketed shoulders hunched.

"A nasty little girl," he observed. "Take the crème-de-menthe away. Drink it if you like."

"And smell like a packet o' hiccorf suckers. I know." Lugg waddled to the coffee table and restored the offending bottle to the cocktail cabinet. "You treat me as a sort of joke, don't you?" he remarked, his great white face complacent. "I'm a regular clown. I make you laugh. I say funny things, don't I?"

His employer regarded him dispassionately. In his velvet house coat, his chins carelessly ranged over a strangling collar and his little black eyes hopeful, he was not by any means an uncomic figure.

"Well, go on, say it. I'm a laugh, ain't I?"

"Not to everyone."

"Wot?" He seemed hurt and also incredulous.

"Not to everyone. A lot of my friends think you're overrated."

"*Overrated?*" The black eyes wavered for a moment before a faint smile spread over the great face. "Reelly?" he said at last, adding tolerantly, "It takes all sorts to make a world, don't it? It's a funny thing, I often give meself a laugh. I think we'd better give 'er up, don't you? It's no use me sitting around dressed like a parcel if company's not expected. That's *makin'* trouble. Mr. Tuke advises me to wear lower collars. One inch above the shirtband, in 'is opinion, is quite sufficient if a gentleman 'as an 'eavy neck. What would you say?"

"What's the time?"

"Close on arf-past. She's not comin'. She's led you up the gardin. That's a woman all over. I don't know what you want to bother with them for. Two blokes 'ave died and are tucked up tidy, and what if there is a lot of talk about your sis and a sleepin' tonic? That's nothin'. Leave it alone. Fergit it. Be a gent and look it in the face and don't see it."

"A sleeping tonic?" Mr. Campion's pale eyes were cold behind his spectacles and Mr. Lugg perceived the pitfall too late.

"A naspirin, then," he said defiantly. "Fergit it. Don't roll in the mud. Don't *bathe* yerself in it."

"When did you hear this?"

"Oh, ages ago. Months it was. Last week per'aps." Mr. Lugg was throwing the subject about until he lost it. "I changed the conversation, if you want to know, same as any gent would 'oo 'adn't fergot 'isself."

"Where was this? At your beastly pub?"

"I may 'ave 'eard a careless word at the club. I really fergit." Mr. Lugg's eyes were veiled and his dignity was tremendous.

"The club!" said Mr. Campion with a force and bitterness which were unusual in him. "All the blasted clubs. Oh, my God, what a mess! There's the bell at last. Let her in, there's a good chap. Where on earth has she been?"

Mr. Lugg raised his eyebrows, or rather the ridge of fat where his eyebrows should have been, and shuffled out of the room. His voice came back from the passage a moment or so later.

"No luck. It's only Miss Amanda. This way, yer ladyship. She's let 'im down. No, 'asn't showed up at all."

Amanda came in full of sympathy. She did not take off the thick ivory silk coat which covered her from throat to toe but seated herself on the arm of a chair and regarded her host enquiringly.

"What do we do now?"

He grinned at her. Her enthusiasm was infectious and comforting and it occurred to him then that she would retain it all her days. It was part of her make-up and sprang from a passionate and friendly interest in all the many and exciting surfaces of life.

"I was considering," he said seriously. "At the moment we face an impasse. The old maestro allows beautiful suspect to slip through nicotine-stained fingers. I had been all over London for that wretched girl and I was lying harmlessly in bed this morning, wondering if the Salvation Army wasn't the next most likely hunting ground after all, when she phoned me. I recognised the jew's-harp voice immediately and promptly fell out of the bed onto the bear I shot in the Afghanistan campaign. She gave her name at once and plunged into business. 'It's Miss Caroline Adamson speaking. Is that Mr. Albert Campion? Oh, it is?' *Light laugh*. 'I don't know if you remember me?' *Pause*. 'Oh, you do? That's divine of you.' *Gasp*. 'Well, Mr. Campion, would you be in tonight about eight if I was to call round? I think you've been looking for me and I think I know what you're interested in. You want me to tell you something, don't you?' *Seductive upward inflection*. 'I'll call then. Oh no, no, thanks, that's sweet of you. No, I won't dine. I just want a little business chat. You understand it will be business, don't you?' *Firm, straight-from-the-shoulder tone*. 'Oh, you do? I thought you did.' *Relief*. I've only seen you once to speak to but I thought I was right about you.' *Unnecessary laugh*. "Well, I've got your address so I'll drop in about eight, then. What d'you want to know where I live for?' *Hur hur hur*. 'I'll come round to you. No, really, I'm on a diet, I am really. About eight then. Righty-ho.'"

He finished his impersonation with a realistic giggle.

"There you are," he said. "I couldn't discover where the call came from. Never try to trace a London telephone call unless you're a superintendent of police. So I washed my hands and face, bought three pennyworth of mimosa for the desk vase, lassoed Lugg into a collar and sat down to wait. When I asked you to come along at half-past nine I thought we'd have some jolly gossip to discuss. Instead of that the little canine has ditched me and here I am, disconsolate and foolish."

"You'd look more foolish if she'd fixed up to meet you outside the Leicester Square tube. It's raining like stink," said Amanda with typical practicalness. "What does she know? It must be something fairly good or she'd never approach you. She must have some sort of information to sell."

Campion glanced at her with mild surprise.

"Without wanting to wound your finer susceptibilities, I should have thought that was fairly obvious," he said at last. "I take it that Miss Adamson knows where Ramillies went when he rushed away from his farewell party at Caesar's Court, and where he got the alcoholic drenching which was so tactfully avoided in Doctor Buxton-Coltness' report."

Amanda looked up. She was quietly pleased with herself, he noticed.

"She may, of course," she said, "but I doubt it. I know where Ramillies went that night. He went to Boot's Hotel."

"Boot's?" Mr. Campion was frankly incredulous.

Boot's Hotel is one of those curious survivals which still eke out a failing existence in odd corners of London's mysterious western end. It had been founded early in the nineteenth century by a retired royal servant, and something of the stuffy, homely dignity of the court of Silly Billy still persisted inside its dusty crimson walls. The place had possessed a distinguished clientele in the days when a fine country lady and her husband were at a disadvantage if their relatives were out of town and could not offer them hospitality for their visit, since hotels which were not also public houses were scarce. But now its period was long past and only its tremendously valuable freehold and the sentiment of its owners stood between it and the housebreaker. So far as Mr. Campion knew, the Fitton family were the only people wealthy enough to face the tariff yet sufficiently hardy to stand the discomfort. There was a legend that hip baths were still provided in the vast bedrooms and were filled from small brass cans by ancient personages in livery, but Amanda said it was a good hotel and gave it as her opinion that once they got rid of the rats it would be very healthy.

"Boot's?" Campion repeated. "Boot's and Ramillies? Ramillies left Caesar's Court and beetled off back down the years to Boot's? Why?"

"To get a little peace, perhaps," suggested Amanda. "He wasn't awfully young. Love and the dance band may have got him down between them. It's not unlikely. Anyway he was there on the nineteenth because I saw his name in the book when I signed mine tonight. It was on the top of the page before mine. (I don't think they're going very well.) I asked George about it. He's that old man in the office place, and he remembers him coming in very well. Ramillies arrived fairly late and went up to his room, and, what's more, George doesn't think he came down again until the next morning, rather late. He's going to find that out for certain. Also—and this is the funny thing—George doesn't think he was drunk then."

"My dear child, he must have been." Mr. Campion was almost dogmatic. "Otherwise no man on earth could have done it in the time. I diagnosed at least a twelve-hour blind when I saw him after lunch. The whole story sounds fantastic. He may have taken a quart of whisky to bed with him at Boot's and privately drunk himself pallid. It's a form of vice which I don't understand myself, but, having seen Ramillies, I'm open to concede that such a form of perversion might conceivably appeal to him. I say, are you sure you've got the right date and the right man?"

"Raymond Ramillies, The Residency, Ulangi," said Amanda, "*and* George described him."

"George also says he wasn't tight," objected Mr. Campion.

"George is a wonderful smart old man." She dropped into her native Suffolk by way of emphasis. "If George said you were tight now I'd take his word for it against yours, and as for the date, if Ramillies went and stayed alone on any other night at Boot's for no good reason whatever, that *would* be astonishing. But if he suddenly got fed up with Caesar's Court and Georgia and the noise and wanted somewhere quiet to sleep, then it would be a perfectly normal thing to go to Boot's, where there's not even any plumbing to uggle-guggle at you from inside the walls. That's all right. That's the kind of thing I'd do myself."

Campion was silent. There was a great deal of common sense in Amanda's remarks. It was the kind of thing Amanda would do herself, and Ramillies, for all his vagaries, came from much the same background as Amanda. He stood frowning down at her.

"Suppose you're right," he said. "Suppose all this is true. Where and when did he get in the condition in which he arrived at Caesar's Court and what in the name of good fortune has Miss Adamson to tell us that is sufficiently interesting for her to think we might buy it?"

"That's what I was wondering," said Amanda. "We ought to get hold of her, you know. This is a filthy tale that's going round about Val."

Campion raised his head sharply.

"It's reached you too, has it?" he said. "Isn't that jolly? New York will get it tomorrow when the Queen Mary docks and Uncles Henry and Edwin will mail their protests from the outposts of empire a couple of months from now. That's Georgia. That's what comes of emancipating the wrong type of female. For a thousand years they breed a species to need a keeper and then they let it off the chain and expect it to behave. Progress has made things damned difficult. Twenty years ago Val would have been forced to bring an action for slander, but nowadays, when we have decided that quarrelling is childish, friendship is the fashion, and we're all one big unhappy family, there's nothing to be done at all except to produce an even better story to contradict the first, and that, let me tell you, is not so frightfully easy."

Amanda slid down into the chair and sat looking up at him gravely. Her heart-shaped face was intelligent and he noticed again in an absent-minded fashion how much her appearance had improved. She would never have Val's extraordinary elegance but there was strength and breeding in her fine bones and her personality was as refreshing as the small clear streams of her own county.

"It's this hand-of-fate method that's the trouble," she remarked. "We can't get at anything, not even the body. I suppose those doctors were all right?"

"Oh, I think so." He smiled at her seriousness. 'They'd hardly risk their own necks. Why should they? No, I fancy they were genuinely fogged, just as I am, and I think that whoever arranged that Ramillies should die (and I'm open to bet that somebody did) knew that any ordinary doctor would be taken in. The P.M. didn't disclose anything at all, you see, not even why the fellow died. I wish that Adamson girl had turned up.''

''You think she meant to come?''

''Well, I wondered,'' he began and shot her a glance which was half amused and half genuinely grateful. ''What a pleasant girl you are, Amanda. Did you deduce that from my reported telephone conversation? You comfort me. Thank you. I need it. I wasn't quite my usual corruscating self this morning. But when she phoned I admit it did go through my mind that she might have a girl friend in the box with her. There was a distinct flavor of third person in the air and if so, you see, the whole thing may be a discreet enquiry to find out just how much I'm interested.''

''In that case there's something definite to know, which is a comfort, and the sooner we find her the better.'' Amanda rose with determination. ''What are you looking like that for?''

Mr. Campion had taken off his spectacles and was staring absently at the carpet. He looked older and, as Amanda had said, a trifle bleached.

''I was thinking,'' he said slowly, ''I was thinking that suppose we do find out who got rid of Sieur Ramillies, and supposing when we do it's not quite such a good telling story after all?''

''Then we shut up about it, of course,'' said Amanda cheerfully. ''It's our hanging. Where do we go from here? If you know anything you'd better tell me. It'll save time and I'm bound to find out in the end.''

He sighed. ''I don't know much. During my little mug round after the elusive Miss Adamson I picked up a crumb here and there. Nothing sensational like your Boot's Hotel bomb. That's the irony of life. Poor old Blest and I go nosing about like a pair of bloodhounds for days on end and discover practically nothing, and you go dancing into your horrible home from home and discover Ramillies' name and address in the visitors' book. Just before you descended on me and we went to the Tulip that night Blest had been round with the useful information that someone besides myself had been looking into a trifling matter in Georgia's past, and since then I have discovered that it was Caroline Adamson. That's one crumb. I then found out from various Aunt Maggies that our Caroline was the daughter of a former employee of Gaiogi Laminoff's and that she began her career at the Old Beaulieu

155

when Gaiogi was managing it. She was the girl who sat in a box in the vestibule and exchanged one's hat and coat for a ravishing smile and an artificial gardenia. After that he seems to have got Ferdie Paul to give her a chance on tour, and when everyone was perfectly certain that although the flesh was beautiful the voice was foul, she landed a mannequin job at Papendeik's. That's the other crumb.''

"It's a bit,'' said Amanda. "Have you been to see Gaiogi?''

"About Miss Adamson? No.''

"But why not? He's the obvious person to go to. He knows more about her than anyone. Let's go now.''

She was already halfway to the door, but paused, when he did not follow her, to stand regarding him with open suspicion in her eyes.

"Can I say something rather rude?'' she said. "If you're thinking that there's the least chance that the story about Val is true you're nuts. You don't mind me putting it like that, do you?''

"Not at all. I agree with you.''

"Thank goodness for that. Let's go to Gaiogi at once.''

"I don't think I would.''

"Why not?''

Mr. Campion looked uncomfortable beneath her steady gaze.

"It's a little question of self-advertisement,'' he explained evasively. "While I admire your forthrightness, Amanda, it gives me pins and needles in the soles of my feet. In view of everything I think Ferdie Paul is our most likely bet. He'll know who she was on tour with. In situations like this the girl friends have a tendency to cling together.''

"All right.'' Amanda sounded dubious. "He has a flat over the Sovereign Theatre, the one Sir Richard built for Lucy Gay. He's not likely to be in at this hour of the night but we can try.''

"How true, my sweet, how true,'' said Mr. Campion and reached for the telephone.

Ferdie was not only in, but in cheerful mood. His thin voice, which suited so ill with his appearance, squeaked heartily over the wire.

"I've got to leave town in forty minutes. Come round and have a drink. I'll tell you all I know about the bit, which isn't much. Is young Amanda with you? She is? Good God, what are you worrying about another woman for? I'll expect you both then, in five minutes. Fine. Good-bye.''

The flat, which a great actor-manager had built for a charming leading lady on top of the Sovereign Theatre, was, if sumptuous in the main, a trifle furtive about the entrance. The back of the theatre possessed a yard, now used by privileged persons as a car park, and in the yard beside the stage door was another, smaller and even meaner in appearance, giving on to a flight of uninviting concrete stairs. Once inside, however, the atmosphere changed, and Campion and Amanda came up in a small hand-worked passenger lift to a front door as impressive as any in Victorian London.

They were admitted by a Japanese manservant, who led them across a narrow hallway to the main living room, which was a quarter as large as a church and not at all unlike one in structural design.

Ferdie Paul, who had employed most of the great décor men of the day in his productions, had not permitted their work to get into his home. The vast untidy room had grown. No man on earth could have sat down in cold blood and visualised such jolly chaos.

Ferdie himself sat on a gigantic chesterfield with his feet up, and around him were manuscripts, books, papers, sketches and even patterns of material, in happy confusion.

On the floor before an open suitcase knelt a now familiar figure. She rose as they came in and stood waiting to be introduced with the same hidden discomfort which Campion had noticed in her when he had first seen her at Papendeik's dress show and later with Ferdie at the Tulip.

"Haven't you met Anna? Surely? Oh, you must meet Anna. She's the most extraordinary woman in London."

Ferdie rose lazily.

"Lady Amanda, Mrs. Fitch. Anna, the Lady Amanda Fitton. Anna, Mr. Albert Campion; Campion, Mrs. Fitch. And now, darling, I shan't need four pairs of socks for twelve hours in Frogland. Would you like to be barmaid?"

He sank down on the couch again, moved a pile of loose papers to make room for Amanda beside him, and waved Campion to an armchair opposite. Mrs. Fitch mixed the drinks. As she moved about her home her position in it was as clear as if she had announced it in lights round her head, and it was odd that the fashionable little hat which she wore on one side of her carefully waved hair, and the fact that her bag and gloves lay conspicuously on the side table, should have made this position even more apparent. She was self-contained and polite without being friendly, yet conveyed that because they were friends of Ferdie's they were delightful and exalted beings on whom it was her duty and privilege to wait.

She was the mistress of the house and the handmaid of Ferdie Paul, and it occurred suddenly to Mr. Campion that what she really represented was an old-fashioned, pre-Chaucerian wife, entirely loyal, completely subject, her fortunes inescapably her husband's own. The notion amused him, since he reflected that in view of all the excitement in the past century over the legal status of females the only way for a man to achieve this natural if somewhat elementary relationship with a woman at the present time was to persuade her to love him and never to marry her.

He glanced at her with interest. She could never have been beautiful and the cut of her dark gown showed ugly little spaniel haunches and plump elbows but her face was placid and there was a veiled expression in her pretty diamond-shaped eyes which might have hidden intelligence. Ferdie was supremely unaware of her save as an added comfort.

"I won't drink, if you'll forgive me," he said to Campion. "I may have a bumpy crossing tonight. I've got to run down to Caesar's Court to catch one of their planes. Bellairs is going over at ten-thirty and we fixed up to share a machine. Do you know Bellairs, the furniture man? That gives me six hours sleep when I get to Paris and then a couple of appointments and I can catch the evening plane back. It's very convenient, this service. I used to have to stagger backwards and forwards once every six weeks. Now I can nip over every three and do the whole thing inside twenty-four hours."

He glanced at his watch and laughed at the other man, his round brown eyes impudent.

"Is your car downstairs? You wouldn't like to run me down to Caesar's Court? It wouldn't take you fifty minutes there and back."

"Not at all. I'd like to." Campion glanced at Amanda

questioningly and she answered at once. "I'll wait for you here if I may." She looked at Mrs. Fitch, who smiled politely.

"That's grand," said Ferdie, obviously delighted at getting his own way. "My car's laid up. I hate cabs. We'll start in ten minutes. Anna, no one's drinking. Give me a brandy."

"I shouldn't." It was the first definite statement they had heard her make. She spoke flatly and placidly.

"Shouldn't be blowed! She treats me as though I was ill already. One small brandy."

She refused to hear him and there was quite a tussle between them, Ferdie laughing and the woman mutely obstinate. In the end he got his drink and sat sipping it, laughing at her over the glass.

"It may be the best thing for me," he said. "It hasn't proved so in the past, but still, one never knows. That's the exciting part of life. Isn't that so, Campion?"

"It adds to the general gaiety," agreed Campion affably. "What about Miss Caroline Adamson?"

"Zut! Before the jeune fille?" Ferdie set down his glass and raised his eyebrows. He looked more baroque and Byronic even than usual, with his dark-skinned face shining and his eyes dancing. "Oh, I didn't know. I was trying to be discreet. I don't know where she's living at the moment but I remember the bit well. She got the sack from Papendeik's when poor old Ray dressed her up as Georgia and took her to the Tulip to annoy his wife. She ran around with Ray a bit, I believe. I say, we ought to go, old man. I'll tell you all I know about Caroline on the way down, and when you get there you can talk to Gaiogi about her. He'll know where she is. If Gaiogi feels like it he can put his hands on anyone in London within twenty-four hours. (Is that case packed, Anna? Send Yusai down with it.) What do you want Caroline for, Campion, or aren't you telling?"

"She phoned me this morning and made an appointment with me which she didn't keep," said Mr. Campion mildly and with perfect truth.

Ferdie Paul stared at him, a questioning smile curling his mouth.

"And when you called the number she gave you they put you on to the zoo?" he suggested, grinning at Amanda.

"That's right, and I answered the phone," she said cheerfully.

"He has had a beastly evening. You'd better hurry. Don't smash the car up. We may go to the races tomorrow."

"Oh no, be careful." The words had escaped the other woman before she could stop them and they saw her for a moment with the visor up. The expression in her eyes was not intelligent. Its mute, adoring stupidity was startling.

Ferdie laughed at her good-humouredly.

"She has a theory I'm going to drop to pieces at any moment," he said, inviting them to join in his amusement at her. "We must go. Have I got everything? Is that contract in the portfolio, Anna? And the sketches? Good. Right. Last plane tomorrow if I don't miss it. Good-bye. Come on, Campion."

He did not kiss the woman but rubbed her solid shoulder affectionately as he passed her and, having said farewell to Amanda bustled out of the room, taking an atmosphere of nervous excitement which was somehow backless and ephemeral, like a methylated spirit flame, with him. As he descended the few steps to the lift they heard his thin voice rising heartily.

"I warn you of one thing; Caroline's a good deal older than you think."

Mrs. Fitch stood watching the door for a moment. In the arrested movement she looked shorter and stockier than ever, but with Ferdie's going her poise increased. The handmaid vanished and the mistress of the house remained.

"He's in a good mood tonight," she remarked. "I do hope he has a flat crossing. A bad one takes it out of him so."

She hesitated and glanced at Amanda, who was still sitting on the chesterfield, looking a trifle over sixteen and very comfortable and content.

"I'm going to have some tea," she said. "Would you like some? You haven't drunk your gin and lime."

Her visitor accepted the suggestion with genuine enthusiasm and, when the tray arrived with a small tin of ginger biscuits, settled down to enjoy them. They made a funny pair, and Mrs. Fitch slid unconsciously into the half-sentimental, half-patronising frame of mind that the consciously sophisticated keep up their sleeves for extreme youth and foolish innocence.

"You're getting married," she said. "That's going to be exciting, isn't it?"

"Staggering, I should think," agreed Amanda, swallowing a piece of biscuit. "Tolerance is the great secret, don't you think?" she added with a graceful effort to keep the ball rolling. "Tolerance and three good meals a day."

Mrs. Fitch did not laugh. Her diamond-shaped eyes narrowed and she looked for a moment almost frightened. She had a curious habit of moving her lips as if she were trying out words and finding them unsuitable, and she sat for a moment holding her teacup and staring over it consideringly.

"You don't want to be too tolerant," she said at last and added feelingly, "if you can help it."

"I suppose not."

"No. Do you know this girl, Caroline Adamson?"

"I've seen her once. She's rather like Lady Ramillies, isn't she?"

"Yes," said Mrs. Fitch and suddenly laughed. The laugh altered her personality entirely. It was revealing and intimate and made her less of an unknown quantity, and Amanda, who was one of those optimists who confidently expect every new person to be a delightful surprise, was disappointed once again.

"I shouldn't be too tolerant where Caroline Adamson is concerned," repeated Mrs. Fitch. "She's not the type of girl you know much about, I should say." She glanced at her visitor dubiously as she spoke, as though she wondered if there was anything on earth of which Amanda knew much. "When you asked me if she was like Georgia Wells I laughed because you're not the first person who's noticed the likeness. You were in the Tulip weren't you, when Ray Ramillies brought her in with those swallows in her hair? When I saw those two women together I laughed until I cried. Gaiogi Laminoff was so cross with me but I couldn't stop. There they were, the two of them, with Ramillies in the middle and Georgia with her new man. It was funny."

She laughed again at the picture recreated in her mind and Amanda echoed her, since it would have been impolite not to do so. Of all the band of personal traitors the sense of humour is the most dangerous. Mrs. Fitch's sense of humour disarmed her and made her careless.

"Oh, Lord, that was funny!" she said. "And that wasn't the only thing. I knew something else, you see. Don't you ever tell Georgia this because she doesn't know, only it does make the story. Long ago there was another man who was taken with Caroline because she looked like Georgia. That makes it funnier, doesn't it?''

She went off into paroxysms of laughter again and uncertainly Amanda laughed with her.

"I ought not to have told you that," said Mrs. Fitch, wiping her eyes before she poured herself another cup of tea, "but I happened to know Caroline long ago when she was a cloakroom attendant trying to get on the stage, and that night at the Tulip I was the only person who knew the other story. That's what made me laugh. Two men! Both Georgia's specials! It *is* funny."

"Who was the first man?"

"Oh, you wouldn't know him. He was long before your time. You were in the cradle when all that happened. Besides, he's dead now. He was a very stuck-up chap. Saw himself as a judge or something. Not at all Georgia's type, nor Caroline's either. But she could tell you something about him if she liked. She's a naughty girl."

She laughed again.

"Don't you repeat this, though. I don't know why I told you except that it was so funny. I've been dying to tell somebody."

"Was Ferdie amused?"

"Mr. Paul? Oh, I wouldn't tell him." Mrs. Fitch looked shocked but the sight of Amanda's face seemed to amuse her again. "There's a great difference between the things you tell men and the things you tell another woman. You'll have to learn that when you get married. Women think the same things are funny while men often don't see anything in them at all."

"Don't you like Georgia?" enquired Amanda innocently, still in quest of the joke.

"Yes, I do, as much as I like any actress." Mrs. Fitch was clearly truthful. "She's very clever. Did you see her in *The Little Sacrifice?* My dear, in that last scene, although it was so farfetched, she was wonderful. I had to sit in the theatre and wait till everyone else had gone. I couldn't go out into the foyer with my face. It was in a state. Georgia is an artist. I spotted her as a winner years before I met her up here."

She paused and added, as Amanda looked puzzled, "I used

to buy for the Old Beaulieu at one time. That's where I met Caroline.''

"Buy?"

"Yes. Linen. Silver. Electric-light bulbs. Novelties. It all has to be done you know. These places have to be looked after, the same as a house.''

"Of course they do. I never realised that.'' Amanda seemed astounded by the discovery and there was a brief pause in the conversation. A chiming clock in the hall struck the half-hour and Mrs. Fitch sighed.

"They'll be just taking off,'' she observed. "I do hope they have a good crossing. Your boy will be back by eleven. He looks strong.''

"Oh, very healthy,'' said Amanda heartily and hesitated, as the conversation seemed to have reached an impasse. "That's very important,'' she added heroically.

"It saves a lot of worry,'' murmured Mrs. Fitch. "You're always fidgeting if you feel they're not well.''

"Ferdie looks disgustingly fit.'' Amanda made the remark sound inconsequential.

"So he may, but all the same he's not strong.'' There was a new tenderness in the woman's voice which was unexpected and her lips moved soundlessly again. "Not really strong,'' she repeated. "He'll see Doctor Peugeot this time, I expect. He usually does. He's too clever and he works too hard. Think, think, think; that's all there is in his work. Some people imagine it doesn't take anything out of one, but it does. The brain uses blood just like the muscles do. It stands to reason.''

She spoke of Ferdie's mind as if it were an incomprehensible mystery to her and it occurred to Amanda that it probably was.

"Have you got a clever man?'' Mrs. Fitch was still misled by Amanda's youth and her tone was gently chaffing.

"Brilliant,'' said Amanda, who believed in taking a firm line.

Mrs. Fitch chuckled.

"Isn't that sweet?'' she said to no one in particular. "Go on believing that and you'll always be happy. Never see round your own man, that's the secret.'' She laughed again a little spitefully. "Even if you have to blind yourself.''

Amanda looked hurt and the other woman handed her the

biscuit tin. It was a conciliatory gesture and her stupid eyes were kind.

"Never mind. You won't have to worry about that sort of thing for a long time yet," she said, "if you ever do. But once you've met a really clever man he spoils you for everyone else."

Amanda said nothing but sat up digesting this piece of dubious information and nibbling her third biscuit.

"Oh, I hope they have a good trip," Mrs. Fitch repeated. "There *is* a clever man for you. Ferdie Paul is in a class by himself. If he told me to jump off the roof I'd know he was right."

Amanda looked up.

"Are you sure that's his brains or is it . . . ?"

She broke off delicately and the woman stared at her.

"No, my dear," she said with sudden sharpness. "It's his brains. There's no silly love stuff about me. I'm far too old a bird." She shook her head, stupidity and pride and a certain doggedness all apparent in her expression.

"I wonder if he's got to the coast yet," she added as she relaxed. "The weather report said 'fair.'"

Mr. Campion and Amanda spent the last hour of the evening driving slowly round the outskirts of the town, which were fresh after the rain.

"Gaiogi wasn't there," he said. "He's come to town and isn't expected back until late. I put Ferdie on the plane. I wondered why he was so pleased when we rang up. He hadn't much to tell about Miss Adamson except what I already knew. You seem to have been more successful. Suppose you repeat that conversation word for word as far as you can?"

Amanda lay in the Lagonda, her head resting on the back of the seat, and the street lamps shining on her triangular mouth as she talked. She made a very good job of her report cutting out only the extraneous matter.

"It was Portland-Smith, of course," she said. "Georgia simply couldn't have had two boy friends who wanted to be judges."

"One would seem to be enough."

Amanda stirred.

"Two women, two Georgias," she announced. "And two

men, Ramillies and Portland-Smith, both dead. It's funny, isn't it?''

"That depends on your sense of humour, my girl," said Mr. Campion. "It's frightening me to death. We'll find Miss Adamson tomorrow.''

But the following day an Essex constable made a discovery.

To the police a corpse is a corpse and murder is a hanging matter, and the whole affair slid out of the shrouding mists of the fashionable world and the gossip of the bridge clubs and came under the glare of a thousand bull's-eyes and the ruthlessly indelicate curiosity of the Press.

Chapter Sixteen

Superintendent Stanislaus Oates of the Central Investigation Department, New Scotland Yard, was one of those happy people who retain throughout their lives a childlike belief in a sharp dividing line between that which is wrong and that which is right. It is this peculiarity which is common to all the great English policemen and is probably the basis of their reputation both for integrity and for stupidity. In his thirty-five years in the force he had acquired a vast knowledge of the incredible weaknesses and perversities of his fellowmen, but, while these were all neatly tabulated in his pleasant country mind, his sense of what was black and what was white remained static and inviolate. He was a gentle man, quiet in speech and possessed of a charming yokel sense of fun, but in spite of this he was as hard, as clear-eyed, and therefore often as cruel, as a child of five.

Mr. Campion, who had known him for eleven years and was very fond of him, still paid him that respect which has a modicum of fear in it.

At a little after five on the day following Amanda's enlightening interview with Mrs. Fitch, Mr. Campion came up on the carpet in Oates's office. Although he was so well known to the superintendent his invitation to "step up for a few words" had been as formal as if he had never set his nose inside the place before, and he was conducted to the visitors' chair with considerable ceremony. He looked round him with quick interest. There was quite a gathering. Besides Oates himself, whose bony smile was even less expansive than usual, there was present Chief Detective Inspector Pullen, a great lump of a man with a squat nose and bright eyes who had spent much of his earlier service in the W Division and was one of the Yard's best bets of the year. He sat, solid and solemn, on the superintendent's right hand, looking, in his dark clothes and unnatural gravity, like a bearer at a funeral.

Detective Sergeant Flood was with him, Campion was relieved to see, but his face, which was kite-shaped, did not lighten as the visitor appeared.

A police stenographer sat in the background and they all four looked up silently as the lean man in the horn-rimmed spectacles came quietly in.

Mr. Campion surveyed the scene, his face amiably blank and a headmaster's-study feeling gripping the back of his neck.

"Well, who's been riding a bicycle without a reflector?" he said in a well-meaning effort to lighten the atmosphere.

Oates shook his closely cropped head at him.

"It's not a very nice business, Mr. Campion," he said. "It was good of you to come. Just one or two questions, if you don't mind."

Campion was familiar with the superintendent's brand of understatement and his eyebrows rose. "Not a very nice business" was unusually strong.

"Oh," he said cautiously. "What's up?"

Pullen glanced at his chief and cleared his throat.

"Mr. Campion," he said, "a young woman has been found dead in circumstances which suggest violence. In the back of a powder compactum in her handbag we found a slip of paper with some figures on it. The superintendent here recognised them as forming your telephone number, although only the first letter of the exchange was given. I will now read you a description of the deceased. If you think you recognise it I shall be compelled to ask you to come with me to view the body."

He had a curious, staccato delivery which was not unlike

the rattle of a tape machine and gave the official words an inhuman quality.

Mr. Campion preserved his famous half-witted expression. It was not quite so misleading as it once had been, since the last ten years had etched lines of character in his face, but it was still serviceable.

"Height five seven, slender build, eyes gray, hair very dark brown, hands and feet well cared for. Age at present doubtful, between twenty-five and thirty-five. Exceptionally well dressed."

Oates leant over the desk.

"That's tall for a woman," he said. "A tall dark girl with grey eyes who was very smart. I asked you to come round because I have a fancy that *was* your telephone number. Do you know her?"

"Yes," said Mr. Campion slowly. "Yes, I think I do. Hadn't she any other papers?"

"None at all. Not a card, not a letter, not a mark on her clothes. This scrap in the powder box may have been overlooked."

He was waiting expectantly and Mr. Campion hesitated. He knew from experience that complete openness is the only thing to offer the police once one is convinced that one's affairs are also their own, but while there is still a chance that things may not be as bad as that it is wisest not to awaken their insatiable curiosity.

"I'd like to see the body before I mention any name," he said.

"Naturally." Oates looked disappointed. "Perhaps you'd like to go along with the inspector now? The identification is holding us up," he continued, relapsing into a more natural manner for a moment. "We can't very well turn her over to Sir Henry until we get that done."

Mr. Campion stirred. Sir Henry Wryothsley, the eminent pathologist, was not called in for the obvious or mediocre.

Pullen heaved himself out of his chair.

"It's a little way out of town, I'm afraid, sir," he said. "Do you mind?"

"Not at all. How long is it going to take me?"

"It all depends on how much you know, my boy." Oates grinned as he spoke. "I think I'll come down with you if you don't mind, Pullen. If she does turn out to be a friend of Mr.

Campion's I may be able to give you a hand with him. He's a slippery witness."

There was general laughter at this, none of it ringing quite true, and Mr. Campion found himself checking up on dangerous points, considering Val's position, Gaiogi's and his own. He had time to notice that the inspector took his superior officer's co-operation in very good part. The two men had worked together for some years and were fortunate in possessing different faults and qualities. As he sat jammed in the back of a police car between the two of them he reflected that they made a formidable team and hoped devoutly that he was going to be on their side.

"It's technically an Essex crime," Oates remarked as they swung down the Embankment. "The corpse was found on a common at a little place called Coaching Cross. Where is it exactly, Inspector?"

"Half a mile off the Epping and Ongar main road."

Pullen rattled the words more cheerfully. In the open air, away from the official atmosphere of the Yard, both policemen seemed to have experienced a humanising change, a loosening of the belt, as it were, and there was even just a hint of the "outing" spirit in their smiles, but Mr. Campion was no more misled by them than they by him.

"It's hardly a common. More of a wood," the inspector continued more conversationally. "A sort of thicket. It's a bit of the old forest, I should say. It's full of brambles and hasn't done my trousers any good. I'm a London cop and my clothes aren't constructed for a cross-country beat. Still, the Essex police say it's a London crime and I think they're right. They called us in straight away, not but what an hour or so earlier wouldn't have hurt 'em."

"Anyway, it's our body from now on," Oates remarked complacently. "If they call us in within three days we pay the cost of the enquiry; if not, it's their county council's pigeon." He paused. "We're talking lightly and there's a poor girl lying dead. I hope we're not hurting you, Mr. Campion?"

The naïveté of the question was disarming and Campion smiled.

"No," he said. "No. If it turns out to be the girl I think it may be, I know her name and that's about all. She was a very beautiful person with a terrible voice."

"This young woman is good looking," said Pullen dubiously,

"but she hasn't much voice left, poor kid, with a damned great wound clean through her chest. It's a funny wound. I don't know if I've ever seen anything quite like it except once, and that was made by a sword. However, that's for Sir Henry to say."

The rest of the drive took place in comparative silence, both parties having indicated quite clearly just how far they were prepared to talk, but as soon as they entered the long cool room at the back of the police station at Coaching Cross Mr. Campion realised that the mischief was done. The canker had come to the surface. Now there was no hiding, no saving of faces nor guarding of reputations. The realisation thrust a little thin stab of alarm behind his diaphragm, but in the back of his mind he was aware of a sense of relief. The pseudo-Nemesis had slipped up at last. The hand of Providence so seldom has a knife in it.

The detective sergeant of the Essex constabulary, who had lifted the sheet from the sharp-angled mass on the table, looked at him enquiringly and he nodded.

It was Caroline Adamson. Rigour had set in before the body had been moved and she lay in a dreadful, unnatural attitude, with one knee a little bent and her spine curved. Her face lay on the sheet so that he had to stoop to see it properly. She was still beautiful, even with the greying flesh shrinking away from the cosmetics on her face and her long eyelashes stiff with mascara, and Mr. Campion who had never quite got over his early astonishment at the appalling waste when death comes too soon, drew back from her with pity.

"Do you recognise her?" Oates was touching his elbow.

"Yes," he said and was aware of a general sigh of relief from the assembled policemen. One more step in the enquiry had been accomplished.

There was an immediate adjournment to the Charge Room, where there was an embarrassment of important police officials. The Essex superintendent, who, etiquette demanded, should receive a place of honour, sat on Oates's right hand at the solid kitchen table which half filled the room. Pullen was beside him, while Flood and the Essex detective sergeant stood behind. A constable perched at the desk, pen in hand.

Mr. Campion sat on the other side of the table before this impressive array and gave Miss Adamson's name and a list of addresses where he had sought her without success.

Oates listened to him with his head a little on one side. He looked like a very old terrier at a promising rathole, and Mr. Campion spoke casually and with engaging candour.

"I didn't know the girl at all," he said. "I only had one conversation with her in my life and that was over the phone yesterday morning, but I'd seen her once when she was a mannequin at Papendeik's and once or twice at various restaurants."

"Yet you knew all these former addresses of hers?" Pullen sounded puzzled rather than suspicious.

"Yes, I'd been looking for her. I thought she might be able to give me a little information on a private matter."

Mr. Campion regarded the London superintendent steadily as he spoke, and Oates, who knew better than any man the advantage of having a willing witness, hurried on with routine questions. He had the statement finished in fifteen minutes and as soon as Campion had signed it the telephone wires began to buzz and purposeful detectives in London went off to make enquiries at the houses where Miss Adamson had lodged.

Oates had a word apart with Pullen and returned to Campion with an entirely unprecedented invitation to take a stroll down the road to see the scene of the discovery of the body.

"It's only a step," he said and added charmingly, "I know you're interested in these things. I've got full instructions. I think I'll find it. Pullen will be along in a moment. He wants a word with Sir Henry on the phone."

On a less uncomfortable occasion his guest might have been amused. Oates in tactful mood was delightfully unconvincing.

They avoided the loitering sight-seers and circumnavigated the Press, and as they walked down the narrow lane together, the flint dust eddying before them and the brown grasses nodding in the hedgerows, the air was warm and clear, soft and sweet smelling. The superintendent breathed deeply.

"If I hadn't been ambitious I might still be getting a lungful of this every night," he said unexpectedly. "This isn't Dorset but it's not bad. That's what getting on does for you.

Nowadays I never see a bit of uncut grass but what it leads me to a perishing corpse. What about this girl, Campion?"

"I've told you practically all I know." The younger man was speaking slowly. "She was once the hat and coat attendant at the Old Beaulieu. From there she went on the stage, where she was not successful. After that she got a job at Papendeik's where there was a spot of bother over a stolen design for a dress and she was sent down to Caesar's Court to show models there, While she was at the hotel she participated in a silly joke on a client and got the sack. This was about six weeks ago. Where she's been since then I cannot find out."

Oates trudged along in silence. His shoulders were bent and his hands were deep in his pockets rattling his money.

"Caesar's Court," he said at last. "Seems like I've heard that name before, quite recently." He pursed his lips, and Campion, glancing up, caught him peering at him out of the corners of his eyes. The superintendent laughed, drawing back his lips from his fine narrow teeth. "I'm a terrible one for a bit of gossip," he said. "It seems to me I heard a funny story about this lad who died in an aeroplane down at Caesar's Court. He died so pretty there wasn't an inquest nor anything. It was about him and his wife and a very clever lady who's the head of Papendeik's, a very clever, pretty lady. She's a sister of yours, isn't she?"

Mr. Campion's eyelids flickered and for a long time he said nothing at all. Oates walked along, jingling his money.

"It's not far down here," he remarked conversationally. "We're to look out for a turn to the left and a cop with a bike. I don't believe all I hear," he added as his companion made no comment. "When a man's safely buried, with a certificate backed by a P.M. report and nobody making any complaints, I know he died as naturally as makes no difference. I just happened to pick up a bit of high-class scandal which fixed it in my mind. That was all. Who was this dead girl exactly? Did she know Ramillies?"

"Yes. I'm afraid she did. She got the sack from Papendeik's when he dressed her up as his wife, whom she resembles, and took her to dine at the restaurant where Lady Ramillies was having supper after her show. Ramillies got hopelessly tight the night before he died and no one knew where he spent the hours between midnight and noon. I thought he might have been entertained by Caroline Adamson. That was why I looked for her."

"Oh." The superintendent seemed relieved. "That accounts for it. That covers the telephone number very nicely. It's funny how I stumble on things, isn't it? I never seem to forget a name. Faces often mislead you but names have a way of linking up. That 'Caesar's Court' stuck in my head. You can't call to mind anyone else who knew this girl besides the landladies at these addresses? Papendeik's, of course; they knew her. What about the Caesar's Court people?"

"That place is run by Mr. Laminoff," remarked Campion without expression.

"Laminoff." Oates turned the name over on his tongue. "Gaiogi Laminoff, a naturalised British subject. He used to run the Old Beaulieu."

"Did he?"

"He did." Oates wagged his head. "It's funny, I should have thought you would have known that, somehow," he said. "There's the footpath and there's our man with his bike. Good afternoon, Constable. Detective Superintendent Oates of the Central Division here. Can you take us along?"

As Mr. Campion stood on the bald path and peered over the superintendent's shoulder through a gap between two bramble bushes at the spot where Miss Adamson had been found, a distressing sense of travesty assailed him. The scene was the traditional *Midsummer Night's Dream* set. There was the overhanging oak tree, the lumpy bank, and even the wings of thorn for Moth and Mustardseed to vanish into, but here was none of the immortal wild thyme, the sweet musk roses nor the eglantine. This was a forest which three hundred years of civilisation had laid bald and waste. The brown grass was thin and there were roughnesses and threadbare patches which suggested that the coaching of Coaching Cross was motor coaching and the place had been frequented by untidier souls than sweet Bully Bottom and his company.

The constable indicated the position of the body and the sordid joke was complete. Unlike Titania, Miss Adamson had laid head downwards on the bank, one leg drawn up and her face cushioned on a tuft of soiled twitch.

The constable, who was a cheerful countryman, forgot his awe for the distinguished London detective after the first three stultifying minutes and presently so far forgot himself as to impart a circumstance which had been delighting his bucolic soul all day. The local detective, gathering clues, had removed at least two barrow-loads of waste paper, cigarette ends, used matches, cartons, tins and other delicacies which had lain defacing the clearing for the past three years. The constable also pointed out with some glee that the ground was so turrible hard it afforded no wheel or footmarks and was so trodden over at the best of times that any information which it might yield was practically certain to be misleading. Oates listened to him with a sad smile and a patience which made Campion suspect him until he realised that the old man was merely enjoying the country accent, and finally sent him back to his post with the gentlest of snubs.

"Poor chap, he's got too much sense of humour for a policeman," he remarked when the man was out of hearing. "He'll stick to his helmet and his bicycle for the rest of his days, lucky bloke."

He looked round him and indicated a fallen tree trunk which might have been a piece of sylvan loveliness had it not been for the remnants of a dozen picnic meals strewn around it.

"Have a sit-down," he suggested, wrapping his thin grey overcoat tightly round his haunches before perching himself uncomfortably upon the wood.

Mr. Campion took up a position beside him and waited for the ultimatum. It came.

"I've always found you a particularly honest sort of a feller." The superintendent made the announcement as if it were an interesting piece of information. "You've been very fair, I've always thought. Your dad brought you up nicely too."

"A proper little Boy Scout," agreed Mr. Campion helpfully. "If you are asking me in a delicate way if I am going to play ball with you or if I would rather not because I am afraid my sister may have murdered someone by mistake and I do not want to assist in her apprehension, let me say at once, as an old reliable firm with a reputation to maintain, I play ball. I did not know the young woman who is lying in your icebox, and what I knew of her did not amuse me particularly, but I don't associate myself with anybody who sticks a breadknife into any lady. I'm against him, whoever he is. I endorse your point of view in the matter. On the other hand, I do not want to be involved in a lot of unpleasant tittle-tattle or scandal in the daily press, nor do I want my innocent friends and relations to have that degrading experience either. Do I make myself clear?''

"Yes," said Oates. "Yes, you do." He was silent for some moments and sat looking at the yellow evening light on the treetops with apparent satisfaction. "Why did you say 'breadknife'?"

"Joke," explained his companion grimly. "Why?"

"It might have been a breadknife," said Oates seriously. "A thinnish breadknife. Still, that's conjecture." He showed no desire to rise but remained with his coat wrapped round him, staring down at his feet, and presently he began to talk about the case with a lack of official discretion which Mr. Campion fully appreciated without altogether enjoying it, since any deviation from routine in such a die-hard must have some specific purpose.

"The local bobby found the corpse when he came past here on a bicycle at ten minutes past eight this morning." Oates began slowly. "He was taking a short cut to a farm down here in connection with some foot-and-mouth regulations. Now I don't know if you've noticed this place, Campion, but it's not very secret, is it? It's simply the first piece of cover which a fellow would come to if he had taken a chance on a lonely turning off the main road."

"Arguing that the fellow who dumped the body need not have had any pre-knowledge of the district?"

"That's what I thought." The superintendent nodded his appreciation of his guest's intelligence. "As a matter of fact the choice of this particular place rather argues that he didn't know the village. Do you know what this is, Campion? This is the local sitting-out acre, the petting-party field. Every decent village has something of the sort. I remember when I was a boy down in Dorset there was a little wood above a disused quarry. Go down there after tea alone and you'd feel like the one child at the party who hadn't been given his present off the Christmas tree. The place was alive with boys and girls minding their own affairs. Now wouldn't that be a silly place to turn up to with a body? You'd walk into trouble the moment you set foot on the grass with a couple of witnesses behind every bush. No, I don't think our feller knew where he was at all. I think he saw a tree or two and

174

thought 'This'll do.' Pullen, who is a good man, saw that at once. He's got the local lads going round talking to country sweethearts now. That'll mean some delicate interviews. Well, that's one point. Then there's another. That girl was stabbed clean through the chest. Sir Henry said the heart was grazed, in his opinion, but he couldn't say for certain until he'd done his examination. We haven't found the weapon, yet she wasn't saturated with blood.''

He paused and cocked an enquiring eye at his companion.

"The sword, or whatever it was, was removed some time after death?''

"Looks like it, doesn't it? They're searching for it now but somehow I don't think they'll find it. If a murderer doesn't throw away the weapon within ten minutes of the crime he's a cool hand and that means we'll never find it like as not.''

The old detective was working up to his argument and Campion listened, fascinated by the placid common sense which is the essence of all good police work.

"Then there's the question of rigour." Oates sounded contemptuous. "I don't trust it. I've known it have some amazing vagaries. But we can't afford to ignore it. Rigour is now well advanced and there's no sign of it abating. That shows the chances are a hundred to one that she's not been dead thirty hours yet. So say the crime took place after one o'clock midday yesterday. She was wearing a black silk dress and a small fur cape. It didn't look to me like a morning getup. It was the kind of outfit you might go to a cinema in.''

Mr. Campion blinked intelligently.

"Had rigour set in before she was put on the bank?''

"No, after. That's the expert opinion.''

"So she must have been brought here within six hours of death?''

"There's no must about it, my lad, and don't you forget it." Oates sounded irritable. "We can only say that the probability is that it was round about six hours after. Yet rigour was well advanced when she was found at eight o'clock. Therefore it's fairly certain that she was killed before 2 A.M. at the latest. As we see it the poor thing was murdered somewhere, probably in London, and the weapon was left in the wound for a time, thus staunching the blood flow. Then, some little time later, say within six or seven hours at least, she was brought down here by car and dumped and the weapon removed. She was wearing high-heeled black patent shoes, when she was found and these were grazed on top of the toes, indicating that she'd been carried face forward, with her legs sprawling behind her. There was also a smear on one of her stockings which looked to me like oil. None of this is proved of course; the whole thing is pure conjecture; but that's how we see it at the moment. You follow where that takes us?''

"Nowhere at all," said Mr. Campion cheerfully, his pale eyes belying his tone.

Oates grunted.

"It takes us to *you,* mate," he said bluntly. "It takes us back to you and your pals, and you know that better than anyone. We've got to go over that girl's immediate past with a magnifying glass and we've got to have a chat with everyone who knew her. It's the motive that's going to put us on to our man and that's what we're after. That's plain speaking, isn't it?''

"Almost homely," agreed Mr. Campion absently. "I've told you all I can, I think. There's one trivial little thing which may be interesting. It's only an impression but they're sometimes useful. I don't think she was alone when she phoned me yesterday.''

"An accomplice?''

"I don't know. An audience, anyway. She hadn't her entire mind on me.''

The superintendent was interested.

"There you are," he said. "That's corroboration. This isn't an ordinary knifing. I said that to Pullen as soon as I heard the details. In the normal way, when a good-looking young woman gets herself stabbed it's a perfectly straightforward human story, but this is different. This is what I call number-one murder. It's an honest, done-on purpose killing for a reason. There was no 'Gawd-I-love-you—take-that' about that stab. Do you know, her dress was rolled down neatly off her shoulders and the weapon inserted as carefully as if she'd been on an operating table. Not torn down, mind you, but rolled.''

Mr. Campion stared at him in natural astonishment at this bewildering piece of information.

"What was she doing while all this was happening?''

"The Lord alone knows." Oates shook his bowler hat over

the mystery. "I tell you, Campion, the poor thing was barely untidy. Her hands weren't torn and there wasn't another mark on her skin. She hadn't defended herself at all. I've never seen anything quite like it." He hesitated and laughed because he was embarrassed at the fancifulness of his own thoughts. "There's a sort of inhuman quality about that killing," he said. "It's almost as if it had been done by a machine or the hand of fate or something. Where are you going?"

Mr. Campion had risen abruptly. His face was expressionless and he held his shoulders stiffly.

"That is a very unpleasant thought," he said.

"It's foolishness. I don't know what possessed me to say such a thing." Oates seemed genuinely surprised at himself. "I'm getting lightheaded in this country air; that's about it. Well, if he's Dracula himself we'll get him and hang him up by his neck until he's learnt his lesson, and I warn you, Campion, there'll be a lot of questions asked around your part of the world."

"I can see that."

"So long as you know." Oates was avuncular. "I'm taking you at your word," he pointed out. "You're working with us. You've never been foolish yet and I don't suppose you will be this time."

"I'm glad to hear it." Campion spoke with mild indignation. "If I may say so without offence, your rustic personality has been ruined by your association with the police. This perpetual 'I know you're a little gentleman because I've got my beady eye on you' embarrasses me. I don't want to shield any murderer. I'm not anti-social. I'm against murder on principle. I think it's unethical and ungentlemanly and also unkind."

"That's all right," said Oates. "But don't forget it. That's all I'm saying."

"I shall probably visit my sister tonight."

"Why shouldn't you?"

"Why indeed? I'm only mentioning it in case you have me tailed and your suspicious nature suspects conspiracy."

The superintendent laughed.

"It's not that I don't trust you, but I wish you were in the force," he said.

"In other words you don't doubt my honour, but you wish

it was a fear of my losing my pension," commented Mr. Campion with acerbity. "You embarrass and disgust me."

Oates was still grinning, the tight skin shining on the bones of his face.

"So long as that's all I've got to do, it won't hurt," he said piously. "Do you know the party you fancy I may come after?"

"No. If I did I should tell you. Can't you see I'm not afraid that you may make an arrest? It's the dust you'll kick up snouting round the rabbit burrows which is my concern."

Mr. Campion seemed to have lost some of his composure and his friend was sympathetic.

"We'll come on tiptoe," he promised.

Campion regarded him affectionately.

"The patter of your little boots will sound like a regiment of cavalry," he said. "Rest assured I'll do everything I can. Frankly, I want this man quite as much as you do."

"Oh, you do, do you? What for?"

"A question of personal affront," said Mr. Campion with deep feeling.

Oates eyed him thoughtfully.

"You were at Caesar's Court when that fellow Ramillies died so suddenly and so naturally, weren't you?" he observed. "And you found the body of that young lawyer fellow who shot himself? He was engaged to the present Lady Ramillies at one time, if I remember. You've got no particular party in mind, you say?"

"No. No one. It may be a Malignant Fate for all I know."

Mr. Campion glanced down the footpath. Inspector Pullen was striding towards them. His heavy face was animated, for once, and the skirts of his dust coat were flapping.

"You have—The Hired Help," said Campion with feeling. "He's got something."

The inspector was delighted. Satisfaction oozed from him.

"Important new development," he announced with a rattle like a machine gun.

"Let's have it. Never mind Mr. Campion; he's going to be very useful."

Pullen opened his small eyes but he did not demure. His news was bursting from him.

"Sergeant Jenner of the local force has found a witness," he said joyfully. "She's a girl who works in the all-night carmen's café on the main road. Her boy's a milk lorry driver from Eye and apparently he's been in the habit of speeding up his schedule to get half an hour or so extra with this little miss. She can't be eighteen. (I don't know what these country girls are coming to.) Anyway, he got in here at one-thirty last night and hadn't to get to town before four, so she fetched him a meal and then they walked down here. She's going to point out the place where they were sitting. As far as I can make out it's over there behind the tree. About twenty to three, or thereabouts, because her boy was talking of having to get on to London, they heard a car stop in this lane and then there was a lot of movement behind them. The young-sters minded their own business and the girl actually saw nothing, but the young man got up, she says, and looked over a briar hedge. She doesn't know what he saw and no doubt it wasn't anything very sensational, but anyway he sat down again and said, as far as she can remember, 'They've gone.' Then she heard the car go off again and they said good night and walked back. This morning when she heard of the crime she was frightened because of the boy friend's schedule irregularities, but when Jenner put it to her direct she came out with it. We're getting on to the boy now. With luck he saw whoever it was who dumped the body. The whole thing may be in the bag within twenty-four hours.''

"I wonder,'' said Oates and added slyly, glancing at Campion, "Don't you leave London. There may be another description for you to identify. Can you see our Nemesis fellow in a bag?''

Mr. Campion said nothing. The familiar stab behind his diaphragm was disturbing and he caught his breath.

"Nemesis?'' said Inspector Pullen with disgust. "He's a two-legged Nemesis, if you ask me, and if he has two legs the chances are he also has a neck.''

Chapter Seventeen

Val and Mr. Campion were in the studio at Papendeik's; not the little office, which was only a semiprivate apartment, but the great studio at the top of the house, which was a holy of holies and looked to Mr. Campion's inexperienced eyes like the inside of a woman's handbag magnified. It seemed to contain everything except a bath, although there certainly was a businesslike sink in one corner of the room, besides a remarkable assortment of tables, cupboards, mirrors and mysterious boxes.

They had chosen this place for conversation partly because it was secret and partly because there was a gas fire and, although it was midsummer, the night was chilly.

Miss McPhail, Val's secretary, who spent her life guarding this sanctuary, had gone home, but Rex was still about in spite of the time, and the three of them were alone in the great house. Val had come back from her little Queen Anne bandbox in Hampstead at her brother's request and they had found Rex still working when they arrived a little after ten. Georgia was expected after her show and they were waiting for her.

Campion sat on the edge of a solid wooden table before the fire directly under a hanging daylight bulb. The rest of the room was in shadow, and the hard, unnatural glare shone down on his dark back and bent head.

Val walked about the room. Her dress was the bright, clear green of cooking apples and she looked young but very brave and capable, with her fine hands clasped behind her and her chin set.

Rex leant against the mantelshelf. He held a small square of chestnut velvet and was playing with it absently, feeling the yielding quality of the material and trying the light on it as he laid it on his arm. It was very quiet in the room and still cold.

"I remember her at the Old Beaulieu," Rex remarked without looking up. "She was very attractive. Not chic, never any class, but a *piece*. Well worth looking at. Her father was Gaiogi Laminoff's accountant. His name was Wilfred Adamson. He died before she left. That was early in '33, I think. Gaiogi Laminoff did what he could for her. He got Ferdie Paul to give her a little part on tour, and I know one September—it must have been that same year—she was hanging round the agents, very sorry for herself."

"Gaiogi didn't take her back?" enquired Campion curiously.

"No, he was shutting the Beaulieu and looking about for capital to start the Poire d'Or." Rex was still speaking in an absent fashion as if he were working round to a point and wondering whether to make it. Mr. Campion, who was liable to moments of irrelevant observation, suddenly saw him objectively, a natty, demure little soul, only effeminate insomuch as sex shocked him for its ugliness and interested him because it shocked him.

He went on talking, still stroking the scrap of material on his cuff.

"Then she came into money," he said. "I don't know if there was a man or not, but for quite a bit she was running round with the dancing boys and driving about in a little car. She even bought one of our models. I used to see her quite a bit. She never said where she got the cash but she certainly had it."

Mr. Campion looked up sharply, enlightenment on his thin face.

"That was in 1934, the year Portland-Smith disappeared?"

Rex raised his head, and his eyes, which were doggy and harassed in the usual way, now had a flicker of excitement in them.

"Yes," he said. "He went off on June the eighteenth. I've always remembered that; it's the anniversary of Waterloo. Caroline Adamson had plenty of money, but long before then. It was early spring when she came round here for a model and she'd had it some time then. I noticed her particularly. She chose a very lovely grey moire which Madame admired and which passed over the heads of the buyers. It's only three years ago. She was broke again early the next autumn, when Gaiogi Laminoff recommended her. She was a good model but not a pleasant girl. She was very bitter about Gaiogi, although he did so much for her. He was having trouble of his own then. The Poire d'Or opened in April or May of '34 and Bjornson had let Laminoff in by that crash of his by the January; it had been coming some time."

"I thought Gaiogi was only the manager of the Poire d'Or?" put in Val, who had paused behind the table.

"No. He had money in it. Bjornson never put up all the money for anything. Besides, I knew Bud Hockey, who was running the music there, and I remember he told me that Laminoff was down for a packet. I know I wondered where the old man had got it from because there was no squeal. His backer, if he had one, was very quiet."

There was a long silence while everybody digested this information.

"You think it was Gaiogi's own money?" said Val at last.

Rex shrugged his shoulders and twisted the velvet into a rosette, holding it at arm's length to admire the effect.

"It looked like it, madame. But he had none when the Beaulieu closed. There was a little gossip about it at the time; nothing exciting, just speculation." He laughed at Campion shyly. "One talks about money," he said. "It's the other subject."

Mr. Campion considered the discovery and Val cut into his thoughts with another of the tag phrases from their childhood.

"There's no proof, but I've lost a ha'penny and you're eating nuts," she remarked.

He nodded. Portland-Smith had shot himself in June and Miss Adamson had been well supplied with money since the previous winter. After the shooting she had become poor again. He did not say the words aloud, but Val, he knew, was following his thought. As with many people of one blood, there was a curious, wordless communion between them which might have been telepathy or an identically similar mental process.

"I didn't know she knew him," said Val.

"Caroline Adamson and Portland-Smith?" Rex hesitated over the names. "I don't know that she did but I think she did. It's merely an impression; something to do with a joke about her being so like Georgia Wells. I can't remember it at all. I doubt if I ever really heard it. It wasn't much, I know; only snack-bar talk."

"You're quite the little gossip, Rex, aren't you?" Val was amused. "A little bit here, a little bit there. It all tells up."

The man wriggled and giggled coyly and his face flushed.

"I've got a very good memory," he said primly. "Besides, I like to know what's going on. But I never put two and two together; it's too disturbing."

An electric bell over the door began to vibrate and Val hurried across the room.

"There she is," she said. "No, Rex, thank you. I'll go down myself. I want to."

The little man bowed elaborately and held the door open for her. His every movement was self-consciously gallant and there was a nervous, chuckling effrontery behind his manner which was quite out of keeping with this or any other situation. He came back to the mantelpiece to pick up his piece of velvet. It lay, a dark pool, on the white ledge, and as his hand hovered over it he suddenly drew back. Then, controlling himself, he took up the scrap and threw it into a wastepaper basket.

"She was stabbed, wasn't she?" he said. "That velvet reminded me. It's very lovely material. Very soft and beautiful to drape. But I don't care for it. Dried blood is that colour, you know. I saw a lot of it in France."

"In France?" Mr. Campion was surprised. The notion of the ladylike Rex as a warrior was incongruous.

" 'Fourteen to '17." Rex spoke briskly. "The Somme and the Marne. I was a Tommy. I never got a commission. It was a long time ago but it cured me of all kinds of things. I've never put up with ugliness or discomfort since. I shall advise Madame against the velvet. All this plum and magenta which is so popular is a great pity, I think. It was the Coronation which introduced it, of course, but I still don't like it. It doesn't make *me* think of royalty."

He giggled again and smoothed his hair.

"Laminoff had some peculiar experiences in Russia, I believe. He doesn't talk about them, but he went back during the Revolution and only came through with his life. He can't stand ugliness either. Have you noticed? Everything has to be easy, delicate and elegant. He'll do anything for it. When the Poire d'Or was actually smashing he wouldn't give up the orchid on each table. Money for its comfort's sake means more than a lot to him."

He glanced at his neat wrist watch, which was gold and very delicate without being at all womanish.

"Beddy-byes," he said unexpectedly. "I shan't be home till midnight. I don't know if I've been of any use. It's only gossip, as Madame says. I don't know anything unpleasant. I don't really want to. Good night."

He giggled again and went out, adroitly avoiding the visitor by thirty seconds.

Georgia was not alone. Campion heard Ferdie Paul's excited squeak before the party reached the second floor. He came in a little in advance of the others, a great wave of nervous energy sweeping into the room with him.

"My God!" he said. "My God, what a schemozzle! One damned thing on top of another!" He sat down on a wooden chest and pulled out a cardboard packet of cigarettes, lighting one from it and pitching the spent match into the furthest corner of the room.

Georgia came in with Val. She was at her loveliest, in a black dress of some soft, transparent material draped over her bosom and flowing out into soft baby frills round the hem and train of the skirt. She looked graceful, womanly and, in some inexplicable way, pathetically bereft.

"Oh, darling," she said to Campion. "Oh, darling. How incredibly depressing. I've had a policeman in my dressing room and Ferdie's had two; one at the plane and one at the flat. What a slut of a girl!"

"Damn it, you can't blame her," said Ferdie from the background. "It's not her fault. She's simply the person who fell through the hole in the floor. She was a good look, too. It's a pity."

He spoke with real regret, no doubt at the thought of beauty wasted.

Georgia sat down on the table close to Campion.

"Two deaths," she said huskily. "Two. But I'm not superstitious. I won't be superstitious. What are we going to do? What exactly does it mean to us?"

Everyone looked at Campion, who bestirred himself.

"It's an awkward position," he said slowly, thinking that it would have been easier for Val and himself to tackle Georgia on the delicate matter which they had met to discuss if a fourth party had not been present. "You see, once the police get hold of a case like this they're so infernally thorough. Everyone who knew Miss Adamson will be cross-examined for days by earnest detectives trying to sound as though they had just dropped in to talk about string. In the end they'll find out every mortal thing the wretched girl has said and done during the last six months. That doesn't matter much, of course. I promised them I would give them any information I came across, and I shall, as anyone else would. But whereas it doesn't matter what they find out if it's relevant, they may so easily get on to all kinds of things which are nothing to do with the case and which, although not criminal, have their awkward aspects. These may make the good dicks red herrings and land us all with a kettle of fish.''

He paused. Ferdie Paul was looking at him with his head a little on one side and a slightly derisive smile, which was tolerant rather than contemptuous, on his curly mouth.

"Exactly!'' he said. "Exactly, my dear boy. And so what?''

"It's about me,'' said Val, coming forward with sudden determination. "It's no good being vague and lawyer-like, Albert. You must say the words in a case like this. Now look here, Georgia my pet, you must not go telling the police that story about me and the cachet blanc. It's a good yarn and amusing and all the rest of it and it doesn't matter who else you tell it to, because everyone we know will see it as you see it and realise that you don't really mean that it's true. But the police may take it seriously and we don't want them going all hysterical and applying for exhumation orders and that sort of thing, do we? It isn't as though they could find anything, we know. There was a P.M. at the time, thank God, but there would be a frightful row which would ruin us both professionally.''

Ferdie Paul, who had been sitting admiring his feet throughout this eminently straightforward statement, now glanced up.

"You're a good girl, Val,'' he said. "A sensible girl and a damned good sort to take it like that. I told you, Georgia, that story was stark lunacy at the time.''

Georgia put her arm round Val. It was a long, slow movement, and laying her dark head gently against the apple-green dress, she allowed two tears, and only two, to roll slowly down her cheeks. It was exquisite, the most abject, expressive and charming apology Campion had ever seen. Georgia seemed to think it was pretty good, too, for she brightened perceptibly for an instant before resuming her mood.

"I didn't realise it,'' she said earnestly. "I've got a blind spot. I didn't see it. That story has got me into terrible trouble, Val, more than you'll ever know, so I have been punished. But if it wasn't for you I'd be almost glad. If it hadn't been for that silly story I'd never have realised something rather awful that was happening to me. Now at least I'm sane again.''

She paused.

"And my darling is dead," she said in her breath, but with a tragic depth of feeling which startled them all by its staggering sincerity.

"Who's dead?" said Val sharply.

Georgia stared at her in genuine bewilderment.

"Ray," she said. "Oh, my dear, you haven't forgotten him so soon? He was the only man I ever really loved and when he died I didn't realise it. I don't want to talk about it or I shall make a fool of myself. Forgive me."

She blew her nose on a little white handkerchief and smiled through her tears.

Ferdie sat looking at her with professional admiration. Then he glanced at the other two and laughed.

"She's a dear girl isn't she?" he said, not without a certain pride. "That's very sweet, Georgia, but get the main idea. Don't tell the police fairy stories, even if you believe them. Val's absolutely right. This thing could make one hell of a stink if the Press decided to risk it, which they might, of course. I don't know. What do you think, Campion? Oh, Lord, what a mess! How long will the police keep at this thing?"

"Until they find out how the girl died." Mr. Campion seemed to consider the question superfluous. "The longer it takes the more ground they'll cover. They're a fairly efficient machine."

"I know." Ferdie was disgusted. "They went along to the flat and frightened Anna Fitch out of her wits. She told them where I was and they met me on the landing ground. Poor old Bellairs was in the plane, too, and he came in for it as well. Among other things we told them when we left, where we stayed in Paris, and who I'd seen during the day. I was convinced they thought I'd done it at least. Then I told them all I could remember about the blasted girl, which wasn't a lot. Apparently Anna had the same questions and so did Georgia. Two o'clock in the morning seems to be the fatal hour. I don't like to think how the girls got on, but I had a nice clean tale to tell for once in my life. Bellairs and the pilot and I were eating respectably at the Bouton." He paused. "They asked me a lot of questions about Gaiogi. Did you put them on to him?"

Mr. Campion blinked before the implied reproach.

"She was last employed at Caesar's Court. Val's had the police round here about her. You employed her too."

"Oh, I see. Of course." Ferdie sighed. "It's bad," he said. "Thunderingly bad. Lousy. However you look at it. She was running round with Ray, you know, Georgia."

"I know." Georgia's voice was very small and quiet. "I know. That was my fault. I was infatuated with Alan Dell. That was a nightmare, a dreadful insane sort of dream. I neglected Ray horribly—don't remind me of it, Ferdie; I've been terribly punished—and he was brokenhearted and picked up that little beast because she was vaguely like me. That's all there was to that."

"Very likely," agreed Ferdie grimly, "but it's very unfortunate in view of everything, isn't it, *dear*?"

Georgia responded to the implied rebuke.

"Must you be brutal, Ferdie?"

"Darling, it's the coincidence." Val spoke with the dogged patience which the other woman seemed to inspire in her. "And it's not only that, either. There's another coincidence which may come out, isn't there? There's nothing in them. For God's sake don't think I mean that. But Caroline knew Portland-Smith too, didn't she?"

Ferdie's shiny eyes opened to their widest extent.

"Did she indeed?" he ejaculated. " 'Strewth! Where did that come from, Val?"

"Rex told me. He seemed to think there was a sort of tale about it at the time. He was very vague but that's the kind of thing the police get hold of. If they're going to ferret out everything we may as well be prepared for it."

Georgia laughed. She seemed unaccountably flattered.

"I never heard that," she said, "but it's quite possible. My dears, that girl was *like* me. That's why you let her model my frocks, Val. If a man was terribly miserable because I'd been a cat to him it was quite natural if he tried to console himself with someone who reminded him of me. Surely the police could see an elementary point like that?"

Mr. Campion, who was listening to the scene with interest, considered Superintendent Oates and wondered.

"I know, Georgia, I know." Val was helpless. "But, dearest, *they're all dead*."

"I say, you know, I say, Georgia! I say! It's bad." Ferdie Paul rose as he spoke and strayed down the room with a peculiar jaunty gait which he adopted when excited. "Shattering publicity if it came out. For God's sake don't go talking about cachets blanc and what not. Look here, the whole thing is nothing to do with you or Val. Let 'em talk to me and Campion. Where were you last night, Campion?"

"Driving round the houses with Amanda."

"Were you? I suppose that's fairly conclusive. I like that kid. Good class is attractive when it's genuine, isn't it? Oh well, then, you're all right. So am I. I've got a blameless twenty-four hours and no extraneous odds and ends to hide, for a change. We'll talk to the police, then. You lie low, Georgia, and don't try to tell any bobby what men will do in love. It's over his head."

Georgia smiled at him affectionately.

"Common old Ferdie," she observed. "My dear, I'm not a lunatic. I may have been a little insane just lately but I've snapped out of it. I've told Val I'm sorry, or at least I've conveyed that I am, and she's forgiven me. The cachet was a silly little bit of nonsense we've both forgotten. That's over. Now none of us has anything to worry about, have we?"

Mr. Campion coughed. There was unusual determination on his face and his eyes were cold.

"I'm afraid it's not quite so simple," he said decisively, turning to Georgia. "There is one other matter which I think we ought to mention while we're about it. It's not my affair but it may come up, and if it does you must be ready for it. The police will find out everything remotely connected with Caroline Adamson. They're certain to discover that she was thought to have known Portland-Smith when he was engaged to you. That's all right, I know, but in the course of their investigations they may stumble on another fact which might make them curious. You were married to Portland-Smith, weren't you?"

The effect of the question was startling. The whole room, with its hard, unnatural light and black-shadowed corners, seemed to contract round the girl in the black dress and round Ferdie Paul, arrested in his walk behind her.

Georgia did not move a muscle. She sat looking at Campion and the colour rushed into her face as if she had been a baby, while her grey eyes were guilty and appalled.

Ferdie Paul's reaction was less restrained. For an instant his plumpish face, with its rococo curves and contours, was frozen with astonishment. Then he leapt forward and took the woman by the shoulder.

"You weren't? My God!"

He conveyed that his particular deity was insane.

"Georgia, you trollop! Why didn't you tell me? When did you marry him? When? Out with it. When? My blessed girl, don't you see how this is going to look?"

There was ferocious urgency in his thin voice and he shook her, unconsciously digging his fingers into her shoulder. Georgia pulled herself away and rubbed the place. She looked utterly pathetic and as guilty as an accused puppy.

"When?" Ferdie repeated mercilessly.

"One lovely rainy April day." The infuriating words tinkled in the quiet room.

"The year he vanished?"

"No. We were married fifteen months, the most miserable months of my life."

"Oh, for God's sake!" said Ferdie Paul.

He sat down heavily on the edge of the table and began to whistle. Georgia went over to him.

"*He* insisted on it being a secret," she protested. "It was his career. Apparently if you're going to be a county court judge the stage is still a bit low to marry into."

"Is it? What was the idea? Was he going to keep you under the dresser all his life?"

"No. When he became this judge person I was going to leave the stage. It was the getting there that might have been mucked up. Besides, we had money to think of."

"Really? You astound me."

Georgia ignored him. She was looking over his head, a half smile on her lips.

"It may sound silly now, but that was the argument at the time," she said. "It seems mad at this distance. Utterly mad. I was so hopelessly in love, Ferdie. He was such a sweet prig. I'd never met anything like him before. He was so secretive, all pompous and shut up inside himself and gloriously narrow and conventional. It was the same thing you like in Alan, Val. You get so sick of it when you're married to it. But at first it was like a heavenly closed door, all stern and secret and mysterious."

"We'll imagine it," said Ferdie.

"Forgive me, but I don't see why you actually married the poor mysterious beast." Mr. Campion put the question diffidently.

"Why does one marry?" Georgia appealed to him for information.

"I know." A dreadful travesty of a sentimental smile spread over Ferdie's face. "So you could have a dear little baby."

Georgia eyed him. "No," she said. "Not necessarily. Look here, Ferdie, you and Val and everybody, you don't understand. I really love them. My whole life is controlled by them. I see everything from their point of view. I love them. I want to *be* them. I want to get into their lives. I'm quite sincere, Ferdie. At the time I'm terribly, desperately hurt. I can't stop it. I'm just the same as any little servant girl helplessly in love for the first time, but *it wears off.*"

She hesitated, looking at them, her beautiful dark face earnest and her eyes imploring.

"It's because I'm a natural actress, of course," she continued, revealing that odd streak of realism which made her lovable. "When I've made a character I've made it and she's done. She's finished. She bores me unbearably. Val, you understand. You've made some divine gowns but you wouldn't wear any one of them for the rest of your life. I can't help it. It's my tragedy. When I feel morbid I wonder if I myself exist at all."

Ferdie regarded her. He seemed wearier and heavier. Only his eyes were animated.

"Don't worry," he said dryly. "You exist." He thrust out an arm and pulled her to his side holding her there as if she were an obstinate child. "You're obsessed by contracts," he observed. "That's your complex. It's got its basis in ordinary inbred female funk. I don't blame you. But if you must sign documents think about them first. A marriage certificate isn't quite the same as a Guild contract. The time clause is different."

Georgia freed herself and walked slowly round the room, her black dress rippling over her strong, slender thighs.

Ferdie was silent for some time. He sat on the edge of the table, his head bowed, so that the inadequacy of his dark curling hair was revealed. He was thinking, and it occurred to Mr. Campion that he had never seen a man think more obviously. The man's brain was almost audible.

"Hey," Ferdie said suddenly, "how the hell did you know?"

He swung round and sprawled across the table, looking up into Georgia's face.

"What?"

"How did you know that you were free to marry Ray Ramillies? Portland-Smith's body's only just been found."

Georgia shied away from him and from the question, but he caught her and pulled her round to face him. There was a tremendous force in the man and his incredulity was so great that they were all as conscious of it as if it had been their own.

"Did you know he was dead?"

"Not exactly—I mean of course I knew. You're hurting me, you fool. I thought he must be."

"You thought he must be!" Ferdie scrambled off the table and stood before the girl, peering into her eyes as if they were keyholes. "Are you telling me that for all you knew you might have been committing bigamy? You're insane, woman. You're mad. You ought to be locked up. You're sex crazy. A nymphomaniac. You're *barmy*! You must have known."

Georgia covered her face with her hand and managed to convey the tragically adventurous innocence of an Ibsen heroine.

"I believed what Ray told me."

"Ray?" This development was a surprise to Mr. Campion and he glanced up sharply. But he had no need to question. Ferdie pounced on the admission.

"What did he know about it? He was present at the suicide, I suppose, egging the wretched chap on."

"Don't, Ferdie, don't!" It was a cry from the heart and Georgia turned to Val for support. Val submitted to the considerable weight upon her shoulder and took the quivering hand in her own.

"This is all too emotional, my children," she said, the quiet authority of her voice surprising herself a little. "Everybody sit down. Now, Georgia, you'll have to explain this. What happened?"

Seated on a hard chair, with her lovely rounded elbows resting on the worktable, in her black dress, tears in her eyes and a foil in apple-green beside her, Georgia evidently felt

191

stronger. She raised her head and the hard light gave her black hair a blue depth and darkened the shadows beneath her eyes.

"I married Richard Portland-Smith in April 1933," she said slowly. "You know how I loved him. I've told you that. We were going to keep it a secret until we could afford to announce it and I could leave the stage. It was a ridiculous, idealistic programme and it failed. We lived apart and met in sordid hole-and-corner ways, stole week ends and did all the things that are absolutely fatal. Gradually we got on each other's nerves and by the end of the year we both realised it was a horrible, unbearable mistake. In September you put on *The Little Sacrifice*, Ferdie, and when I played that part I realised for the first time what real unhappiness means. I was caught, I was trapped. My lovely, lovely life was spoilt. I'd ruined it and there was no escape ever."

"Ramillies was over here then, wasn't he?" Ferdie made the remark without spitefulness.

"It wasn't only Ray." Georgia leapt to her own defence with childlike eagerness. "It wasn't. I'd say if it was. I'm not ashamed of love. It's a beautiful thing that one simply can't help. Ray and I did fall in love at first sight but I was desperately, helplessly miserable before. Richard was fantastically jealous and mean about it. He was petty and disgusting. He listened at doors, even, and got possessive and revolting. I begged him to let me divorce him, or even to divorce me, but he wouldn't. His filthy career came first every time. I can't tell you what it was like. He went off in October for one of his walking tours and the relief of being without him was like kicking off a pinching shoe. Ray was so very sweet. He was going back in a few weeks and he spent most of his leave hanging round the theatre. I loved him. He was so strong and happy and extroverted. When Richard came back he really had become impossible. He'd got parsimonious suddenly and was narrower than ever. After a while I began to realise the dreadful truth. He was going off his head. It must have been in his blood all the time and being piqued brought it out."

She passed her hand over her forehead and her eyes were pained and sincere.

"We had fantastic rows, dozens of them. It was unspeakably sordid and degrading. He used to try to make me jealous. It was so piteous. I never actually saw him with Caroline Adamson but he used to rave about women, reviling the whole sex and generally behaving more and more like a lunatic. I bore it as well as I could but it made life impossible. I was physically frightened of him. The subject of divorce sent him into a ferment. He wouldn't even hear the word. Finally I was so utterly miserable that I went to a firm of private detectives in Rupert Street, but they couldn't find a thing. Apparently he really was insane, and simply worked all day and lived on sardines. He sacked his servant and lived like a hermit. There's a name for that sort of mental trouble. Melancholia, or dementia praecox, or something. Meanwhile the detectives were horribly expensive and quite useless, and at last in despair I called them off. And then, in June, quite suddenly, Richard disappeared. I couldn't believe it at first. I went about like a child crossing my fingers and praying that he'd never come back. I had *suffered*, Val."

The other girl looked down at her and there was a bewildered expression in her eyes.

"She had, you know," she said to Ferdie Paul. "She really had."

He met her glance and a faint smile passed over his curly mouth.

"Astounding, isn't it?" he agreed. "Go on, Georgia. I believe you're doing your best. Don't lie. Let's have the full strength."

Georgia shook her head.

"You don't know me, Ferdie," she said tolerantly. "I couldn't lie about Ray. That was my real love affair. When he came back I knew that this was the true thing. It was about six weeks after Richard had gone and I was still quivering in case he came back. Ray walked into my dressing room one night and stood looking at me. You remember how he used to stand, all lean and exciting and sort of gallant. We didn't speak. It just happened. I cried all over him. I was so—so happy."

Ferdie Paul chuckled involuntarily, and, half shamefacedly, because she was heart-rendingly sincere, they joined him.

"What a life you have!" he said. "Then what?"

"He wanted to marry me at once, of course." Georgia ignored the interruption. She was used to being misunderstood. "So I did, of course. I held him off as long as I could and then I saw it was no use, so I had to tell him everything."

"This was all after Portland-Smith had disappeared? You're sure of that?"

"Ferdie, I am not lying. My dear, can't you see I'm not? I'm being wonderfully frank. I'm telling you the absolute, literal truth. I'm not sparing myself. This is what actually happened. It was November when I told Ray I was married to Richard—on Guy Fawkes night as a matter of fact. I remember, because we'd had a party for little Sinclair, who was silly and didn't like it. Ray was adorable with him, and I suddenly saw what home life could be with them both, and it was too much for me altogether. I told Ray and he was kinder than I can possibly describe. He simply laughed in that slightly devilish way he had and said I wasn't to worry."

She pressed her handkerchief to her lips and shook her head.

"After that it wasn't so frightfully easy. I loved him with all my soul, you see, and yet . . . and yet . . ."

"And yet you do like a contract," said Ferdie easily. "You're a remarkable girl, aren't you? So respectable at heart. Ray went to find him, I suppose. Did he find him?"

"We-ell . . ." Georgia was evidently coming to the crux of her story and was considering the light in which to present it. Presently she threw out her hands in a particularly charming gesture of renunciation. "I'll tell it simply," she said. "If you don't understand you've never really loved. Ray was absolutely convinced that Richard was dead. He said he would never have left me for so long if he had been alive, and of course that was true. Besides, knowing Richard in that insane brooding mood of his, I couldn't help feeling that it would be just like him to go off and die somewhere secretly, revenging himself on me by leaving me in doubt. He was like that in the end, all mad and tied up and mean in soul."

"When you got the secret door open you found it led to the junk cupboard," Val remarked dreamily.

"The *cellar*, my dear! Old bottles and damp newspapers and frightful white crawly things." Georgia threw the bagatelle over her shoulder happily. She and Val were dear friends again and she was so glad. "Ray hurled himself into the search. He worked like a lunatic. You know how energetic he was, Ferdie. *You* saw him, Albert, over that idiotic gun. Once he wanted a thing he wanted it more than anything in the world. He scoured the country for unidentified bodies, but he couldn't find a trace of him until just before Christmas, and then he found Richard.''

"Found him?"

The words were jerked from Mr. Campion, who had been standing quietly by the fireplace listening to the scene with his habitual politeness.

Georgia met his eyes steadily.

"Yes," she said. "He found him in a crevasse in Wales. He'd been mountaineering or something. People often go to mountains with broken hearts; they're so comfortingly solid. Anyway, he'd fallen and been lost for months. Ray wouldn't let me go to see him because of the filthy things that happen to bodies. He simply gave me his word of honour and I took it. We married on January the fifth, by special licence, as you know. As my marriage to Richard was secret I called myself Sinclair.''

"In fact, as far as you knew, you committed bigamy." Ferdie strode down the room. "If this comes out you're done. It mustn't, of course. I don't see it need. We shall all hold our tongues for our own sakes.''

Georgia rose. She was angry and her cheeks were bright.

"It *was* Richard," she said. "Ray gave me his word of honour.''

"Don't be silly, dear." For the first time Ferdie betrayed an unintentional irritation. "Portland-Smith was found in Kent with a bullet through his skull. His papers were found on him. The coroner decided the bones were his. You drove the poor brute off his head and he killed himself. That's the truth of that. See a few facts now and again. Don't let 'em cramp your style but don't kid yourself all the time.''

"That is not true." Georgia was gentle. "Ferdie, you're sadistic. You enjoy hurting me. My dear boy, Ray *proved* to me that the body in Wales was Richard's.''

"How?"

"He went down in the train with a woman who was also travelling to identify the body. He recognised her as the wife of an old sergeant-major of his, a perfect fiend of a hag who'd led her wretched husband such a ghastly life that the poor creature ran away from her. Ray knew because the man had been to him and borrowed some money to get to Canada and Ray had lent it to him. The woman was mad to identify this body to get a widow's pension, and so of course Ray was in a cleft stick. Once this woman had decided that her husband was dead the man was free from her forever. Besides, if Ray had put his foot down and insisted that it was Richard, we couldn't very well marry immediately, could we? After all, it was only he and I who had to be satisfied. We were the only people to whom it really mattered.''

"Except his parents and his clients," murmured Mr. Campion tactlessly.

"Oh? Had he got people?" Georgia was both startled and contrite. "He was over thirty. I never thought of him as being someone's child. How disgustingly selfish of me! But I was so, so terribly in love. Well, Ray saw it was Richard, and the awful woman, who was sick at the sight of the body and couldn't look at it, insisted that it was her husband, and so Ray didn't interfere, I think it was rather nice of him. He told me the whole story and even took me to see the woman, who had some dreadful little hovel in Hackney. She convinced me utterly.''

"That it was her husband?"

"No, of course not. She convinced me that she had persuaded herself that it was. She was unbelievable. I sympathised with the wretched man in Canada. Then she went into the most gruesome details and Ray had to take me away. Then, of course, since I was sure, Ray and I married.''

There was a long pause after her husky voice had died away. Ferdie sat looking at her, his chin resting on his hands and his face morose and inscrutable.

Mr. Campion was shocked. There are some people to whom muddled thinking and self-deception are the two most unforgivable crimes in the world.

Val patted Georgia's shoulder absently.

"How did *he* dare?" she demanded suddenly. "He had an enormous amount to lose.''

"Oh, Ray was like that." Surprisingly it was Georgia herself who answered. "Ray was a natural adventurer. That's why I adored him. He risked everything all the time. He didn't care. So long as he achieved his objective he didn't care how dangerous it was.''

She went on talking happily, sublimely unconscious of the tacit admission she was making.

"Ray just wanted Georgia and he didn't care what he did to

get her. He was so young always, so brave, so gloriously dangerous.''

"He was a damned fourflusher," said Ferdie Paul. "Dangerous is the word. What happened when Portland-Smith's body was discovered? That tarnished his word of honour a bit, didn't it?"

"Oh, I was frightfully angry with Ray." Georgia spoke involuntarily, adding with maddening gentleness, "Until I realised that there'd been another mistake, and anyway it didn't really matter then. I was so terribly upset about poor Richard at the time. I only remember the best in people, you know.''

Ferdie Paul rose to his feet with what appeared to be a considerable physical effort.

"Yes, well," he said heavily, "let's all hope she never gets into the witness box. Now look here, you people, there's only one thing we need all remember and that is that this particular mess is nothing to do with us. We can be as helpful and as polite as we like. The more helpful we are the better. It looks well. But the affair is not our business. It's quite obvious what happened to Caroline Adamson. She went around with a dangerous lot, the dregs of the fur and the restaurant trade and the lower West End mob. Heaven knows what scrap she got herself into. They're a nasty crowd to monkey with and she was a pretty piece. We're all right if we don't go and jump into it. Get that well into your head, Georgia.''

"I have, my dear." There was a flicker of shrewdness in Georgia's tweed-grey eyes, but it vanished almost at once. "I should probably be very good in court, you know.''

"You wouldn't." Ferdie's brown eyes were intensely earnest. "Don't for pity's sake get that idea in your head. You wouldn't. D'you remember that blank-verse play you would try one Sunday? You do? It would be like that only a million times worse. Take my word for it.''

Georgia shrugged but she looked chastened.

"I see things so clearly," she said and laughed at herself. "Even when I'm wrong.''

It was nearly two in the morning. Campion had the Lagonda in the drive and Val's man was waiting in her famous grey Daimler with the special body. As Georgia lived in Highgate she went home with Val, while Campion dropped Ferdie at the Sovereign.

THE FASHION IN SHROUDS

As the two women settled down in the soft grey-quilted depths of the car, which was like a powder closet inside, shut away from the chauffeur and as exquisitely feminine as a sedan chair, Georgia linked her arm through Val's.

"Ferdie's quite right," she said with a return to the more truthful mood, which she kept for the few women she recognised as her equals. "If we simply smile and do all we can for everyone without actually doing anything, it may be all all right. I do hope so. It'll all pass. We'll laugh about it when we're old women."

"I hope so," said Val soberly.

"Oh, we shall." After her ordeal Georgia's spirits were reviving and she was dangerously optimistic. "I'm so glad all that about Ray and Richard has come out at last. It's been half on my conscience. I hate secrets. It was dangerous, but it didn't matter as it happened. I simply didn't care at the time. You don't, do you? Nothing else seems to matter. That's why Ray and I got on so well together. In that respect he was feminine too. He was the only man I ever met who really understood how my mind worked. His own was the same. Oh, my dear, it's going to be hell without him."

She was speaking quite sincerely and Val glanced at her out of the corner of her eye. Georgia was aware of the scrutiny in spite of the shifting darkness.

"I've got rid of Alan," she said, adding in a burst of truthfulness which was more than half pure generosity, "in a way he got rid of me. We had a dreadful row the day after the memorial service, of all indecent moments. He simply abused me, Val. Not noisily in a way you could forgive, but quietly, almost as though he meant it. It was about that cachet story, as a matter of fact. It had come round to him again, fifteenth hand. Someone got tight and tried to tell it as a joke. I said that I was sorry and that you did understand but he was just quietly unreasonable, and suddenly, while he was talking I came to my senses. I saw him objectively. He's not my type, Val. He's 'all on one plane.' Then, of course, I realized what I'd done. I ought to have looked after Ray. He was the only man I ever loved and I let him die. It's terribly tragic, isn't it?"

"It has its disastrous aspects." There was humour in Val's dry little comment, which robbed it of much of its bitterness.

"There's a word for you, Georgia my pet. You're a proper cough drop, aren't you?"

"Darling, how vulgar. I thought you were going go say bitch."

Georgia was laughing but broke off to sigh.

"Isn't it odd?" she said presently. "Have you noticed that women like me who have dozens of men in love with them spend such an astounding amount of time alone? Here am I, under thirty-two, a pathetic, brokenhearted widow, utterly deserted and yet God knows I've had enough men hysterical about me. I like your brother, Val. He doesn't approve of me. Men who don't approve of me always intrigue me. I can never understand why it is and that keeps me interested in them."

"Albert?" said Val dubiously. "What about Amanda?"

"Oh yes. The pretty little red-haired child." Georgia was thoughtful. "Isn't it tragic when you think what all these babies have got to go through?" she added, sighing. "All the hurts, the heartaches, the wretched emotional agonies which make one mature."

"Darling, I don't know and I don't care. It's nearly half-past two. Don't you live somewhere along here?"

"No, it's miles further yet." Georgia peered out into the darkness. "I love my little house," she remarked. "Ray and I adored each other there. When I get sentimental I think of it as a little shrine. Don't be angry with me, Val. After all, I've given up Alan. You can have him now if you want to."

Val was silent. The car sped on down the faintly lit street and only now and again, when they passed a street lamp, was her face visible.

"Don't look like that." There was a note of panic in the childish phrase. "Val, don't look like that. You're grim. You're frightening me. Say something."

"Can you see that you've put that man out of my life forever?"

The words were spoken unemotionally and Georgia considered them.

"No," she said at last. "No, honestly I don't see that, darling. Not if you love him. Nothing in love is forever, is it? Be reasonable."

They were two fine ladies of a fine modern world, in which

their status had been raised until they stood as equals with their former protectors. Their several responsibilities were far heavier than most men's and their abilities greater. Their freedom was limitless. There they were at two o'clock in the morning, driving back in their fine carriage to lonely little houses, bought, made lovely and maintained by the proceeds of their own labours. They were both mistress and master, little Liliths, fragile but powerful in their way, since the livelihood of a great number of their fellow beings depended directly upon them, and yet, since they had not relinquished their femininity, within them, touching the very core and fountain of their strength, was the dreadful primitive weakness of the female of any species. Byron, who knew something about ladies if little enough about poetry, once threw off the whole shameful truth about the sex, and, like most staggeringly enlightening remarks, it degenerated into a truism and became discountenanced when it was no longer witty.

"Love really can rot any woman up," Georgia observed contentedly. "Isn't it funny?"

"Dear God, isn't it dangerous!" said Val.

They drove on in silence, both of them thinking of a very different thing from the common disaster which they had met to discuss and which, had they been less preoccupied, must have terrified them by its imminence and its tremendous risk.

Chapter Eighteen

Mr. Campion, arriving home a little before three in the morning full of the deepest misgivings and secretly uneasy because the police had not called upon him to identify anyone whom the amorous lorry driver might have described, found, instead of the expected detective, Lugg and Amanda in the kitchenette eating bacon and eggs.

"The poor kid's got to get to work at the factory by seven-thirty termorrow." Lugg's greeting was reproachful. "I thought at least I'd give 'er a bit of breakfast. What will you 'ave yourself? Eggs or a mite of 'erring? I've got a lovely little tin 'asn't been opened above a couple of days. I was savin' it for when I fancied it.''

The kitchen was warm and odorous, and Mr. Campion, who suddenly felt he had been too long among the sophists, sat down on the other side of the enamel-topped table and glanced at his lieutenant with satisfaction. She was rosy with sleep but bright-eyed and very interested.

"I've been here since ten, sleeping in a chair. I thought I'd better wait in case you needed any help. What happened?"

He gave her the rough outline of the momentous interview, while Lugg sizzled contempt and bacon fat in the background.

"So you see," he said at last, "Portland-Smith was being blackmailed. That emerged with a blinding flash and a smell of damp fireworks. No one who heard Georgia's story of the six months before he vanished—heard it with anything besides his ears, I mean—could possibly have missed that."

"Who blackmailed him? Miss Adamson?"

Amanda's untroubled logic was comforting after the tortuous mental fancywork of the past three hours.

"She was in it; I think that's certain." He spoke decisively and paused, a shadow of embarrassment passing over his face. She caught his expression and grinned.

"I'm getting a big girl now," she said. "You can mention it in front of me. It was the usual story but 'she had her auntie Jessie underneath the kitchen sink,' I suppose? When and where did all this happen?"

"I don't know, of course." Mr. Campion sighed and his lean face looked less weary. Amanda was easy to talk to. "He went off on a walking tour in October and came back all peculiar. He seems to have been batty about his wife at this time and she evidently loathed him, so I take it that a solicitous Caroline who resembled the Dear Unkind might easily have had a walkover. That angle is a job for Blest. I'll get hold of Portland-Smith's itinerary and Blest must go round all the pubs he might have stayed in. That should put us on to it. But we must be prepared for it only leading us to the girl, and I'm more than certain she didn't do it alone. It was too opportune. The whole thing has a curious organised flavour, like everything else. Portland-Smith was caught and bled until he took the shortest way out, poor beast. All this evening I've been quaggly in the middle of the thought of that fellow. He must have had hell's delight.''

"Very nice dick work, but it's unsatisfactory," remarked Mr. Lugg, flopping another egg onto the plate before his keeper. "There's no fear of blackmail nowadays. It's Mr. A and Miss X and three years, yes, yer lordship, thank yer very much. You don't even read the papers.''

"That's where you're wrong, you with your mammy's eyes, poor hideous woman." Mr. Campion spoke without resentment. "It's because of the anonymity rule that I'm certain the whole thing was a more subtle affair than would at first appear. Miss Adamson's own methods were just plain abominable. I gathered that much when she phoned me. There usually is a third, negotiating party in this sort of case and it's pretty obvious that this particular third was the brains of the act. You see, Portland-Smith was a barrister, i.e. he had the one kind of job which makes the anonymity rule a trifle less than useless. He couldn't go into the Central Court at the Old Bailey calling himself Mr. X, at least not with any marked success, unless of course, he wore a false beard or a cagoulard hood, either of which might so easily have been misunderstood.''

"Oh well, if you say so, cock. I can't talk about trade risks." Mr. Lugg was magnanimous. "I'll do you a bit o' bacon.''

"I suppose the threat was divorce information for Georgia," Amanda observed. "That might have cooked his county court ambitions. Was it done purely for the money? How much had he got?''

"I don't know exactly, but I think he must have got through about four thousand pounds in the last six months of his life. He died broke. I had taken it that he'd been wallowing in diamonds, costly furs and ballet shoes of champagne, but it seems not." Campion spoke lightly but his eyes were not amused. "All the same, I don't believe money was the primary motive, although somebody thought a lot about it. Our Caroline did, for one. I may be braying in the wilderness, but whenever I consider the events in the round I smell fish. It's fishy that Portland-Smith should have been driven to suicide just as Georgia met Ramillies, and fishier still that

Ramillies should have looked up his ancestors just as Georgia fell for Dell. I may merely have a beastly mind, of course, but it shouts to heaven to me.''

Amanda nodded gloomily.

"A.D.'s back at work," she observed. "He looks a bit tempered but he's making up for lost time. We're getting the old atmosphere back. Sid's like a dog who's discovered he's got his collar on after all. I say, Albert?''

She sat back from the table and remained looking at him, her face scarlet and her honey-brown eyes embarrassed.

"She couldn't possibly have persuaded *them* to do it, could she?''

"What? Persuaded each succeeding boy friend to do in the retiring chairman?" Mr. Campion was impressed. "That's a very beautiful idea, Amanda. It's got a flavour of the classics. Lovely stuff. All clean, ruthless lines and what not. But I don't fancy it for a bet. It belongs to a more artistic age.''

"I find that very comforting," said Amanda candidly. "Would you like some more to eat?''

The downstairs button sounding a cuckoo-clock device in the hall outside forestalled Mr. Campion's acceptance. Lugg paused, frying pan in hand, his eye ridges raised.

"Eh?" he demanded.

"That damned owl again," said Mr. Campion. "Go and see who it is.''

"Three o'clock in the mornin'?" Lugg's little black eyes were startled. "'Ere, is your aunt in London, yer lady-ship?''

"My dear fellow, you could chaperone a regiment of Georgias." Amanda was cheerful. "Don't put on a collar. Decolletage is perfectly all right at this time of night. Buck up.''

The cuckoo called again and Lugg surged to the door.

"I've laid them eggs there and I want to see 'em when I come back," he said warningly. "I'm coming. I'm coming.''

"His mother instinct is strong, isn't it?" commented Amanda as he disappeared. "Who is this? The police?''

"I don't know." Mr. Campion looked uneasy. "I don't like this show, Amanda. I'd feel much happier if you were out of it. You don't mind, do you?''

Amanda laughed at him. "Don't drop the pilot," she said.

203

"I'm the only disinterested intelligence in the whole outfit. My motive is nice clean curiosity. I'm valuable. Listen."

It was Lugg's breathing, of course. The noise of it came up from the stairs like a wind machine. As he reached the flat door they heard him speak.

"On a bicycle?" he protested. "That's a nice way to get about! Would you care for an egg or a nice fresh bit of 'erring?"

Mr. Campion and Amanda exchanged startled glances and were on their feet when the visitor appeared shyly round the doorpost. It was Sinclair. He looked smaller than ever in his grey suit, his hair untidy from his ride in the wind.

"It's stinkingly late," he said. "I hope you don't mind, but I thought I might find you up, and it seemed important."

He was evidently excited but his self-possession was extraordinary and he reminded them both of some little old gentleman in his old-fashioned ease. Amanda made room for him on the edge of her chair and pushed rolls and butter towards him.

"That's all right," she said affably. "What's up? New developments?"

"Well, I don't know." Sinclair glanced questioningly at Lugg and, receiving Campion's reassuring nod, hurried on. "It's about Ray. I say, they—they're not going to dig him up, are they? That's why I came at once. I didn't like to wait until the morning if there was anything I could do to stop them. It's such a filthy thing to happen."

"My dear chap, don't worry about that." Mr. Campion had caught a glimpse of the horror behind the small white face. "That's all right. That won't happen. And even if it did there'd be a tremendous setout first. The Home Office would have to move, for one thing, and that takes weeks even if everyone there happens to be awake. What put the idea in your head?"

Sinclair looked relieved and afterwards a little foolish.

"I'm sorry to have come so soon," he said. "I didn't know this, you see, and I got worrying. Georgia came in just now. I was waiting up for her; I often do, as a matter of fact. She was a bit hysterical, I'm afraid, and she rather frightened me. I hadn't heard of the murder of this girl friend of Ray's. I read the case in the evening papers, of course, but she hadn't been identified then. Georgia wept over me and I finally got it out of her that she was afraid the police might get suspicious over Ray's death. That upset us both, naturally. Then I suddenly realised that I knew something that might help, so I got out my bicycle and came down to see you. I didn't want to go to the police if it wasn't necessary.''

"Jolly sensible," encouraged Amanda. "Eat while you talk. There's nothing like food when you're rattled; even if it gives you indigestion, that takes your mind off the main trouble. It's actually about Ray, is it?''

"Yes." Sinclair accepted the plate which Lugg placed before him, showing a certain amount of enthusiasm. "It's about old Ray getting tight that morning. I've been thinking. Perhaps he wasn't so tight, you see.''

They stared at him and he hurried on, wrestling with his bacon in between remarks.

"I don't know if you knew old Ray very well," he said shyly, "but I did and I saw him pretty tight dozens of times. He used to weep, as a rule, and then thresh round a bit and finally sleep. I never saw him as chatty as he was on that day and yet so sort of thick and unsteady." He hesitated. "I don't want to sneak on the old man," he said, "but he told me something one day in strict confidence which may be rather important. It was about courage.''

"Courage?"

"Yes." Sinclair flushed. "He used to go a bit kiddish and earnest at times. He was nuts about courage. He thought it was the one really big thing. He'd done some pretty brave stunts, you know, and I think he was frightfully proud of them really. We were talking one night about six weeks ago when he suddenly told me something and made me swear I'd never repeat it. I don't like doing it now, but he is dead, and my hat, I'd hate them to disturb him. Ray told me that in spite of everything he did about it there was one thing that put the wind up him. He said he had a complex about flying.''

"Had he, by George?" said Mr. Campion with interest.

Sinclair nodded.

"So he said, and I believed him, because he was pretty well sweating when he told me. He said he used to make himself go up now and again, but he couldn't stand it and he used to get the breeze up for days, both before and afterwards.''

"There are people like that, of course," put in Amanda,

"but it doesn't seem possible in Ramillies. Why on earth did he take on this big flight?"

"I asked him that," agreed Sinclair, nodding to her, "but as a matter of fact, though, I understood pretty well. It was because of the flight that he told me about the complex. He was so jolly scared that he had to tell someone. I've felt like that about other things. What he actually said was that he'd arranged the whole business because he thought that as flying was the one last thing in the world that he was afraid of he ought to make one great effort to cure himself of it once and for all." He blushed. "That wasn't true, though. Old Ray used to pretend a bit. You know how people do. As a matter of fact he didn't arrange it. The government did that. He was asked to make the flight and it would have looked stinkingly bad if he'd refused. He was simply telling me to make it sound all right to himself."

He sighed for the weaknesses of man and the perversities of circumstances.

"Your idea is that he died of shock induced by fright, I take it?" enquired Mr. Campion with interest.

"Oh no, I think he took something." Sinclair was innocent of any attempt at dramatic effect. "You see," he continued awkwardly, "he went on talking to me for quite a bit. He explained how frightfully brave he was in everything else except this, and then he said that in a way he was really extra brave over the flight, because he knew someone who could give him a drug to make him perfectly fit and confident throughout the whole thing. It was quite easy, he said. You just took it in your arm and you felt a bit rotten for four hours and then you suddenly felt magnificent and that lasted for about a day. He pointed out what a temptation it was, and then he said he wasn't going to give in to it and that he'd made up his mind to make the flight without."

"I see." Mr. Campion's pale eyes were darker than usual. "Did he mention the name of this stuff?"

"No. He wouldn't tell me. He just said he knew someone who could see he got it if he wanted it. I half thought this person, whoever it was, had found out how scared old Ray was. I think he'd told them. But he didn't want to go on talking about it to me and so naturally I didn't mention it."

"Four hours feeling rotten and then a day feeling fine?" Amanda repeated the words dubiously. "Is there such stuff, Albert?"

"I've never heard of it. It sounds to me like a tale from someone with an unpleasantly perverted sense of humour." Mr. Campion's precise tone was grim. "You think Ray succumbed to the temptation after all, then, Sinclair?"

"He might have done, mightn't he?" The young voice was very reasonable. "When I heard that he'd cleared out in the middle of the farewell party, I thought at once that it was probably because he'd suddenly realised that he couldn't face the flight after all, and had dashed up to town to get hold of this drug stuff somewhere. That would have been frightfully like him."

"There you are." Amanda was sitting up. "There you are. That's it, Sinclair's right. Ramillies left the party in a blue funk, went to Boot's to be quiet and attempt to pull himself together. In the morning he found it was no good and he went round to Miss Adamson, who gave him this stuff. He must have taken it round about noon. Probably he began to feel peculiar almost at once and told that story about being tight in order to cover up any obvious ill effects. That must be right, because the flight was timed for four. Don't you see, the murderer would have expected him to die in the air. Ramillies thought he was going to feel fine in four hours and instead of that it killed him. Miss Adamson realised what had happened and tried to blackmail the person who had given her the drug for Ramillies. She used you as a threat and got herself killed. It all fits in."

"I know, I know, my dear, but there's no proof." The words escaped Campion reluctantly. "I'm sorry to be so unhelpful but there's no proof that he went near our Caroline after he left Boot's. Besides—and this is vital—what was it? What was the stuff? There was a P.M., you know, and an analysis."

"That's irritatingly true." Amanda was deflated. "I thought we were on to it. It's frightfully good, though, Sinclair. Part of the truth is there. Don't you think so, Albert?"

"Yes." Mr. Campion still spoke cautiously. "Yes, there was no mention of alcohol in the report on the body, and the entire story points to him having been poisoned somewhere in town. And yet what about that badge in the plane?"

"The Quentin Clear?" Amanda had the grace to look startled. "I'd forgotten it. I've still got it, too. A.D.'s never enquired about it. That's odd. You're right. We shall have to consider that. And yet I don't know, though. It was an obvious plant, wasn't it? We decided that at once."

"Is that the badge of the Award?" Sinclair was interested. "It's frightfully good, isn't it? What did Mr. Dell get it for?"

"The first Seraphim." In spite of her preoccupation there was tremendous pride in Amanda's statement. "It's only given for exceptional pioneer work in aviation design. Look here, Albert, it does fit in. Whoever gave Miss Adamson the stuff to kill Ramillies would naturally be there watching him, and when they saw that the man was going to die in the plane before she went up they planted the Quentin Clear there to pin the thing on A.D. How's that?"

"Not bad, for the one 'disinterested intelligence,'" said Campion and grinned as she grew fiery at the dig. "I don't know. I don't know, my hearty young betrothed. I don't really like to think."

He leant back in his chair and sat there, his head jutting forward and his hands in his pockets. For a long time he did not look up.

At four the morning papers were on sale outside in Piccadilly and they all went down to get them. The story had made the wrong side headlines on the front pages, most of which also carried studio portraits of Miss Adamson, looking beautiful and more like Georgia than ever. Much of the published account was unusually accurate and fitted in with the superintendent's own version, but there was one interesting new development. A formal police appeal, boxed and leaded, took the pride of place in every double column.

In connection with the death of Miss Caroline Adamson, late of Petunia House, W. 2, whose body was found yesterday morning on a piece of waste ground at Coaching Cross Essex, the police are anxious to trace the whereabouts of two men, both of medium height and very heavy build, who are thought to be in possession of a small four-cylinder car of some considerable age. These men were observed by a witness near the scene of the discovery at 3 A.M. approximately on the morning of

Wednesday, July 21st. Information should be lodged at any police station.

As they stood in the Circus, with the thin cold wind of dawn drawing its fingers up their spines, they looked up from the papers and stared at each other.

"Two shortish, very fat men in an old car?" translated Amanda in bewilderment. "They don't fit in at all. We're all wrong. It almost looks as though it was nothing to do with our business after all. It's another incredible coincidence, another manifestation of the hand of Providence."

The words struck an answering note in Lugg's mysterious consciousness. He looked over his paper with that plump, gratified satisfaction at a chance to shine which in the dog world is the peculiarity of the hound.

"'Providence, 'aving the advantage of knowin' both the strengths and the weaknesses of men, 'as a facility for unostentatious organisation undreamed of by our generals.' Sterne," he said. "That comes out of my book. What's the matter, cock?"

Mr. Campion was staring at him with fascinated excitement.

"What?" he demanded.

Mr. Lugg obligingly repeated this latest fruit of his labours in the fields of culture.

"Tell you anythink?" he enquired with interest.

Mr. Campion put an arm round each of his two younger lieutenants.

"Yes," he said and the old enthusiasm returned in his voice and in the gleam behind his spectacles. "Yes, my secondhand scholar, it does. Look here, I'll drive you down to work, Amanda, and I'll phone you in the lunch hour. We can drop Sinclair and his bicycle on the way. And when I come back, Lugg, I'll want a bath, a clean shirt, and you ready for outside work. We start, we stir, we seem to feel the thrill of life beneath our keel."

Amanda laughed with pure excitement.

"Seen his taillight?"

"Not yet," said Mr. Campion, "but the Lord be praised I've seen his wheels go round."

Chapter Nineteen

Sir Montague Paling, the chief commissioner, who was a soldier and a gentleman and everything that phrase implies, phoned his superintendent of the Central Criminal Investigation Department early in the morning.

"Oates? That you? You still there? Good man. Good man. About this girl-in-the-wood case of yours; is there a foreign element in that?"

"We don't know yet, sir." Stanislaus Oates tried to suppress any placatory tone which might have crept into his pleasant country voice. "Pullen found a quantity of drugs in her flat last night. We're working on that angle with Wylde at the moment."

"Who?"

"Detective Inspector Wylde, sir—Narcotics."

"Oh yes, of course. I didn't catch you. Oh well, that's very promising. What is it? Cocaine?"

"No sir. Morphine. Quite a bit of it. Seven or eight ounces."

"Really? She was a distributor, I suppose? Yes, yes, that's satisfactory. I phoned you because I've had a private word from the Colonial Office. The girl was the mistress of one of their fellers who died the other day, and, while they don't want to interfere in any way, of course, they do hope we'll be discreet. No need to drag up a lot of mud if it's not necessary. We know that as well as anyone, don't we?"

"I hope so, sir."

"Good man. Good work, Oates. Advise me from time to time. Good-bye."

The superintendent in charge of the Essex side phoned Superintendent Stanislaus Oates five minutes after the commissioner had returned to his breakfast.

"We've taken Robin Whybrow, the lorry driver, over his statement again, Superintendent, and he's remembered that one man was hatless. He only saw him up against what light there was in the sky, remember, but he says the top of his head was all crinkled, like as if he had curls. I don't know if it's worth nothing."

"Eh? I dunno. Every crumb means something to an empty spadger. No news of the car?"

"Not yet there isn't. We're working on it."

"Nor the weapon?"

"No. I don't think we ever will find that. Sorry to disappoint you, but we've combed that place. Still, we're working on it. I'll give you a call the moment anything crops up. I thought I'd let you know we were keeping busy."

"Oh yes, fine, thank you very much. Good-bye."

Oates wrote down. "One bloke seen in dark may have curly hair" on his blotting paper, added an exclamation mark and drew a ring round it. He glanced absently at the teapot on his desk, his sole sustenance for twenty hours, and, resisting it, took up the telephone again.

Sir Henry Wryothsley was happy to hear from him. The fine precise voice which was so impressive in the box sounded bright and enthusiastic.

"I'll bring it round myself as soon as it's finished. I've been working all night. A lovely wound. Oh yes, definitely. Obviously sole cause of death. I'm working out the specifications now. I'll read you the opinion. It gives it in one. Are you listening? Don't take it down; I'll bring the report round. Listen. '1. The cause of death was the wounding of the main blood vessel of the heart and the consequent internal bleeding. 2. The wound on the wall of the chest, penetrating the main heart bag, was caused by a sharp-pointed two-edged instrument approximately six tenths of an inch wide. 3.'—and this is interesting, Oates—'the blow was delivered practically straight.' "

"What?"

"I know. The direction is all but dead level. I'll talk to you about it when I see you but for the present take it from me she was lying peacefully on her back when it was done, and so far I don't see any trace of an anaesthetic or anything else. I'm doing the analysis myself. The only other mark was a slight contusion high up on the left side of the neck, but it's very faint. What? Oh, I don't know, old boy. I don't know at all. Before midnight and after midday. I daren't be more specific. I'll come round. Good-bye.''

Meanwhile Georgia was phoning Val.

"I simply threw myself on his mercy, my dear, and he was charming. He says he'll do all he can and I am not to worry. He was very sensible and very sweet. Government people so often are. Did you meet him?''

"I think I did.'' The line was bad and Val's high voice sounded very far away.

"Old, but rather nice. Slightly doggy, with a sprouty moustache. Just like his name. Don't you remember?''

"I can't hear you.''

"Oh, it doesn't matter, darling. This line is abominable. I only phoned to tell you I'd fixed everything and it's all going to be hushed up, so we needn't worry any more, thank God. Toddy Towser's going to see to everything. Isn't Toddy a perfectly vile name? Good-bye, sweet.''

Val phoned Mr. Campion, and the steady buzzing echoing in the empty flat answered her. As she hung up the receiver the little white instrument in her panelled room at Hampstead rang once more and she pounced on it eagerly, but it was only Rex again.

"Lady Papendeik is with the inspector now.'' He was gabbling in his annoyance. "Everyone in the place is talking about drugs. I'm doing everything I can, madame, but I simply cannot guarantee that some wretched vendeuse won't blurt it out in confidence to the first trade buyer who comes in. One wouldn't think they'd be so vulgar but one can't be sure. Marguerite Zingari has had hysterics and handed in her resignation. What would you advise?''

"I'll come, Rex, I'll come. Since your last message I've been trying to phone my brother. Never mind. Keep them all quiet if you can. Don't worry. I'll come.''

Val sounded calm and her authority was consoling. The little man's theatrical sigh was magnified over the wire.

"I shall be relieved,'' he said. "This is appalling. Such frightful disorganisation. Can I send the peach 'Fantastique' to Lady B.? I can't be more specific over the phone, can I? She's asked for it, but you know that we did say that next time, in view of the past, we ought to have a trifle on account. Lady B. B for bolero.''

"I'll leave it to you, Rex." Val sounded breathless. "I should be tactful but firm. I'll come down at once."

She hung up and made one more attempt to get Campion's flat. There was still no reply, and she phoned the Junior Greys and left a message for him.

The Daimler was at the door and she was setting a small black hat at precisely the right angle over her left eye, characteristically giving the task the same intelligent care which she would have bestowed upon it had she been summoned by the Last Trump and not Rex's shrill alarm, when Papendeik's rang through again. It was Tante Marthe herself this time. The ugly voice betrayed that faint trace of accent which the telephone always seems to accentuate.

"Val, my child, there is an inspector here. He is at my side now. Do you remember that mannequin, Caroline, the one we got rid of? She has got herself murdered, wretched little girl. The police seem to think she may have had something to do with drugs, and they are enquiring about them from all former employers. Do you remember anything about some morphine? There was something, my dear, wasn't there? I seem to remember it."

No policeman on earth could have mistaken Madame's warning tone, and Val grew hot and then very cold again.

"The inspector says it is purely a matter of form," Tante Marthe concluded, speaking apparently from dictation.

"I'm coming right down, darling. I'll be with you both in fifteen minutes." The high voice was brisk and cheerful, and Val rang off.

While she was riding through the streets Gaiogi Laminoff stood in his amusing sitting room and telephoned Mr. Paul.

"Ferdie, my dear fellow, listen to me for a moment." The Russian's voice was sibilant and charged with all the emotional force of his dramatic race. "Have you seen the papers? I have had the police here at my house. Yes, here. My dear Ferdie, it is not at all funny. I am not laughing. They have found some drugs in the girl's flat at Petunia House, and they have found out that Ramillies took up the lease of that flat. I have told them nothing, naturally; it is not my affair. The abominable girl was only here for six weeks. But for everybody's sake, Ferdie, keep Georgia quiet. That story of hers about the cachet—it won't do any good, you know. Things are bad enough as they are."

"You're telling me," said Ferdie Paul and hung up.

The obliging Sinclair succeeded in getting a call through to the Alandel works and bore the instrument in triumph to his parent. Dell's secretary, who had been trying to get Papendeik's all the morning without success, put the incoming call through to the inner office in all innocence.

"Alan"—Georgia's tone was motherly—"I wouldn't have disturbed you, dear, but don't you think you ought to ring up Val?"

"Hallo, Georgia. Ring Val? Why?"

"Oh, darling"—she was reproachful—"don't you read the papers? She's frightfully worried and upset. That murdered girl was one of her mannequins, the one who stole my dress, you remember. Papendeik's are bound to be positively bristling with police. It will be frightful for her. You know how temperamental these artist people are. A phone message from you would probably help a lot."

There was a long pause from the other end of the wire, and Georgia began to feel dubious.

"This is just between ourselves, of course," she said hurriedly. "I'm only trying to help you both, my sweet. Of course I haven't said a word to her."

She heard him laugh. It was one of those short explosive laughs associated in her mind with an embarrassed expression and a change of colour.

"What a *dear* you are, Georgia, aren't you?" he said.

She was surprised and gratified. She laughed herself.

"It's funny to hear you say that. Do you know, Alan, everyone who has ever loved me has said that in the end. Oh well, you ring her, darling. She'll be frightfully pleased. Good-bye, Alan. I say, give the poor sweetie my love."

He rang off, a little abruptly, she thought, but put it down quite seriously to eagerness on his part to condole with Val. She sighed. There was a tremendous satisfaction in being magnanimous, so much satisfaction that she sometimes wondered if there wasn't a catch in it somewhere.

Val had not expected any friendly offer of assistance from Dell, but had only hoped for it. She was, therefore, not surprised when he did not ring her.

*   *   *

Just before noon a little girl with ferret's eyes in an innocent face stepped out of Papendeik's, where she was employed in the sewing rooms with nearly two hundred others and turned into a public telephone booth. Within a minute or two a fat young man with a superior manner and disreputable clothes was listening to her with interest in a corner of an editorial mezzanine floor.

"It's drugs. Madame was with the police an hour and they took a statement." The squeaky voice was thin with excitement. "Madame's shut up in the studio now and no one can get near her. They say she's crying and we're wondering if she's going to be arrested. If this is useful, I get the usual, don't I?"

"Have I ever let you down, kiddo?" The pseudo-American accent was slick. "Step on it, baby. Keep your ears open. So long."

At about the same time, in a glass cubicle on the other side of the same floor, a far more elegant personage was listening to a far better accent.

"Well, my dear"—the instrument's voice was crisp—"that's all I know. I was actually in the Tulip when it happened. Ray Ramillies brought this girl in actually *disguised* as Georgia Wells and there was nearly a frightful scene, and then poor Ray died and now this girl. Dangerous? Of course I know it's dangerous. But isn't it exciting?"

Mr. Campion's call to Papendeik's came through to Val while her employee was still in the phone box in Oxford Street. Val was in the studio, and Miss McPhail, who was both discreet and practical, hurried out of the room and planted her solid back against the door, casting suspicious glances at anyone who ventured within twenty feet of it.

"Albert?" Campion knew at once by the very control in Val's voice that she was badly rattled. "The police have been here. They've found the morphine I told you I had. It was in Caroline Adamson's flat."

"My dear girl, you told me you destroyed it."

"I know I did. I couldn't find it when I came to look for it. I took it for granted that it had been mislaid. It never dawned on me that someone might have pinched it."

"Oh, I see." He sounded comfortingly unalarmed. "Oh well, it can't be helped. She saw what it was and thought it

marketable, I suppose. I was all packed up in little doses, was
it?''

"Yes, I'm afraid it was. I say, I told the police.''

"Oh, you did? I daren't ask. Good, that's good. What did
you tell them? The full strength?''

"Yes, everything. I gave the name of the woman we
sacked on suspicion of smuggling it and the firm in Lyons
from whom we bought the bale of silk. They took it all down
and I signed it. I say, Albert?''

"Yes, ma'am?''

"The men—the inspector had someone called Wylde with
him—weren't exactly matey after I'd told the story.''

"Old Pullen? Not offensive, surely?''

"What? Oh no, just reserved. 'Yes' and 'no' and that sort
of thing.''

"The atmosphere changed, you mean?''

"Yes, it did rather. Is that bad?''

"Oh, Lord, no.'' His tone was hearty, but not entirely
convincing. "The police are always like that when they get a
new bit of information. They've got to go home to Poppa and
see what it means, that's all. That's all right. That's nothing.
I'm glad you told them. Tell 'em every mortal thing. You
haven't suppressed anything, have you?''

"No, nothing. At least, I didn't mention the cachet blanc.
Ought I to have?''

"No.'' The word sounded considered. "No, I don't think
so. If things stew up a bit more before this evening we'll go
along to see Oates and have a showdown, but it may not come
to that. You did tell them everything else?''

"Yes, I did. I did, dear. You sound suspicious.''

"I'm not. Only you told me you destroyed that muck.''

"Oh darling''—Val sounded helpless—"this really honestly
is the truth, all of it.''

"May all your designs fail if you lie?''

"May all my designs fail if I lie.''

"Right, that's fine. Now, is Rex about? I want to know if
anyone saw that girl at a night club recently.''

Rex was summoned by Miss McPhail, who seemed to have
got it into her head that Val was in danger of being kid-
napped, for she only admitted one person at a time into the
room, and then only after a keen visual "frisking.''

Rex did his best, but it was not very helpful.

"I've only seen her at the Tulip," he said. "I'll enquire if you like."

"Will you? Make a list of any names and phone it to the Junior Greys. Don't leave any other message; just the list of clubs where the girl may have been seen. If you would do that? Thank you. Look after my sister. There's nothing to worry about. Good-bye."

He rang off and felt for another twopence. His face was sharper than usual, and for once his natural indolence had vanished. Oates could not speak to him at once and he waited and rang again. He rang every five minutes for half an hour, and when at last he got hold of the old man, he gathered that Pullen had been before him, for conversation was not easy.

"I'm so rushed, Mr. Campion. If you haven't anything relevant to tell me I'll have to ask you to excuse me. You know how it is. I haven't slept since it broke."

"You should take a shot of morphine," said Campion and plugged in a question while he still had the other man's attention. "Have you had the P.M. report? What was the weapon? Go on, that can't be a state secret. Damn it man, I'm likely to help you. What was the weapon?"

"A long double-sided blade six tenths of an inch wide. That's all I can tell you, mate. Sorry. Good-bye."

Campion hung up. He was whistling a slow, mournful little tune which went painfully flat in the middle and his eyes were troubled. He went out to the hotel bookstall, obtained another pocketful of pennies, and returned, still whistling. He was soothed by getting on to the hospital immediately. Also, Sir Henry Portland-Smith was unexpectedly easily found. The old man was evidently curious and his fine voice sounded eager.

"I wondered if I should hear from you, my boy. I was thinking of you this morning. Have you any news for me?"

"No proof, sir." Campion had to drag his mind round to this half-forgotten angle of the case which yet remained the other man's main interest. "But I think it's fairly obvious now that the cause was blackmail."

"Blackmail." There was no question in the word, only enlightenment and considerable relief.

"I haven't finished by any means. It's still in the air. I can't tell you the details over the phone. I'll call on you when I've got it straightened out a bit. I really wanted to bother you for a piece of information. How long does morphine take to kill?''

"What kind of morphine?"

"I don't know. White powdery crystals."

"Diluted and taken subcutaneously?"

"No. By the mouth."

"How much?"

"God knows."

"What?"

"I have no earthly means of finding out."

The old man laughed. "I can't help you, my boy. I'm sorry. Thirty-six hours, perhaps."

"Really? As long as that? You wouldn't expect fatal results in four hours?"

"Well, I don't like to say on such vague grounds. You'd get some effect in four hours, you know. Perhaps even coma."

"I see. There would be a protracted period of coma, would there?"

"Oh yes. That is, in straight morphine poisoning. But there might be other conditions present, you see. Those would have to be considered."

"Yes, of course. But if you saw a man take—well, say a rice-paper container full of morphine crystals you wouldn't expect him to throw a fit four hours afterwards, bite his tongue and pass out?"

"No, I shouldn't. I should expect him to be sick. If not you'd get sleep, and afterwards no reflex action, slow pulse and so on, and finally coma."

"No fit?"

"No, no, no convulsions. At least I shouldn't say so. If you could be more specific I could help you. Post-mortem would find it, you know."

"It would?"

"Oh, certainly, if it was competently done. Bound to. Sorry I can't help you more. You'll come and see me, will you?"

"Yes, I will. I can't give you a date, unfortunately, but I'll come."

"Then we'll have the whole story?"

"Yes." Campion's voice was unusually sober. "The whole story. Good-bye. Thank you enormously."

"Not at all. I'm afraid I've been most unhelpful. These things depend so much on circumstances. As far as it goes the instance you give sounds most unlikely, but one can't tell. Odd things happen in medicine. Good-bye."

"Good-bye," said Mr. Campion.

Oates was eating a sandwich when Pullen's call came through to him. The superintendent's eyes were hard and bright with the nervous "second wind" which comes after the first intolerable desire for sleep has been overcome, and he held the receiver at some little distance from his ear. The inspector's machine-gun delivery was apt to be paralysing when received at short range.

"One of Wylde's men had dug up a band-boy friend of the girl's," Pullen rattled. "He has some story about her offering dope openly to anyone who seemed likely to have any money. It all sounds very amateurish. Wylde's seeing the man now. I don't like the dope angle myself. All the stuff came directly from Papendeik's. We mustn't lose sight of that."

"What?"

"All the dope we found came from Mrs. Valentine Ferris, I told you that last time I phoned, sir. There is no evidence to show that Adamson had any more than this in her possession. Wylde is inclined to believe Mrs. Ferris' story about the smuggling. His people are looking up the woman she sacked on suspicion. He thinks the name is familiar to him."

"Ah." Oates sounded unhappily convinced. "That leads us back to the swells."

"Looks like it. Still, that alibi of Laminoff's is not satisfactory, is it? He's a fat man, you know. I've got it here. Will you check it with yours? 'Six-fifteen, left Caesar's Court. Six thirty-five, Savoy cocktail bar. Seven-forty, Tulip Restaurant. Eight-fifty, the Tatler Theatre to see Mickey Mouse programme (alone). Eleven approximately the White Empress. Four-thirty A.M., left the White Empress for Caesar's Court in taxicab. That's the White Empress Club in Grafton Street."

"I know. The high-class all-alien dive. No reliable witnesses there, you feel?"

"Not one." The machine gun was vehement. "Every one of 'em would swear each other out of hell."

"I suppose they'd try. You'll go over them, of course."

"I was going down there now. I'll ring you at two-thirty. Good-bye, sir."

By a coincidence Gaiogi Laminoff was telephoning Matvey Kuymitchov, manager of the White Empress, at the same time that the two policemen were considering his alibi. He also was a trifle worried but not over the same matter.

"Matvey," he said, "you have in your hall some little birds in a gold cage shaped like a basket. Will you tell an old friend where you got them? They are charming."

Kuymitchov was delighted to oblige. He rattled off the name of the importers of the golden canaries and explained that the firm were also part owners of the cage-making company.

"I know them very well, Excellency. They are not easy people to deal with, but if you want some, perhaps I could get them for you."

"Would you do that, Matvey? That would be kind of you. I should appreciate that." The faint note of irony was well suppressed. "Can you get me sixty cages, each containing two little birds, to be delivered here by the thirtieth?"

"Sixty cages?"

"Yes. I went through my dining room just now—not the main dining room, but the little romantic one in the flower garden—and it depressed me. It is sad, Matvey. It is almost gloomy. I want it to be essentially gay, and I thought that if over each table there was one of those little basket-shaped gold cages it would make it look a little happier. Don't you think so?"

Matvey laughed. "It is not very practical," he said. "You will get tired of them."

"Of course I shall. Then I shall get rid of them. But meanwhile they will look gay. Sixty cages by the thirtieth. You won't disappoint me? Tell the firm to send a little boy to look after them. You will see they are all there?"

"I will. You are an extraordinary person."

"Not at all." Gaiogi's laugh was infectious. "I was depressed. Now I feel quite happy."

Mr. Lugg phoned Mr. Campion by appointment. Mr. Campion was in the private office of the Boiled Owl Club and Mr. Lugg was in a small basement room which looked as though some thoughtless person had built four walls round a gipsy encampment.

"Not a sossidge, cock." The thick melancholy voice was just audible above a chatter like the din of a monkey house. "Ma Knapp was no good at all. Thos. is inside again, so he can't help, poor chap. I've been to Walkie's and to Ben's and I dropped in at Conchy Lewis'. Not a sossidge anywhere."

"Have you tried Miss King?"

"I 'ave. Just got out alive. If Mr. Tuke ever 'ears of this I'll never 'old up me 'ead again. Mud-rollin', that's what I'm doing. They was all very pleased to see me. It was like old times."

"That must have been ever so nice. Keep your mind on the job."

"I am. My Gawd, you're grateful, aren't you? Here am I with me pockets sewn up mixin' with dust I've shook orf my feet for ever. What d'you think I'm doin' it for? What luck your end?"

"Nothing yet. Phoebe gave me the Starlight, the Fish, the Newspaper, the Enraged Cow and a staggering dive called the All At Home. I've had a morning long after the night before. All a blank. Look here, try straight food with a smear."

"Smear meanin' filf?"

"Yes. I was wrapping it up for you. Ollie is the man you want. Ollie Dawson of Old Compton Street. Take him a bottle of kümmel."

"It is kümmel? I thought 'is fancy was dressed crab? I'll take both. Righto. Any more dope?"

"Dope? Oh, I'm sorry, I was on the other book. Yes, one thing. Listen. A long two-edged knife, very narrow indeed."

"Ham and beef type?"

"That's about it. My hat, you're horrible. All right then. Phone me at four at the Dorindas in the Haymarket. I'm keeping Pa Dorinda as a last hope. Good-bye."

"Good-bye, cock. Good hunting."

"Yoicks to you, sir. Good-bye."

Amanda, who had been sitting over the telephone in her private cubbyhole at the works for considerably over an hour, was commendably good-tempered when at last her fiancé kept his promise.

"Never mind," she encouraged with all the boundless

energy of youth in her voice. "Never mind. Keep at it. I've got something. It's a bit negative. You know the Clear, the badge? I say, that was Sid. Yes, Sid. He pinched it from Georgia. The sight of her wearing it turned him up, as I thought it would, and he pinched it off her lapel during the crush after lunch. He didn't want to go into a lot of explanations, so he put it where someone who knew what it was would be bound to see it. He did that at once, while the plane was still empty."

"Did he though? That was a bit roundabout, wasn't it?"

"Not really." She sounded embarrassed. "He's only a bit touchy on the subject of his snappy pinching. He's shy about it. The accomplishment wasn't thought a lot of at his school. At your place they probably thought it was clever and funny; at his they didn't. It's a social question. I got it out of him this morning."

"I see. That means the deity in the machine may not have been near the hangar at all?"

"I know. But so few people were there before Ramillies, were they? I say, A.D. has been trying to get you all the morning, but he's out now seeing Gaiogi. I think he wants to ask if there's anything he can do."

"If there is I'll let him know. Good-bye, Lieut."

"Good-bye."

Detective Inspector Wylde of Narcotics had a soft, friendly voice and a habit of lowering it when speaking on the telephone. Superintendent Oates had to concentrate to hear him.

"I've had a little talk with Happy Carter," Wylde murmured. "I'm afraid it's not down our street at all, sir. We shall go on working on it, of course, until further orders, but I thought I'd let you know what the situation is. This girl Adamson certainly wasn't in touch with any of the big people. It looks to me as though she stole the stuff, or had it given her, from someone at Papendeik's, and simply tried to make a bit on the side."

"Oh, I see. Thank you very much, Inspector." Oates was gloomy. "You'll just cover every angle, won't you? We don't want anything to slip through our fingers at this stage, do we?"

"No, of course not, sir, but I think you'll find it's not our pigeon. All right, sir. Good-bye."

He had barely replaced the receiver when the Essex superintendent was on the line again.

"Nothing at all to report." The cheerful voice sounded unwarrantably pleased with itself. "We've practically stripped the clearing and there's no weapon of any sort, unless you'd count three tin openers and a bicycle pump. I reckon the seat of the mystery is at your end, as I said all along. Mayhap if you could get on to the motive now we might learn something."

"Mayhap we might," agreed Oates grimly. "We've had the medical report and none of the usual reasons apply."

"Fancy that, now. Oh well, we'll go on looking. So long."

"Wait a minute. No news of the car?"

"No, no, not a sign of it. The petrol stations can't help us. There's plenty of traffic on our roads just now, you know. We've been on to the lorry driver again and he can't add to his statement. He only heard it, you see. Still, he knows engines and he sticks to his story. He says it was four cylinders, missing on one, and there was a body rattle like a sackful of old iron. But there's plenty o' they about at this time of year."

"You're right, son. The woods are full of 'em. The boy's evidence isn't worth the paper it's written on as it stands. It's seeing that's believing; that's what they say."

"So they do, so they do. I don't know if it interests you, but Glasshouse for the three-thirty. It's a local horse. Sure to do well. Oh, perhaps not. I only thought it might. Good-bye."

Oates hung up, considered a few moments, sighed and recalled Sir Henry Wryothsley. The pathologist seemed surprised at his question.

"The Richmond Laboratories?" he repeated. "Why yes, I think so. I've never had any reason to doubt them. I can't give you any firsthand information, unfortunately. They don't do my stuff. But a big place like that is sure to be pretty sound. What's the trouble? Anything I can do?"

"No trouble at all." Oates was suspiciously casual. "I was only curious. It's not this affair we're on now. Another matter. If these people did a rushed analysis they'd be bound to find anything fairly obvious, would they?"

A laugh reached him. "What do you call fairly obvious?"

"Well, acute morphine poisoning, for instance."

"A fatal dose? Oh, Lord, yes I should say so, if they tested for it. Why don't you ask 'em? Parsons is the man there. He's a good chap. Frightfully conscientious. Ask him. He's not chatty. He'll be discreet if you tell him so. Ring him up."

"Perhaps I will. Thank you very much. Sorry to trouble you."

"Not at all. Have you been through my report? It's interesting, isn't it? I've got one or two theories. I'll put them forward when I see you. I've got to rush back now. My assistant's calling. We're doing a Stass-Otto. Good-bye."

Sergeant Francis Gwynne, hopeful product of the Hendon Police College, caught Inspector Pullen just before he settled down to write his report. The young man was diffident.

"I took up the angle you suggested, sir, and I've found one interesting piece of gossip which may or may not be of some use to you. . . ."

"Come to the horses," snapped the machine gun, who was irritated by the accent which he insisted on considering, quite erroneously, as unmanly.

"Well, sir, I saw Madame Sell of the big hairdressing firm just off Bond Street and she tells me that there has been a story going about for some weeks now concerning the death of Sir Raymond Ramillies and Mrs. Valentine Ferris of Papendeik's. Apparently Lady Ramillies and Mrs. Ferris were quarrelling over the same man, and on the morning of Ramillies' death Mrs. Ferris gave Lady Ramillies a cachet blanc—a sort of aspirin in a rice-paper case—for herself but instead of taking it the woman gave it to her husband. According to the story it was the last thing he had before he died."

"This is only gossip, you say?" Pullen was loth to show his intense interest.

"Yes sir, but I thought I'd better let you know at once in case it was useful."

"It may be. I can't say. I'm going up to the superintendent now. I'll mention it to him. That's all right, Gwynne. Carry on. That may be of some use."

Meanwhile Rex wrestled with the newspapers.

"Lady Papendeik authorises me to state that she is extremely sorry that she cannot help you any further. The whole matter is in the hands of the police. I am really very sorry but I myself know nothing. No sir, nothing at all. Miss Caroline Adamson left our employ some weeks ago. I really cannot remember if she was dismissed or if she resigned. Yes, that is my last word, absolutely my last word."

He rang off, only to pick up the receiver again as the instrument buzzed once more.

Val's attempts to find her brother brought her in despair to Amanda's office wire.

"No, Val, not since lunch." Mr. Campion's fiancée was intensely sympathetic. "What's the matter? Reporters?"

"Oh, my dear, they're everywhere." Val sounded despairing. "We're in a state of siege. Four women have actually got into the building at various times by representing themselves as clients. The staff is hysterical. Tante Marthe's had half a bottle of champagne and gone to sleep. You don't know where he is at all?"

"No, not at the moment, but he's on the job. If you could only hang out for a bit he'll see you through. Lock the doors if you have to. Shall I collect A.D. and come and help you? We could always barricade the windows."

"No, my dear." Val was almost laughing. "It's not as bad as that yet. I'll send out an SOS when the party begins to get rough. You think Albert's doing something?"

"Doing something? He's moving heaven and earth."

"Your faith is very comforting."

"Faith nothing," said Amanda. "It's the old firm. We're invincible."

It was four o'clock when a reluctant Oates, with Pullen at his elbow, got on to Papendeik's.

"Is that Mrs. Valentine Ferris? This is Superintendent Oates of the Central Department, New Scotland Yard. Mrs. Ferris, I wonder if you'd mind coming down to see me? Yes, at once, please. I'll send a car for you. It's nothing to get worried about. We just want a little statement."

"But I've told you all I can about Caroline Adamson." The high clear voice was nervy now and very much on the defensive.

"I dare say you have, ma'am." Oates was avuncular but

firm. "It's nothing alarming. I just want to have a little talk with you, that's all."

"It is very important? The house is surrounded by reporters. I daren't set my foot outside the door."

"I'm afraid it is, ma'am. Very important. Don't worry about the press, ma'am. We'll get you through them all right. You'll be ready, will you? Thank you very much. Good-bye."

"Good-bye," said Val faintly.

At four o'clock Papendeik's phoned Mr. Campion's flat without result. At four-one Papendeik's called the Junior Greys, but Mr. Campion had not come in. At four-three Papendeik's called Mr. Campion's fiancée again, but she had not heard from him. At four-five and a half Mr. Campion called Oates and, on hearing that the superintendent could not speak to him, sent him a message which not only brought the eminent policeman to the phone, but sent him and Inspector Pullen, to say nothing of a couple of plain-clothes men, hurtling down to 91 Lord Scroop Street, Soho, like a pack on the scent. Mr. Campion's original message sounded cryptic to the secretary who took it.

"Ask him," he had said, "ask him if one of his fat suspects had curly hair."

Chapter Twenty

In summertime the streets of Soho are divided into two main species, those which are warm and dirty and jolly, and those which are warm and dirty and morose. Lord Scroop Street, which connects Greek Street and Dean Street, belongs to the latter category. Number 91 was a restaurant with high brick-red window curtains and the name HAKAPOPULOUS in a large white arc on the glass. The main entrance, which was narrow and a thought greasy, had a particularly solid door with a picture of a grove of palm trees painted on the glass, while the back entrance, which gave on to Augean Passage, was, as the local divisional superintendent put it in a moment of insight, like turning over a stone.

Inside, the restaurant was strangely different from its exterior. The main room which possessed a gilt-and-mahogany staircase rising up into mysterious blackness above, was indubitably shabby, but it was not a bare shabbiness. There was a cold darkness, a muffled quiet in the big curtain-hung-room. All the tables were half hidden, if only by shadows, and the carpet, the Victorian hangings and the columns to the ceiling were all so thick and dusty that the smell of them pervaded the place like a kind of unscented incense. It was this quality which met one as one entered. The quiet swooped down on one as does the quiet of a church, but here there was no austerity, only secrecy: not the exciting secrecy of conspiracy but the awful, lonely secrecy of passion, the secrecy of minding one's own business. It was not a pleasant room.

The divisional superintendent, a grizzled friend of Oates, who knew and rather loved his district, arrived at the back door at the moment that Oates and his company arrived at the front. This happy co-operation avoided the suggestion that anything so unfriendly as a raid was intended, and the two parties, save for those four men who were left to hang about the entrances, met in the shadows of the main dining room, where there were only two customers, four-fifteen in the afternoon not being a busy hour with the house.

Mr. Lugg and Mr. Campion came out of their obscurity as Oates arrived. They had been sitting in a corner and their appearance had some of the elements of a conjuring trick, so that Pullen glanced round him suspiciously.

"Anyone else here?"

"No one. Only this lad." Mr. Campion's murmur was as discreet as the room itself, and they all turned to stare at the waiter on duty, who had come sidling out from behind a column. He was a small furtive person in an oiled tail coat and dirty tablecloth and he took in the nature of the visit in a single wide-eyed glance. Then, shying away from them like a field animal, he sent an odd, adenoidal shout up into the pit of darkness above the staircase. He was answered immediately and there was a tremor in the walls above and every chin in the room was raised to greet the newcomer. After a moment

of suspense he appeared, and a small, satisfied sigh escaped
Inspector Pullen.

Fatness and curliness are relative terms, but there is a
degree at which either condition becomes remarkable. In
each case Andreas Hakapopulous strained the description to
its limit. He was nearly spherical, and the oily black hair,
which carried the line of his stupendous nose to a fine
natural conclusion somewhere about six inches above the top
of the back of his head, was curly in the way that the leaves
of the kale are curly, or Italian hardwriting, or the waves
surrounding an ascending Aphrodite in a Pre-Raphaelite
painting.

He came downstairs daintily, like a big rubber ball, bounc-
ing a very little on each step. His welcoming smile was more
than friendly. It had a quality of greasy joy in it and he
winked at the divisional superintendent with such convincing
familiarity that Inspector Pullen had to glance at the other
man's unbending stare to reassure himself.

"We will all 'ave a nize bot'le of wine." The newcomer
made the suggestion as if he were announcing a rich gift to
the Police Orphanage. "Louis, quickly. A nize bot'le of wine
for everybody 'ere."

"That'll do." Oates was not amused. "We want a few
words with you only, Mr. Hakapopulous. Will you please
look at this photograph and tell us if you have ever seen the
girl before?"

Andreas Hakapopulous was not abashed. He stood balancing on the last step but one of the staircase, exuding a strong
odour of jasmine and an ingratiating affectionateness which in
that particular room was almost unbearable. He put out a
shapeless hand for the pasteboard and looked at it with a
casual interest which, although unconvincing, was also,
unfortunately, negative.

He peered at Miss Adamson's lovely, languorous face for
some moments and finally carried the photograph under the
window, where he held it at arm's length.

"Euh!" he said at last. "A nize little bit. Who iz shee?"

"We're asking you." The divisional superintendent put the
words in briskly. "Come along, Andreas. Don't be a b.f.
We're not interested in your theatricals. Have you seen her
before?"

"No."

"Wait a minute." Oates was smiling sourly. "Have you seen the papers?"

The Greek perceived his mistake and rectified it jauntily.

"She might be a girl who was found dead somewheres," he said. "I don' know. I see something this morning. I don' take much account of it."

"Yes, well you clean up your memory, my lad. Where's your brother?"

"Jock iz upstairs."

Andreas kept his smile and his soft, satisfied tone. He was neither sulky nor reproachful. A divisional plain-clothes man went up to find the other member of the firm and a minor inquisition began in the dining room.

"Now, Mr. Hakapopulous, think carefully: have you ever seen that girl in the flesh?"

"In the flesh?"

"Yes. Have you see her?"

"No."

"You understand me, don't you? Have you ever seen the girl alive?"

"Has she been 'ere?"

"That's what I'm asking you."

Andreas smiled. "I don't know," he said. "So many girls come 'ere. I don' think I ever saw 'er before."

Pullen thrust his chin out and butted into Oates's enquiry.

"Have you seen her dead, by any chance?"

"Dead?" Andreas raised his eyebrows.

"You heard what I said."

"Dead? No."

"Look here, Hakapopulous." The name was cramping to Pullen's staccato style but he took it manfully. "Do you want to come inside and think it over? You know what the inside of a cell is like, don't you?"

Andreas laughed aloud. It was a little teetering giggle which displayed his magnificent teeth.

"Excuse me," he said. "I tell you I don' know the girl. Ask someone else. Don' let's quarrel. We understand each other. I have not seen the girl except in the papers."

"I see." Oates took up the questioning again. It made an interesting picture in the gloom, the lean grey-haired policeman with the eyes which were as bleak and honest as the

North Sea, and before him, supremely happy in his security, the monstrous Latin, smiling and guileful.

"Mr. Hakapopulous"—the old super was always studiously polite—"you have several private dining rooms here, haven't you?"

"Yes, for business conferences." Andreas made the statement with unblushing simplicity.

"For business conferences?"

"Yes."

"Very well." The glimmer of a smile passed over the superintendent's thin lips. "We're not going into that now. Where are these dining rooms?"

His question was answered somewhat precipitately by the hurried return of the divisional detective, who made a startled announcement from the head of the staircase.

"Painting?"

Pullen was across the room in an instant. The Greek's smile broadened.

"That is so," he admitted placidly. "We do a little redecoration. My brother makes a 'obby of it."

"Does he?" Oates was very grim. "We'll go up there please."

"Why not?"

The entire company mounted the staircase, Campion and Lugg dropping in behind the procession. They came up into a dark, quiet passage which had four solid doors on either side and a small half-glassed one at the far end. The doors were all numbered very plainly, odd on the left and even on the right. Number eight alone stood open. In the passage the atmosphere so noticeable in the room below was intensified. It was not unlike the box of a very old theatre. Muffling festoons of drapery hung everywhere, and the strong smell of turpentine issuing through the one open doorway came as a relief. With the turpentine fumes came a little song. Jock Hakapopulous was singing at his work.

They found him on a stepladder, his head protruding through a hole in an old sheet which was tied about his tremendous middle with a blind cord. Apparently he wore no shirt, for his great forearms were naked save for a thatch of long soft black hair. He was engaged in painting the cornice, and his head, which was exactly like his brother's, save that it was bald, was very near the ceiling.

The room was uncompromisingly bare. There was not a vestige of furniture in it anywhere. Even the walls had been stripped and the dirty boards of the floor were furred where linoleum had been removed.

Oates avoided Pullen's eyes and a gloom descended on the raiding party. Andreas indicated the visitors.

"The police," he said unnecessarily. "They want to know if we seen a girl."

"That'll do." Pullen snapped out the admonition and the pantomime with the photograph was repeated.

Jock Hakapopulous was even blander than his brother. He too was ingratiating but he was an older man, and there was an underlying capability about him and a dreadful rat intelligence which was not only not negligible but, somehow, in that atmosphere, alarming.

He too professed himself unhappy not to be able to oblige. There were so many girls in the world, he said. One was very much like another. He himself had no use for women.

The divisional superintendent remarked that this fact would hardly seem to emerge from his police record, and both brothers were inordinately amused.

Since there was nothing to be seen in number eight, always excluding Jock Hakapopulous in his drapery, which was a sight with merits of its own. Mr. Campion and Mr. Lugg drifted away from the police party and explored the other rooms. As soon as they opened the doors the story was evident. Every dining room was suspiciously clean and there were uneven, discoloured patches on the wallpaper where furniture had been removed and replaced. Every room on the floor had been recently rearranged.

"They've got the police cold." Mr. Lugg made the observation through closed lips. "There's not much those two don't know. Where are you going?"

Mr. Campion did not reply. He had opened the half-glass door and was already some way down a flight of dirty stairs which he had discovered behind it.

When Oates joined him five minutes later he was still standing at the foot of the staircase looking out of the back door into the small yard which gave on to Augean Passage. The old superintendent had left the Greeks to the pack and he came down to Campion, holding the skirts of his coat closely round him like a fastidious woman.

"Lumme," he said expressively.

Mr. Campion nodded. "A corner of our picturesque London," he observed. "Mind that swill can. See what this is?"

Oates glanced up the staircase and then out into the yard again.

"A convenient getaway," he said. "Getaway or, of course, a get-in. Trusted clients take the back stairs, I suppose. Let's get out in the air. I don't really fancy the atmosphere of this place. They're a couple o' daisies, aren't they? How did you come to stumble on them?"

"Old-fashioned footwork. Lugg and I have been round every fishy club and suspicious eatery in London. What do you think?"

"About them?" Oates jerked his head upward and smiled with his lips only. "They know something, don't they?" he said.

It was not effusive thanks but Mr. Campion knew his Oates.

He led the other man across the yard to an open shed which he and Lugg had inspected less than an hour before. The plainclothes man inside looked up from the car which he was examining, shamefaced disappointment in his smile.

"Well, here it is, sir," he said, "such as it is. I was just coming in to report."

The superintendent walked round the machine, his shoulders hunched. There it was indeed, a nondescript four-seater Morris Twelve which had been someone's pride in 1929 and was still serviceable. The most irritating thing about it was its cleanliness. There were certainly a few traces of vegetable litter in the back, but the leather upholstery had been recently scrubbed and the paint positively scraped. Also, which was even more depressing, it possessed four new tires.

Oates said something under his breath, nodded to the man and came out into the yard again. He looked at Campion.

"I hate this kind of outfit," he said. "Did you see anyone in that house except those two and the waiter?"

"No," said Campion. "And yet, of course, there must be other people about; kitchen staff and so on."

"That's what I mean." Oates was spiteful. "They're all there somewhere. The place is full of people. We'll find 'em, of course, but it's like a rat warren. The whole house is so darned furtive you never know if the chair you're leaning on hasn't someone curled up in the bottom of it. They're all the same, these places—cold, dark, dirty and alive. They get on my nerves. Come on, we'll go in.''

They picked their way to the back door through a miscellaneous collection of kitchen refuse, dirty delivery trays and fresh supplies of greengrocery. Campion was in front and in the doorway he stopped abruptly, so that the superintendent ran into him.

''I say,'' he said.

Oates peered over his shoulder and an exclamation escaped him. At Campion's feet was a basket half full of cabbage leaves and among them, its bright blade gleaming wickedly against the green, was a long, thin, doubled-edged knife, about six tenths of an inch wide at the shaft.

Oates took up the basket without a word and went upstairs. The entire company had moved down to the main room again and as they passed along the passage curtains sighed dustily around them and the carpet swallowed up their tread.

Pullen looked down at the knife and for the first time during his visit a gleam of satisfaction appeared in his face.

''Ah,'' he said, ''that's something like, sir. Yes, indeed. Now then, you two.''

The brothers Hakapopulous regarded the discovery without interest. Jock had removed his sheet and now stood clad in a torn singlet and a disreputable pair of trousers. His great neck flowed from his jowls and swelled into a double roll at the top of his spine.

''Don' you like it?'' he enquired. ''We got a dozen of these. Show 'im, Andreas.''

Andreas Hakapopulous was delighted to oblige in any way. He threw open the drawers of his sideboard. He invited Inspected Pullen and his friends into the unholy mystery of his dreadful kitchens. Jock had underestimated his possessions. They found twenty-seven knives of the same pattern in various parts of the establishment and the elder Hakapopulous took up one of them and balanced it in his hand.

''Nize little knife,'' he said as the filtering light from the top of the window glistened on his shining face.

'' 'Andy. They're very popular just now in the trade. We get them from Loewenstein in Ol' Compton Street. He tell me the other day he sells more of these knives to restaurants than any other kind. Sharp, you know. She goes through a tough ol' chicken as though she was a little bit o' butter.'' He wiped the blade affectionately along his forearm and Mr. Campion, who was not unimaginative, turned away.

In the shed, where the car stood, the police held a brief conference. Pullen faced the two superintendents while Mr. Campion nosed about discreetly among the rubbish in the background.

"I'd like to pull 'em in at once, sir, all three of them." Pullen spoke earnestly. Lack of sleep had changed the key of his machine gun rattle and his eyes were angry. "They're lying, of course, but you can't seem to get at 'em in a place like this. You can't see 'em, for one thing. I'd like to get 'em into the light. Jock has a record as long as your arm, and Andreas has been inside half-a-dozen times to my knowledge. That little waiter chap might be made to squeal too," he added, not without a certain grim anticipation. He glanced across at Campion and gave him a conciliatory smile. "It makes you wild when you see it under your nose and can't lay your hands on it, don't it?" he demanded. "The job was done here if it was done anywhere and you can see how it was done."

"Those two wouldn't kill in their own house," said the divisional superintendent, unaware that he was making a nice distinction.

"No, no, they didn't do the killing." Oates made the pronouncement out of the fund of his vast experience. "They had a corpse wished on 'em. They're accessories after the fact."

"*And* they've had two days to clear up the mess." Pullen was bitter. "Let's get 'em inside," he said. "No arrest, of course; just a little friendly chat. They know something."

"Of course they do." Oates was laughing in spite of his weariness. "You'll leave someone to go over the house. That's your pigeon, Super."

"Righto." The divisional man grinned. "God knows what I'll find," he said. "Half-a-dozen stiffs, I shouldn't wonder."

Pullen went off to superintend the exodus and Oates looked at Campion.

"We'll go back together, I think," he said. "Not forgetting Master Lugg either. I want to talk to you two. I was just going to see your sister when you phoned. Don't worry; I put her off." He paused. "We don't want to make trouble," he added presently. "You'll come along, will you?"

"Right by your side," said Mr. Campion. "I'm not leaving you."

At ten o'clock on the same evening he had not gone back on his word. Lugg had returned to the flat for sustenance and a relief from his collar and shoes, but in a corner of the superintendent's office Mr. Campion sat on, and because of his service, and because he might be even more useful, no one disturbed him. Oates remained at his desk. The hard artificial light made him look old and his shoulders were prominent under his chest.

Four hours intensive questioning in the little office next door had elicited a number of things from the Hakapopulous brothers, among them the fact that the respectability of their establishment was, in spite of several extraordinary miscarriages of justice in the past, absolutely above reproach. They agreed, moreover, that they had used their car not only in the small hours on the morning of the twenty-first, but on every other morning for the past two years. A car, they explained, was indispensable for an early visit to Smithfield or Covent Garden, and, if one was to provide one's customers with good clean wholesome food, personal marketing was the only way to avoid economic ruin. Both brothers professed themselves charmed by the photograph. It reminded them of several customers, they said, and offered names and addresses to prove it. As for the redecoration—well, it was about time. The house was just a little old-fashioned. Had the inspector noticed it? It was indeed a coincidence that they should have chosen just this particular time to make a start, but then one must begin sometime, and the summer air carried away the smell of the paint.

It was an unequal contest. The police were handicapped and knew it. Their one forlorn hope, the lorry driver, had let them down badly. He had been rushed from Coaching Cross and had arrived eager to help. For a long, wearisome hour he had watched the brothers parading in half darkness in company with half-a-dozen or so other well-nourished aliens, only to confess himself "a bit muddled" at the end of it. In despair Pullen had dismissed him and returned to the direct attack.

The brothers remained friendly, oily and untired. Although the whole story was clear for anyone to read, and no one appreciated that fact more deeply than themselves, they knew that so long as they kept their heads they had nothing worse than inconvenience to fear. They were both men of tremendous physical stamina and mental agility. Moreover their experience of police procedure was considerable. Nothing was new to them. Any deviation from the beaten track of police questioning brought a bland demand for their solicitor and the farce began again.

At a little after eleven Pullen came in to Oates. He was hoarse and irritable, and there was a limpness about his appearance which suggested that a portion of the grease of his captives had somehow got on to himself.

"Nothing," he said savagely. "Absolutely nothing. Something's happened to that race since they did all that marble work."

Mr. Campion grinned and looked up.

"Those two are 'wide,' are they?"

"Wide?" The inspector threw out his arms expressively. "Not only do they know all the answers, but they enjoy giving them. I've got my hands right on it, you know. Chorge! That makes me wild."

He looked like an exasperated setter and Mr. Campion sympathised with him.

"How about the other chap?" he enquired.

"Him?" Pullen showed the whites of his eyes. "Have you ever had a long serious talk with an idiot child? He ought to be in a bottle, that's where he ought to be, in a jar. Flood's got him now. He's gentle, is Flood. They were matching cigarette cards when I left 'em. God give me strength!"

Oates sighed. "Sit down, Inspector," he said. "Mr. Campion's got a fag on him. Now we'll see what Flood's up to." He took up the telephone and made the enquiry. The instrument crackled back hopefully and Pullen jumped up. "Oh." Oates was interested. "Is that so? That's better than nothing, Sergeant. *Is* he? Yes, I dare say. Yes. They often are, these fellows. Yes. Well, bring him up here." He hung up and cocked an eye at Pullen. "Flood says he's weak-minded, but his mouth is moving," he said. The inspector sat down again and bit at his cigarette.

"It's in our hands," he said. "That's what pips me."

Louis Bartolozzi came in with Flood, who treated him as if he were certified, that is to say with great tenderness.

"Sit there," he said, stretching out a great bony arm and planting a small chair in the exact centre of the room. "Put your hat under it. Now are you all right? There's the superintendent."

Louis smiled faintly at the gathering and looked as though he were going to be sick.

"His mother was half Italian and half Rumanian and his father was probably French," explained the sergeant, consulting his notebook. "He was born in the Boro', he thinks, and he can't speak any other language than—er—what he does."

"Street Arabic," exploded Pullen and laughed unpleasantly, relapsing into bitter silence as Oates glanced at him.

"He remembers a girl in room number eight on Tuesday," Flood continued softly. "That's right, isn't it, Louis?"

"Da girl in da room, a nize pretty girl, yes."

"On Tuesday night? Last Tuesday?"

"Ver' like. Y'know we have a lot of people come there. Rich people. Nize girls, some of dem. Smart, y'know."

"In room eight on Tuesday last?"

The wide-eyed stare on the man's face became intensified.

"Tuesday, yes, every day."

"That's how he keeps going, sir." Flood looked at Oates apologetically. "Perhaps I'd better read you what he's said so far. He thinks he recognises the photograph but can't be sure. He remembers a girl in room eight on Tuesday last. She came in alone and ordered a meal. She must have been expected, but he doesn't know how the rooms are booked. He took her some food and never saw her again."

"Never saw her again?"

"No sir. He can't remember if she was gone when he went in again or whether the door was locked."

"But it's only two days ago!" roared Pullen. "He *must* remember."

Flood looked at his protégé helplessly. "He doesn't seem to," he said.

Louis seemed paralysed, but after a moment of complete vacancy he burst into sudden and excited speech.

"She was annoyed," he said. "Wild, y'know. Feller hadn't come. Somethin', I don' know."

"Annoyed, was she?" Oates sat up. "When was this? What time of the evening?"

The little creature, who looked as if he had never before been above ground, gave the old man an ingratiating smile.

"In the evening, yes, tha's right."

"What time? Was it still light?"

An elaborate shrug answered him. "In the evening."

Oates turned to Flood. "Any more?"

"No sir, not really, I'm afraid. He thinks people did use the back stairs, but he doesn't seem to notice people getting in and out of the place. When they're there he waits on 'em. He works very hard, sir."

"I don't doubt it, son." Oates's smile at Flood was half amused and half affectionate. "All right, take him away. See what you can get."

The sergeant collected his charge and shepherded him out again.

"That would look nice in the witness box, wouldn't it?" Pullen spoke with feeling. "You'd throw that to counsel as you'd throw a dog a bone."

Oates shook his head. "No, I see," he said. "I see. That explains the Hakapopulous calm. There's nothing very useful there except that it's fairly clear now what actually did happen. She went there by appointment and somebody came up those back stairs and killed her, probably with one of the restaurant's own knives, leaving the body for the Greeks to deal with. One of the brothers must have found her, and, not wanting any trouble—heaven knows they understand trouble, those two—they cleaned up the mess in their own way. Frankly I'm inclined to take my cap off to them. They've been thorough. When they went to market I suppose they slung the body in the back of the car, drove a little further out, dumped it and probably returned to do their shopping without raising an eyelid. They're that kind."

Mr. Campion stirred in his corner.

"If I might suggest," he said slowly, "if your man—I take it it was a man—came into that place up the back stairs he must have known his way about. Ergo, he's been there before. Do you think Flood's little packet of trouble could recognise a photograph?"

"That's an idea, sir." Pullen shot up. His energy was amazing and it flashed through Campion's mind that one could almost see his body pumping it out. "It won't be evidence but it might be useful. If we could only get something to jolt those greasy beggars in the next room out of their damned complacency it would be something."

Oates unlocked the drawer in his desk and took out a bundle of photographs. They were all there, taken from illustrated papers or begged or borrowed from servants; Val, Georgia, Gaiogi, Tante Marthe, Ferdie, Alan Dell, even Mr. Campion himself. Pullen gathered them up.

"I'll mix 'em with the usual," he said. "We'll see."

As the door closed behind him Oates swung round in his chair and looked at Campion.

"You're still on the blacking?"

"Yes," said Campion with a complete lack of hesitation which was unusual in him. "It's blackmail all right, guv'nor. Think of it. What a place for a transaction of that kind! Complete safety. Complete secrecy. Our Caroline has used that place before for the same purpose. Andreas recognised her immediately and it wasn't a good photograph if one had only seen her dead. Besides, my dear chap, how could she get into the place alone if they didn't know her? If this little Louis person is any good and he's been there long I should be very much inclined to show him a photograph of Portland-Smith. Don't you see, someone knew that place well. Whoever he was, he got Caroline Adamson to book a room there by promising her money. Then he sneaked across the yard and slipped up the stairs. He need not have met anybody. It was made for him. It was a place where muffled figures were always slipping in and out. The Mazarini mod used to use it for a paying-out place last year; did you know that? That's where Mazarini used to pay his thugs for services rendered on the racecourse."

"Is it? I didn't know that. When did you hear that?"

"This afternoon, from the friend who gave me the name of the place as a likely dive."

"Oh, I see." Oates glanced at the younger man with a smile that was only part amusement. "You and your friends," he said. "*All* your friends."

Mr. Campion's expression grew serious.

"I don't mind my friends' troubles," he remarked feelingly, "but I draw a line when they get mixed up with the family."

They were still eyeing each other when Pullen came in. He

walked over to the desk and laid the photographs down without a word. His heavy face was blank and his eyes looked bloodshot.

"Well, did he recognise anyone?" Oates was hopeful.

"He did." The inspector could barely trust himself to speak. "He knew 'em all. Why shouldn't he? They're all fairly well-known people. He knew Miss Wells and Mr. Dell and Mrs. Ferris and Laminoff, of course. He'd waited on every one of 'em, he said. He also recognised a photograph of the ex-Emperor of Germany, Sergeant Withers of the K Division, and the portrait of you, sir, as an inspector. He's worse than hopeless. Flood seems to understand about half he says, but I'm hanged if I do. I'll go back and have one more talk to those perishing Greeks. I can't keep 'em here all night without charging 'em and although there's plenty we could hold 'em for I don't see much point in it. They won't run away. Why should they? I don't suppose the boys on the car have phoned yet, sir, have they?"

"No, nothing. That's a forlorn hope, Inspector, I'm afraid. We didn't get on to it soon enough. I'll leave you to it. I've had forty-eight hours solid and I'm no longer intelligent. If you want me you know where you can find me."

The phone bell answered him, and he pounced on the instrument hopefully, all trace of weariness receding from his eyes. Mr. Campion had seen the same phenomenon in the face of an angler who had noticed a nibble when he was just about to wind in his line.

"What? Yes, Superintendent Stanislaus Oates here. Yes, Sanderson speaking? Yes. You have? Really? Good man. She saw 'em, did she? Splendid! Saw the two brothers lifting a girl into the car? She thought the girl was what? Oh, drunk. Yes, of course. Fine. Bring her round. She's just what we want. What? What? Oh. Oh, I see. Oh. What a pity! No, no, of course. Of course not. Well, yes, yes, you may as well. Yes, Inspector Pullen will be here. Yes, righto. Good-bye."

He replaced the receiver and grimaced at them.

"You heard that, did you? They've found a witness who saw the Greeks carry a girl out of the back door at two in the morning of the twenty-first. She thought the girl was drunk and took no notice of them. Unfortunately she's a vagrant and not a good witness. We could never put her in the box. She'd be discredited in five minutes. They're going to bring her round, but I don't see that she's going to help. There you are, Pullen. I'm sorry, but what do you expect in Augean Passage?''

The inspector thrust his hands into his pockets.

"It's always the same with these cases," he said. "Still, I'll get back to those two. This might rattle 'em. There's a chance. If only they'd play ball we might get a description of the man. That'd be something.''

"If they saw him," said Mr. Campion.

Both men turned to look at him and spread out his hands.

"With a back entrance like that, why should anyone ever have seen him? Why shouldn't he have come and gone like any other of the shadows in that rats' nest? No one need ever have seen him there that night.''

"Except the girl," put in Oates. "She saw him and she knew him. We're back where we started, Mr. Campion. It's motive we want; motive and Miss Adamson's friends.''

"Give me a week." The demand was out of the younger man's mouth before he realised he had spoken. "Give me a week, Oates, before you stir up the dovecotes. The chief won't like it if you do, the Colonial Office will be furious. What's the good of an exhumation order? What's the good of an unholy stink? What's the good of smearing all this appalling mud over people who don't even dream it exists? Give me a week, only a week.''

"It'll take a week to get the Home Office to move," said Oates.

Chapter Twenty-one

On the Sunday Amanda gave a formal sherry party to mark the breaking off of her engagement to Albert Campion.

It took place at her cottage on the river near the Alandel works and was one of those elaborately masochistic gestures which the modern cult for the proper sublimation of all the more commonplace emotions has made fashionable among the highly civilised.

Coming, as it did, at the end of one nightmare week and at

the beginning of another, it seemed very appropriate and was almost, as Tante Marthe said, the only conceivable kind of celebration which one could decently bring oneself to face in the circumstances.

No one knew the cause of this new trouble, and most people were too worried to care, but the first impression, which was that young Pontisbright had put his foot down, was dispelled. The mischief lay between the two parties most concerned. So much was evident as soon as one set foot in the house.

Amanda's house was like Amanda inasmuch as it was both small and astonishingly rational. The main room, which, with a little kitchenette, comprised the whole of the ground floor, possessed one glass side which opened on to a steep lawn running down to the river, and was otherwise individual inasmuch as the furnishings had been taken over complete from the prim old lady who had lived there before, and had been made comfortable and attractive with anything which had taken Amanda's fancy, from a nice piece of machinery to a two-foot bowl of marigolds. The result of this marriage of tastes was a big, odd room in which a fine "tea-chest" clock and a plush-framed photograph of Edward VII in a kilt lived in harmony with an architect's drawing table and a magnificent Van Gogh.

Hal Fitton, Earl of Pontisbright, supported his sister at the gathering. He stood by her side, grave and old-fashioned as he had always been. At twenty he was a sturdy, serious young man with the family's eyes and hair and a double dose of the family's composure. The situation was one which appealed to his youthful sense of the dramatic, while appeasing his individual mania for decorum. He was very nice indeed to Mr. Campion and frequently spoke to him, making it even more clear than if he had said so in so many words that the dissolution of the proposed partnership had been a matter of mutual arrangement, and that nothing unpleasant had been said or even thought on either side.

Amanda was at ease, if a trifle brittle, but Mr. Campion was not so good. He looked hunted rather than harassed and there were fine lines running down his cheeks from ears to chin, as if his facial muscles were under particularly good control.

Val was inclined to be bitterly amused. She had come over

with most of the others who had been lunching at Caesar's Court and she was, as never before the complete professional woman, hard, experienced and aware of her responsibilities. Her tailored silk suit was a minor miracle. She looked unapproachable and, had it not been for her essential femininity, severe.

Ferdie Paul was there. He had come over with Gaiogi and his wife, and he stood in a corner, his quick brown eyes interested. Val fascinated him and the paralysing decency of the whole procedure evidently took his fancy, for he watched the brother and sister with a smile that was part genuine admiration.

Georgia arrived alone, her chauffeur driving. She caused a little sensation by appearing in white muslin, blue bows and a picture hat, which, although decorative and eminently suitable to the weather, were out of keeping both with the last mood in which anyone present had seen her and the unfortunate nature of the gathering.

"Mon Dieu!" said Tante Marthe aloud and turned away with interest, having caught sight of her own discreetly clad, silk-caped figure in a convex mirror.

Gaiogi alone seemed to appreciate the essential preposterous charm of the main idea of the party. He behaved as if he were at the funeral of an old enemy, looking about him with a kind of mock solemn relish. Too, he alone seemed to have shaken off the real bond of calamity which encompassed them all. If ruin threatened, for him it was at least not yet. He talked earnestly in a low voice about trivialities and was delighted with Hal, whom he obviously took to be a particularly interesting English "piece." But if Gaiogi could forget the main situation, the others were not so fortunate. After the first overbright five minutes the morale broke down. The room was littered with Sunday papers and by the time Dell arrived, looking if anything a little more worn than Campion himself, the post-mortem upon them was in full swing.

The cheaper press carried little new about the actual mystery. The Hakapopulous brothers had burst upon the world two days before and the photograph of "Mr. Andreas Hakapopulous, who had been questioned by the police in connection with the death of beautiful Caroline Adamson (Miss Adamson was once a mannequin at a famous dress

house)'' was still vivid enough in everyone's mind. So far
the name of Ramillies had not appeared in print in connection with the case, and the references to Papendeik's had
been most carefully confined to the bare fact that the dead
girl had once been in their employ, but what the laws of
libel restrained in print had not been silenced in conversation, and the feature, or magazine, sides of the family
Sundays were littered with evidences of the trend of popular
thought.

There was in particular an article by Lady Jevity called
"My Life as a Mannequin. How I Saved Myself from the
Dreaded Drug Habit. The Canker of the Upper Classes"
which came as near being actionable as anyone dared go, and
a catchpenny indictment headed "Hands Off Our Girls!" by
Honest John McQuean, which began "In a little country
morgue a lovely girl lies dead" and ended with typical
inconsequentiality, "Will no one tell them drugs and lovely
dresses are snares for little moths?" printed in gothic letters.

Most of the other papers had something in the same vein
but *Oliphant's News* had taken another and more ominous
line. They had merely written up Val very thoroughly. There
was no reference to the crime in their article at all, but the
house of Papendeik received a full-page spread adorned with
Val's photograph and a press picture of Georgia in a Val
negligee. This publicity was a trifle suspicious in itself, but
the writer of the copy had infused a touch of melancholy into
her account which gave the whole thing the dreadful flavour
of an obituary notice and left the uninitiated reader with the
uncomfortable feeling that the end of the story would be sad
and that he must wait until next week for it.

Georgia brought the ball out into the open field in her own
unmatchable style.

"It's very sweet of Alan, you know," she said, smiling
across at him. "Most people in his position would just keep
away from us all, wouldn't they? I don't mean anything
personal by that, Amanda. I know you and Albert just don't
want to get married and that's all there is to that. Besides,
you've got a family and a village and traditions and that sort
of thing. But I mean, poor Alan is nothing to do with this
and he could so easily just stay away, couldn't he? We all
are a bit leprous just now. It's got to be faced. Do you

know, my dears, I've been astonished. Quite a lot of people have been really awfully nice. Which reminds me: what's the time?"

"Half-past six," said Ferdie, who appeared to be the only member of the party still coherent. "Got a boy friend?"

"No, just a food appointment." Georgia nodded to him but glanced out the front windows immediately afterwards and smoothed down her muslin frills with an expression of such tender artlessness on her lovely face that several people glanced at her sharply. After her original pronouncement normal reticence seemed a little affected and people began to talk freely.

"I am ill," said Tante Marthe. "I feel the end of the world is coming, and I do not care what I wear for it. Don't you know anything at all, Albert? We haven't even seen you for two days."

"Albert's had troubles of his own," said Val absently and bit her tongue as he turned to look at her with sudden darkness in his eyes.

"Ciel! Yes. But what a time to choose!" Lady Papendeik spoke to herself, but the events of the last week had destroyed a poise which had lasted half a lifetime and the words were audible. Hal heard them and so did Amanda, and their reactions were precisely similar. Hal replenished Lady Papendeik's glass and Amanda began to talk about her house. There was not a lot to be shown, but she did the thing thoroughly, displayed the convenience of the white gas stove, the sink and the cupboard in the kitchenette, the stairs to the two little bedrooms, the bathroom, and her own newly invented electric geyser. There were several interesting labour-saving features, all of a startlingly practical rather than a merely gadgety character, and Gaiogi began to chip her gently about her domesticity, avoiding most adroitly any errors of taste which the nature of the occasion might have invited.

"But, darling, it's mad to live here *alone,*" said Georgia, innocently spoiling everything. "It's all so sort of honeymoon, isn't it? What do you do about service?"

"Oh, a char, you know." Amanda spoke with determined cheerfulness. "She's a good old thing. She lives just down on the highroad and she doesn't come when I don't want her. I go away rather a lot. I'm off to Sweden tomorrow."

"Really?" It was Gaiogi who spoke, but everyone had

heard and there was a moment of embarrassment as her immediate personal difficulties were recalled to everyone's mind. Hal moved over to her side.

"I have persuaded my sister to come with me to visit the Tajendie works," he said primly. "Alan, you approve, don't you?"

"Oh yes, rather. Very useful. We must keep in touch with what the other fellow's doing." Dell spoke dutifully but his eyes strayed curiously towards Mr. Campion, who met his glance with studied disinterest. Campion did nothing, nor did he speak, but at that moment everyone was aware of him. He stood looking at Dell and there was a wave of unrest in the room as it passed through most people's minds that perhaps this lean, affable person was not entirely reliable in his present mood. It was a sort of telepathic warning that he was not taking his personal disaster with quite the same decent casualism that everyone else was prepared to afford it and they were all, in spite of their own worries, a little embarrassed by it.

Georgia alone seemed unaware of the signal. As usual she was entirely occupied with her own point of view.

"You just shut the cottage when you go away, do you, Amanda?" she said.

"Yes, it's very convenient. In the country but with all the amenities of town." Amanda's satisfaction had a trace of hardness in it. "I'm off tonight. I go home to Suffolk first and we sail on Tuesday. I'm looking forward to it."

"My dear, of course you are. I wish I could do something like that, but then you haven't got children, have you?" Georgia sighed and looked out of the window again. Her beautiful face was troubled and her eyes were gentle. "I wish to God I *could* go away and get out of it all," she went on quite sincerely, forgetting the unfortunate inference. "I bet you do, too, don't you, Val? My dear, let's *rat*. Let's bunk and go to Cassis and lie in the sun."

"Darling!" The protest escaped Val before she could prevent it and as Georgia gaped at her she added with the quiet bluntness of exasperation, "For pity's sake, sweetheart, shut up. Things are bad enough."

"I wonder if you realise how bad they are, my dear." Mr. Campion's soft observation from the other side of the room made them all turn to him. He was leaning over the drawing table, his strong, sensitive hands, which no one seemed to have noticed before, gripping the sides of the board. His natural vacuity of expression had vanished and he had taken off his spectacles. He looked vigorous, deeply intelligent and by no means unhandsome in his passionate sincerity. "I don't like putting it to you as baldly as this," he said, clipping his words a little. "It's not a jolly subject to rake up at this particular party, of all times. But you terrify me. You appal me, standing around hopefully as you discount this and that little private awkwardness, packing it away in the back of your minds as not really important while you blind yourselves to the terrifying fact that these little awkwardnesses all mounting together make up one tremendous and overpowering sum, awkward enough to ruin every one of you. At the actual moment you're all comparatively safe. The libel laws protect you and the police enquiry is at its beginning. But my enquiry is nearing its end. I don't intend to rat to the police but the methods I have used are ordinary orthodox methods and what I know tonight they are bound to know soon, certainly by the end of the week. There is nothing to stop them finding out everything if they consider it necessary to pursue the enquiry, and as long as the murderer of Caroline Adamson goes free they will consider it necessary."

"What do you know?" Tante Marthe's question was sharp and unexpected, but no one in Mr. Campion's audience looked round at her.

"I know a number of interesting things." He was very earnest. "Several of them are criminal and the rest are, in varying degrees, unfortunate. For any one of them to be set down in print would be a considerable embarrassment for one of you, but for all of them to come out would be a catastrophe for the whole crowd of us. Let me tell you something. I know, and the police will eventually know, that Richard Portland-Smith was driven to suicide, not deliberately but by accident. The fact that he committed suicide was fortuitous. The idea behind that blackmailing was the desire to ruin him, to get him out of the way. I know that a carefully arranged frame-up, involving Miss Adamson, was staged for him at the Green Bottle Hotel at Shelleycomb on the Downs in October 1933. I know that one other person was present on that occasion besides Caroline Adamson and that that other person was a woman."

"A woman?" Georgia spoke faintly but Campion ignored her.

"I know," he went on, "that Portland-Smith used to meet this second woman in a back room in Hakapopulous' restaurant in Lord Scroop Street and that there he paid her all he had. I also know that this woman was not the main instigator of the plot. She merely did the work and took the money, half of which she paid to Caroline, who threw it away, and half of which she kept herself and invested most unprofitably. I know that Ramillies was murdered. I know that he left Caesar's Court in the middle of a party because he was so frightened of the approaching flight that he couldn't bear himself any longer. He went to Boot's Hotel and spent the night there in an agony of apprehension, and in the morning he went to see someone who knew his phobia and who gave him a hypodermic injection, promising him that the effects of it would be discomfort for four hours followed by a feeling of happy irresponsibility and freedom from fear. I know that the flight was unexpectedly postponed for an hour and that therefore Ramillies died on the ground when he should have died in the air. But I also know that any accident of this sort was anticipated by the fact that his specialist was at Caesar's Court in response to an invitation to sample the amenities of the place at the management's expense. I know that Miss Adamson was killed because, having been taught to blackmail once, she saw in Ramillies' death an opportunity to blackmail again. I know that she visited Hakapopulous' restaurant thinking to receive money and met a knife instead."

He paused and looked round. They were all watching him. Georgia stood with tears on her cheeks and her eyes wide, but the others were all imperturbable, their faces strained but expressionless.

"That is the criminal side," said Mr. Campion. "Now we come to the merely interesting but unfortunate. I make no apology for digging up these facts about you all. My principal care has naturally been for my sister and in her interest I have done my best to satisfy myself of the whole truth of the story. I've told you that I shan't squeal to the police, and I shan't, but, as I say, my methods of enquiry are the same as theirs and they are doing now what I did a week ago. Some of these facts are relevant and some of them aren't. I don't know yet which are which, but I shall know, and should the police

248

come to discuss them the entire world will know. I know, for instance, that you, Gaiogi, received a small but mysterious backing for the the the Poire d'Or. I know that you, Dell, have an enormous sum of money invested in Caesar's Court. I know that you, Georgia, have all the money you possess in the world in the same place. You too, Ferdie, have a packet there, and so has Val and Tante Marthe. Then there's Rex. Rex has a lot of money, Tante Marthe. He's your senior partner, isn't he? Then Caroline Adamson's father was a friend of Gaiogi's and when he died Gaiogi promised to keep an eye on the girl. I know lots of little odd things which may mean nothing, but which have come out in my enquiry, personal things which perhaps don't matter very much to anyone but those concerned. I know Georgia's first husband is playing in a concert party in a third-rate watering place. I know the name of Ferdie's doctor in Paris. I know the White Empress Club is financed by Gaiogi, and I know that Val was criminally careless to leave some seven ounces of morphine where any member of her staff could steal it. None of these may matter very much, but they won't look jolly in print, with ghouls like Honest John McQuean and Lady Jevity underlining them. There's only one way to save the worst of the mess and that is to get the murderer into the hands of the police immediately. Fortunately one can only hang a murderer once. One body is sufficient to inaugurate the ceremony. If the police can only get Caroline Adamson's murderer they won't go into the death of Ramillies. That is why I am still here. I shall make one last attempt. If I fail—and I warn you I'm not too hopeful—then I'm through. I don't care what happens to me or to anyone else. I'm finished.''

He glanced across at Amanda.

''God knows this business has cost me enough,'' he said.

Nobody spoke for a long time. Young Pontisbright was white and angry and the others were thinking the swift, absorbing, lonely thoughts of self-preservation. It was an appalling minute and the incident which ended it was mercifully ludicrous. Tires crackled in the flint road outside and Georgia started. Everybody looked out of the window and Gaiogi laughed abruptly. A long black chauffeur-driven car had pulled up outside the garden gate. The tonneau was nearly all glass and the three occupants were clearly visible. Two of them sat side by side in the back. One was Sinclair and the other was Towser. They had been to Whipsnade and had called back by appointment for Mama, forced to waste her time at a tiresome formal party. Even at that distance it was evident that the outing had been a success. Towser spoke to the chauffeur, who smiled faintly and sounded the horn. Georgia did not say good-bye. She picked up her little pale blue handbag and her long gloves and walked out of the cottage in her demure white muslin, her bows and her picture hat. She looked beautiful, sweetly feminine and virginal, as she went off on a new adventure, tears still on her cheeks.

Dell walked over to Val and led her out onto the little lawn behind the house. There was a gate leading into a flat meadow there and he piloted her through it. The atmosphere had been so electric that there seemed nothing odd in his behaviour. Her instinct had been to get away at all costs and his appearance at her elbow merely made the going easier, but out in the warm air, with the world green and rational about her, the sensation of nightmare wore off, leaving her battered but aware again of life as it was in the daylight.

"He's very cut up," Dell remarked as they stepped onto the turf.

She nodded. "I've never seen him like that before. It's rather unnerving when you see someone you know so well go all out of character. He's frightened, too, I think. Things aren't good."

"No," he said. "No. Yet they may not be as bad as he seems to think. We can only hope, you know."

He was comfortingly calm and Val glanced up at him. She was relieved to see that he was at least not embarrassed by their recent personal upheaval. She tried to consider him objectively, and saw only that his hair was going grey and that he looked tired. In common with most modern-thinking women she was pessimistic where her own emotions were concerned and she found herself acutely conscious of her attitude towards him. She was still most painfully in love with him. He still created in her that unaccountable excitement and exquisite sensitiveness which would seem to have some psychic or at least some chemical origin, since it had no birth in reason, but she still shrank from investigating him. She still recoiled from the secret door which Georgia's Pandora instinct found so irresistible in all men. A living room or a junk cupboard? The risk was too great to take. Her own exacting intelligence, her own insufferable responsible importance, weighted her down like a pack. She was desperately aware that she wanted something from him that was neither physical nor even mental, but rather a vague moral quality whose very nature escaped her. It was something of which she stood in great need and her fear was not only that he did not possess it but that no one did. Her unhappy superiority made her feel lonely and she turned from him so that she was not looking at him when he spoke.

"I wanted to talk to you, Val. Do you mind if I talk about myself?"

The question was so unlike him and yet so much to be expected that her heart sank.

"Oh, that's all right," she said. "I think we can almost take that as read, don't you?"

"What?" He was astonished and his bright blue eyes were amused. "What do you think I'm talking about? Georgia?"

"Aren't you?"

"Well, no, I wasn't exactly." He was laughing a little. "I wanted to talk about myself. This is my trouble, Val. I am in love and I want to marry, but there are difficulties, my own mainly. I don't want a mistress or a companion. I want a wife."

Val paused in her walk. She was surprised. She held her head stiffly and her eyes were interested. Her business people knew her thus and in certain Parisian quarters the attitude was viewed with deep respect. Madame was alert.

Dell smiled at her. He seemed to find her charming.

"It's not so easy," he said. "Wives are out of fashion. I love you, Val. Will you marry me and give up to me your independence, the enthusiasm which you give your career, your time and your thought? That's my proposition. It's not a very good one is it? I realise that I've made a fine old exhibition of myself with Georgia Wells which has hardly enhanced my immediate value in the market, but I can't honestly say that I regret the experience. That woman has maturing properties. However, that is the offer. In return— and you probably won't like this either—in return, mind you (I consider it an obligation), I should assume full responsibility for you. I would pay your bills to any amount which my income might afford. I would make all decisions which were

251

not directly in your province, although on the other hand I would like to feel that I might discuss everything with you if I wanted to; but only because I wanted to, mind you; not as your right. And until I died you would be the only woman. You would be my care, my mate as in plumber, my possession if you like. If you wanted your own way in everything you'd have to cheat it out of me, not demand it. Our immediate trouble is serious, but not so serious as this. It means the other half of my life to me, but the whole of yours to you. Will you do it?''

"Yes," said Val so quickly that she startled herself. The word sounded odd in her ears, it carried such ingenuous relief. Authority. The simple nature of her desire from him took her breath away with its very obviousness and in the back of her mind she caught a glimpse of its root. She was a clever woman who would not or could not relinquish her femininity, and femininity unpossessed is femininity unprotected from itself, a weakness and not a charm.

He pulled her towards him and her shoulders were slim and soft under his hands.

"It's the only unfashionable thing you've ever done, Val."

Her eyes were clever as a monkey's and sunny as a child's.

"My fashions are always a little in advance," she said, and laughed in that sudden freedom which lies in getting exactly what one needs to make the world that place in which one's own particular temperament may thrive.

They walked on through the meadow and, finding the road, came back to the front of the cottage. Georgia's chauffeur had driven away and the Lagonda now lay first in the line. The sight of it brought the general situation back to their minds with an overpowering sense of dismay. Dell was holding Val's elbow and he pressed it encouragingly.

"We'll get by," he said. "Come on."

Their first impression was that the party had dwindled. Ferdie was talking to Hal about jujitsu and Gaiogi and Tante Marthe were standing together in more serious consultation. The three glass doors on the lawn stood wide, and through them, on the edge of the river's bank, Mr. Campion was listening to Amanda. Ferdie looked up as Val came in and his glance followed her own to the two on the lawn.

"Hallo," he said suddenly. "What's this? A reconciliation? That lad's in a nasty state. I thought she was going to take pity on him when she took him out there.''

"I don't think . . . .'' Hal began stiffly and paused abruptly as the conversation on the lawn took a sudden turn.

As Amanda ceased to speak Mr. Campion took her hand and raised it to his lips with a gallantry which might or might not have been derisive. Amanda recovered her hand and hit him. It was no playful situation but a straight broadside attack delivered with anger, and the noise of the impact sounded clearly in the room.

"Indeed,'' murmured Gaiogi with an embarrassed laugh, and added instantly "Good God!''

Campion had picked up his ex-fiancée and they saw him poised for an instant with the girl over his head. He said something which no one caught, but which possessed that peculiar quality of viciousness which is unmistakable, and then, while they all stared at him, pitched her from him into the deep river with a splash like a waterspout. He did not wait to see what became of her, but swung away and strode up the garden, the imprint of her hand showing clearly on his white face. As they reached the water's edge they heard the roar of the Lagonda.

Amanda's comment as she swam ashore and was lifted, breathless and dripping, onto the lawn by a bewildered gathering, was typical of her new mood.

"Not everybody's form of humour,'' she said briefly. "Will you all go and have a drink while I change?''

Tante Marthe accompanied her and Val made helpless apologies to Hal, who was devastatingly polite.

"He's not taking it very well,'' he said. "Frankly I was afraid something like this might happen. Anyway, she'll be out of the country for a bit. It's really nothing to do with you, Mrs. Ferris. Please don't worry about it. Fortunately there was no one here who could make a gossip paragraph of it.''

"He's obviously off his head with worry,'' put in Alan Dell hastily. "That résumé which he gave was most enlightening. He evidently knows what the police intend to do. I heard this morning that there was talk of an exhumation order for Ramillies' body. What he said is quite true. If there is no arrest the enquiry may turn into a long ordeal for all of us. A murder is the one and only thing which cannot be hushed up in this country.''

Amanda's brother regarded him with a curious little smile on his young mouth.

"Believe me, I appreciate that," he said. "If you'll excuse me I'll just have a word with my sister."

Ferdie looked after his retreating figure.

"There's not much that that kind of kid in that kind of position couldn't hush up, is there?" he said. "What was the row about? Anybody know?"

And Gaiogi, who had been listening with his bright eyes on Ferdie's face, shrugged his shoulders.

"That is how it should be," he said.

Val laughed uneasily.

"I thought you were going to say, 'What is a little murder to disturb an aristocrat?' Gaiogi," she murmured.

The Russian looked at her steadily, his round eyes intelligent.

"Among clever aristos, what is it?" he said.

Chapter Twenty-two

Ferdie Paul was on the telephone when Mrs. Fitch brought Campion in. The room was much tidier than usual and struck cold after the warmth of the summer streets, but Ferdie himself was slightly dishevelled in his anxiety.

"Well, do what you can, anyway, old boy, won't you?" he said into the instrument, his thin voice carrying a world of nervous force and irritability behind it. "Yes, I know, but it's not a pleasant experience for any of us, is it? You were an old friend, that's all."

He hung up and glanced at Campion, the welcoming smile fading from his face as he saw him.

"Hullo, you all right?" he enquired.

"All right?" Mr. Campion threw himself down in the armchair which Mrs. Fitch pulled up for him. He barely remembered to thank her but she did not seem to notice the omission. "Yes, I'm all right. I'm alive, anyway. The corpselike effect is induced by lack of sleep."

"It's getting you down, is it? I don't blame you." His host

was grimly amused. "Have a drink, Anna, for God's sake, dear, get the man a snifter. Don't hang about. Don't hang about."

If Mrs. Fitch resented his tone she did not show it. She mixed a drink on the sideboard and carried it to the visitor, who took the glass from her absently and set it down untasted. He looked like a skeleton in a dinner jacket. There were blue hollows round his eyes, while the skin stretching over his jaws seemed to have pulled his lips back a little. His normal affability had vanished completely and a sort of spiteful recklessness, which was wrong in him, had taken its place. Ferdie watched him, his shiny eyes laughing a little contemptuously in spite of his friendliness.

"Your girl friend swam ashore last night," he remarked.

"Did she?" Mr. Campion was profoundly disinterested.

"They have nine lives, all of 'em." Ferdie was not intentionally tasteless, but the little joke amused him. "You forgot the brick," he said.

Mr. Campion did not smile.

"You said you wanted to see me?" he enquired pointedly.

Ferdie raised his eyebrows and turned round to frown at Mrs. Fitch.

"Just a moment, dear," he said, every tone in the request indicating that she and everyone else in the world exasperated him unbearably. "Shut the door behind you. I've asked Mr. Campion round here to talk. You don't mind, do you? We shan't be long."

Anna Fitch went out obediently and Ferdie got up and shook his loose clothes.

"You're taking that engagement bust of yours too hard," he said. "I was talking to Georgia on the phone just now. She said Val seemed to be very worried about you. Still, that's your affair," he added hastily as his visitor prepared to rise. "I didn't phone all over London simply to tell you that no woman's worth it. You'll discover that in your own time. I've got my hands full at the moment. This is all pretty nasty, Campion, isn't it? Where's it going to end? We're in the soup, aren't we?"

Mr. Campion sighed. "It's comforting to find that someone realises that," he said bitterly. "These silly women don't see what's stewing up for them. They haven't savoured the

Hakapopulous variety of stink. They don't know what it's like. Their innocent little snouts don't register anything stronger than cheating at bridge. The home secretary is considering the exhumation petition now, I believe.''

"Oh, he is, is he? I was afraid that was coming," Ferdie spoke gloomily but his eyes were still bright with interest. "I've been trying to pull a few strings myself, as a matter of fact, but there's an ominous frigidity on all sides which doesn't feel too healthy. Still, supposing the police do get the order through, what can they expect to find? Wasn't there a P.M. at the time?''

"Yes, but the police aren't satisfied.'' Mr. Campion made the statement wearily. "They've got the report of the first P.M. and in it there's a mention of a hypodermic puncture in the left upper arm, yet the analysis found nothing to account for this. Not unnaturally, the police feel they'd like their own man to go over the ground again. They've got the viscera from Richmond now, as a matter of fact, and it's in Wryothsley's lab, but he wants to see the rest of the cadaver.'' He laughed briefly at the other man's expression. "I'm sorry to be so forthright, but there you are. That's the sort of detail which next Sunday's press is going to dish up with comment. Meanwhile, if there is anything in the body which was overlooked in the first P.M., Wryothsley will find it.''

Ferdie looked up. "There's always a chance that there's nothing to find,'' he observed but his optimism was not convincing.

"The 'unknown drug'?'' Mr. Campion sounded derisive. "Don't you believe it, guv'nor. There ain't no such thing. What they don't find they'll deduce, same as I have, and that deduction, if it doesn't give them proof, will certainly give them the lead they want. It's going to be an almighty mess.''

Ferdie Paul wandered about the big cold room. His body looked heavier than usual as his shoulders drooped and his chin rested thoughtfully on his chest. After a while he came to a pause before Campion's chair and stood looking down at him.

"*I* haven't any illusions, you know, Campion,'' he said at last. "*I* see the danger. *I've* got the wind up all right. But, if you don't mind me saying so, my business has trained me to

256

keep a bit quieter about it than yours has. Also, of course, I'm not personally touched by it as you are. I'm not a fool, though. I've lived with it for over three weeks and I've had my mind working. It's a question of proof now, isn't it?''

"Practically." Mr. Campion met the other man's eyes and seemed to make the reservation unwillingly.

"You mean you don't actually *know*. Is that it?'' Ferdie was merciless and Mr. Campion was forced to hedge badly.

"Well," he said, "since Val is so closely involved the police don't trust me entirely. Why should they? Then this row of my own broke on Friday and, frankly, I made a fool of myself, got tight and that sort of thing, and after the exhibition I put up I fancy the super may be wondering if I'm the white-headed boy after all. Still, I'm fairly well acquainted with police movements. Just now they're concentrating on the Hakapopulous pair. Inspector Pullen has worked it out that whoever murdered Miss Adamson must have known the restaurant very well or had at least used the back entrance before. They've decided that she was killed about eight in the evening. Just now he is spending his time trying to get the Greeks to identify photographs of everyone who has ever had anything to do with the poor wretched girl. Jock Hakapopulous is still as resilient as a sphere of solid rubber, but Andreas, I understand, is showing signs of wear and tear. Those two are holding out because of the accessory-after-the-fact charge, of course.''

Ferdie perched himself on the edge of the table and the light behind his thin hair made his curls look forlorn and inadequate.

"Campion," he said quietly, "who do you think it is? Does your idea coincide with mine?''

Mr. Campion raised his weary eyes.

"That's a very delicate question," he murmured cautiously.

"Because it involves a friend of mine, you mean?'' Ferdie's driving force was tremendous. The air seemed to quiver with it.

"Well, yes, there is that aspect, isn't there?''

"My dear chap"—the other man was exasperated—"I have many friends but I don't stand for 'em through thick and thin. I'm not superhuman nor am I a sentimental bloody fool. What put you on?''

"A quotation from a letter of Sterne's," said Mr. Campion.

257

He spoke dreamily and when his host stared at him went on, his tired voice precise and almost expressionless. "Lugg of all people produced it at four o'clock in the morning. All through this business I've been bewildered by a curious hand-of-fate quality which has pervaded the whole thing. I noticed it first when I found young Portland-Smith so very conveniently dead and yet lying in the one spot where no murderer could possibly have put him. I said something about it being 'like Providence' and Lugg suddenly produced the key. This is the quotation. It gives it to you in one. The truth is startlingly obvious when you consider it. 'Providence, having the advantage of knowing both the strengths and the weaknesses of men, has a facility for unostentatious organisation undreamed of by our generals.' It's a smart-type remark and just like a sophisticated parson, but it contains the key of this business. See it? 'Unostentatious organisation.' That's the operative phrase, while the recipe for same is given earlier: 'knowing both the strengths and the weaknesses.' That is how it was all done."

"My God, you've got it, Campion!" Ferdie was watching him with fascinated interest. "I think you're right. I thought you were three parts fool but I take it back. This is what I've been groping for. This explains *how*. Yes, I see it in the main, but I thought when you were talking yesterday you said that Portland-Smith's suicide was not intended?"

Mr. Campion rose.

"It wasn't," he said. "The intention was merely to get him out of the way of Georgia. He was round her feet. No one knew they were married, remember. You didn't yourself, even. In the beginning it was simply a little intrigue to break up an engagement of which Georgia was obviously tired and yet which, for some reason or other, she refused to dissolve. There was no great underlying scheme about it. It was just a little plot to end an unwise alliance. Portland-Smith was evidently nuts about the woman and I fancy the idea was either to get it into his head that he could never afford to marry her or, failing that, to get it into *her* head that he was unfaithful and not worth worrying about. Anyway, the original plan was merely to make a decisive sort of row between them. Unfortunately the 'unostentatious organisation' technique was not then perfected and, as with many beginners, the tendency was to work too large, while of course the

258

unknown fact that the two were married altered the whole scale of the thing. However, it provides a fine example of the method itself. The recipe lies in the strengths and the weaknesses, remember. A frame-up was arranged. Portland-Smith was in love with Georgia and she was unkind. Therefore a girl who resembled Georgia had a chance with him. That was a weakness in him. He was a barrister and therefore unable to take any real advantage of the anonymity law, so that he was peculiarly susceptible to blackmail. That was another weakness. Of the two women employed to do the dirty work the elder, who arranged the whole thing and who in my opinion needed no more than to have the idea as a money-making scheme put up to her, had a passion for money and that particular type of mind which can see the sufferings of others and regard them without comprehension, seeing them only as an interesting spectacle. That in her was a strength. Unfortunately, however, the blindness which made it possible for her to have undertaken the project at all was too much for the scheme altogether. Unconscious of the effect she was really having on Portland-Smith, she hounded the poor beast to death, and her boss, the original perpetrator of the little row, found Georgia's unwanted fiancé permanently removed. Whether this astounding success encouraged him or not I don't like to think, but I imagine that, once one has accustomed oneself to the idea of causing death, the convenient finality of that means of disposing of an obstacle might outweigh all other considerations. Anyhow, when Ramillies became a howling nuisance, the 'unostentatious organisation' method was put into practice again. Again the strengths and the weaknesses of men were all carefully utilised. Ramillies was so afraid of flying that he believed in the perfectly preposterous story of a drug which would make him feel seedy for four hours and magnificent for twenty-four. That was a weakness. Caesar's Court is one of the few places in England where the organisation is so perfect that, should anything arise there which the manager desired to hush up, every possible facility for doing so could be instantly afforded him. That was a strength. Then there were interested government officials there who could lend their influence to avoid any scandal if there seemed no real cause for one. That was the strength of the occasion. It was all very prettily thought out. Think of the doctor. Buxton-Coltness is an unmitigated snob and he was flattered by the invitation to

Caesar's Court and availed himself of it promptly. That was a weakness in him. He is anxious to please all important people and is in the peculiar position of having the kind of fashionable practice which permits him to take little risks which an ordinary G.P. might hesitate about. That is a strength. See what I mean?"

"Yes, I do. You're right, thunderingly right." Ferdie was trembling in his interest. "What about the last case?"

"Caroline? Oh, that was the same thing. I mean it was done in the same way. But it was a murder of necessity. Caroline attempted to blackmail her old colleague of the Portland-Smith business and, since anything that involved that elder woman would of necessity also involve the man, the old original god in the machine, she had to be silenced. This time the strengths and the weaknesses were brilliantly employed. He was becoming more experienced, I suppose. Caroline needed money badly. She had a job, no protector. This need blinded her to the tremendous danger of going alone to the Hakapopulous restaurant. However, she had been there before with her colleague to interview Portland-Smith and she thought she was going to meet a woman, the woman who had stood by the telephone while the wretched girl rang me up as a threat. Still, real need of money was her weakness. Then the Hakapopulous brothers could not afford an enquiry into their business, they were people who simply could not risk a murder investigation on their premises. That was their weakness. But their strengths were equally useful. Those two are crooks with the real crook temperament which half enjoys a tremendous risk. Also they are experienced. They've cleared up a mess and destroyed evidence before. Added to this, they're both used to police cross-examination and they know all the answers.

"There you are. That's how the whole thing was done: by brilliant, unostentatious organisation. He organised his crimes and relied on the strengths and the weaknesses of other people, none of whom had the least idea of the way in which they were being used, to protect him. The fact that he could do it shows the sort of chap he is: shrewd, sophisticated, quite without conscience and probably under the impression that he's superhuman, in which respect he's insane, of course."

His voice died away and there was silence in the room.

"The man's a genius," said Ferdie presently and sighed.

"Look how he runs that place," he added. "What a pity, Campion. What a cracking pity!"

Mr. Campion lay back in his chair again. He looked exhausted.

"Have you known this long?" he enquired at last.

"It's been forcing in on me for a bit. I've been afraid of it, yes. After all, when you're in the thick of a thing like this you can't help your mind working on it, can you?"

"Got any ideas?"

"I don't know. I've been thinking." Ferdie paused and looked at his visitor. "Forgive me, old chap, but I haven't really taken you seriously before. I've been working on an idea of my own. I didn't know *how* he'd done it, you see; all I knew was that he *must* have done it, and of course I saw why."

"You did? I didn't. I don't. That's the thing I don't understand now. I can't see why on earth he should get rid of two of Georgia's boy friends, one after the other, simply because she'd set her heart on someone new. It's not feasible. That's where the whole case goes to pieces and becomes fantastic."

Ferdie laughed softly.

"You haven't got the full story, old boy. You've got some of your facts wrong," he said. "All he did was to remove two men who were dangerous to Georgia's career. That was the thing Ramillies and Portland-Smith had in common. Damn it, Georgia's had plenty of love affairs which didn't end fatally! Look at that fellow Dell. Portland-Smith was a strong-minded chap who'd set his heart on being a county court judge. You never met him, did you? I did. I can't describe that chap. He was one of those pompous, pigheaded, thick-skinned fellows. You knew he'd get his own way if it was only by nagging for it or simply sitting next it until it became his by squatter's rights. You saw that in his eyes. If he hadn't been removed he'd have removed Georgia in the end. He just happened to be that sort of chap. Ramillies was a different bloke but just as dangerous. He was the 'scatty beaver' breed; you know, half-built dams in every square foot of stream. He wanted Georgia out on that swamp of his and when he got her there he played old Harry with her. Did you see her when she came back last time? Oh, terrible. Half frightened, half demoralised, figure going, God knows what. Ramillies was wild, you know, reckless, slightly crackers. He'd have ruined her if she'd stayed out there any length of time. Besides, she was terrified of him."

He hesitated.

"Just before the flight excitement he'd got some hold on her too, I fancy. I think he got some information out of that girl."

"Out of Caroline Adamson?"

"Yes, I think so."

"About the fleecing of Portland-Smith?"

"Yes. I imagine he was using it to get Georgia out to his infernal swamp and to keep her there for some time. At least that's what I think."

"I see." Mr. Campion's hollow eyes were hard. "But why?" he demanded. "Why this concern for Georgia and her career? Why Georgia?"

Ferdie slid off the table and walked down the room. He looked unhappy and embarrassed but there was still a hint of amusement on his shining rococo face.

"She's a considerable artist, you know," he said. "She makes a lot of money. He didn't see he was running any risk, and he wasn't until he had to wipe out Caroline. She's a valuable property, Campion; a great possession."

"To *him*?" Campion was insistent.

"I think Gaiogi Laminoff had better tell you about that himself, old boy," said Ferdie Paul. "Good heavens, haven't you ever looked at 'em?"

"Do you mean that she's his daughter?" Mr. Campion seemed taken completely off his balance.

"You talk to him, old boy," said Ferdie Paul.

There was a long pause during which Mr. Campion lay back in his chair, his face blank. Ferdie was more practical.

"Campion," he said suddenly, "look here, this is a jam. We're all in it. None of us want any more of a row than we can possibly help. I'm not asking you to shield anybody. That's too darned dangerous, I see that. But if we could avoid the worst it would at least be something. We might at least save ourselves the flood of dirt in the newspapers. Let's get hold of him. Let's get him up here and get the whole truth out of him and then put it to him plainly. He's up in the clouds. He doesn't see where he stands. I bet you he doesn't realise the danger. He's probably thinking about table decorations or illuminating the bed of the river by the swimming pool. His sense of proportion has gone to pot. If we got him here, in this room, and talked to him we could get the facts into his head.''

Mr. Campion passed his fine hands over his face.

"Get him to sign something, you mean?" he said dubiously. "Sign something and go to Mexico or some other place undiscovered by the extradition agreement?"

"Well, yes," said Ferdie slowly, "unless, of course, he has some other idea. . . . After all, that would be better than the police way," he added defensively.

"I think perhaps we ought to see him," agreed Mr. Campion hesitantly. "Between us we've got quite enough to prove the truth to him, if not to a jury. What did he use in that hypodermic on Ramillies? Did he get Caroline to do that? She may have swallowed the whole story, as did Ramillies himself, of course. Women will believe anything about medicine. It was a hell of a risk.''

"I suppose it was. It all depends what it was. The police may never find out.''

"That's so, but they'll do their best." Mr. Campion spoke bitterly. "They'll go round to our pet chemists, our doctors, our personal friends, making what they consider are discreet enquiries, until no one will give us so much as a packet of bicarbonate of soda without looking at us as if we were buying prussic acid. That's what I mean. The police are so damnably thorough. Our lives won't be worth living.''

Ferdie took a deep breath.

"We'll get him up here," he said. "After all, Campion, once the police are satisfied about him they'll stop hounding the rest of us. We must do it. There's no other way, is there?"

"We could try. Is he suspicious?"

"I'm not sure." Ferdie stood considering the practical aspects of the project. Now that the moment had come it was he who took command. Mr. Campion remained in his chair, his head sunk between his shoulders, weary disillusionment in every line of his thin body. "He's at home tonight," said Ferdie at last. "He rang me up just before you came. I don't think we'll beard him there. We don't want a row down there if we can help it. We've all got too much precious cash in the darned place. Look here, I'll go down now and fetch him. You'd better not come. If he sees you he'll spot something.

I'll bring him back here and we'll have it out, alone, where we can't be disturbed. How's that?''

"I'll leave it to you." Mr. Campion sounded listless. "The Lagonda's in the yard. You can take it if you like."

"My dear good chap, pull yourself together." Ferdie was reproachful. His own energy was boundless. All trace of his old lackadaisical manner had vanished and he seemed possessed of an enthusiasm which might have been undergraduate had it not been for its obviously nervous origin. "Never lend your car, your shoes or your girl friend. I've got my bus in the garage. I say, Campion?''

"Yes."

"I think we're going to pull this off with luck."

"I hope so."

Ferdie stood looking at him.

"I don't want to offend you," he said, "but I'm an experienced sort of bloke, you know. I know a lot about women. That girl of yours is going to Sweden tomorrow, isn't she? Do you know what train?"

"They're going from Harwich. They'll motor over. It's not far from their place. It's the early boat, I think." Mr. Campion made the confidence unwillingly and Ferdie did not move. He made an odd, uncouth figure standing there looking down, a quizzical expression on his face.

"Send her some flowers."

Mr. Campion began to laugh. He laughed with savage amusement for quite a long time. Ferdie appeared hurt.

"Women like that sort of thing," he said.

"I'm sorry." Mr. Campion sat up. "Forgive me. It's got its damnably amusing side. In fact it's not a bad idea. If there was time I'd do it. I could phone them, of course, couldn't I?"

"Send some from the Court. They've got the best florist in England down there. I'll do it for you myself when I collect Gaiogi, if you like." Ferdie seemed completely oblivious of any incongruity in the two errands. "What will you have? Roses?"

"A pot of basil would be nice." Mr. Campion's interest in life seemed to have revived for an instant and his smile had a curious intensity of derision.

"You're a fool, you know." Ferdie was perfectly serious. "Send a straight armful of red roses and a card with a sentimental message down to the boat and it'll work miracles. Women are like that. Their minds run on those sort of lines. Give me the card and I'll send it with the flowers. She's sailing for Sweden from Harwich tomorrow early? That's all I need know. They'll do the rest. Her name's Fitton, isn't it? Right.''

Mr. Campion took out his wallet and found a card.

"You think a message, do you?" he said, a trickle of amusement in his voice.

"I do, and not a rude one either." Ferdie was emphatic. "Say 'A happy journey, my dear' or something of that sort."

Mr. Campion wrote obediently and looked up, his pencil poised.

"You're an extraordinary chap, aren't you?" he said. "You keep your mind very mobile, what with one thing and another. A murderer to be apprehended here, an engagement to be patched up there. It's amusing how you find the time, really."

Ferdie took up the card.

"You're too conscious of the personal angles, my dear fellow," he said. "You let yourself be obsessed. 'Amanda— You'll never forget me—Albert.' That's all right. Bit didactic but not bad. You know the girl, after all. Very well then, I'll send the roses from the Court, collect Gaiogi and persuade him to come back here. We shall be back before eleven. You'll wait, will you? Good man. We'll put it to him."

He hurried out, and Mr. Campion, his plans made for him, was left alone with his thoughts. The room was very quiet and still cold and the noise of the traffic below sounded far away, a remote sea in another world. He heard the front door of the flat shut behind Ferdie and then, after a long pause, Mrs. Fitch came in.

She did not speak but moved quietly about the room, tidying up odds and ends, replacing books in their shelves and plumping up the cushions on the couch. There was an indefinable air of neatness about her, a suggestion of making all safe in her very walk, and a finality in the pat of her plump hands on the upholstery.

When she came to Campion's side in her tour of orderliness she looked down at his glass.

"You haven't touched your drink," she said. "Would you like a nice cup of tea?"

"No, thanks. I'm all right."

"You don't look it. Been to bed lately?"

"No, not for a night or two."

"What a pity you lost that girl." Mrs. Fitch had gone past him now and had reached the untidy muddle on the end of the sofa table. Her tone was conversational. "She was a nice little thing. No sense of humour but very good class. Pretty hair, too, but I don't expect you want to talk about her. Now look here, the whisky is there on the side. There's some gin and French and a little Advocaat and some more siphons in the cupboard underneath. If you want more glasses ring for them and the Jap will bring them in. There's plenty of cigarettes in that red box on the shelf."

"You're not staying to meet Gaiogi?" Mr. Campion put the question idly but she looked at him sharply, her glance unnecessarily square.

"No," she said. "No, I don't think so. I'll just get my coat and then I'm off."

He heard her giving some last instructions to the Japanese boy in the kitchen and then she popped in again, a dyed ermine coat hanging from her shoulders.

"Good-bye," she said.

"Good-bye. I'll give your love to Gaiogi, shall I, or haven't you forgiven him?"

"I don't know what you're talking about." She was smiling at him boldly. "Gaiogi's always been very kind to me. I worked for him long ago at the Old Beaulieu. He was very generous to work for. Always putting me on to things. He's not a bad old stick."

"Yet he lost your money for you at the Poire d'Or. It was quite a packet, wasn't it? Two or three thousand pounds. Unlucky money."

She stared at him and for a moment he thought he was going to see her angry. Bright patches appeared in her cheeks and her mouth was pale round its make-up. Suddenly, however, she laughed and a flash of the insouciance which is the keystone of her profession appeared in her smile.

"I've learnt a thing or two since then, ducky," she said.

She did not display her hands but his eyes were drawn to them. They were ablaze with stones. Her square ugly neck was alight, too, and the clips on her dress shone with the unmistakable watery gleam of the true diamond.

"Well, I'm off," she said and paused abruptly as the phone began to ring. She took up the receiver and listened for a moment. "Yes, all right, all right," she said. "What's the matter? I see, dear. It's Mr. Paul," she added, holding the instrument out to Campion. "He wants you. Something seems to be up."

"Hullo, Campion, is that you?" Ferdie's voice sounded loud and unsteady in his ear. "I say, can you come down here at once? Yes, I'm at Caesar's Court. I've just arrived. Look here, I can't tell you over the phone because of the girl on the house exchange. You understand? You come down, will you? Yes, just as soon as you can. There's an unexpected development in that business we were discussing. Very unexpected. I don't know what we'd better do, quite. What's the name of that man you know at Scotland Yard?"

"Oates?"

"Yes. I wondered if I'd ring him and tell him to come down here. No, I tell you what, you come down yourself first and then we'll have a conference. Hurry, old man, won't you? It's a question of time, I'm afraid. You'll be down at once, will you? Righto. I won't do a thing till you come."

"What is it?" The woman put the question as he hung up the receiver.

"I don't know." Campion sounded puzzled. "He seems upset about something. He wants me down there at once. I'd better go, I suppose."

"It's not like him to get windy," said Mrs. Fitch and led the way into the hall. As they went down the stairs together she sighed. "It's a nice old flat," she said. "Are you going by car?"

"Yes, I've got the bus down here."

"Give me a lift as far as Marble Arch, or aren't you going that way? It's just as quick this time of night. Would you mind?"

"Not at all." Mr. Campion seemed almost bored.

She scrambled into the front seat beside him and he swung the car out of the dark yard into the blazing Circus. He drove recklessly and she gripped the side.

"Here, don't break *my* neck," she said, laughing. "Put me down at the cinema, will you?"

"Got a date?" he enquired.

"You mind your own business," she said. "There we are. Pull right up. What do you expect me to do? Jump for it?"

"I'm sorry." He stopped outside the cinema and the commissionaire opened the door and helped the woman out. Her jewels flashed in the lamplight and he touched his cap respectfully at the tip she gave him.

"Well, good-bye," she shouted. "Cheer up."

Campion did not answer her but let in the clutch and swung out from the curb, missing a bus by inches.

The Lagonda continued her breathless speed through the town, which was enjoying a temporary lull in the traffic before the theatres closed. Campion sat at the wheel, the light from the dashboard shining up on his expressionless face. The hooded car was like a little quiet universe inside the larger world. It possessed the same atmosphere which had been so noticeable in Ferdie's flat, a cold loneliness, an air of going away. It seemed very doubtful if Mr. Campion was thinking at all. He drove brilliantly but apparently without interest and if he was consumed with a burning interest to discover what new disaster Ferdie might have brought to light in Gaiogi Laminoff's tight little kingdom he showed no sign of it.

He left London behind and travelled through those little townships which crowd on tiptoe round her skirts, jostling each other in their efforts to get close, and yet each retaining its essential characteristics, never merging either with a neighbour or with the mother city. He shot through Maidenhead at last and came swiftly into darker Berkshire. There was less than half a mile to go now. He had one long straight strip of tree-hung road, a dip and a humpbacked bridge, and then the turning and the long drive. This was Money's Acre: quiet reserves, well-kept grounds, protected reaches of river, here and there a little cottage like Amanda's built for working folk but dressed expensively and kept for pleasure, here and there a club or a discreet roadhouse, but country air and cool, unobscured starlit sky.

For the first time the Lagonda had the road clear. Nothing passed her and there was a gap in the oncoming traffic. He raced through the tree-hung stretch, bounced over the humpbacked bridge and slowed down for the turn. It was then, just at that moment when he was aware of the silence, of the lonely peace of his little world, dark in the midst of darkness, and when the brilliant lights of the Court sprang into sight through the shrouding elms, it was then that he felt the movement so close to him, so warm, so familiar and yet so horrible in its very intimacy. Someone was breathing on his neck.

He trod on the brakes and brought the car up with a scream and a jerk which stopped the engine and sent her slewing across the bend. The steering wheel caught him in the stomach and as he turned he saw for an instant the face captured by the upward ray of the dashboard light. The soft glow touched the unfamiliar under-curves, the nostrils, the insides of the arches of the eyes.

He did not speak. There was no time. The light glancing blow which, in the illegal science of the Kempo, has a very sinister name, touched the nerve centre behind his ear and he stiffened and slid forward. As Mr. Campion went out into the darkness a single thought ripped through his mind with the dazzling clarity of revelation: *This is why the knife went in at a right angle. This is why Caroline Adamson lay so still.*

Chapter Twenty-three

The headlights of the Lagonda described a wide arc over the grey meadows and laid yellow fingers on the boles of fine old trees as the great car swung round and crept smoothly on to the main road again.

She took the quarter mile to the winding lane with the same swift efficiency which she would have afforded had her master been in command, passed the white gate through which Val and Dell had come up out of the green field together, and slid quietly to a standstill in the dark road outside Amanda's cottage. The lights went out and the engine died away.

It was a fine night with stars and a fine rain-promising wind. The flowers in the cottage garden nodded together like small white ghosts in the shadows and there were whispers in the grass and in the leafy billowings of the trees.

The small house waited with that forlorn secrecy which is the peculiarity of all empty houses. The windows shone like beetles where the starlight touched them and the chimneys showed squat and smokeless against the cloudless sky.

The door of the car opened noiselessly and a figure remained motionless, half in and half out of the driving seat, as the twin searchlights of a traveller on the highroad behind him climbed up to the stars, sank and disappeared again; leaving an inkier blackness behind.

The wind in the trees freshened and the whispering among the leaves grew more intense. The figure moved. It vanished behind the car, melted into the uncertain silhouette and reappeared an instant later on the other side. There was a moment of tremendous noise as the door catch clicked. The tiny alien sound seemed to silence the roar in the treetops, but there was no other movement. The cottage remained dead and the fussy wind built itself about it caressingly.

There was a long pause which seemed interminable as the figure remained webbed inextricably to the black shadow which was the car. Afterwards came the sound of effort, breathing muscles straining and once the single scrunch of a shoe on the loose flint road. Then out of the larger shadow came the other one. It was monstrous, horrible, a nightmare shape, topheavy and enormous, limp arms flapping, the head of an elephant, and, when it turned, the great beak of a gigantic bird ending incongruously in a shoe, vividly describable against the holey curtain of the sky.

It advanced falteringly down the path until, outside the first window, it turned miraculously into two, a long figure on the ground and a thicker one bending over it.

There was the thin, alarming sound of splintering glass, then another pause while the whole world seemed to listen, then breathing again and the swift rattle of a window sash and a scrambling sound as the upright figure pressed into the darkness of the house and was swallowed by it.

The night grew older. The wind dropped and sprang up again. On the highroad headlights climbed to heaven and shied away again. Down in the river an otter swam by and a rat paddled about in the mud. Amanda's house crouched beside the figure on the path. They were both very quiet, very lonely, very dead.

The little creak which the door made as it swung open was

the creak of wood and started no shuddering questions in the night. A cedar by the field path opposite creaked back in answer.

The breathing had begun again and once more the monster rose up out of the blackness and there was the clatter of a heel on tiles. The door swung wide and the night rushed into the little house, carrying dust and a crumpled leaf or two and a white petal in its surging drapery, which floated over the tea-chest clock, brushed the Van Gogh and scattered the papers on the desk. The monster struggled on. Safe within protecting walls, it was less cautious. It moved more quickly and when it cannoned into the table ledge it whispered an imprecation. The door of the kitchenette stood open and a circle of glowing blue beads on the top of the stove cast just enough light to show the way in. The monster stooped under the lintel and bowed to the ground.

For a long time there was swift movement in the kitchen. Gloved hands fastened the small window and drew both blinds and curtains. The heavy mat was kicked up over the crack beneath the door and finally the inner door, through which the night still poured, exploring every corner in silent busyness, was closed and the blackness was almost complete.

The man lit a match and found the light switch. Mr. Campion lay on the floor. He was breathing regularly and his fair hair was tousled. He looked as if he were sleeping after being very tired. The man who bent over him laid a finger on his pulse and straightened himself immediately. Then he replaced his glove and turned off the lighted gas jet. Evidently time was precious, for he completed his arrangements hurriedly. He stripped off Campion's jacket, folded it into a pad and opened the oven door.

The shining cupboard was partitioned with iron shelves and he removed them hastily, stacking them carefully beside the sink. He arranged the pad carefully over the sharp edge of the oven's iron surround and returned to the man on the floor. It was not an easy operation to force the head and one shoulder into that tiny cavity while maintaining a fairly natural position but he accomplished it presently and settled the long thin legs with care, drawing up one knee under the body and pulling the loose trouser cuff into a likely fold.

He turned on the gas tap almost as an afterthought and stood back to look at his handiwork while the thirty jets poured choking death into the tiny space. The man he was going to kill stirred. He breathed deeply and at one time seemed to be struggling to rise. Once, even, he spoke. The thick voice was the first human sound in the cottage and it set the walls quivering, but the rushing gas was louder. It swelled up into a roar, a cascade, a relentless torrent of whispering noise. The body on the floor grew still again, the muscles relaxed and the leg which had been drawn up slithered a little.

The man who stood watching with a handkerchief pressed over his nose drew a visiting card out of his waistcoat pocket and looked at the scribbled message it bore.

"Amanda—You won't forget me—Albert."

It seemed miraculously appropriate and he folded it in two and tucked it into the livid hand which lay across Mr. Campion's breast.

In his mind's eye he saw the headlines on the morrow. "Suicide after Broken Engagement." "Tragic Discovery in Lady Amanda Fitton's Riverside Cottage." That was the strength of the Press; it jumped to the obvious scandal in all scandals. That was the weakness of the Earl of Pontisbright's position; any scandal in his family *was* a scandal. Mr. Campion had taken his broken heart badly; that had been his weakness. The Lady Amanda Fitton was of sufficient social importance for everyone concerned to sympathise with her youth and to hurry through the inquest, with its inevitable verdict, as swiftly and decently as possible; that was her strength.

Now, however, it was still the time to hurry. The Lagonda in which the cinema commissionaire had seen Mr. Campion leave Marble Arch alone must remain where it was, a silent witness for the next passer-by to note, but Caesar's Court was less than ten minutes by the field path. He took a last look round, satisfied himself that there was no betraying sign for the first inquisitive police constable to observe, and moved quietly to the light switch.

His fingers were actually on the bakelite when he noticed the phenomenon which sent the blood streaming into his face and passed a white-hot hand over his head and spine. The door to the living room, which was not a foot away from him, was opening inwards, very slowly, and even as he stared at it the stubby nose of a police revolver crept quietly round the jamb.

At the same instant there was a commotion behind him as the food cupboard burst open, as heavy footsteps sounded in the room above, as the garden door was flung wide, as the whole house burst into sudden swarming life, and a young voice, savage with indignation, sounded clearly in his very ear.

"If you've killed the old man I'll never forgive you, Ferdie Paul," said Amanda Fitton.

Chapter Twenty-four

"Perhaps you'd care to be sick, sir," said the plain-clothes man helpfully.

Mr. Campion declined the invitation gracefully, and Amanda grinned at him. On the other side of the room Mr. Lugg, still padding about in stockinged feet, turned away from the Van Gogh, which seemed to fascinate him, and leant over the superintendent's chair.

"He put a lot of faith in that solicitor of 'is, didn't 'e?" he remarked. "It'll take more than a lawyer to explain that fancywork in the kitchen. No wonder the pore little legal gent looked a bit on 'is dig. It's cost the country a mint 'o money, too. That'll pile it on for Mr. Paul. Still, a very nice police turnout; I will say that. If you'd done a murder, cock, you couldn't 'ave bin looked after better. Busies 'ere, busies round the Sovereign watching Mr. Paul hang about the theatre until it was time to do 'is bit of telephoning from a call box, busies in the yard watching Mr. Paul gettin' in the back of the Lagonda, busies phoning up the report, busies on motorcycles, busies at Caesar's Court, busies all round the perishin' country. And yet 'e might 'ave spiked you in that car. I don't blame you for drivin' so fast. Still, you would do it. I 'ad a look at you first thing to see if you was dead."

"They kept as near the car as they dared." Oates looked

across at Campion apologetically. "You seemed fairly safe while you were going at that pace. I didn't think he'd attack you, for his own sake. And don't you talk so much," he added, glancing round at Lugg. "Mr. Campion asked for police protection and I gave it to him. The way you tell the story it sounds as if we were all agents provocateurs."

"I knew he'd come here." Hal Fitton spoke from the fireplace. "Amanda and I were both convinced of it. I actually saw him take the idea yesterday. You handed it to him on a plate, of course. I thought you were going to overdo it with that river business. He's pretty shrewd."

"He's so sharp he cut hisself." Sergeant Flood could not resist the observation and hoped the lateness of the hour would excuse the breach of discipline.

"That's it exactly," said Amanda, beaming at him. "That's what we hoped. What will you do now? Will the Hakapopulous brothers split?"

Oates rose.

"They might," he said. "They'd recognise Mrs. Fitch anyway. Still, I don't think we shall have to bother much about him. He's a sick man. He may not even come to trial."

"That's what put you on to him, isn't it?" Hal glanced at Campion. Now that he had shelved his tremendous dignity of the previous afternoon his youth was very apparent.

Mr. Campion stirred himself. He looked ill and exhausted.

"Oates found it," he said. "He had the list of people Ferdie Paul had seen in Paris and one of them was Doctor Peugeot, the great diabetic biochemist. That explained a lot. If Ferdie Paul was an insulin-taking diabetic the death of Ramillies ceased to be so much of a mystery. It also explained why he was so happily convinced that he was perfectly safe."

"It's indetectable, is it?"

"Practically. A blood-sugar test must be taken within five minutes of death to trace anything unusual even. That's what I meant when I said he'd slipped into it, Oates. It was so abominably simple for him. Once Ramillies had confessed his fear of flying to him, all Ferdie Paul had to do was to tell him the kind of tale he wanted to hear. He had the method of

274

killing in his hand twice a day. He knew enough of Ramillies'
character to realise that the man would hang on until the last
minute and finally give way, and he prepared accordingly. He
backed his judgment as to what the other man would do.
After all, that's the basis of most business methods. If
Ramillies hadn't been really so frightened, or if he had been
a stronger character, he wouldn't have gone creeping round
to Ferdie at the eleventh hour and the scheme would have
fallen through. Ferdie put his money on the chance that
Ramillies was the sort of man he thought he was, and he
happened to be right. I should think he gave him a dose of
about two hundred D.S. units and after that nothing could
have saved him, unless someone had spotted the conditions
and dosed him up with some sort of vasopressin, Tonephin
or something. As it was, of course, the wretched Ramillies
had no idea he was dying."

"Paul's a peculiar sort of chap." The old superintendent
was buttoning himself into his coat as he spoke. It was nearly
dawn and there was a cold mist over the water meadows.
"He's got exalted ideas of his own importance. A lot of them
have. It's the commonest type of what you might call the
'elaborate' killer. I've seen it before. George Joseph Smith
was one of them. They honestly think a bit of their cash or a
bit of their convenience is worth someone else's life. I don't
suppose we shall ever know the full ins and outs of the
motive, shall we?"

"We do. He told me." Mr. Campion was battling with
sleep. "I'll come up in the morning and make a full report.
He gave me the whole motive so frankly that I sat there with
my eyes popping; terrified out of my life he was going to do
me in on the spot. He told me the full truth and fastened it on
to Gaiogi Laminoff with a single magnificent lie. Who are
Georgia Wells's parents, by the way?"

"She's only got a father," said Amanda, who knew everything, as usual. "He runs a touring company in Australia and
is a bit low, so Georgia keeps him dark. She sends him all her
press cuttings. Ferdie didn't try to palm Georgia off on
Gaiogi, did he? The poor little man can't be more than
fifty-five. Did he?"

"He hardly committed himself." Mr. Campion spoke wearily. "It was in character, though. He told Ramillies the truth,
you know, except for the one stupendous lie."

THE FASHION IN SHROUDS

" 'After four hours you'll feel fine,' " said Amanda. "He had a sort of sense of humour, but not very kind. What about the woman? Will she stick to him? I wonder."

Mr. Campion glanced at Oates, whose thin lips curled sourly.

"I don't think we shall hear of her again," he said. "She was on her way when Mr. Campion left her at the cinema to come here. I've seen her sort before. They're not a wholly bad lot, but they get sort of used to looking after themselves. Paul knew that better than anyone. Oh, he said one funny thing, Campion. He gave me a message for you. I nearly forgot it. He said: 'Tell Campion it's interesting to see his recipe works both ways.' What did he mean by that?"

"The strengths and the weaknesses of man," Mr. Campion laughed and there was genuine regret in his tone. "He forgot the catch in it, poor lunatic," he said. "It's Providence who has the advantage. The rest of us haven't the divine facility for correct diagnosis. Providence would hardly have fallen for our broken hearts, for instance."

"Talking of our broken hearts," said Amanda when the last of the company had departed and the Earl of Pontisbright was assisting Mr. Lugg to make beds upstairs, "where is my ring? It was Aunt Flo's, you know, and the stones are thought to be real if not large."

Mr. Campion turned out all his pockets and discovered the missing token. Amanda stood balancing it in the palm of her hand and he looked up at her.

"Go on. Put it on. I'll be happy to marry you if you care for the idea," he said. "And then when I'm fifty, and feeling like a quiet life, you'll go and fall with a thud for some silly chap who'll give us both hell."

Amanda hesitated. She looked very young indeed, her red hair standing out like an aureole.

"Cake love, you mean?" she said dubiously.

"Call it what you like." He sounded irritable. "The only thing is, don't pretend that it doesn't exist or that you're immune."

Amanda regarded him with great affection.

"Cake makes some people sick," she remarked cheerfully. "I'll tell you what we'll do: we'll pop this tomorrow and buy some apples."

He brightened.

"And comfort ourselves," he said. "That's an idea. Do you know, Amanda, I'm not sure that 'Comfort' isn't your middle name."

ABOUT THE AUTHOR

MARGERY ALLINGHAM, who was born in London in 1904, came from a long line of writers. "I was brought up from babyhood in an atmosphere of ink and paper," she claimed. One ancestor wrote early nineteenth century melodramas, another wrote popular boys' school stories, and her grandfather was the proprietor of a religious newspaper. But it was her father, the author of serials for the popular weeklies, who gave her her earliest training as a writer. She began studying the craft at the age of seven and had published her first novel by the age of sixteen while still at boarding school. In 1927 she married Philip Youngman Carter, and the following year she produced the first of her Albert Campion detective stories, *The Crime at Black Dudley*. She and her husband lived a life "typical of the English countryside" she reported, with "horses, dogs, our garden and village activities" taking up leisure time. One wonders how much leisure time Margery Allingham, the author of more than thirty-three mystery novels in addition to short stories, serials and book reviews, managed to have.

Murder Most British

With these new mystery titles, Bantam takes you to the scene of the crime. These masters of mystery follow in the tradition of the Great British crime writers. You'll meet all these talented sleuths as they get to the bottom of even the most baffling crimes.

Special Offer
Buy a Bantam Book
for only 50¢.

Now you can have an up-to-date listing of Bantam's hundreds of titles plus take advantage of our unique and exciting bonus book offer. A special offer which gives you the opportunity to purchase a Bantam book for only 50¢. Here's how!

By ordering any five books at the regular price per order, you can also choose any other single book listed (up to a $4.95 value) for just 50¢. Some restrictions do apply, but for further details why not send for Bantam's listing of titles today!

Just send us your name and address and we will send you a catalog!